Ben Allsop, who is currently aged 13,
English and reading thriller novels. He went to Anthony Bek Primary
School in New Houghton near his home, and now attends Shirebrook
Comprehensive School. He has always had one life ambition - to have a
book published. This has already happened and in April 2005, when his
first Frank Ward novel, *Sharp*, was published and sold very well. The
book and the young author had a lot of publicity, securing large articles in
newspapers, radio interviews and book signings.

A lover of creative writing, Ben also writes poetry and had a poem
published in an anthology as well as a short story. Shortly after, Ben
started a sequel to his first spy mystery bringing his dangerous creation
back to the pages. This is 'The Perfect Kill.'

At the moment, Ben is working on his third novel, this time a
completely different story altogether. It will be a crime 'whodunit.' Ben is
a lover of detective fiction and reads novels by Agatha Christie, Colin
Dexter and several other authors.

To Anne + Mike,
Best wishes and
fond memories of
a happy cruise
aboard the Black
Prince

Ben Allsop
9th October 08

BOOKS ALSO BY THE SAME AUTHOR -

<u>Frank Ward Novels</u> -

Sharp
The Perfect Kill

<u>Short Stories</u> -

The Midnight Stalker(short story published in 'Telling T.A.L.E.S. From Nottinghamshire.')

<u>Poetry</u> -

Death of a Soldier (published in '2007: A Poetry Odyssey.')

<u>Coming Soon</u> -

The Baltic Mystery (a murder mystery thriller)

THE PERFECT KILL

Frank Ward is back …

BY: BEN ALLSOP

Published 2007 by arima publishing

www.arimapublishing.com

ISBN 978-1-84549-183-3

Printed and bound in the United Kingdom

Typeset in Garamond 12/16

arima publishing
ASK House, Northgate Avenue
Bury St Edmunds, Suffolk IP32 6BB
t: (+44) 01284 700321

www.arimapublishing.com

For my mother, Sally, for without her, this book would not exist.

B.A

CONTENTS

1/ DANGER IN PARIS

BEING A SPY is one of the most dangerous and thrilling careers available in the world. Often you will get to travel around the globe to exotic locations on an assignment, and you will face sinister enemies and terrifying experiences. Yet, despite the dangers and risks that a government agent has to take, Gaëlle Dumas actually found it an exciting profession, that most of all, she enjoyed.

Gaëlle was a secret agent working in the French Direction Générale de la Sécurité Extérieure (DGSE). Its headquarters are located at 141 Boulevard Mortier in Paris 20th. The building is often referred to as *La piscine* ("the swimming pool") because of the nearby Piscine des Tourelles of the French Swimming Federation. She was an agent working in the Directorate of Intelligence section, which meant she was a field spy who gathers intelligence from the enemy and investigates the knowledge gained.

Currently, she was on a mission. Two highly powerful French cruise missiles containing real life nuclear warheads were stolen on a test launch a few days ago. The French military were flying the two missiles on a routine examination flight and they were originally carrying dummy warheads. However, an insider in the military had switched the dummy warheads for the real things. Somebody had then manipulated the flight of the missile and had obviously sent it off course. It was then that some criminals must have taken them. God only knows what they intended to do with them. If one of those was launched into the middle of Paris or London or Washington DC for instance, billions would perish in the atomic explosion. The French Secret Service were determined to find them and had every agent in the Directorate of Intelligence section searching for the machine. The Direction de la Surveillance du Territoire, the French agency concerned with terrorism within the country, was also searching for the missing technology. NATO said it was crucial to recover the device before it got into enemy hands.

Gaëlle sat on the front balcony of her large flat overlooking Paris whilst eating her morning breakfast. The sun had come out and she immediately knew that it was going to be a nice day. The Eiffel Tower loomed above the other buildings, dominating the sky. It stood proudly as one of the world's most famous landmarks. She sipped her cup of black coffee and finished her two croissants and placed her knife and fork down neatly in the centre of the plate.

Gaëlle Dumas was very beautiful. Many of her past lovers had complimented her on her looks. She had fine, dark brown silken hair that fell heavily to the shoulders. Her face was very pretty and showed a light tan. Her cheekbones were slightly raised. Gaëlle's eyes were level and deep blue underneath the long, feminine eyelashes. Her small nose had a slight tilt to it, the mouth was delicate and the smile could break hearts. Her breasts were small and jutted out proudly from her body. She was dressed in a green shirt and light brown trousers. Gaëlle wore a pair of beige shoes on her feet. She admired the view from her balcony and then collected her glass and plate and put them in the sink.

It was another day, she thought. Another day to search for the missing missile technology. She made her bed and pulled her small semi - automatic pistol out from underneath her pillow, slipping it into the hip holster that was concealed underneath her trousers. She checked in her mirror above her dressing table to make sure that one could not notice the slight bulge of her gun in its hidden place.

It was as she was about to leave her apartment in the block of flats that she heard the sound of growling engines from the street below. Curiously, she dropped her keys onto her bed and walked purposefully across her bedroom towards the balcony. She leant against the rail and saw four identical black Toyota Altezza's pull off the road and come to a stop outside her flats. The cars all had black tinted windows, making it impossible to see inside the vehicles. A car door opened and a tall Chinese man who appeared to be in his mid thirties emerged from the first Toyota, and looked up at Gaëlle on her balcony. There was something about his eyes that instantly made Gaëlle feel uncomfortable. They were dark brown pools that seemed to be like corridors that led to hell. The whole face had a cruel quality about it. He stared at her and his wide mouth split into a sickening grin. He turned away and shouted something in Chinese to the men in the cars behind. Instantly, several men climbed out of the cars. They were all Chinese and dressed in dark black business suits. They came around to the man who had got out first and they looked up at Gaëlle. It was then she knew something was definitely wrong.

She rushed back into her bedroom and grabbed her keys and locked the door. Then, gripped by fear, she pulled a small coffee table towards the front door and pushed it against it. Gaëlle headed back out onto the balcony and watched as the Chinese men hurried off the street and into the flats.

By God, they were coming for her!

'*Merde!*' Gaëlle swore in French. She sat down on the bed and cleared her head and tried to think about the situation logically. *Who were those men? Why were they after her? What did they intend doing to her?* The last thought frightened her the most. She pulled up her right trouser leg and gripped the butt of her Browning 9mm and she held it in her right hand, her finger resting on the curve of the trigger. She could hear the men thundering up the staircase, shouting out in Chinese. She had to escape. There was no chance she could fend off all of them with only her small gun. They probably had sub - machine guns. She felt like being physically sick. She needed help.

It was then a thought sprung into her mind. She smiled and moved over to her bed and threw the sheets off her bed and immediately got to work. The Chinese men had already reached her flat. They hammered their fists on the door and shouted things out in Chinese. Gaëlle was determined not to be put off. She began to join the sheets together using powerful knots. Her hands worked fast and the men outside were now beginning to kick the door down. The front door began to shake and she watched as the coffee table against it was beginning to move out of place. The hinges were starting to come loose.

Gaëlle's heart skipped a beat. *Stay focused,* she willed herself. Thirty seconds later, the knots had been successfully tied in the bed sheets and she ran onto the balcony and tied one end around one of the bars on the railings. The banging on the door was getting louder and more aggressive. One of the hinges had snapped and the table had been knocked over. Any moment now the door would break free from its hinges and it would come crashing down. The Chinese assassins would march into the room, 9mm Heckler & Koch MP - 5's slung around their shoulders, ready to burst into rapid fire if anything moved.

Gaëlle than looked over the railings onto the street below. *Would it work? Would the sheets actually lower her down onto the pavement? Or would the knots break and make her plummet three storeys to her death?* She turned and looked back at the door.

It was about to collapse! She had to take the risk. It was too late for anything else now. They had her trapped! Gripping the knotted sheets with both hands, she checked that the other end was knotted firmly. Then, the last hinge on her door broke and it fell to the floor. The

Chinese men burst into the room, trampling over the door. One of them saw the target leap over the balcony, holding onto the knotted sheets for dear life.

'She's getting away!' One of the men screamed in Chinese, and the assassins all rushed across the room and onto the balcony. They watched in astonishment as Gaëlle slid down the sheets like a fire-fighter down the pole and land safely on her feet. She let go of the sheets and sprinted across the road where her Venturi Fetish Electric Sports Car was parked. The car was the fastest electric sports car in the world and could accelerate from speeds from 0 - 60 in five seconds. It's top speed was one hundred and five miles per hour. It was painted in a metallic dark blue, and at first glance, it evoked sensuality and femininity. Its outlines, combing angles and smooth curves made it a unique alternative to a super car. The Venturi Fetish was ahead of other cars, being noiseless, reliable and safe. It was a beauty and Gaëlle's pride and joy.

She opened the car door and slipped into the cream leather driving seat and immediately started the engine. The engine came to life and growled loudly and then hummed. Gaëlle glanced up at the Chinese hit men on her balcony. Most of them had rushed back downstairs to get into the Toyotas parked outside. They were going to follow in hot pursuit. She had to get away. Gaëlle Dumas slammed her foot down on the stainless - steel accelerator and the Venturi pulled away from the kerb and tore down the road, leaving a small cloud of dust behind her.

High up in the sky, a AH-64D Apache Longbow US military helicopter glided over Paris. Developed by the American Army in 1997, The Apache Longbow is the only combat helicopter in service with the ability to rapidly detect, classify, prioritise and engage stationary or moving enemy targets at standoff ranges in near all-weather environments. The Apache Longbow's advanced avionics suite gives combat pilots an unmatched advantage over enemy threats through the integration of the Longbow fire control radar, advanced Hellfire missiles, and an advanced avionics suite. The Hellfire heat - seeking missiles were housed underneath the cockpit along with the machine guns. This particular helicopter had been modified to have a larger storage area in the back for special flights.

Frank Ward, Agent 27S in the American Central Intelligence Agency sat crouched in the back of the military helicopter, examining aN Armalite AR - 50 sniper rifle. He was the ace of the CIA and the best shot in the agency. It was why his chief, the Director of the CIA, had chosen him especially for this important mission. He was to protect Gaëlle Dumas, an allied French intelligence agent from a group of Chinese Triad hit men who had been hired to eliminate her. He had to ensure that she stayed alive as she knew some vital information that would be of extreme importance to the US government. Ward had to shoot the enemy with the sniper rifle from up in the helicopter. It wasn't going to be easy at all. With the movement and slight swaying of the helicopter, it was going to be difficult to get accurate shots.

Ward slipped on a pair of black leather gloves as his palms were beginning to perspire. He needed to get a grip on the rifle. He held the rifle and looked down the telescopic sight, his right eye pressed against it. His left hand held the guard and his finger rested on the trigger. The right hand supported the back of the gun. Comfortable with the sniper rifle, he got into a position which would give him the best view. He put the Armalite AR - 50 down for a moment and reached up and pulled the sliding door across, revealing a magnificent view of the streets of Paris. Immediately, the wind rushed at him and whistled through his ears. He turned his head and shouted to the two RAF military pilots in the cockpit of the Apache Longbow. 'I'm ready,' he announced. 'Lower the 'copter a bit. I need to focus on the road and find the French agent.'

The co - pilot in front nodded and looked back at the brave CIA spy in the back of the helicopter, balancing the sniper rifle on his knee. 'Affirmative, 27S!' The US combat aircraft descended slightly so that Ward could get a better view of the many roads. Frank Ward looked through the sights and focused on cars as they tore down the road. He had been told to look for a dark blue sports car with the roof down. It had to be nearby. He scanned the many streets and roads and then he saw it. The speeding blue French sports car was accelerating down a straight road at about ninety miles per hour. The driver was a young lady. He saw two black cars with tinted windows behind her, driving at around the same speed. It had to be her.

'Keep it steady,' Ward instructed, focusing on the first car behind. 'I've found the girl. She's driving a blue Venturi Fetish. Try to match her speed and don't shake about too much or I'll miss. I've only got limited ammunition for the rifle.'

'We'll try, Agent 27S,' the co - pilot explained. 'I can see the car.'

Ward assumed the correct position and balanced the rifle on his right knee to prevent it from moving too much. He looked down the scope and zoomed in on the car behind the Venturi. Before he pulled the trigger, another black car hurtled around a bend and came up behind the other two. Another followed. There were four cars in pursuit now. He had to take action. Ward concentrated on the first car, not allowing himself to be distracted by the wind blowing through his ears, or the rotor blades spinning rapidly above. He aimed at the driver's head in the first car. The car moved out of the sight and then came back in again. Ward pulled the trigger. The windscreen shattered and the driver's head exploded into a gory mess. The car stayed straight for a moment and then it veered off to the left and crashed full speed into a concrete wall. The bonnet crumpled and grey smoke billowed out of the engine.

Frank Ward smiled. One down, three to go. The French agent in the Venturi Fetish roared around the next corner at high speed, and the other three cars followed, despite the first car having crashed. Ward couldn't get a good shot at the cars in pursuit from behind. He took his eye away from the scope.

'Head over to these buildings,' he said urgently. 'We'll be ahead of them, and then I can line up a good shot.'

This time the co - pilot said nothing and jerked left and soared over the row of houses below. 'Hover for a few moments,' Ward ordered, looking back down the scope to see the blue Venturi accelerate down the road towards the helicopter. The Apache Longbow hovered in mid - air sideways, giving Ward the perfect vantage point to pick off his next target. He looked down the scope again and aimed at the front left tyre of the black car directly behind. Satisfied with the shot, he squeezed the trigger and watched the rubber explode. The driver's face was contorted with fear and shock as he frantically struggled with the wheel and the Toyota Altezza began to lose control. The vehicle went all over the road, swerved, and hit the car on the opposite side of the road at full speed. A long black skid mark was printed on the tarmac, and the Toyota turned over on its back, surrounded by shards of broken glass and twisted metal. The two remaining Toyotas continued travelling behind their target, unconcerned about their friends in the two crashed cars. They stayed close and the Venturi Fetish disappeared underneath the combat helicopter.

Ward extracted the empty magazine and slipped a fresh one into the barrel of the rifle. 'Turn around and get ahead of them. There're still two more cars to take out.'

The familiar voice of the co -pilot in the cockpit said, 'Whatever you say.' The US military helicopter turned around and tilted its nose slightly as it glided through the air. The 'copter got ahead of the two enemy Toyotas and then flew over the French agent's Venturi. Ward had a good view of his targets again. He looked down the scope and focused on the Toyota behind the Venturi. The passenger's head emerged from the lowered tinted window and fired violent bursts of his 9mm Heckler & Koch MP - 5's at the girl in the sports car. Ward had to act quickly. A finely placed shot from the assassin's sub - machine gun and the French agent would be dead and Ward would have failed his mission. Ward zoomed onto the tyres and then decided it might be a risky option. The car was right behind the Venturi. The burst tyre would probably send the car into the back of the blue sports car. Ward decided not to go for the tyres, and instead focused his aim on the petrol tank. The explosion might even take the car out behind as well.

Frank Ward pulled the trigger for the third time, and the Toyota burst into flames and torrents of black smoke. The flames engulfed the Chinese killers inside, and as the spectacular explosion finished, the wreck of the car rolled over and came to rest in the middle of the road, flames licking around the burnt out remains. The driver in the Toyota behind had noticed the sniper in the Apache Longbow helicopter and had managed to break away from the explosion before it managed to catch the car in it. Ward was going to have to eliminate it. The Venturi Fetish and the remaining Toyota Altezza were now pushing the hundred mark. The helicopter was moving well, but it was getting harder to shoot accurately. He had less than a second before the target would move out of sight.

Beads of glistening sweat were gathering on Ward's forehead. A drop trickled down past his cheek and hung from his chin for a second and then it dropped onto his neck. He could feel his arms aching from the weight of the rifle and his right knee was going numb. He had three rounds left in the rifle and then that was it. He had no spare clips for the gun. He had only brought two with him. Ward didn't think he would need any more than that. Frank Ward wiped his eye and put it against the scope of the sniper rifle and focused on the last Toyota. Two men were leaning out of both sides of the car, their machine-gun bullets spraying the back of the Venturi. They might shoot out a tyre or even hit the petrol tank. Ward zoomed in on the cruel face of the Chinese murderer behind the wheel. He swallowed and fired one of his three rounds. The Toyota swerved suddenly to the right and Ward's sniper shot went slightly wide and missed.

Ward swore and bit his lip. He didn't have much more time. The Venturi would explode in a few moments! Frank Ward zoomed back in on the driver and aimed straight between the eyes and pulled the trigger. The shot went a few inches above the driver due to the movement of the helicopter. A spider web formed on the Toyota windscreen and the driver screamed. He glared at the sniper up in the 'copter and shouted instructions to the gunners in the back of the car.

Damn it, Ward cursed himself. *Missed again!* Ward had to get an accurate shot this time. He had no choice. If he missed, the gunman would continue shooting until the Venturi exploded. Ward put his finger back on the trigger and looked into the scope. He had to get a good shot. The life of the French agent all depended on this last bullet. Ward aimed at the driver, took a deep breath, and pulled back on the trigger. The windscreen of the Toyota vanished as if hit by a monster fist and for a moment, it looked as if the Chinese killer had grown a third eye above his nose. He stared up glassily at the sniper in the US combat aircraft and blood spilled down his face. The Chinese men's head crashed down against the wheel. The passenger tried to move the body so he could steer the car and prevent a crash. The dead driver had jammed the controls. The Toyota slid across the road and smashed through the railings beside the sea. The car sailed in the air for a few moments and crashed into the icy water. Water filled the car through the smashed windscreen, and in seconds it began to sink to the bottom of the sea like a sunken tomb.

Ward felt like jumping up and shouting to the heavens. *He had done it! His final shot had been accurate! His mission was complete!* He looked down at the beautiful French girl in the sports car. He put the rifle down on the floor and pushed a small rope ladder out of the side of the combat helicopter. It dangled in mid air, the wind blowing it wildly. 'Keep above the sports car. I'm going to lower myself down. Thanks for the helicopter.'

With that, Ward turned around and gripped the top of the rope ladder. The force of the wind was incredible. He nearly lost his grip and fell to his death. He put both his feet down onto a step and clung on for dear life as the aircraft thundered through the sky, doing one hundred miles per hour. Several insects hit Ward's face at high speed as he held onto the strong rope ladder as it blew about wildly in the wind. He swallowed, blinded by dust and dead flies as he began to move his feet down the ladder, his gloved hands gripping onto the sides. He was a few metres above the speeding sports car. He looked up at the two RAF pilots in the cockpit of the AH-64D Apache Longbow. These had large headphones strapped over their heads. They signalled to Ward dangling from the swaying ladder, hanging from the back of the helicopter. Ward smiled and moved down the ladder unhurriedly and carefully, and then he let go and allowed himself to drop into the luxurious leather passenger seat beside the attractive Agent Gaëlle Dumas of the French Secret Service. She turned and looked at him in astonishment, her delicate mouth open in awe. Finally, she closed her mouth and turned away from the handsome figure who had just dropped into her Venturi Fetish.

'Who are you?' She said in good English.

Frank Ward turned to face her, and it was then she recognised him and realised how incredibly handsome he was. The American looked calmly at her with his watchful grey - blue eyes that had a ruthless touch about them, yet appeared friendly as well. The mouth was wide and cruel, the nose was straight. He had a tanned complexion, and a very faint scar showed above the right eyebrow. This was partly concealed by a thick lock of black hair that hung above the right eyebrow out of place, like a comma. The jaw was set in a hard, decisive line and the expression on the face was authoritative but cold.

'I'm Frank Ward, Agent 27S,' he said stoically, 'I've been sent over here by the Central Intelligence Agency to protect you. Somebody has put a price on your head, Miss Dumas.'

Gaëlle swallowed and looked at the American spy, the very man who had just saved her life from the Triad assassins sent to kill her. She felt like reaching across to him and plunging her soft lips down upon his. Of course, she was too embarrassed to do so. 'Thanks for saving my life,' she said gently. 'I feel that I owe you something for your work.'

Ward looked at her, and the mouth that had before been cruel split into an attractive smile. 'I suppose you can give me something.' Ward said, looking up at the sky thoughtfully as if thinking, 'Pull over,' he added decisively.

Gaëlle nodded and slammed her foot down on the brake and slipped into the parking zone. The military helicopter roared overhead, the ladder dangling down from it. She turned off the engine and they gazed at each other hungrily for a few moments. Slowly, Ward brought his face close to hers and she wrapped her arms around his neck. Their lips touched, and Ward's mouth obliterated hers. Gaëlle made a soft moaning sound as his tongue penetrated her lips and began to wrestle with hers. They kissed passionately for a few moments and Ward's mouth moved away and he kissed her several times on her right cheek. Eventually he pulled away. 'You won't be safe at your apartment for some time.' He told her. 'Come to my hotel and I'll protect you until you leave the country.'

Gaëlle smiled and said, 'I'd love to.' The sun beamed down on the two new lovers in the blue Venturi Fetish as Ward's mouth forced down upon hers.

2/ MIDNIGHT INTRUDERS

THE NAME 'HONG KONG' means 'fragrant harbour,' and is derived from the area around present-day Aberdeen and Wong Chuk Hang on Hong Kong Island, where fragrant trees were once abundant and widely exported. The landscape of Hong Kong is fairly hilly to mountainous with steep slopes. It is on the coast of China, and part of it is a small island, and the rest is a narrow strip of land called the New Territories, which are in turn connected to mainland China across the Sham Chun River (Shenzhen River). In total, Hong Kong has 236 islands in the South China Sea, of which Lantau is the largest. Hong Kong Island itself is the second largest and also the most populated. Ap Lei Chau is the most densely populated island in the world.

Hong Kong's climate is subtropical and prone to monsoons. It is cool and dry in the winter times which lasts from around January to March, and is hot, humid and rainy from spring through summer. It is warm, sunny, and dry in Autumn, and occasionally suffers from typhoons. The ecology of Hong Kong is mostly affected by the results of climatic changes. Hong Kong's climate is seasonal due to alternating wind direction between winter and summer. It has been geologically stable for millions of years.

With a population of about 5,841, 000, it is a very crowded and busy place to live. Hong Kong is on the coast of China, and part of it is a small island, and the rest is a narrow strip of land called the New Territories.

Hong Kong has been governed by Britain since 1842. It was handed over to Chinese rule in 1997. Hong Kong has a fine harbour surrounded by mountains. The capital is Victoria, and another busy city is Kowloon. It is a fascinating mixture of East and West. The people in Hong Kong live by trade, fishing and farming. Despite the huge apartment buildings and houses constantly being built, there is still barely any room for the millions of people who crowd this small island.

The United States of America moved one of their large top - secret government laboratories from Tokyo, Japan to Hong Kong in 2001. With the amount of military technology being developed, they soon needed a much larger headquarters. The new US government lab is a massive complex surrounded by a tall electrified fence with only one entrance. It is heavily guarded. In the middle of the complex are the main laboratories where new chemical weapons are being produced, and next to it is the testing facility where cruise missiles are launched on test flights carrying only dummy warheads. Next to it are all the offices of the main personnel, and then a large block of computer rooms and monitoring stations where the US officers use space satellites to relay area images of land for military purposes and covert operations.

It was just approaching midnight, and a small olive green jeep pulled off from the quiet road on the east side of the US laboratory. Unnoticed, it turned left and silently crept up to the electrified entrance of the complex. A long barrier and sealed gates were preventing the jeep from entering the site. A small kiosk where security men would examine anybody entering was on their right. Nobody came out to question them or ask for identification. The men in the jeep - all clad completely black from head to foot - slowly climbed out of the vehicle and the driver turned off the quiet engine. They crouched down and moved stealthily towards the door of the kiosk led by the man who had driven the jeep. They all had small Browning 9mm's holstered on their belts. The driver of the jeep seemed to be the leader of the group and he moved towards the small window. He reached down with a gloved hand and his finger touched the trigger of his Browning. Slowly, he lifted his head and examined what was inside.

Two security guards dressed in green camouflaged uniforms were seated inside on swivel chairs beside a bank of computer screens and monitors, relaying CCTV footage. Both of their eyes were closed and they made gentle sounds as they slept. One of them had his feet up on a small desk next to him, his face partially hidden. They both had an American Ingram MAC M11 sub machine gun slung around their shoulders. A small map of the complex was pinned onto a notice board on the wall. The driver turned and looked at the other three men and said something to them in Chinese.

This was going to be very easy, he thought.

He stood up and gripped the door handle and gently pushed it open, holding his Browning in his right hand. The door had made a slight creak as it opened, but the sound didn't seem to make the sleeping guards stir. He turned around and motioned to one of the other men to follow him inside. One of the men came up behind the leader, and silently they crept inside the kiosk. The leader whispered something to the man behind him and he reached inside his pocket and removed a piece of silver garrotte wire and held it at both ends in his hands and smiled. The other guard did the same. Slowly, they circled around both of the sleeping guards and moved the wire around their necks and pulled back violently.

The guards' awoke instantly and realised what was happening. Quickly, they moved their hands up and pushed their thumbs underneath the garrotte wire to prevent it from digging deeper into their necks. They made frantic screams and moans as they tried to pull free and escape. The two men in black jerked backwards with the wire, trying frantically to strangle their victims. The men used their hands and thumbs to keep the wires away from their throats, but it became harder and harder and they gradually became weaker and weaker. They were going faint and dizzy and their minds went all cloudy. Numbness crept up their bodies and their neck felt as if it would snap at any moment. Their faces went red, then blue and saliva trickled down the corners of their mouths. The guards' eyes had a glassy stare to them and suddenly blood burst out of their mouths and fell down their chins. Their mouths opened in disbelief and slowly their eyes rolled upwards. Satisfied that both guards were dead, the two killers removed the garrotte wire and put it away. The leader signalled to the other two men to come inside.

The leader of the group was Kazuki Masaharu, a Chinese hit man and mob boss of a Triad gang, which is an organisation based in Hong Kong that recruits criminals for various crimes and hired killings. Their activities include drug trafficking, money laundering, illegal gambling, prostitution, car theft and other forms of racketeering. A major source of triad income today comes from counterfeiting intellectual property such as computer software, music CDs and movie VCDs/ DVDs. They also trade in bootleg tobacco products. However, Kazuki and three of his most hardened criminals had been recruited for a very special job tonight. His men had already blundered a hit earlier today on a French agent in Paris. He wasn't going to fail another mission again. His boss didn't enjoy being given bad news.

Tonight, the boss had requested them to steal an important piece of hi - tech missile guidance hardware that directed the course of all types of cruise missiles to their programmed targets. A cruise missile is basically a small, pilot-less airplane. Cruise missiles have an 8.5-foot (2.61-meter) wingspan, are powered by turbofan engines and can fly 500 to 1,000 miles (805 to 1,610 km) depending on the configuration.

The military purpose of the cruise missile is to deliver a 1,000-pound (450-kg) high-explosive nuclear warhead to a precise location - the target. The missile is destroyed when the warhead explodes. Since cruise missiles cost between $500,000 and $1,000,000 each, it's a fairly expensive option of defence. Usually their missions are to destroy ships, aircraft, enemy land and even dams. However, depending on the size of the warhead, they could be used to destroy much larger targets such as towns or cities.

Kazuki Masaharu and his Triad associates had to steal the guidance system for their boss from the US laboratory. His team were getting paid five thousand American dollars each which they would then transfer into yen, the Chinese currency. They had to pull it off - they needed the money after a bank robbery failed and two Triad gang members were shot dead.

Kazuki was fairly tall, probably six foot, and his whole body looked menacing. His face was rather round and the skin was an oily, translucent yellow. The eyebrows were black and arched above the two steely brown eyes that looked like gun barrels. The nose was thin and fine and ended a few centimetres above the small mouth that showed cruelty and authority. The jaw was slightly raised and clean cut. He seldom smiled or laughed, and his face was always sombre and never showed any happy emotions. His black hair was quite long and was slicked back immaculately with a comb. He wore a dark black stealth-outfit that covered all of his body except the head. It allowed him and his men to remain camouflaged and unseen in the darkness. The arms bulged with muscle, the whole body was kept in good shape and the build resembled that of an athlete.

Kazuki's men got to work and crouched down whilst searching the two bodies for weapons or anything of importance. They found only two hidden knives in their shirt cuffs, a small flashlight and a set of keys. Two of the men took the Ingram machine guns from the stiffened corpses and slung them around their shoulders.

Kazuki moved over to the control panel beside the window and scanned the buttons for a moment before flicking a switch. Slowly the barrier began to rise with a gentle humming sound. Kazuki turned abruptly to his crew of Triad associates and handed one of them the keys to the jeep outside.

'Get the vehicle started,' he barked in Chinese. 'I'll open the gate.'

The men turned on their heels and climbed back into the military jeep outside the kiosk. One of the men started the engine and it came to life immediately. Kazuki Masaharu pressed another button on the bank of machines. Slowly, the electrified gates opened, leading straight into the compound. Kazuki then rushed out of the small kiosk without giving a final look at the two strangled guards sprawled on the floor and got behind the wheel of the stolen olive green jeep. Steadily, he drove it through the gates and headed past the office block, the only sounds being the crunching of gravel underneath the tyres and the gentle purring of the engine. Kazuki turned on the headlights to cast a small amount of light to guide him in the darkness and turned the wheel slightly and headed left towards the middle of the compound, where the weapons laboratories were located.

The other three men in the jeep all held heir guns closely and kept their fingers on the triggers. They scanned the darkness for movement, sound or even the slightest glisten of gun metal in the moonlight. If they saw any guards or security, they were prepared to open fire and shoot them dead. Kazuki didn't want any witnesses or messy killings. He had told his crew this job required lots of stealth and discretion. All their guns, as well as the Ingram's, were silenced.

The jeep continued towards the laboratories, and Kazuki smiled. *So far it had been easy.* There was a security guard ahead controlling the grounds, unaware of the intruders in the jeep coming towards him. As he turned around and saw the glare of the headlights, one of the Triad's in the jeep fired two silenced rounds directly into his chest. The guard's eyes widened, and he clutched his gory wound on his chest before he doubled over and crumpled onto the ground. The jeep went past the body, the lights catching the corpse as a pool of blood gathered around it. The jeep was nearly there now, and on the way they had only encountered one guard on the grounds.

Ahead of the moving vehicle, a huge building dominated the sky. There were very few windows as far as Kazuki could see. *This must be the government laboratories,* thought Kazuki. *This is where the boss said the guidance system would be kept.* The jeep crept up to the secret building and unnoticed, Kazuki pulled the jeep up against the right hand side of the building and turned off the engine. He scanned the darkness for guards or security, and then he jumped out of the vehicle and withdrew his silenced Browning and ordered his men to get out of the jeep.

'We'll head 'round the back,' Kazuki announced quietly in Chinese. 'It might not be as heavily guarded as the main entrance.'

The men all nodded and moved as a group around the sides of building, staying close to the walls and keeping within the shadows. A Chinese man wearing an elaborate white coat and gloves emerged from the back entrance of the weapon facility, and walked unhurriedly in the opposite direction. Kazuki and his men remained silent, and once the scientist was out of sight, they started moving again towards the back of the building without making any noise. There was a discreet entrance to the laboratories around the back of the building as Kazuki had imagined. Kazuki crouched down beside the double doors and looked up at a combination lock on the right hand side of the door. He reached inside his stealth jacket and removed a key - code cracker that he used on multiple bank robberies to crack safes. It was capable of cracking pass - card locks. It had an advance processor built inside that cycled through thousands of possible codes in seconds before finding the correct combination. Kazuki Masaharu, the Chinese Triad gang leader, inserted the device inside the card slot at the door, pressed a button and almost instantly the buttons on the cracker flashed green and red. In seconds the combination on the door had been found. The great silver doors opened with a faint hiss and Kazuki and his team proceeded inside, the doors closing behind them automatically.

The intruders immediately found themselves in a large dark room, the only light source from a small bullet - proof window on the left of the room. Several large oil drums and chemical canisters were propped up against the walls along with a few wooden crates. They were all marked with various hazard symbols - 'highly irritant', 'corrosive', 'toxic'. They were all different types of chemical weapons which were being built inside the US government laboratory. Two of the men produced the flashlights they had taken from the bodies of the dead guards in the kiosk, and aimed the torches at the floor, moving them around the room. There was nothing of interest in here, so Kazuki moved purposefully towards a stainless steel double door at the end of the wheel, and slipped inside, followed by his crew of men.

The next room was brightly lit and much larger than the first room. This one was white and covered with several workbenches, desks, chairs and tables. The floors were covered with shiny tiles and the walls were cream and plain. The whole room resembled that of a hospital ward, minus the beds. The room smelt like a hospital, too. There were several strange smells in the air - smells of chemicals, dangerous liquids and gases. Two Chinese men dressed in white coats like the one Kazuki and his men had spotted outside, were sitting at desks, making furious notes on pieces of paper.

The one nearest to the door spotted the intruders clad in black immediately after he heard the door close. He looked up from his jottings, and his mouth opened in shock. He stopped writing immediately and dropped his pencil. Kazuki pointed the barrel of his Browning 9mm at his forehead, and flicked off the safety catch.

'Stick 'em up and stay quiet,' Kazuki instructed coolly. The other three men focused their aim on the other man sitting furthest away. He looked extremely frightened and raised his hands up quickly. The other did so too, but more reluctantly.

Kazuki stood there, his dark gun-barrel eyes blazing with excitement, balancing his gunning arm on his other for accuracy. He waited for the scientist to say something, anything, before he pulled the trigger. He didn't. Calmly, Kazuki motioned towards the wall at the far end of the room.

'Walk over to that wall and face it, keeping your arms where we can see them - now!'

Kazuki sensed the fear written on their faces as they turned around and walked slowly towards the wall, their arms above their heads. They stopped at the wall and stayed quiet. 'Good,' he said firmly. 'Where's the missile guidance system?' He demanded. 'If you don't talk we'll riddle your bodies with bullets. Now where is it?'

The second scientist was the first to answer. 'It's in the next room - in the safe behind the painting.' Kazuki smiled and nodded at his men as if giving them a silent instruction. The three Triad thugs grinned too as if understanding the message and then Kazuki pulled the trigger four times and shot the second scientist repeatedly in the face. He caught a glimpse of realisation spreading across the man's face before it disappeared into a gory mess and exploded. The defenceless man had thrown up his arms and covered his face as if to catch any additional bullets before his body slumped against the wall and fell to the floor. The other scientist screamed in shock after watching his college brutally shot and then turned around and faced the intruders. Two of the men fired a rapid burst of rounds of the Ingram sub - machines gun, and the bullets ripped into his chest and flung the man across the room like a rag doll. Before his body hit the ground, Kazuki sadistically emptied the entire clip of his silenced Browning into the man and then all was silent. The white walls and tiled floors were smeared in blood like something out of a terrifying horror film. Kazuki Masaharu lifted the barrel of his Browning to his nose and moved it underneath both his nostrils, sniffing delicately at the fresh smoke as it came out of the gun. Then he smiled again, extracted the clip, inserted a fresh one and looked at his team proudly.

'Good work,' he said. 'Let's get what the boss wants and leave before anybody discovers the bodies.'

The Triad crew ran across the laboratory and pulled open the door at the end of the room. They were now in a small, modern office decorated in stainless steel plate tiles, and carpets of red plush. Against the wall was a silver bookcase, and next to it, an ornate desk topped with a glass surface. Kazuki Masaharu remembered what the scientist had said - the missile guidance hardware was locked up in a wall safe behind a painting. Sure enough, there was a small piece of artwork on the wall, framed in gold. He smiled again and lifted the picture off the wall and put it down carefully onto the desk. The front of a safe with a combination lock in the centre of it, had appeared in the wall in its place. Kazuki grinned and withdrew the key code cracker from his pocket which he had used earlier to break into the building. He attached it onto the combination lock and flicked a switch. Immediately, the gadget began searching for the correct combination.

Kazuki turned to face his crew of brutal killers. 'Stand outside and keep guard. If anybody comes in, blow 'em to hell!', he ordered in Chinese. The hard - faced thugs nodded and marched out of the office under their chief's instructions.

Beep.

Kazuki looked at the key - code cracker. Yes, a light had flashed green. The first code had been found. The cycle of the codes continued.

Beep.

Another code had been located. This went on for a further ten seconds and then there came a soft buzzing noise and the safe door flung open. There wasn't much inside - stacks of papers, folders and a small metal briefcase.

That must be what the boss wants, thought Kazuki. He reached inside, pulled the briefcase out and closed the door. Kazuki pocketed his key code cracker and went into the next room where his team were waiting.

'I've got it,' he announced, and they sprinted back out of the door, ran out of the dark room and found the stolen military jeep waiting for them outside. Kazuki jumped in the passenger seat and ordered one of his men to drive. The vehicle started immediately and the driver reversed and drove out of the compound.

When the jeep was well out of the US government lab, Kazuki moved his fingers on the locks until the briefcase opened and looked inside at the machine. The missile guidance system was basically a small black rectangular box slotted in a space in the dark velvet lining. He took it out and the lid opened electronically, revealing a glass panel with digital numbers and a few wires to connect with computers.

Kazuki smiled, and for the first time in his life, laughed out loud. He was going to be rich. The boss would be so pleased with his new toy.

3/ AN UNEXPECTED VISITOR

THE AIR BRAKES of the Boeing 727 VIP airliner grumbled down slowly, and the undercarriage emerged underneath the craft and thudded into place. The Boeing was now beginning its slow descend back to land.

'*Please remain seated,*' came the youthful voice of the stewardess on the speaker, '*we are approaching Paris airport. We will land in a few minutes.*' The stewardess then repeated what she had just said in French.

Seymour Andrew Cartwright, the new Director of the Central Intelligence Agency, sat in one of the luxurious brown leather seats, extremely comfortable and relaxed. He sat next to the window whilst sipping his black coffee and watched the magnificent view from high up in the sky and wished he could enjoy it, and maybe even get a quick nap before the plane landed.

There was no chance of that, though. Cartwright had many serious matters on his mind at the moment. He couldn't sleep or rest or relax. Anyone looking closely would see signs of strain under the grey commanding eyes.

Cartwright looked nothing like his predecessor. He was somewhere in his mid or early fifties, and had a hard, lined weather - beaten face, a face that Frank Ward and many other agents had grown used to since the man's arrival at the service. It was strict, but calm, and showed signs of lack of sleep and tiredness. The skin was however, luminous with health, pink and well scrubbed. His face was topped by receding black hair, and featured a pair of bright, commanding eyes. He was dressed in a well - worn dark-grey suit, a stiff white collar shirt, a loosely tied red tie, and a small linen handkerchief inserted into the pocket of the jacket completed the picture.

He had been nominated by the USA President to take on the role of the DCIA, following the death of the previous head of the C.I.A, and he was officially confirmed in the job by the Senate four months ago.

It had been a difficult time since Cartwright's predecessor passed away due to a sudden unexpected heart failure, but since his death the Central Intelligence Agency had moved on, and the position of the DC.I.A was replaced shortly after. In the meantime the Chief - Of - Staff temporarily took over the position, and dealt calmly with any situations the United States faced, and conducted the covert operations.

Now, both the C.I.A and Cartwright had a crisis on their hands. Two French BGM - 109 Tomahawk cruise missiles containing live nuclear warheads had disappeared a few days ago, and apparently last night, a missile guidance system had been stolen from a US government lab in Hong Kong, China. The guidance hardware had been recently built as part of a multi - million dollar project to safely control the courses for the flights of all types of cruise missiles to their targets. It was America's most valuable defence - and a vital piece of equipment for defending the country. The guidance system was going to be programmed onto all of the US's nuclear submarines, military ships, and fighter aeroplanes. Basically, it had the power to control the flight paths of cruise missiles and programming the missiles for their target destinations. In the wrong hands, the missile guidance system could be used against America - the US submarines, ships and fighter planes could be reprogrammed to attack their own country. Missiles containing nuclear warheads could be launched into major cities in America, killing thousands, millions.

Just imagine the human casualties!

Cartwright took a deep breath and tried to calm himself. He raised his large china cup up to his pale lips and sipped at his coffee. The refreshing, but bitter taste relaxed his headache slightly. He placed the cup back down on the saucer and laid his head back against the reclining leather chair. He closed his eyes for a few moments, the whining of the aeroplane engines drumming in his ears.

Thank God the Central Intelligence Agency had Agent 27S, Cartwright thought.

Frank Ward was a remarkable agent of the very highest loyalty. Cartwright had never met a person like him. He was a professional - he would take orders without question and kill a man if this was required, although Cartwright sensed Ward didn't like killing in cold blood. As far as his dossier goes, Ward is fully trained in hand - to - hand combat and all known martial arts, including *judo* and even the Japanese *kendo*. Ward is also experienced in boxing and is accurate with knife throwing. He is the best shot in the Agency and is familiar with all types of guns and arms - this was why Cartwright chose him to protect the French spy a few days ago. He knew Ward wouldn't let him down.

Now, with a much bigger crisis on the plate, there was only one man Cartwright could rely on to recover the missile guidance hardware. That one man was Ward.

Fifteen minutes later, the Boeing 727 private jet had landed at Paris Airport, and Seymour Cartwright stepped down from the aircraft, shielding his eyes from the sun, followed by two men. One of them was Grunther, an SAS man assigned as a bodyguard to Cartwright. The other was Walter Greaves, a short, well - mannered American who was Cartwright's close friend and Chief Of Staff.

It was warm and scented in Paris today and Cartwright smiled and thought of the rainy climate back in America at the moment. Cartwright and the other two men walked unhurriedly across the airfield towards the terminal building. When they reached immigration, Cartwright produced his passport and so did Greaves and Grunther, and the official behind the desk wished them a happy stay in Paris.

Once all the signing of papers and checking of passports was done, they were met at the front of the airport by a black Rolls - Royce Phantom and a stocky dark - skinned uniformed chauffeur. The chauffeur finished loading the boot of the Rolls with Cartwright's two suitcases, saluted lazily, and then opened the rear door for them and motioned for them to sit back and relax.

He drove the luxurious car effortlessly and sensibly through the hectic streets of Paris, apparently taking his time. Cartwright leaned forward and after a while asked the chauffeur if they were near Ward's hotel yet.

'*Oui, Monsieur ,*' came the reply.

Cartwright grunted and reached inside his jacket and removed a packet of Marlboro cigarettes. He slit open the plastic wrapper with his fingernail, selected a cigarette and lit it with his battered Dunhill lighter. He inhaled the smoke greedily through his flared nostrils and waited anxiously for the Rolls - Royce to arrive at Frank Ward's hotel.

Sure enough, the Rolls arrived at the luxurious *Le Meurice* 5 - star hotel within minutes as the chauffeur had promised. The hotel looked very elegant and was between the Place de la Concorde and the Grand Louvre, opposite the Tuileries Garden, only a few steps from the Garnier Opera House and the jeweller's shops in the Rue de la Paix and Place Vendôme. As Cartwright climbed out of the Rolls, he became envious of Ward's expensive way of living. The uniformed bellboy met Cartwright and the others on the hotel steps and the chauffeur handed him the two leather suitcases.

'May I wish you a pleasant stay here at *Le Meurice* hotel, *monsieur*,' said the bellboy.

'*Merci, monsieur,*' Cartwright said. He produced a small card and handed it to the bellboy. 'I'm looking for a Monsieur Ward. He's staying at this hotel. Can you direct us to him.'

'*Oui, Monsieur.*' The bellboy turned abruptly and walked purposefully up the steps towards the grand entrance followed by Cartwright, Grunther and Greaves. As soon as they stepped through the golden automatic doors, they found themselves in a magnificently decorated lobby. The floor was covered in cream and beige mosaic tiles and on either side of the walls were two marble columns with golden candelabras sitting proudly on top, the flames flickering in the light. The lobby was obviously decorated in an 18th century style that seemed so sophisticated and expensive. A small oak table was against the wall at the far end of the lobby with a crystal vase on top of it, holding dozens of red roses. Above it, a massive glass mirror hung upon the wall in a thick, golden frame like those in a ballroom.

Cartwright swallowed and instantly felt uncomfortable in the elegant lobby. He felt that the people wandering the corridors were looking down on him. The bellboy led them through several more corridors and up and down grand staircases with ivory banisters, each floor having a particular style where space and silence are the primary luxuries.

Eventually, they came to a door at the end of a corridor with a brass plaque attached to it reading in bold capitals: 'MASSAGE ROOMS.' Cartwright and Walter Greaves, his loyal Chief Of Staff, exchanged glances. The bellboy knocked on the door and without waiting for a reply, pushed it open and motioned with a sweep of his gloved hand for the three men to go inside.

'Monsieur Ward is in the first room on the left,' the bellboy said in English with a thick accent.

'Thank you,' said Cartwright and they moved inside the room which was basically a relaxation chamber. There were a number of reclining chairs against the walls with men and women lying on them, listening to classical French music on a CD player above them. There were a number of rooms leading from it, and at the far end was a huge window overlooking the spa which was built around an inner courtyard. Grunther, the SAS agent, pointed out a door on their left which the bellboy had told them to enter. Hesitantly, Cartwright opened it and they stepped inside.

A tall man of a muscular build lay on a massage table in the corner of the room, naked except for the blue shorts he wore. He might as well have been dead. He wasn't moving. A pretty young blonde woman was bent over him, pouring a colourless liquid over her hands. She rubbed them together furiously and then flexed her fingers like a pianist before bringing them down hard on the man's upper back. She began to massage the sterno - mastoid and trapezium muscles at the back of his neck, digging her thumbs deep into the flesh. The girl leaned forward and worked with her hands, trying to release the tensions on his spine and relax his muscles. The blonde masseuse looked down at her patient and surveyed the fine body that she admired even more than her own boyfriend's. It was bulging with muscle, not fat, and the arms were strong and powerful. There were a few cuts down his back, and as she noticed underneath the faint tan, a 3 - inch scar that ran down the side of his chest. There was an ugly wound on his left arm, it looked like the man had been shot. Curiously, while the girl worked hard on his neck, she wondered what kind of profession this man was in. It was obviously something extremely physical, which would explain the numerous injuries on the man's well - built body. Maybe he was a policeman, or possibly a bodybuilder or maybe a football player, or a solider?. It would certainly explain the awesome muscles on his biceps and hamstring.

The thoughts of the masseuse were interrupted by the sound of people behind her. She stopped what she was doing and turned her head around slightly. Her brow furrowed as she studied the three men gathered around the doorway. Walter Greaves broke the silence.

'May we speak to Monsieur Ward please.' At the mention of the name, the patient on the table turned his head and looked at the familiar faces, 'in private.' The girl turned to face the handsome man on the table.

'It's alright, Dominique,' Ward explained. 'Would you leave us for a few moments.'

Dominique, the blond masseuse, nodded and walked out of the room without question. Grunther closed the door behind her and Ward stretched his back and flung his bare feet over the side of the table. He slipped his feet into a pair of slippers on the tiled floor and pulled on a white hotel bath robe to conceal his near-nakedness. Cartwright caught sight of the wound on his left arm before he pulled the robe on.

'Morning, 27S.,' Cartwright said, smiling. 'I've heard of your success in protecting the French agent. Good work. How's the arm?'

Ward felt the wound and winced in pain. He had been shot three months ago on his first mission, whilst avenging the death of his brother, Joe. It was gradually healing, although after his mission was complete, he spent several weeks in hospital to recover.

'Getting better, Sir,' he replied, sitting down on the table. He acknowledged Greaves, his closest friend in the CIA, and the other man, whom he had never met before. He ran his hands through his black hair and looked at Cartwright, his chief and boss, whom he admired greatly. 'What are you doing here, Sir?' He enquired.

Cartwright's face looked sombre and he glanced quickly at his watch. 'Something big has come up, 27S,' he said regretfully without giving any clues as to what it might be. 'It's serious or I wouldn't have come out here myself to talk to you personally. Meet me at the hotel restaurant at eight o'clock sharp and we'll discuss it over dinner,' Cartwright turned around and gripped the door handle. 'Now I'll leave you to finish your massage.'

Frank Ward grinned and watched the three men walk out of the room, slipped off his slippers and his bath robe, and lay face down on the board ready for Dominique to return. He closed his eyes and began to think what kind of job Cartwright had got for him this time. He hoped it was going to be something exciting and thrilling. He liked those kinds of missions the best - especially the dangerous ones. Those were the best of all.

4/ DINNER WITH THE DCIA

SEVERAL HOURS LATER, following the thorough massage in the health centre, Frank Ward lay between the thick golden sheets of the king - size double bed in the Deluxe Double Suite, overlooking the Rue du Mont Thabor. It was a magnificent room, decorated in a sophisticated French elegance with gracious 18th century furnishings, luxurious fabrics, mouldings and a two-metre bed in which Ward and Gaëlle Dumas, the French secret service agent, lay together, naked, kissing each other passionately on the mouth.

Ward held her tightly in his strong arms, her small breasts squashed against his chest, wrestling her tongue violently with his. She made soft moaning sounds and ran her fingers through his short black hair, securing her legs around his waist. She moved her mouth away from his and moved her soft lips across his right cheek and kissed him several times. Ward took his left arm away from behind her neck and slowly, gently, he moved his hand down the curve of her spine and stroked the cheeks of her buttocks. Gaëlle was about to kiss him hard on the lips again when a bleeping sound came from underneath the untidy pile of clothes, strewn around the room. Frank Ward heard it straight away and pulled away from her.

'What is it?' she said, pulling the sheets up to her neck, concealing her breasts.

Ward walked across the room hurriedly, and began to toss clothes around searching for the bleeping object. Eventually, he found what was making the noise, and he retrieved his stylish cell phone and pressed a button. The bleeping stopped.

'It was my cell alarm,' he announced, 'I've got to have dinner with my chief downstairs in half an hour.'

Gaëlle looked disappointed, and tried her best to conceal it. 'I suppose you have to go then.'

'Yes,' Ward turned and walked towards the spacious, marble bathroom. He stopped when he reached the door and faced her, smiling. 'I'll expect to find you in bed when I return.'

Gaëlle laughed, dropping the covers revealing her nakedness. With that, Ward had disappeared into the bathroom, followed by the sound of water from the shower-tap moments later.

Precisely fifteen minutes later, Ward stood before the grand mirror on the dressing table. He fastened the black bowtie around his stiff collar, paused for a moment and examined his reflection in the glass. His grey - blue eyes stared back at him calmly, and his dark hair was combed immaculately and parted to the left, although the usual lock of hair hung inches above his right eyebrow, resembling a thick comma. Behind it, his scar showed faintly underneath his light tan.

He slipped the straps of his leather shoulder holster around his right armpit and collected his gun of choice - the reliable old Beretta 84FS Cheetah that he had been first issued with when he joined the Central Intelligence Agency. The Beretta was a simple blowback pistol that had received many improvements, such as a decocking device, a hard chromed barrel and a reshaped trigger guard. The slide and barrel are made out of steel and the frame is made out of aluminium alloy. It is capable of holding a maximum of 10 - 13 rounds and over the past months he had gradually become more accurate with it. He couldn't imagine being equipped with a different gun - he was comfortable with the Beretta and it was easy to conceal in a holster. He weighed his gun professionally in his hand and before putting it into the holster pouch, he flicked on the safety catch.

He walked over to the door and collected his expensive white linen dinner jacket from the golden stand and pulled it on over his cotton shirt and buttoned it up. He moved over towards the marble - topped table and took out a red carnation from the vase. He fitted it neatly through his button hole and turned back towards the mirror for the last time, to check whether his gun showed underneath his jacket. It didn't, so he reached inside and withdrew his gunmetal cigarette case, put a cigarette in his mouth and lit it promptly with his battered old lighter. He blew a cloud of smoke out of his nostrils like some kind of dragon and turned and looked at Gaëlle, who was lying in bed, her back propped up with pillows, reading a novel. Her brown hair hung around her face and she casually pushed it aside.

'I'd better be off,' Ward exclaimed, inhaling the smoke.

Gaëlle slipped a bookmark in-between the pages and closed the novel. She looked up at Ward, who was now standing on the threshold.

'I'll be in the restaurant. I've got my cell phone. Call me in case your Chinese friends come back again. Don't open the door to anyone - I'll knock three times.'

Gaëlle grinned, revealing her beautiful, pearl - like teeth. 'Okay. I'll be asleep when you come back,' she yawned and covered her mouth. 'I'm feeling very tired.'

'Fine,' he said. ''Bye.' With that, he disappeared through the door and closed it behind him softly.

Frank Ward saw Cartwright waiting for him beside the grand double doors of the Restaurant Le Meurice as he came unhurriedly down the close-carpeted wine-red staircase.

Their eyes met and Ward saw the calmness behind the hard, tired grey eyes of his chief. They showed understanding and for the first time, they seemed less sombre, and more relaxed. Cartwright's thin mouth split into one of his rare smiles and he extended his right hand as his best agent came towards him.

'Good evening, Frank,' Cartwright said as Ward took his hand in his. Ward was rather shocked to hear his chief call him by his Christian name. He only used it on informal occasions such as now. 'You're just on time. Now, shall we dine and discuss your latest mission, or have a drink in the bar first?'

Ward released Cartwright's clammy paw and felt the hungry pain in his chest. He said that he would prefer to eat first. A formally dressed steward met them at the doors, his arms behind his back. The steward led them into the restaurant after Cartwright had explained they had booked, and he motioned towards a vacant table for two. The steward politely pulled back the comfortably cushioned chairs and lit the candle in the centre of the table delicately with a match. Once the flame got going he blew the match out and handed them both a broad black menu with the words 'Restaurant Le Meurice' printed on the front in gold script.

While Cartwright busied himself with finding his reading glasses in order to choose from the menu, Ward took the chance to look around the restaurant. It was certainly the most classy and stylish restaurant he had ever seen. The large room was filled with ornate gilding, antique bevelled mirrors, Louis XVI period crystal chandeliers and large bay windows framed in rare marble. The two Michelin star Restaurant 'le Meurice' recreated the lustrous effects of this period's architectural detailing. Landscape paintings on the wall and a ceiling depicting a blue sky with angels create an uplifting, open feeling. The floral-infused decor echoed the Tuileries Garden, with chairs and curtains in floral patterns of green, yellow and salmon. The china, specially designed by Limoges for

Le Meurice, matched the mosaic patterns on the floor. Against such a background, guests feel as if they have been invited to a private dinner hosted by Louis XVI. Once Ward had looked around the lavishly decorated room, he took a quick glance at the menu and immediately decided on what he was going to have.

'What do you fancy, Frank?' Cartwright said without moving his eyes off the menu.

'I feel like the grilled salmon served with salad and Beluga caviar,' he replied decisively. 'Salmon is a favourite of mine.'

Cartwright put the menu down beside his plate and seemed to have made up his mind. 'It sounds nice. I'll have the same. Drinks?'

'Champagne?'

'Excellent!'

The steward who had met them at the doors appeared with a notebook and pen in his hand. Cartwright explained what they wanted and asked for the finest champagne on offer. Once the steward had scribbled his notes down on the paper he grinned and hurried off towards the kitchen.

Now Cartwright's face was serious and he sat, his shoulders hunched over the table, his eyes meeting squarely with Ward's. 'Let's get down to business,' he said. Ward looked up immediately interested. 'As you know, a few days ago, two nuclear warheads were stolen by international terrorists. Both French Intelligence and the C.I.A have been searching the world for them without success. You rescued the French agent yesterday from those Chinese thugs. They were our leads and we believe that they had been hired by whoever had stolen the warheads. On the same night, the new cruise missile guidance system was stolen from a US government lab in Hong Kong. There have been no witnesses and several guards and technicians have been killed. The guidance system was removed from a safe.' Cartwright paused as the steward returned with the bottle of Bollinger champagne and began to pour into two glasses. Ward took the chance to think about what Cartwright had just said.

Surely both the theft of the warheads and the guidance hardware are connected? But who had stolen them? S.C.I.E.R.D perhaps? (S.C.I.E.R.D was an international terrorist syndicate that Ward had battled against before. He believed that it no longer existed after the Sharp affair).

Both glasses were filled to the brim with the champagne, and the steward placed it in the middle of the table and walked away. Ward reached for his glass, feeling the satisfying coldness against his fingertips, before lifting it to his lips. He sipped it, and placed it back down onto the table waiting for his chief to continue the briefing.

'As you know, the guidance system was a new development for the US, controlling all our defence programmes. You've read all about it back in Langley. It was due to be unveiled next week. Now, we can only assume that whoever stole the warheads had something to do with the break-in at the Government testing facility last night in Hong Kong.'

'That's what I was thinking.'

'So we can only believe that those Chinese thugs who were after the French girl also were in on the theft of the warheads and the guidance system.'

Ward raised his glass, tilted his head back and drank slowly and sensibly. He favoured Bollinger champagne - he thought of it as the best and often drank it on special occasions. 'Were any of the Chinese men identified? I shot a few from the helicopter but a few would have survived.'

Cartwright nodded discreetly. 'Yes. All of the men were identified. The French Direction Générale de la Sécurité Extérieure looked them up on their files. Most of them were from the Chinese Triads. Others were just random killers.'

'Did the French Secret Service interrogate the survivors?'

'Yes,' Cartwright replied mildly, 'but they all kept their mouths shut. None of them talked, but they found a piece of crumbled paper on one of them.'

'What did it say?' Ward enquired, rubbing his thumb up and down his now empty champagne glass.

'It was a business card for the Kraken International Cooperation. Ever heard of it?' Cartwright asked.

'Of course,' he said softly, 'A massive chemical company that creates and ships all sorts of fuel around the world. The multi million empire also provides America, England and France with rocket fuel to launch space shuttles. The company makes the explosives and chemical elements found in warheads and nuclear bombs. As far as I am aware, the Kraken International Cooperation was taken over a few years ago by the French multi billionaire and industrialist, Claude Victor. Victor is perhaps the wealthiest man in Europe, especially since he brought the Kraken Cooperation. You can't help seeing and hearing about him every time you open the newspaper or turn on the television.'

Cartwright listened to Ward's explanation. 'Your story goes together with mine. Victor seems to be America's best ally at the moment. He is supplying us with the explosives needed to create our guided missiles, and he is also working with the NASA space programme. This is why I'm shocked that it seems Victor may be involved with the theft of the warheads and the guidance system.'

Ward was about to refill his glass with champagne when he heard what his boss had just said. 'Victor?' He exclaimed, his voice filled with shock and confusion. 'Why would he have been involved?'

Cartwright shrugged. 'I don't know either, Frank, but the evidence points to him. It seems that he is connected with those Chinese thugs, despite whether he was behind the whole theft. I don't understand it but I cannot afford to take any risks. If Victor has got the warheads and the guidance system, he could launch them right at us and America would be defenceless. Remember, the Kraken International Cooperation makes the explosives used in nuclear warheads; supposing he goes and packs those two stolen cruise missiles with even more explosives. Maybe even enough to wipe out the whole country! That is precisely why I'm sending you to investigate Claude Victor.'

Ward's brow was furrowed and he rubbed his chin and thought about it. So this was going to be his latest mission. His new assignment was to go after Claude Victor, the richest man in the world and a possible threat to the world. But why? If it was he who hired those Chinese hit men, why would he do it? What would he gain? His thoughts were interrupted by the steward who came with a stainless steel trolley on wheels, two dome - shaped platters covering the plates. Ward and Cartwright looked up. The steward collected the two starter plates and replaced them with their meals. Cartwright looked down at his dinner - grilled salmon with salad and caviar.

'*Merci.*'

'*Appréciez votre dîner, Messieurs.*'

Ward started straight away and cut a piece of the salmon and popped it into his mouth. It was very fresh and it tasted as if it had just been taken out of the sea. He swallowed it, took a sip of the champagne, and collected a bit of lettuce on his fork.

After a few moments of silence while the two men began their splendid meal, Cartwright asked, 'How much do you know about Claude Victor, Frank?' Ward looked up at his chief and took a sip of his champagne before starting on the excellent Beluga caviar. He washed the salmon down with the Bollinger and began to search his brain for information. 'Quite a lot actually. I read the official autobiography last year. He is the child of a wealthy French media mogul and a poor American girl. He was raised, during his childhood, mainly in Paris, but his father moved around often with his job. His mother committed suicide when Claude was six years old, although some believe his father, Jean, may have had something to do with her death. Afterwards, Claude was brought up by his father alone. He was always an intelligent child, an enigma to teachers and other students. He could calculate the most difficult sums in his head within seconds, and his understanding of science was amazing. He had an interest in chemistry when he was a child, and at school he would practise various dangerous experiments. As he finished school, he was a very brainy student, excelling in mathematics and science. He studied at university and took up media courses under the encouragement of his father, Jean. Claude was a very quiet young man and didn't talk much or have many friends. He was short tempered and tended to get violent with anyone who came near him. While he was at university, he was testing a scientific theory of his own in the laboratories when something went wrong and the experiment exploded. The explosion was horrific, burning down the entire university and severely burning Claude. His whole face was basically blown off, his skin burning. The university sued Jean for millions, leaving him nearly bankrupt. Claude was left in intensive care for a year due to the burns all over his body. Claude begged his father to pay for plastic surgery to restore his looks. Jean refused, having no money at all, having lost his career and television empire. Claude announced he never wanted to see his father again. Jean was upset and angry so he pulled out a gun and shot himself dead. Claude inherited his father's mansion which he sold for a million, which he then used to buy back his father's media empire. With all the money, he had plastic surgery and skin transplants to repair his face, arms, legs and chest that were affected in the explosion. However, the surgery was not a success, leaving Claude looking like a freak - the living dead even. Controlling his father's empire for a further ten years, Claude was now a wealthy man, having power over television, radio, magazines and newspapers. Soon he became bored with being a media mogul. He sold his empire for far more than he had originally paid and then continued his scientific research. He made a massive discovery in biology, earning him millions. As his interest increased in his work, he brought the Kraken International Cooperation and he soon became a billionaire, providing countries with various chemicals and fuels needed for defence and attack. Within months, Claude Victor became one of the wealthiest men alive, owning huge luxurious mansions and estates around the world. He also has a massive collection of sports cars, helicopters, boats and even two jumbo air jets. He donates millions to charities. The public adore him and admire him.'

Cartwright shovelled a spoonful of caviar into his mouth and looked up at Ward who had already finished his meal. 'That's pretty much it,' he said conclusively. 'He's gone from nothing to everything, being one of the most recognised faces in the world.'

Ward grinned and laughed out loud. 'People can't help recognising his face. He looks like a zombie!' Cartwright chuckled too and his face went serious again. 'Well, enough joking,' he said, 'Victor may be a criminal just putting on an act. Like I said, I'm not prepared to take any chances. Not if it means putting America on the line. If there is a chance Victor has anything to do with this whole thing, we must look into it. The French Secret Service think the same too - that's why they are assigning the French agent, Miss Dumas to work with you on a joint mission,' Ward smiled at this point, being glad to work with Gaëlle again. 'Victor is holding a party at his castle fortress in the French Alps tomorrow evening to announce his engagement with his girlfriend, Linda Pascal. You and Miss Dumas will attend under the cover of reporters of a new space magazine. Find out as much as you can and search the place if possible for information. Miss Dumas will receive her briefing tomorrow with my opposite number. The President and the Director of National Intelligence would have my head on a plate if they knew I was sending you after Victor. Don't fail or mess up, 27S or we'll both be out of our jobs.'

With that, Cartwright wiped his lips with a napkin and got up out of his seat. 'Goodnight, Ward.' Ward said goodnight back and watched his chief disappear through the restaurant doors. He grinned and finished his third glass of champagne. So, a new mission! It sounded exciting as well. He had a new cover and a female ally. He couldn't wait until tomorrow night. He got up out of his chair and moved purposely out of the restaurant towards the bar.

5/ UNDERCOVER

THE 2006 CHEVROLET CORVETTE Z06 COUPE cruised down the cliff - top road, high up in the freezing French Alps.

Frank Ward took his eyes off the icy road for a few minutes and gazed at the snowy Mount Blanc, also known as *La Dame Blanche*, the highest mountain in Western Europe. He could visibly see the large castle fortress up on the white hills, belonging to Claude Victor, the owner of Kraken International Cooperation. It only looked small from the road, but Ward could imagine how large Victor's castle actually was. They were nearly there now. Gaëlle Dumas, the lovely French spy was sitting next to him in the leather passenger seat, admiring the fantastic view of the mountainous land covered in thick sheets of snow. She was wearing an expensive light blue silk dress, the curves of her fine breasts showing proudly underneath the material. She wore elegant diamond earrings, square - cut, and a matching diamond bracelet. She wore no more jewellery. Her beautiful light brown hair was put up neatly this time , instead of falling to her shoulders, and her finger nails were painted in blood-red varnish.

Ward's heart was beginning to thump hard against his chest. His adrenaline was pumping up like it always did at the beginning of a new assignment. He had to keep his cool tonight or his cover and Gaëlle's would be blown. They were supposed to be reporters of the new *Space Triumphs* magazine. The cover was all set. It was just a matter of whether it would fool Claude Victor.

Frank Ward jerked at the wheel of the platinum Chevrolet Corvette and turned sharply around the next corner, ending in a skid which he corrected immediately. The speed - o - meter was just pushing sixty. His car had always been one of his main hobbies, and during his free time, he loved to get away from it all and just relax in his precious American sports car.

He bought the Chevrolet Corvette Z06 Coupe last month, brand new. It had cost him $66,000, but it was worth it. It had replaced his old BMW Z8, which he sold for far less than it was worth. He was glad to see it go.

The Chevrolet was something different altogether. It was silver, the seats were all leather and the interior was a magnificent ebony colour. The sports car is powered by a 6.0-litre V8, generating an impressive 400 horsepower. A six-speed manual transmission is standard. The Chevrolet is a convertible, and the car includes a manually operated soft top.

The car could accelerate to exceptionally fast speeds and the brakes were excellent. It was Ward's pride and joy. The Z06 frame is made entirely of hydro-formed aluminium (the standard Vettes have steel rails), with a magnesium engine cradle, and its fenders are formed from ultra-light carbon fibre. As a result, and despite a much heavier engine and drive train, the Z06 weighs 50 pounds less than a standard Corvette coupe.

The CIA Weapons & Gadgetry Department had fitted a few complimentary accessories into the sports car. Hidden behind both wing mirrors of the car were two poison dart guns, that were fired manually by buttons on the dashboard. They were used to take out enemies in cars alongside you. The poison on the tip of the darts causes death in three seconds. Underneath the drivers seat in a secret compartment was a weapons tray, holding a .357 Magnum pistol, a flat - throwing knife and a fragmentation grenade. Ward was comfortable with the Magnum, and like his small Beretta 84FS Cheetah, he was highly accurate with it. He didn't carry it around with him though. It was far too bulky and difficult to conceal. He thought it to be a useful gun not only to take out people but even vehicles. A well aimed shot to the bonnet of a car and it would stop it in its tracks. The Chevrolet Corvette was also covered in a thick armoured casing, making it immune to bullets, fire and explosion damage. Finally, behind the rear licence plate was a tear-gas duct, capable of temporarily blinding enemies and injuring them sufficiently. The car was Ward's own 'toy' and he was very proud of it. Since he bought it last month, it had served him well, both on duty and off.

Ward was beginning to think about Claude Victor, the richest man in the world and possibly a terrorist employing Triad gang members. If he was responsible, what motivation would he have to steal the two nuclear warheads and the missile guidance system? What did he intend doing with them? He didn't like it. He could launch them at anywhere in America using the guidance hardware, and the US defences wouldn't be able to stop it in time.

Stop it, 27S! Wake up! Surely Victor didn't steal the warheads and the missile technology.

Claude Victor's medieval castle fortress was on top of Mount Blanc, only accessible by helicopter or the cable car station at the bottom where visitors were taken up to the very top. The castle looked hundreds of years old. Two large turrets were located at either side of the building. The towers and many ancient battlements were all of weathered, grey stone covered in layers of green moss and decay. There were a number of old - fashioned slit windows, covered in dark glass, which was possibly bullet - proof. There were many large courtyards around the building as well as a few gardens on each side. On top of the roofs and balconies were large search-lights which were being operated by security - the men looked the size of ants in the distance. The roof, now coated in layers of snow, was made up of worn slate tiles. There was a new addition to the fortress on the right hand side.

A large helipad area had been built on a raised platform. A small helicopter was positioned on the helipad, presumably belonging to Victor himself. On the left was the cable car station which had been built into the rock leading down to the station at the bottom of the mountain.

Ward continued down the road in the metallic silver Chevrolet, following the directions Cartwright had given him last evening. A few minutes later Ward drew up to the cable car station at the bottom of the Mountain, the aerial link to Victor's castle fortress high up in the Alps. A large car park was beside it for the visitors. Ward spotted a few Lamborghini's and Ferrari's among the vehicles. The Chevrolet came off the road and edged up towards the building, the thick sheet of snow crunching underneath the tyres. Two security men dressed in red ski jackets saw the sports car come to a halt in the car park and they came over towards it unhurriedly. Frank Ward opened the car door and climbed out to meet the two men.

'We are guests at Claude Victor's party tonight,' Ward said, motioning with his right hand towards Gaëlle who was getting out of the car behind them. 'Can we take a ride up to the castle?'

The two guards in the ski jackets were hard - faced men. One of them had a broken nose and a build like an ox. He resembled some kind of professional wrestler. The first man came forward. 'Invitation?'

Ward nodded slowly and reached inside his black tuxedo jacket and removed the two invitations and handed them to the first guard. The other men examined them to make sure that they were genuine, and he stuffed them into his trouser pocket and gestured towards the large station. 'This way please.' The two guards turned and trudged slowly through the snow towards the station. Ward locked the Chevrolet Z06 Corvette and activated the safety mechanisms, which sent electric stunners to the door handles. Anybody who touched them would receive a nasty electric shock. He joined Gaëlle and they followed the two guards towards the entrance.

'Victor's got an interesting place up here in the mountains,' Ward said quietly to Gaëlle. She looked around on full alert, watching everybody for any suspicious movements. Her gun was concealed in a holster hidden underneath her lovely silk dress. They stayed close together. Ward looked at the steep slopes of Mount Blanc. There were a few ski routes on the east side of the castle fortress, leading down into the valley below and into the village. He memorized each route individually; which one was easiest, which was the fastest and which seemed most hazardous, just in case he needed to make a quick escape.

The two guards showed them inside the large cable station where they went down a few cold steps into the terminal room where the bull wheel was assembled. This is connected to an electric motor in order to drive the gondola lift on the cable, joining both stations. It was very cold in this room, and Ward noticed Gaëlle shiver. They moved through the double doors and out onto the platform where a black and red cable car was waiting for them. The first guard gestured for them to go inside with a wave of his arm while the other disappeared inside an office. Ward thanked the security man as they stepped inside the gondola lift and they gazed out of the windows, overlooking the massive drop to the valleys below. The car shook slightly and after a faint noise the aerial lift began to move on the loop of steel cable. It was a fantastic feeling to be high up in the sky, the ground so far away it seemed that one was flying. Frank Ward looked around inside the car and moved over to Gaëlle. 'Don't say anything about business, Gaëlle, while we are inside the cable car,' he whispered quietly. 'It's wired for sound.'

Gaëlle looked around cautiously and nodded gently. She spotted the small bug transmitter and microphone cell taped into the top right hand corner of the car. It was certainly suspicious. If Claude Victor had nothing to hide, why was be being so meticulous at listening into other peoples' conversations. Was he expecting to be investigated by intelligence communities? There was definitely something wrong. Ward took one last look at the hidden mike and then at the castle fortress which stood firmly at the top of the mountain, high above the villages nearby. It was lively with people already. Guests who had already arrived were assembled outside the large oak doors studded with bolts. Others had already gone inside to get a drink or wait in the ballroom for Claude Victor's announcement of his engagement to his girlfriend. Ward spotted many celebrities amongst the crowd. He guessed that there were going to be well over one thousand people invited to the party. Media groups and television cameramen were getting their equipment ready outside the front of the castle. As the cable car drew into the station, Ward's eyes met with those of a gargoyle on one of the castle balconies.

The cable car came to the end of the line and stopped suddenly causing the car to jerk slightly. The doors opened automatically with a hiss and a tall man wearing a dark suit met them on the platform. He was a beastly looking kind of man with fierce predator features and a well built body. The man's arms were as wide as his legs and great muscles bulged underneath the tight fitting jacket. His eyes were wide and like dark, black pools that showed only anger and hatred behind them. The eyebrows were thick and hung above his evil eyes. The nose was large, like the rest of his body, and his nostrils were constantly flared like some kind of animal scenting fire. The mouth seldom smiled and was quite ugly and small. It looked misplaced on the face amongst his other features. The lips creased into a sickly smile, revealing rows of immaculate white teeth. 'Welcome to Claude Victor's Engagement Party. I am his head of security, Marcus Hillman, 'he extended a large, powerful hand, 'I hope you both enjoy yourselves this evening.'

Ward took the hand. It felt as if the man squeezed hard enough he would crush Ward's hand to bits. It was so strong. 'My name is Frank Ward,' he announced. Gaëlle moved forward. 'This is my colleague Fiona Bennett. We are both reporters for the *Space Triumphs* magazine.'

'Excellent,' Marcus Hillman said mildly. 'The reception will be in the ballroom in a few moments. Would you like to go inside the castle, please. The bar is open.'

'Thank you.'

As Ward and Gaëlle walked past him up the stone steps of the gondola station, he noticed the faint crease underneath Hillman's right armpit; a bulge that he recognised as that of a concealed gun. *Why would Victor's staff carry guns? Surely it wasn't necessary for the security to be armed with such weapons. After all, Claude Victor was only a successful business man, and not a criminal who steals warheads and missile guidance technology.* Even more suspicious than before, Ward thought of the hidden bug transmitter in the cable car. Again, his adrenaline rushed through his body. He sensed danger around him. He had to presume that other security men were armed too. If things went out of hand, he had his Beretta with him. It was at least some comfort although he didn't intend using it tonight. If he was going to kill, he was going to make it as silent and discreet as possible. He would also make it look like an accident. The least amount of kills the better. This job required stealth; nothing else. If he was found out he would certainly be killed. Maybe even tortured to death.

Hillman led Ward and Gaëlle out of the station and up towards the castle and disappeared amongst the crowd of guests and television crews that were gathered outside the large doors. Ward turned to Gaëlle. 'Let's go inside and get a drink at the bar before Victor addresses his guests in the ballroom.'

Gaëlle looked at him and said, 'Okay.'

They walked through the thick, heavy doors that brought them immediately into a long corridor, the stone floor lined with wine-red carpet. Against the walls were tall candelabra, their flickering flames casting light upon the dull stone walls. Old water - colour paintings were framed on the walls, the colour yellowing with age. They followed the twisting corridor and came to a massive room with a marble floor, designed in a checkerboard pattern. It was brightly lit around the room with lights, including the spectacular golden chandelier that hung from the ceiling. A huge tapestry was draped on the centre wall beside the two slit windows. On the right side of the room was the bar, all metal surfaced and modern looking. It looked strange amongst all the other ancient styles which decorated the ballroom. At the far left was a grand stone stairway with a wide landing and a balcony, overlooking the marble floor and the bar area.

This was obviously where Claude Victor was going to give his engagement speech, thought Ward. The ballroom was filled with party guests and the worlds media, running around to and fro. Ward and Gaëlle moved over to the bar. The barman came over to them and smiled. 'Yes, sir?'

'Russian vodka, please. With ice and a thin slice of lemon peel. Got it?'

'Yes sir. And the lady?'

'Just a shandy, please.'

The bar man nodded and got to work. It was then Ward felt a hand grip his shoulder from behind. His body went cold and he turned around instantly, coming face to face with a tall, skinny man that resembled the living dead. The extremely pallid skin, which was almost certainly white, looked as if it had been stretched over the small, bald skull. The grey eyes were drawn far back into their sockets, making the 'man' look like some kind of mutated alien. Thin veins showed underneath the ghastly transparent skin, almost bursting out. The eyes stared directly into

Ward's, glassy and unblinking; and only then did a smile form upon the deformed mouth. The nose was thin and slightly crooked like that of a witch. Maybe it was broken. The smile revealed the very few teeth, hanging from the gums, all dead and decaying. His whole body looked as if it was dead. No life or movement was shown. Frank Ward wasn't even sure whether the man was actually breathing. 'Good evening,' the man said calmly in a thick French accent, extending a large bony hand. 'I am Claude Victor, your host for this evening.'

Ward forced a smile and took the bony hand in his. It was so deathly cold and clammy. Surely it was not alive. 'I'm Frank Ward, and this is my friend Lucy Bennett. We both work for the *Space Triumphs* magazine.'

Gaëlle Dumas, a.k.a Lucy Bennett, came forward and exchanged warm smiles with Claude Victor. Ward noticed the resistance in her face as he offered her his hand. The barman came and handed them their drinks. Ward sipped at his Russian vodka, looking Victor squarely into his grey eyes.

'Is your magazine covering tonight's big event?' Victor enquired, standing straight with authority, his hands behind his back. He was very tall, perhaps six foot two. 'Of course,' Gaëlle exclaimed. 'Our readers admire you and everything you've done, especially aiding NASA with their research.'

Victor grinned, revealing the ugly gums, holding very little teeth. 'Excellent! My work with NASA has taught me many things. I've benefited hugely from my career. I also provide England, America and France with explosives used to make warheads for attack and defence purposes.'

'Yes I know.' Ward decided he was going to light a fire under Claude Victor and make him sweat. He thought that if he mentioned the missing warheads, Victor's reaction might give the game away. 'I suppose you know all about the missing warheads,' he said casually.

Ward studied Victor's face. The smile had vanished and the face looked as if it had just been slapped. He stared hard into Wards eyes, suspiciously and then narrowed them. A smile returned to the face but the eyes remained watchful and anxious.

'What do you mean?' He asked.

'They were stolen a few days ago by a group of terrorists. Maybe it was the Chinese Triads.' Again, the mention of the Triads made the smile vanish from the face. The eyes were filled with venom, and a look of doubt spread across his face. *Who was this man? Did he really know, or was it just a coincidence?*

'Perhaps,' Victor said coolly. There was an awkward pause for a few moments while Victor stared hard into the back of Ward's skull. They were joined by a beautiful woman in her early thirties. She had golden hair that was quite short and fell to her shoulders, emerald eyes and a sensual mouth. Her figure was fantastic and slim. She wore a low cut black dress and a pair of designer shoes with high stilettos. A diamond necklace hung above the top of her dress. The attractive girl put an arm around Victor.

'Come on darling,' she said softly, 'it is time to make your speech.' Claude Victor turned towards his soon-to-be fiancé. 'Yes darling. I don't suppose you've met our new friends Mister Ward and Miss Bennett?'

The girl smiled and came forward. She shook their hands in turn and said, 'I'm Linda Pascal. I'm delighted to meet you both.' She then turned towards Victor. 'Come darling. Everybody is waiting for us.'

Victor nodded and followed Linda Pascal through the crowds of people gathered in the ballroom. He stopped and looked briefly at Ward, his vicious eyes shooting daggers, and then he hurried off towards the stone staircase. Ward finished the rest of his vodka in one solid gulp and handed the cocktail glass to the barman. He faced Gaëlle. 'Victor is definitely hiding something,' he said decisively. 'I suspect that our superiors were correct. Victor may be connected with the theft of the warheads and the guidance system. He may also have been the one who put a hit on you back in Paris.'

Gaëlle nodded and finished her drink. 'It certainly looks like it. We'll have a look around the castle once Victor has finished his speech. With the party going on in the ballroom, we should be able to get a good look around the grounds without being noticed.'

'We'll have to be careful,' Ward replied. 'There will still be guards patrolling the place. They are all armed as well. Victor's got his own little army up here in the mountains. There's also searchlights monitoring the courtyards and the gardens. I noticed them before we came in.'

Their plans were interrupted by the creepy voice of Claude Victor on the landing above the marble floor. He was standing there with Linda, his eyes surveying the crowds watching him, a phoney smile fixed on his thin lips. 'Welcome everyone!' Victor exclaimed. 'I thank you for your presence here tonight as my dear love, Linda and I announce our engagement to our friends, family and the press. I also thank you for the constant support that you have given me throughout this joyous time. I have worked hard over the years, my life dedicated to science and other people who need me the most. Throughout my life, my aim has been to do good in the world, and to make a fantastic discovery. I have done that. I have donated almost half of my fortune to charities that need it more than I do. I aim to end all world hunger, give the poor and homeless roofs over their heads. I hope to send many astronauts to the moon so we can continue our understanding of outer space. Throughout all this time, Linda,' he turned towards her and put a long arm around her shoulder, 'has supported me hugely and has given me love and pleasure. Tonight, in view of you all, I will show how much I am devoted to Linda. I will give her an engagement ring that signifies not only my love for her, but the many more years we shall spend together.' Victor reached inside his trouser pocket and removed a small case. He opened the lid, removed the diamond ring and slipped it onto her finger. Then he turned towards the crowd and grinned as photographers clicked away at their cameras, and he kissed Linda full on the mouth. The whole crowd cheered and applauded. Victor pulled away and faced his guests. 'Again I thank you for making the journey here this evening. Now, you can party in the ballroom and feast in the dining hall. Cocktails are available all night.'

The crowd continued to applaud, and Claude Victor and Linda Pascal waved to the guests and exited through a door on the landing followed by Marcus Hillman, the man who had greeted Ward and Gaëlle at the cable car station.

Hillman closed the door behind them, shutting out the noise of the crowds in the ballroom. He inserted a key into the hole and locked it. Victor and his new fiancé Linda walked unhurriedly down the stone staircase leading down to the bottom rooms of the ancient castle. 'Now darling,' Victor said calmly. 'I'm meeting with a few business associates in the conference room. You return to the party and play the hostess for a while. I'll be back in an hour.'

Linda was disappointed but tried not to show it. 'OK. But don't be long. You don't want to neglect your guests and the press do you?' Claude Victor grinned and kissed Linda gently on the cheek. 'I won't.' With that he beckoned Marcus Hillman to follow and they continued down the stairs, leaving Linda alone.

It was darker and damper as Victor and his right hand man, Hillman moved towards the cellars of the castle, where his conference room was located. Nobody ever came down here. Only Hillman and Victor himself had keys. Victor turned towards Hillman. 'Put all the guards on full alert. I believe that there may be a spy at the party. He goes by the name of Frank Ward. Tell them to find him and question him. I don't want him to spoil the party for my guests.'

Hillman nodded and took out his cell phone and dialled in a number. A few moments later it was answered. 'Find Frank Ward,' he instructed. 'He may be a government agent ... no don't kill him, just make him uncomfortable ... Just make sure he is taken care of ... I'll be in the conference room with the chief ... No, don't disturb us.'

Hillman put the phone away and grinned. 'They have gone after him, Sir. He won't be a nuisance to you any longer.' Claude Victor grinned and laughed out loud, his voice echoing against the mouldy stone walls.

6/ 'STEALTH IS THE GAME'

THE TWO SPIES stood by the bar, watching the guests talk and dance on the marble floor, music blasting from the modern speakers that were jotted around the room.

Linda Pascal, Claude Victor's fiancé came elegantly down the stone staircase and into the ballroom, where she mingled with the celebrities and gave interviews to the adoring press. Ward sipped at his second Russian vodka, wondering where Victor and the Hillman chap had gone to. Why had he gone away and completely ignored his guests? Maybe he was just finishing some work for the Kraken International Cooperation? Or maybe the American missile guidance system was about to switch hands? He couldn't afford to take that chance. He would have to find Victor and see what he was up to.

Frank Ward turned to Gaëlle, conscious of a security guard dressed in an immaculate suit across the room watching them suspiciously. 'Perhaps we should split up now and see what we can find out,' Ward suggested, finishing his drink.

Gaëlle nodded and glanced over her shoulder at the security guard. 'Maybe it is for the best. There is a guard behind me watching us both carefully. Do you suppose they've found out who we really are?'

Ward put his empty glass back down on the bar. 'Yes. I've noticed. If we have been found out, we'd better get moving. We've got to search the castle and find out what Victor is really up to.'

Gaëlle bit her lip. 'Right. I'll search the east side of the castle. You search the west. Wait.' She reached inside a hidden compartment in her dress and removed something shiny and handed it to Ward. 'It's a lock pick,' she said. 'I've got one as well.'

Ward grinned. 'Thanks.' With that, she turned around and headed for the exit of the ballroom. Ward glanced back at the guard. His eyes were focused on him. Ward ground his teeth.

Damn! If Victor was onto him, they would have less time than he thought.

Frank Ward took one last look at the security man and turned and headed towards another exit that led out onto one of the castle balconies. It was snowing slightly, and a flake brushed against his cheek. It was a cold night and he shivered. Jagged icicles hung from the battlements above, like daggers ready to fall. Ward glanced over the side of the stone balcony. It was a terrific view. The ravine was covered in an immaculate sheet of snow; a thick blanket of coldness. The mountainous terrain was steep and uneven. Mount Blanc stood above the other rocky hills and cliffs, taller and greater. Ward looked at the two gondola stations, linked together by the cables. That was the only way back down, but it was going to be heavily guarded. They'd never make it alive that way. It was then he remembered the three ski routes leading down the steady slope. He had remembered which one was the easiest and less hazardous. When they needed to escape, taking the slopes might be the best and most discreet option. The only problem was his skiing was a little rusty.

Ward walked unhurriedly across the balcony, making his footsteps gentle. The snow crunched slightly underneath his feet. He was like a wild animal - alert and ready for a fight. He stopped and hid in the shadows. He heard the sound of footsteps nearby. Ward steadied his breathing, remaining as quiet as possible. He slipped on a pair of black leather gloves and removed his Beretta 84FS Cheetah from the pouch of his shoulder holster and held it uncertainly in his right hand, his finger on the trigger. He would shoot anything that moved. The footsteps were getting nearer. There was a faint creaking sound as a door opened. Ward turned his head slowly and watched the security guard who had been spying on him in the ballroom, come down the balcony, a Walther P99 fixed in his hand. He looked around, his dark eyes searching in every direction. Finally, he reached up to his earpiece walkie - talkie.

'I've lost the him,' the man said softy. 'He must have headed into the west courtyard… No, don't sound the alarm. We don't want to upset the guests. Search all the courtyards and gardens and upgrade the security. Contact me once you find him.'

With that, the security man turned around and disappeared back through the door. Slowly, Ward slipped out of his hiding place and looked left and right. The coast was clear. Like a panther, he moved cautiously down the balcony and came to a small flight of stairs that led into a deserted courtyard.

There was nobody in sight.

All was silent.

Frank Ward gripped the stairs and rushed down them, his watchful eyes scanning the area and the bridge above the courtyard. There were two guards standing on the bridge, one operating the large search light, the other keeping a look out for intruders. They both carried pistols and small sub - machine guns. Ward moved his finger up and down the trigger, trying to decide whether to shoot them both or try and slip past them, and the glowing beam of the searchlight which raked the courtyard grounds. If he was caught in the light, his presence would immediately be given away. He could pick off the patrolling guard first and then shoot the one on the searchlight before he spun around. He decided against shooting them both dead.

Stealth is the game, he told himself.

He waited until the patrolling guard had his back turned and then he rushed down the stairs and into the courtyard. He stayed close to the wall to avoid the searchlight which was monitoring the grounds. When the beam moved away from him, he slipped underneath the bridge and stayed there where neither the guards nor the search light would find him.

Now how was he going to get out unseen? Could he create some kind of distraction? No, that was a foolish idea. He would just have to sneak past when the guards weren't looking.

Ward bit his lip. He had no idea whether to make a run for it. He didn't know whether the guards were looking in the right direction or not. He edged out from underneath the bridge. Currently, the searchlight was focused at the other end of the courtyard. If he managed to get up against the wall and creep back in to the next courtyard in the shadows, he might just go unnoticed. He would have to remain silent, though. Ward moved out into the courtyard creating as little noise as possible whilst moving in the shadows away from the circular beam of the search light that focused on the ground and the walls. He could hear one of the men receiving instructions via his earpiece walkie - talkie. '...*Non, nous n'avons pas vu l'Américain encore. Vous devez avoir été erroné. Il pourrait avoir retournéà l'intérieur du château.*'

Frank Ward, who was fluent in French, clearly understood what the security guard was saying. They hadn't spotted him yet and they believed that he must have gone back inside the castle.

So the guards didn't know he was here. He wasn't going to allow the search light to give away his hiding place now.

Keeping his back against the stone walls, Ward stayed in the darkness, barely visible to the human eye. He controlled his breathing and took small, gentle steps so as not to make a noise in the snow. He was nearly there now. He was nearly at the end of the courtyard. Ward stopped when he reached the end of the wall and looked up at the bridge that connected the two balconies together. The guard on the searchlight had taken a break and lit himself a cigarette. The other one was facing the other way, talking to a colleague through his walkie - talkie.

It was time to make a move.

Frank Ward slipped behind the wall and immediately found himself in a smaller courtyard with a grand water fountain in the middle, made of concrete. A figurine of a naked woman was on the top, water spraying out, the eyes staring at Ward glassily. A single guard was walking around the fountain, his right hand resting on his gun holstered at his waist. There was a small stone office built into the courtyard, which appeared to be the control station that supplied the electricity for the search lights. Ward peered over the wall. There was a man inside the office at a wooden desk, writing on some papers.

Maybe the man wouldn't notice if Ward took out the guard silently in the courtyard. Ward watched the patrolling guard carefully, remembering his every move and noting when he would have his back turned. Like a predator, he waited until the time was right to strike. The guard was coming past the fountain again. He turned forty five degrees and continued walking, out of view of the man in the office.

One, two, three, strike! Ward leapt forward, holding his Beretta by the muzzle. He grabbed hold of the man's collar with his left hand and brought the butt of his gun down upon the shaven head with all his might. The guard didn't have time to react or alert the man in the office as the gun smashed down upon his head with force, cracking his skull like a boiled egg. He grunted and stumbled to his knees, blood and gore leaking out of the hole in his head like a piñata. He reached up towards his head, closed his eyes and fell face first into the snow.

All was silent. Ward watched as the life vanished from the body quicker than he had imagined. He looked up at the small glass window of the office. The man was still hunched over the desk, scribbling furiously with his pencil. Ward collected his Beretta and looked down at the dead body, a pool of blood staining the snow. He would hide the body later and cover up the evidence. But first, he had to take care of the man in the office.

Stealthily, Ward moved past the fountain and towards the stone office. He crouched down as he edged underneath the window and came towards the wooden door. The man inside was possibly armed. Ward would have to act fast as soon as he opened the door. He decided on subduing the guard with his bare hands - he might need the bullets in his Beretta when he makes his escape. He didn't have any spare ammunition any way. Frank Ward stood up and gripped the handle with his gloved hand, his other clenched ready to attack. He made sure he was ready and he pushed open the door.

The naked single bulb that hung from the ceiling revealed the side of the man's face as he looked up from his work. He looked a vicious brute - possibly a Hungarian. He had a heavy moustache that drooped over the snarling mouth. His sadistic eyes widened and he immediately reached for his Colt .45 that was laid on his desk beside an ashtray. Ward saw the gun on the table and immediately acted. He lunged out with his left fist, catching the Hungarian directly under the chin, almost lifting the man off the ground. His head tilted backwards and blood trickled down from his mouth. The Hungarian thug fell back against the wall dropping the Colt. It clattered harmlessly to the floor. The guard's eyes were filled with anger and he charged at Ward and punched him in the chest. Ward groaned and ignored the pain, smashing the man across the face with his fist again. The man's body jerked backwards and he stumbled onto the desk. Frank Ward stiffened the fingers on his left hand and advanced on his enemy, bringing his hand down upon the offered neck. There was an awful snapping sound as the neck split and the guard smashed his head against the wall and slid to the floor, sluggishly. He was already dead before he reached the ground.

Ward breathed heavily, came around the desk and turned over the body. The eyes were blank and staring at the ceiling. The mouth was open, fixed in disbelief, fresh blood trickling down the pale chin. Ward swallowed and frisked the body professionally. He took a set of keys from the man's pocket and looked at a door that led into a storage room beside a row of filing cabinets. He would hide the two bodies in that room, then lock them inside and dispose of the keys. That way, it may be a few hours before the corpses are found, giving Ward the chance to escape. He hauled the body up from underneath the armpits and dragged it across the cold stone floor towards the door. He tried the keys in the lock until the door opened and he dumped the Hungarian inside. He then hurried back out into the courtyard and did the same with the other body. He covered up the blood near the fountain with clean snow and then went back inside the office.

Now, time to disable to the search lights. Frank Ward removed a concealed knife from his shirt cuffs and moved towards the metal control box. He opened the cover, revealing several green and red electronic wires, all connected to a circuit. Ward grabbed a bunch of wires and smartly severed a few with the blade. He looked out of the window. The guards operating the search lights on the balconies were now trying to figure out what was going on. The search lights had all gone out. One of the security men was telephoning his chief, asking whether it was a technical fault. Ward grinned and closed the cover. He could now roam around the courtyards in complete darkness and find another way inside the castle. He had to find what Claude Victor was up to.

Quickly, Frank Ward ran out of the office and locked it behind him before tossing the keys into the snow. Then, he glanced around and headed for the stairs.

Gaëlle Dumas of the French Direction Générale de la Sécurité Extérieure, slipped the lock pick into the keyhole and gripped the door handle. She peered through the small gap.

There was nobody in sight. She opened the oak door completely and advanced inside the room, holding her Browning 9mm, fitted with a silencer. She was now in an elegantly furnished drawing room, designed in an old fashioned style. There was a grand stone fireplace in the centre of the room surrounded by a black marble hearth. Green leather armchairs and settees were dotted around the room in front of the fireplace, the classic grand piano in the corner of the room. A painting hung above the mantelpiece depicting a violent scene of war. Men were being impaled with spears and others having their heads cut off by swords. It was a truly ghastly sight.

Gaëlle looked around the room, looking for cameras or bug transmitters like those in the cable cars. She couldn't allow herself to be seen. She had remained stealthy so far. She began to think about Frank Ward. She saw the security guard in the ball room follow him out onto the balcony. *Had they killed him? Or even worse, captured and tortured him?*

She didn't want to think about it. Gaëlle walked further into the room. There didn't appear to be any installed microphones or surveillance equipment. She walked over to the cabinets and pulled out drawers, sorting through papers and documents for anything suspicious. Most of them were business orders for the Kraken International Cooperation. She shut the drawers and moved over to the shelves of books. They were all old poem books and well - thumbed adventure novels. It was then that she noticed a piece of folded paper in-between two books. Gaëlle pulled it out and read it. It said, 'OPERATION LAUNCH.' She read it over and over again, trying to make sense of it. Finally, not knowing whether the information was useless or not, she stuffed the note into her expensive handbag.

'Stop right there, missy!' Came a loud voice from behind her. 'Turn round slowly and drop the gun.'

The noise made Gaëlle jump. *She had been caught searching through Victor's desk and shelves. The game was over.* She swallowed and dropped her Browning to the floor.

'Good,' boomed the voice again. 'Kick it away from you and face me. Then you can explain what you are doing in Monsieur Victor's office.' Gaëlle Dumas pushed her gun away and it slid across the carpet underneath a green armchair. Obediently, she turned around slowly and found herself staring directly down the barrel of a pistol, trained on her. Marcus Hillman, Victor's Head of Security, flicked off the safety catch and a sick smile formed onto his lips.

Hillman came forward, the grin now vanished from his face. The oak door opened behind them. Gaëlle looked past Hillman and saw two security men come into the room. One was armed with a gun, and the other had a sharp stiletto knife.

'Seize her,' Hillman instructed, his furious eyes focused on her; the gun in the hand perfectly still. The two men came past him and grabbed Gaëlle, holding her arms tightly against her back. She struggled at first, and the man with the knife came forward and held the sharp blade to her throat. 'Don't move,' he hissed, his disgusting animal breath blowing into her face. 'Or I'll draw a neat line across your throat with the stiletto.'

Hillman watched the two thugs hold her still, his gaunt face remaining serious. 'What are you doing in Monsieur Victor's office?' Marcus Hillman demanded, his voice flat and uninterested.

Gaëlle's eyes narrowed. 'I'm not talking, you monster!' She turned away from him. Hillman snarled and his open palm smashed across her face with force. Gaëlle gasped and a tear emerged from her eye. Hillman's teeth glinted in the light of the candelabras; bared like some kind of vicious animal. 'Don't talk to me like that!' Hillman shouted. He paused for a moment and smiled. 'You'll talk later in the dungeons. I can be very persuasive when I want to be. Besides, your friend Mister Ward will be joining you very shortly.'

Gaëlle swallowed and wiped the tear from her face with her free hand. *So they had got Frank. Either that or they were going after him.* The two goons herded her towards the office door followed by Marcus Hillman closely behind. As they approached the door, the guards didn't notice as her hand disappeared inside her handbag for a few seconds. She withdrew it immediately before they noticed, and held the small white cyanide pill in her clenched fist.

They weren't going to got a word out of her. All hope was lost now. It would be easier to end it all painlessly and quickly rather than endure the torture of Hillman and his men. Frank Ward wasn't going to rescue her this time. A shape moved across the concrete balcony above the garden, the flower beds and trees all coated in layers of white snow.

Frank Ward stopped in the darkness and got his breath back. *There were no longer any more searchlights to betray his presence,* he thought. *He hoped the security team believed it to be a technical fault. The longer he could keep Victor's men off his back, the better.*

Ward advanced stealthily towards the thick, oak door and slipped his hand inside his trouser pocket and removed the lock pick Gaëlle had given him back in the ballroom. He inserted it into the lock, and after patiently twisting and turning the pick, the door pushed open softly, revealing an empty marble corridor. He looked around him and above for cameras and walked cautiously forward, following the route of the hallway.

There didn't appear to be anybody around.

He stopped as he reached the end of the stone wall and peered over the side. Some of the party guards were preparing to leave and heading unhurriedly towards the exit. Others stood in the grandly decorated room, talking and gossiping whilst sipping champagne. Then he saw the two guards at the other side of the room, standing in front of a large double door, listening for instructions through their ear - piece walkie-talkies.

Had they spotted him yet? It didn't look like it.

Ward looked around him and waited until a group of guests headed towards the door. He would try and walk along with them and then try and get past the guards unnoticed. It was definitely worth the chance. He *had* to find Claude Victor and see what the hell he was up to.

Ward took a deep breath and looked back at the security guards. They weren't looking in his direction - they were too busy chatting to each other. Frank Ward sneaked out from behind the wall and moved in and out of the crowds of celebrities and media.

Had they seen him? Had Victor's men recognised him as an impostor?

Ward managed to sneak past the guards standing at the double doors and moved towards another door on the right hand side of the room.

Quickly, he picked the lock of the door again and slipped inside, closing it with exaggerated quietness. He was now inside a 'Prohibited Area,' beyond the double doors. It was obvious that not many people came down this corridor. The wine red carpets were beginning to mould, and the stone walls were damp and grimy. The old paintings were faded with age and caked in layers of dry dust.

Frank Ward withdrew his Beretta from his holster and held it in his right hand as he followed the narrow passageway. Eventually, he came to the end of the corridor and found himself at the foot of an ancient stone staircase. Slowly and gradually Ward moved down the spiral staircase in short steps, pointing the Beretta ahead into the darkness. As he reached the older parts of the castle fortress it became darker. Unable to see, Ward reached inside his pocket and withdrew his battered cigarette lighter and flicked back the rusty metal jaws. The lighter produced a tiny flame that flickered in the shadows.

It wasn't much light, but it helped him see where he was going.

A few minutes later, following the crumbling staircase, Ward found himself on another balcony, high above another large room that looked better cared for than some of the other parts of the castle. A huge crystal chandelier hung from the mosaic ceiling, creating a massive amount of light. Ward replaced his well - used lighter and squatted down. He heard voices coming from the room below the balcony. He couldn't see anybody yet, but Ward crept up to the edge of the raised platform and watched what was happening down below.

There was a massive conference table surfaced with gleaming metal which reflected the light of the chandelier. The room had clearly been refurnished. The furniture was of a high quality and before the table, a map of Europe was on a large screen, and beside it, a plasma screen television for video conferences. Behind the table, was an enormous window overlooking the glorious French Alps. Snow flakes were beating against the pane. The glass of course was impregnable and six inches thick. It would take a cannon or something like that to get through it. Covering the window, were modern blinds, that were presently open, allowing small amounts of light into the meeting room. Fourteen identical leather chairs were assembled around the long table, facing one another. Each chair was filled with serious looking Chinese men dressed formally in evening dinner jackets, staring grimly at one another. Agendas and glasses of water were placed in front of each person at the table. Claude Victor, the wealthy owner of the Kraken International Cooperation, sat at the head of the table, his long, pointed hands laid out in front of him. He surveyed each individual man at the table with his cruel, watchful eyes and then sipped at his glass of water. Ward noticed that six or seven security men were positioned at each corner of the room, Italian Spectre M4 automatic firearms slung heavily around their broad shoulders. The Chinese men had noticed the sub machine guns and some were glancing nervously around the table at each other.

The long doors at the end of the conference room opened and Marcus Hillman emerged and walked purposefully towards Claude Victor at the end of the table. The Chinese men looked up as the door opened. Hillman stood beside his chief, his arms behind his back. He leant towards Victor's ear and whispered something quietly. Victor nodded and a sick smile formed onto his twisted mouth.

Ward's eyes narrowed and he moved his head back behind the stone pillar out of view. *What had Hillman just whispered to Victor? Why did Victor smile? Was Gaëlle o.k, or had she been caught?* A chill ran down his spine and he shivered, although he wasn't cold. He suddenly felt uncomfortable and wondered where Gaëlle was.

The Oriental gentleman sat opposite Claude Victor was wearing a dark blue jacket and seemed to be the leader of the other Chinese people gathered around the conference table. A large, bulky silver briefcase was laid out on the table in front of him. Victor eyed the man opposite him carefully and a grin formed upon his disfigured mouth. 'Now that we are all here,' Victor began, his sinister voice loud and audible, 'we can begin the exchange. But before our little deal begins, I want to discuss your failed attempts on the French agent's life a few days ago, that have ultimately led to a security breach tonight at my castle.'

Kazuki Masaharu, the leader of the Triads in Hong Kong, looked up and stared at his boss, Victor, with his gun-barrel eyes. 'It was an unfortunate incident, Monsieur Victor,' Masaharu explained. 'My men arrived at her address in Paris as instructed and we broke in and raided the building. The female spy managed to lower herself down from her balcony with knotted sheets and escaped in her vehicle. My people chased after her immediately, but a number of my Triad gang members were killed by an unidentified assassin with a sniper rifle in a helicopter. After wrecking all of my Toyota cars, the assassin vanished with the girl. There was nothing we could do.'

Victor drummed his bony fingers on the table and looked up at Marcus "Menace" Hillman, his hired killer and Head of Security. 'I am not pleased, Masaharu. The girl has showed up at the party tonight with an American who calls himself Ward. I suspect that the man Ward is an agent of the CIA and the "unidentified assassin" who killed your men several hours ago.' Victor gestured with a wave of his arm towards "Menace" Hillman. 'My Head of Security has just informed me of the girl's capture. The American is being hunted down by my security as I speak. Let's just hope that neither of them have made contact with their headquarters or I will lay the blame on your head Kazuki Masaharu.'

Ward swallowed. So Gaëlle had been captured, just as he had thought. *God only knows what they are doing to her!* Cartwright's hunch was correct. Claude Victor was not the wealthy, loving businessmen that he made himself out to be. Instead, he was a gangster; a criminal who would kill and steal to get whatever he wanted.

'Now,' Victor said, his voice now soft and calm. 'I congratulate you on your success on stealing the two French cruise missiles, armed with live nuclear warheads. I believe you have also brought me another present.'

A smile plastered on his lips, Kazuki Masaharu unfastened the silver briefcase and pulled back the lid, revealing a small black box inserted into the velvet lining. Victor's glassy eyes lit up as the lid lifted automatically revealing a silver panel with digital numbers flashing, used for downloading coordinates. Two wires were held inside, for connecting to a computer or laptop.

'The American missile guidance system, Monsieur Victor,' Masaharu announced. 'Worth millions of dollars, this piece of intelligence hardware can interfere with the launch of cruise missiles, torpedoes, warheads and bombs. New courses can be plotted and coordinates of targets can be programmed into the device by computer software.'

Ward went cold all over. He felt dizzy and nauseous. The stolen missile guidance system was about to change hands. Victor had been behind the whole thing, just like the hit he had put on Gaëlle Dumas, the French agent several days ago. The Chinese criminals around the table looked at each other, showing interest. Victor stared at the device capable of chaos and destruction within the wrong hands, and summoned a guard behind him. The security man, a muscular brute of a man, came up to the table, carrying a heavy leather briefcase. He came and handed it to Masaharu at the end of the table, and took the missile guidance system and gave it to Claude Victor, who was busying himself lighting a cigarette. Kazuki Masaharu opened the heavy case, revealing stacks and stacks of new, crisp *yaun* notes, the Chinese currency.

'There's two million *yaun* in that case, Masaharu,' Victor told him, exhaling a fine cloud of smoke through his nostrils. 'It's all in twenties, but nevertheless, it's difficult to trace.'

This time, it was Kazuki Masaharu who smiled. 'Thank you, Monsieur Victor. It has been a pleasure doing business with you.'

Victor nodded slowly, the smoke from his cigarette sketching a chalky line up to the ceiling. Two guards unlocked the double doors at the end of the conference room and motioned the Chinese Triad mobsters to leave. The men got to their feet and walked purposefully towards the exit. Victor got up out of his chair and held out his pale, bony arm and shook the Chinese gang leader's hand.

'Goodbye, Monsieur Victor,' Masaharu said, heaving the briefcase crammed with money off the table.

'Goodbye, Masaharu. Spend the money wisely and enjoy it. No doubt I will be requesting your services very soon.'

With that, Kazuki Masaharu bowed and followed his crew of men out of the room. Claude Victor drew in a lungful of smoke and killed the cigarette in an ashtray on the conference table. He turned towards Marcus "Menace" Hillman, the murderer and convicted killer who served underneath his orders.

"Menace" Hillman was born in Nice, France on 9th May 1972. His parents were both quite poor and struggled to bring up young Marcus Hillman along with his other three brothers and two sisters. His father, Francois, was a criminal. When Marcus was only seven years old, his father was involved in a smuggling operation. As the local police and law enforcement surrounded him and his men, they gunned him down after Francois killed two policemen. Devastated and ashamed of her husband's past, Marcus's mother moved away with the children in order to protect them. As Marcus and the other children grew older, she told them that their father had disappeared years ago. However, young Marcus could remember when his father was shot dead years ago. When he was seventeen, Marcus ran away from his home and family and lived on the streets for months. Needing money for survival, Marcus Hillman got involved with a local crime gang. He was paid well by the thugs and robbed shops, houses and even killed a few men. He did this for years, until he was arrested during a bank heist. He escaped prison after strangling a guard and joined the crime group again. The police gave him the nickname "Menace" and even now, his closest friends still call him that. Victor was glad to have him in his employment. He was a cold -

blooded killer, and strong both mentally and physically. He was a handy man to have around; he was so useful that Victor had paid for him to undergo plastic surgery and gene therapy so he could work under his employment without being bothered by the police. Despite his loyalty to his chief, "Menace" made Victor very nervous and uneasy. He was a disturbing character. "Menace" Hillman seemed to be obsessed with death and the art of torture and pain. He was an expert in various types of physical and mental torture and often tried to break his own record for keeping his victims alive for a long time whilst inflicting as much pain as possible, probing sensitive organs such as the genitals. Currently, his record was forty two hours and thirteen minutes. Despite his mania for death, "Menace" was the perfect bodyguard and chief executioner.

"Menace" Hillman stood there now, next to his boss.

'Let's go and see the girl in the interrogation cell,' Victor said. 'We'll get as much out of her as possible. Once I'm satisfied with the information, I'll give her to you to do what ever you want with her.'

"Menace" grinned, his eyes showing madness. 'I would like that very much, Monsieur Victor.'

With that, the two criminals headed towards the doors, followed by the security guards. Once everybody was out of the room, Frank Ward stepped out of the shadows and snaked down the stone staircase leading into the deserted conference room where earlier Victor and the representatives of the Chinese Triad society were gathered. He gripped the door handle, and cautiously advanced into the corridor. Reaching for his Beretta, Ward bit his lip.

He had to get Gaëlle out of here, he thought. Either that or she would endure hours of endless torture in the cell before dying a painful and lonely death. He wasn't prepared to let the woman he loved die in such a horrible way. Fuelled by determination and anger, Ward followed the dancing shadows of Claude Victor and "Menace" Hillman whilst staying close to the stone walls of the castle fortress.

7/ ESCAPE FROM DEATH

LURKING IN THE shadows, Frank Ward, Agent 27S, followed Claude Victor and his right - hand man, Marcus "Menace" Hillman. He kept a reasonable distance between them as so not to alert them to his presence. Ward felt the urge to pump Victor and "Menace" full of bullets from behind and have done with it. They were both criminals who had stolen two nuclear warheads and the American missile guidance system.

God only knows what they intended doing with them!

He decided on not to shoot them both. That way he would never find where Gaëlle was being held captive. Also, Victor's army of guards would kill him before he could escape the castle fortress high up in the French Alps.

Victor and "Menace" led Ward down a small staircase into a gloomy passageway. There were a few old lamps on the walls, creating small amounts of light. On either side of the hallway, Ward could make out thick, oak doors studded with nails. There were barred windows in the doors, showing the interiors of what looked like ancient dungeons for the castle's medieval use centuries ago. The smell was horrific and Ward willed himself not to vomit. It smelt like decaying flesh. A large, black rat scurried across the cold stone floor and disappeared through a hole in the wall.

Ward's body went dumb. He began to think of the hundreds of innocent men and women who would have been brought here and locked in the dungeons. People would be chained to the walls, starved and dying. They would endure hours of physical torture. The blood - thirsty guards would beat them, stab them, poison them, and leave them to die in great pain. As he passed another dungeon door, he thought he could hear the shrill scream of one of the prisoners.

He shivered. Ward crept down the hallway, staying in the shadows and away from the lamps on the walls. Victor and "Menace" Hillman had stopped at the end of the passageway now, and they unlocked the door and stepped inside. Ward drew closer and wanted to see if Gaëlle was alright. The frightened girl was sitting in the corner of the room, scratching the walls with a piece of stone. Tears had spoilt her makeup, making her beautiful face look a wreck. She got up immediately, her face contorted with anger.

'Let me out of here, you monsters!' Gaëlle screamed.

It was then Ward noticed the bruise on her cheek. Somebody had hit her, and damn well hard.

"Menace" Hillman grabbed hold of her arm and pushed her without effort onto the floor. 'Shut up, spy!'

Claude Victor crouched down beside the crying woman on the floor and lifted her chin up so that her eyes were staring directly into his. 'You know too much, Gaëlle Dumas,' Victor hissed. 'Too much for your own good. Now you will tell me what you know or I will be forced to hurt you - severely. I can be *very* persuasive, my dear girl.'

With that, Victor removed a whip from his trouser pocket and held it tightly, the silver hooks on the end glinting in the light. 'Talk or you'll receive ten lashes of my whip,' he threatened, grinning sadistically. 'If you still don't talk, you'll receive another ten. I will keep on going until you tell me what I want to know, even if it means lashing every bit of skin off your body!'

Gaëlle swallowed, and looked at the sharp hooks on the end of the rubber whip. She imagined the amount of pain it would cause her. She imagined those hooks digging into her flesh and ripping her skin from her back. Still, she wasn't going to betray her country and the French Direction Générale de la Sécurité Extérieure. Bravely, Gaëlle Dumas gathered up saliva in her mouth and spat at Claude Victor, catching him straight in the eye. 'Go to hell, you fiend!'

Victor cursed, reached up to his eye and wiped his face. He raised his whip above his head, and in uncontrolled anger, lashed out on the girl's exposed back. Gaëlle screamed - louder than she had ever done before. She slipped onto the cold floor and could feel the blood pouring down the deep cut in her skin. Beads of sweat were gathering on her brow and more tears were forming in her eyes.

'You've just made matters worse,' Victor snarled. 'For that, you will receive ten whips before we even start the interrogation!'

Gaëlle moaned softly. She concentrated hard, trying to prepare herself for the next lash across her bare back. Sure enough, Victor's whip struck hard against her back again, partly ripping through her dress; blood seeping through the fine material. She screamed loudly.

'Nobody will hear your cries for mercy!' "Menace" Hillman cackled, as Victor raised the whip for another attack.

Gaëlle fought against the pain and clenched her teeth until she thought that they might break.

It was all too much. Opening her clenched fist, Gaëlle moved the small cyanide pill towards her lips.

'Enjoy a lonely death, Miss Dumas!' Victor exclaimed, brandishing the whip.

Just before he was about to lash out at Gaëlle for the third time, Frank Ward leapt through the threshold and caught hold of Victor's arm. Stunned, Claude Victor didn't have time to react. Ward tightened his fist and slugged the villain hard in the face and pushed him backwards where he fell into "Menace" Hillman. The two criminals tumbled over and fell onto the stone floor, causing "Menace" to drop his small automatic gun. Ward came forward as "Menace" dived for his weapon. Lashing out with his shoe, Frank Ward kicked "Menace" in the face and pocketed his gun, training his own Beretta on both of them.

'Move and I'll kill you both,' Ward hissed. 'My trigger finger is a bit edgy this evening.'

"Menace" Hillman glared at Ward, blood trickling down both of his nostrils and down onto his lip. Claude Victor wiped a bit of blood from his mouth, and held up his arms. Steadily he climbed to his feet.

'You must be Frank Ward, the American agent of the C.I.A,' Victor said gently.

'And you must be Claude Victor, the French murderer and terrorist.'

Victor's mouth twisted into a ferocious snarl. 'You'll never leave this place alive, Ward!'

Gaëlle got to her feet and watched Ward have the two villains at gunpoint. Ward turned briefly and looked at her, gesturing with his eyes towards the door.

'Go outside, Gaëlle. I don't want to get Victor's blood all over your dress.'

Gaëlle nodded and stepped outside.

Ward aimed the Beretta at Victor's head. 'Goodnight, Victor,' Ward spat, squeezing the trigger.

Before Ward had chance to shoot, Marcus "Menace" Hillman dived on him, wrapping his powerful hands around Ward's throat. Ward grunted in surprise and fired blankly with his Beretta 84FS Cheetah. The single round bounced harmlessly off the stone wall. The two men struggled, fighting for possession of the gun. "Menace" lunged at Ward, his fist connecting with his jaw. At the same time, Ward elbowed his opponent in the chest and threw him backwards against the wall of the dungeon, before kicking him with a karate manoeuvre. "Menace" cried out in pain and stumbled, smashing his head against the stone. He groaned, his eyes open in disbelief. Then, the killer slid to the floor, unconscious.

Frank Ward spun around to take care of Claude Victor, but the gangster burst out of the door and sprinted down the passageway into darkness. Ward looked down at "Menace" Hillman and straightened his dinner jacket. He stepped out of the depressing cell and shut the door behind him. Gaëlle Dumas was standing outside, her hair dangling down over her face. She was shaking with fear.

Poor girl, thought Ward. He came over to her slowly and put an arm around her shoulder, comfortingly. 'Are you okay, Gaëlle?'

She wiped a tear away from her pretty face and nodded slowly. Ward examined the severe cuts on her back. 'Your back looks nasty,' he told her. 'When we get out of this bloody place I'll take you to have those looked at properly.'

Gaëlle swallowed and winced with the pain. She opened her hand and showed Ward the cyanide tablet. 'I nearly took this tablet,' she confessed, jerking back more tears. 'I couldn't bear the pain any longer. If you hadn't intervened, I would, I would...' Gaëlle paused and covered her face as she began to cry again.

Frank Ward came forward and embraced her trembling body. She held onto him tightly. He looked directly into her eyes, and it was then he realised how incredibly beautiful the woman was, even with her makeup smudged. She was so perfect in every way; attractive and gorgeous. He admired her courage and bravery above everything else. She really was a tremendous girl. He loved her more than any other girl he had ever loved before. Gaëlle was just - special. His face serious, Ward wiped away the tears, and without warning, forced his mouth down upon hers, crushing her lips in an affectionate kiss. Passionately, their lips moved together; their tongues exploring in each other's mouths.

Ward pulled away and said softly, 'I love you, Gaëlle.'

She smiled. 'I love you too, Frank,' she replied.

Ward held her hand in his. 'Gaëlle, will you....' Before he could finish his proposal, there came the sound of frantic voices heading down the ancient staircase, their feet hammering on the stone.

Grabbing her by the hand, Ward ran to the end of the corridor and pulled open a heavy, oak door, leading to the outside of the castle. They were on a balcony, not that far from the ground. Ward couldn't tell exactly - the ground was just covered in white so he couldn't estimate the distance. 'Quick! Hurry!'

Gaëlle rushed down the balcony, clouds of snow gushing into her face. Ward stopped by the door as he saw two men jump down the stairs. The first man pointed at him and withdrew a hunting knife. '*Là il est* ! *L'espion!*'

The man with the knife approached him; the blade glinting in his deranged eyes. He made a clumsy lunge at Ward with his deadly weapon, but Ward counter-moved the attack and dodged to the left. Frank Ward circled his opponent, judging him carefully; predicting when he would make another attack. A few seconds later, the killer dived at him again, aiming for Ward's throat. Quickly, Ward grabbed hold of his opponent's arm, and with extreme force, wrenched it backwards. There was a sickening crunch and the assailant dropped the knife, wailing in agony. Ward thought that he might have broken the man's arm. He didn't really care.

The second man was on him in a flash, throwing punches aimlessly at Ward. The guard hit Ward hard in the chest, causing him to groan softly. As he came to hit him again, Ward moved out of the way, and the man flew over the edge of the balcony, screaming as he plummeted down the side of the castle.

Ward closed the door, hopefully barricading any more guards inside. He caught up with Gaëlle, who had nearly got down the balcony and onto the ground. He put an arm around her. 'We've got to get the hell out of the Alps before Victor's men get to us,' he explained. 'We need to inform our superiors of Claude Victor's criminal connections with the Triad society.' Ward gestured towards the cable car station, where a gondola was already waiting to head back down the mountains. 'You take the cable car down and collect my Chevrolet Corvette. I'll distract the guards.'

Gaëlle took his car keys, her face showing concern. 'How will you get back?'

Ward turned around and showed her a small concrete hut beside the car park. A pair of skis were leaning up against the wall. 'I think there's some skiing equipment in there. I'll ski back down to you.'

Gaëlle was stunned. 'You're crazy!' She cried. 'It's suicide!'

Ward shrugged and walked purposefully towards the hut, his feet crunching in the powdery snow. 'It's a risk I'm willing to take. Now go - Victor's men will be on their way to intercept us!'

Gaëlle didn't bother arguing. She rushed through the snow, her stiletto shoes, digging into the snow. Ward looked back up onto the courtyard balconies. Three guards were assembled, one of them holding a small sub - machine gun. He aimed at Ward and let off a rapid burst of fire, sending up a spray of snow. Ward ducked and rolled over, climbing to his feet immediately. He sprinted into the hut before more shooting commenced, and bolted the door.

A bulb hung from the ceiling without a shade. Frank Ward looked around at the equipment gathered in the small room. There were padded gloves, ski jackets, water - proof trousers, skis and poles and eye protection goggles. Ward picked out the things he thought would be necessary for his descent down the Alps. Quickly, he stripped out of his black evening tuxedo and slipped on the warm ski jacket and trousers. Dressed suitably, he unbolted the door and stepped out into the freezing cold. He dug his poles into the thick snow and fitted his boots into the skis, making sure that they were properly assembled. Ward took his small Beretta and fitted it safely in his trousers in case he had to use it. Then, he slipped on the large goggles that rested over his focused eyes.

Let's do this, he thought. Taking a deep breath, he pushed forward and glided through the layer of white, sending up an occasional spray of snow whilst he moved. He worked hard and meticulously, desperately trying to keep upright and gain enough speed at the same time. He flew around a corner, past a few trees and looked up into the starry sky. He saw Gaëlle in the gondola, gliding down the cables slowly towards the bottom of the mountains. He smiled and began to think about her.

God, what a woman! He loved her passionately and was even about to propose marriage back in the dungeons. *It was silly now, though. What would he have done if he got married? Get a different job? Have children? Hell no!* He didn't want to be tied down. But Gaëlle was just so pretty, courageous and sexy…

Break out it! he scolded himself. He needed to concentrate on skiing. He hadn't done it for years. He remembered the first time he fitted on skis and hit the slopes. When he was a teenager and still at high school, the Physical Education Department took him and a few other children to Aprica in Italy, where they stayed for a week in a Bed and Breakfast chalet high up in the mountainous Alps. He remembered his old teacher, Mister Oldham, instructing him on how to put all the gear on and ski at various speeds. He was a great influence on Ward, and before long, Ward was the best skier in the group and received a trophy. He still had that very trophy back in his home in Langley Falls, Virginia. As he zoomed around a tree, he remembered the advice Mister Oldham had given him all those years ago. He would say, 'Use the "snow plough", Ward. It helps control your speed. Form a V - shape position by sliding both skis tails apart an equal distance while keeping your ski tips together. This position creates resistance as you go downhill and slows you down.'

Remembering the helpful advice, Frank Ward used the "snow plough" manoeuvre as he approached a rocky area ahead. He slowed himself down to a speed he was comfortable at for the time being, and safely avoided the dangerous obstacle. Once Ward had passed the hazard, he put more weight on his poles and leaned forward as he gradually regained speed.

Hell, he was going fast now!

Blood rushed through his ears, and wind hit him hard in the face, making him feel dizzy and nauseous. Now, he saw the three runs ahead, that he had memorized earlier. He thought back to decide which one was the easiest, and turned left and veered down the GREEN RUN. After all, his skiing was a bit rusty. The GREEN RUN was practically simple with easy turns and few obstacles on the track. Noises came from behind him. He turned around. A figure on skis was behind him, one hundred yards away. He slowed down again to get a better look. No, there were three men on skis now! Victor's men! Ward knew it was just a matter of time before they figured he had taken to the slopes. He hoped Gaëlle had got back down the mountains safely. He didn't want anything to happen to her.

Ward tried to lose them. There was no point in making an attempt at shooting them with the Beretta at this stage - his shots would be too inaccurate and far away. The only thing he could do now was ski as fast as he could without stopping. He zig-zagged around a bunch of trees and continued down the track, sending waves of powdery snow into the air. The sound of the men in pursuit was becoming louder. Ward wove around a tight bend, tougher than before, and stayed within the route, following the green flags marking out the path. A cracking sound came from behind him. Ward spun around to face the men, wondering what the sound was. He then saw one of the men pull out a shiny silver object and point it towards him. A gun! Ward continued forward as fast as his skis would allow him. A shot sounded nearby, followed by another which went harmlessly into the snow. He could hear the men cursing over the sound of the skis and the wind whistling.

Ward now found himself speeding downhill in a fast descent. The men were still after him, occasionally letting off a few inaccurate rounds of their guns. Their shooting had been bad so far - but how much longer could he keep on going? He was tiring already, and sweat was gathering in his warm clothes. He willed himself to continue for he knew he would die if he stopped. Driving forward down the mountain, Frank Ward drew in deep breaths.

One of the men, clearly a talented skier, had managed to get ahead of the others. He was only a few metres behind Ward. *Did he have a gun too?* If so, he must act quickly! Without taking chances, Ward used the "snow plough" technique to slow himself down before spinning around to face the enemy skier. A look of menace flashed on the man's face as he removed a small automatic from his belt and directed it at Ward. Quickly, Frank Ward lifted his left ski pole out of the snow and pointed it threateningly at the enemy like a sword. He then proceeded to lunge forward with the stick - the pointed end of the ski pole impaling the skier in the chest. He screamed and fell to the ground, rolling in the snow leaving a trail of blood behind him. Ward faced north again and picked up speed with the nearest guard now out of the way. He could hear one of the enemy skiers behind shout something. Ward ignored them for now and tried to keep a distance between them. The further away they were, the more difficult it would be for them to put a bullet in his back!

Everything was becoming a blur as Ward gathered up speed. The area surrounding him was just a mixture of brown, green, and of course, white. The snow was covering his goggles and obstructing his vision. He swore and reached up to wipe the snow away from his goggles. It was then he lost control of the skies, and without warning, he was thrown to the ground and began falling, falling and falling until he smashed his head against something and was knocked out cold.

Ward explored the pain in his body and could taste blood in his mouth. He knew that his leg hurt - how badly, he didn't know. He opened his eyes and pulled off the plastic goggles that had caused him to crash. He was lying on his back in a mound of snow, his head leaning on a small rock. That must have been what had sent him unconscious. He lifted his head up, and could feel a small amount of blood matted in his black hair. He had a headache, but apart from that, the blow to his head hadn't been fatal. He couldn't have been out cold for too long. He could hear the distant voices of Victor's men on skis nearby. They must be looking for him. Moaning, he eased himself up so that he was sitting upright in the powdery snow. He felt the snow with his gloved hand and his mouth creased into a smile. The snow had saved his life. It had broken his fall. If it wasn't for the snow, he would most certainly be lying here dead for weeks before anybody would discover his body. He imagined what he would look like lying here after a few days. His face would be a light blue, so clear and vivid; like the face of a supernatural being. His hair would be covered in layers of snow, and frozen icicles would dangle from his nostrils. His slim built body would be stiff and rock hard like a statue, until, after weeks, it would be buried under heaps of snow never to be seen again.

Ward shivered and put the thought out of his mind. Concentrating hard, he climbed heavily to his feet and inspected his skiing equipment. He had lost one of his poles for certain, the other lay in the snow a few metres away from where he stood. His wooden skis were still attached to his feet, but one was broken in half. They were no good to him now. He sat back down again and unfastened the useless skis from his heavy boots and hid them underneath a nearby tree, burying them so that Victor's men wouldn't find them. Then, he got back up again and removed his Beretta from its hidden place. He walked on the track, lost in the mountain, roaming the mountain. He could see his ski prints in the snow like train tracks. Taking off the safety catch, Ward listened to noises around him, watching out for the enemy skiers that had chased him down Mount Blanc. He began to realise how hungry he was. He hadn't eaten a thing at Victor's reception. *Never mind*, he thought. *There'll be food back at the hotel. That is, if I ever make it back to the hotel alive.*

Suddenly, something hit him hard on the back of the skull, causing him to fall forward into the snow. Frank Ward turned his head briefly to see his attacker, and before he could make out the face, a strong fist hit him in the nose, sending him crashing onto the ground. His nose was bleeding freely and trickling down to his lip. He wasn't sure whether it was broken. He looked up and focused his eyes at the person who had just hit him. It was a tall man of a similar build to Ward with golden hair and bright blue eyes. He was possibly a German body builder. His arms were as wide as tree trunks and his muscles showed underneath the expensive ski jacket. He was directing a gun at him, so that Ward was looking right down the barrel of the pistol. '*Sie, Spion!*' The man shouted. 'Put your arms behind your head and keep them there.'

Ward bit his lip and did as he was told. He tried to plan out a strategy of escaping which would certainly be death. At the moment, everything was useless. He was defenceless and couldn't reach for his gun. But wait! His small 'messy' knife was hidden in the heel of his right boot. He had transferred it from his shirt cuff earlier when he changed into his skiing gear. The 'messy' knife, as they were called, were blades no more than a few inches long. Every field agent in the Central Intelligence Agency would be equipped with one of these deadly weapons in cases of emergency such as capture or torture. The concealable knives could be used to quickly injure guards allowing the captured agent to escape. However, instructors who made the weapon described the results as being very gory and 'messy.'

If only he could manage to get hold of the hidden tool. He would have to come up with a distraction of some sort.

The German guard said: 'Now, stand up slowly and come with me back to the castle. Claude Victor wants to talk to you. If you refuse, I am ordered to kill you.'

Ward nodded and started to get to his feet. 'Fine. First, would you let me tie my laces on my boot. It appears to have come undone.'

The guard looked at the unfastened boot and then stared suspiciously at Ward. He steadied his aiming on the gun and said quietly: 'Go ahead. Don't try anything or you'll get the first one in the eye.'

Frank Ward smiled and said 'Thank you', before beginning to tie the laces on his right boot. Slowly, gradually, he moved his hand down towards his heel and unlocked the secret compartment. Ward clasped his thumb and index finger around the tiny weapon and holding it in his left palm, continued tying his boot. Once it was done, he climbed gingerly to his feet and walked unhurriedly up the steep slope, the German behind him, holding the cold muzzle against his neck.

Everything was going perfectly to plan, he thought. *Now all he had to do was get the timing right and strike.*

He counted to three and taking his chances, spun around and pushed the gun out of the way. Luckily, Ward had caught the unsuspecting German off guard, and had forced the Walther away from his body. He lunged with his left fist and caught the man under the chin, virtually knocking his head clean off his body. The neck was open for attack. Ward dived on him with the blade, slashing with the 'messy' knife at the man's throat. The German screamed and screamed and tumbled into the snow with Ward on top of him. Before he knew it, blood was everywhere. It was all over Ward's clothes, the German and the snow. The German was dead within seconds, his neck nothing but a gory mess of red. Ward heaved himself of the body, and dropped the knife into the snow. He looked down at the man he had just killed and turned away before being violently sick.

He hated killing - it was by far the worst part of his job. Altogether, he had killed eight people, including those of past assignments. He remembered the first time he killed and the feelings of remorse he had suffered. Now, over the past months of continually murdering enemies, he tried to dismiss these feelings. In his career as a D.O agent in the C.I.A, he had found it to be unprofessional. He now knew that those he killed were themselves killers and often deserved it. He never took pleasure in killing and often attempted not to think about it. However, every time he slept, he would have frightening nightmares that were so vivid that they might be true. All previous men he had assassinated would come back to haunt him, especially the sinister Howard Sharp, the drug baron who had ruthlessly killed Joe, the younger brother of Frank Ward.

Now, Ward began unfastening the skis from the bloody corpse and attaching them onto his own boots. His heels clicked inside and he stood up and pulled the blood - stained goggles from over the German's head and fitted them above his own eyes. He wiped the blood from the visors and prised the two Leki Titanium ski poles from the stiffening fingers. The poles were a better quality than the others he had used to descend down the mountain. With all the new gear, Ward pushed himself forward and glided down the steep white slope, easily manoeuvring around the bends at controllable speed.

***

Thirty minutes later, after Ward's exhausting descent down the rocky sides of Mount Blanc, the town Chamonix in Haute-Savoie was now in sight. The buildings were illuminated, and the distant sound of traffic in the early hours of the morning echoed over the mountainous terrain.

Frank Ward saw the town, and with deep relief mumbled: 'Thank God!' He had never felt so tired and weak in his entire lifetime. Even the many hours in the gym and the strict exercise routines every morning had not prepared him for such an adventure. His body stank of perspiration - he could smell it himself. His whole body was covered in layers of sweat, and glistening beads had gathered on his forehead. As he reached the bottom, he dropped his poles and clumsily, drunkenly, stumbled forward and caught his breath. His bicep muscles were very painful as were his hamstrings. He unfastened the skis from their boot bindings and trudged through the snow. Only a few more yards to Chamonix! The noise was growing louder. He wiped a bit of blood from his chin, wondering whether it was his own or the German's he had killed up in the mountain. Ward began to think about Claude Victor. What was he going to do with those warheads? The possibilities could be fatal. He obviously had an army of some sort up there protecting him, consisting of French, German and Hungarian killers. Ward suddenly felt a hatred build up inside him for Victor. He wanted to grab him by the throat and shake him crazily until his hideous eyes rolled up and his grotesque tongue protruded from his lips...

Just then, Ward caught the sight of beaming headlights as he crossed the road. There was a screeching of tyres and Ward threw up his arms to shield his eyes from the bright light and identify the driver who had nearly run him over. The driver was a female. He couldn't make out the face. Slowly, he shuffled towards the driver's door as a gorgeous figure emerged from the platinum 2006 Chevrolet Z06 Corvette.

He couldn't believe it, *it was Gaëlle!*

Her beautiful light brown hair caught the moonlight, and she smiled, lovingly and then looked concerned as she saw the crumpled man approach her. 'Need a lift? You look a bit rough. Looks like I bumped into you just at the right time.'

Ward smiled, gratefully. 'I've never been so pleased to see you. Get us back to the hotel, I'll explain in the car. Victor's definitely up to something.'

Gaëlle nodded. 'Frank - you're hurt. What did Victor's men do to you?'

Ward wiped the mixture of sweat and blood from his face and looked up into the mountains. 'Victor wants us both dead. They nearly got me on the slopes. Quick, put the keys in the ignition and put your foot on the accelerator. Men are probably on their way down in the cable car.'

Gaëlle didn't argue and switched on the engine. As she was about to climb into the driver's seat, Ward grabbed her by the arm and pulled her close to him before plunging his lips upon hers forcefully in an affectionate, passionate kiss. They kissed for a few moments, standing there in the middle of the road. Slowly, reluctantly, he pulled away and whispered into her ear: 'Thank you. You saved me.'

Gaëlle grinned and got behind the wheel of Ward's Chevrolet Corvette. As he got in beside her, she looked him squarely in the eyes and said: 'Now, we're even.'

Without a single word, she slammed her foot down on the stainless steel pedal. The engine roared loudly, and the car tore down the road leading away from the town of Chamonix and Claude Victor's castle fortress. Alas, neither of them knew that their undying love was about to be destroyed in less than twenty - four hours.

8/THINGS THAT GO BUMP IN THE NIGHT

THE FOLLOWING MORNING, Frank Ward of the Central Intelligence Agency was feeling much better, and only had a minor headache. Gaëlle had advised him to visit a doctor to examine the injury to the back of his head and the various severe cuts and bruises around his body. She had even given him the address of a local surgery! However, Ward had told her that he was feeling good and the headache would easily be cured with an aspirin, some hot black coffee and some buttered French farmhouse bread. He wasn't particularly hungry this morning.

Reluctantly, he flung his naked body out of the golden sheets of the king size bed, and began to perform his regular exercise routine, beginning with twenty five toe touches. The rest included, twenty slow press ups, enough straight leg lifts until his muscles screamed to stop, and twenty sit ups. He had completed his morning workout in five minutes, which had become almost a ritual since he started in the American Army years ago. He showered for ten minutes in hot water and slipped on a complementary hotel bath-robe before heading out onto the spacious balcony overlooking the jagged hills of Rue du Mont Thabor.

Gaëlle Dumas was sitting out by the table, topless in order to achieve a perfect suntan. She was idly reading the paper, occasionally turning over a page and having a sip of her freshly-squeezed orange juice. She had already finished her breakfast, and Ward's farmhouse bread and coffee was waiting for him. He sat down next to her and took a big bite out of the bread. 'Good morning,' he said softly, whilst busying himself lighting the first cigarette of the day. He clamped the Malboro cigarette between his teeth, held it there firmly and lit it with his battered Dunhill lighter. 'I told you I'll be fine.'

She glanced up from her paper, her breasts and chest already showing signs of tan. 'Whatever, you say how you feel. What exactly happened last night? Did you find anything out?'

Ward exhaled a lungful of smoke through his flared nostrils and finished his mug of coffee in two solid gulps. 'I did. I happened to find Claude Victor's conference room, hidden in the lower section of the castle. I overheard a meeting with him and a group of Chinese Triad gang members. It turned out that Victor was the one who put the price on your head. He also happens to be the one who stole the American missile guidance hardware from the testing facility in Hong Kong, and the two nuclear warheads.'

Gaëlleput her paper down furiously and gazed out over the gardens. 'I knew it!' She exclaimed. 'I suspected him right from the moment I saw him. He just looked so scary and evil. But why did he want me dead? Why would he pay a group of professional guns to wipe me out?'

Ward looked thoughtful for a few moments and finished his first slice of the bread. He said: 'Perhaps you knew too much to stay alive. After all, your superiors assigned you to recover the two warheads. Maybe he thought you might find him out so he went for the easy option to eliminate you before you could learn anything about his criminal activities.'

'You must be right. But I don't understand what he wants to do with them. He's a famous scientist and even funds NASA projects. Surely he doesn't intend firing them at other countries?'

Ward swallowed. 'I don't know and I don't really care. All I know is that he is a murderer, a thief, and a gangster working with foreign criminal syndicates and organisations. It still makes him a threat, and I will kill him.'

'What happened next?'

Ward poured himself another mug of dark black coffee. 'I followed him and that "Menace" chap down to the dungeons where I found you. Once I had freed you, I found some skiing gear and hit the slopes, choosing the Green run, which was the simplest of the three. After a while, Victor's heavies caught up with me. I injured one, but then I fell and can't remember what happened next. I suppose I must have hit my head and knocked myself out. However, I killed one of Victor's guards and managed to make it down the rest of the mountain. That's where I found you.'

Gaëlle gave him a hard, meaningful look. 'You're lucky to be alive. You could have easily died up in the Alps.'

Frank Ward ignored her and stirred his coffee slowly and mechanically before placing it on a china saucer. 'Anyway, what did you find out?' He enquired.

Gaëlle removed the piece of folded paper from her pocket and pushed it across the table towards Ward. He picked it up and opened it, reading the block capitals. He put the paper down, a confused expression written on his face. 'Operation Launch?'

She shrugged dumbly. 'I can't make sense of it either. I found it in Claude Victor's office. "Menace" Hillman caught me but he must have forgotten to take it from me.'

Ward got up and changed into a light blue cotton shirt, black trousers and a pair of black leather Italian shoes. He collected his leather shoulder holster and fitted it underneath his left armpit and added his Beretta to the pouch. He walked back onto the balcony and looked at Gaëlle. 'If my hunch is correct, Victor will already have a professional hit team searching Paris for us. We've got to send mutual reports to our respective chiefs. Contact the Head of the Direction Générale de la Sécurité Extérieure and tell them we are going to headquarters. Tell him to inform Cartwright. I'll get the Z06 out of the garage and I'll be waiting out front.'

Gaëlle said: 'OK,' and got up and walked purposefully through the living room of the Double Deluxe Suite towards the old fashioned telephone. Frank Ward put on a comfortable navy linen jacket to hide the gun, and said goodbye before he vanished out of the room.

A little later, Frank Ward and Gaëlle Dumas were making their way towards the Operation Room on the higher levels of the modern building, which was the headquarters of the French Secret Service (DGSE). They summoned an elevator and stepped inside and selected the floor.

The Operations Room was one of the most secret rooms in the building, where only VIP personnel and Head of Divisions would gather to discuss matters that currently threaten France. Seymour Cartwright, the new D.C.I.A was also there, discussing the Claude Victor assignment with the man holding the same position in the DGSE. Neither of them talked as the lift ascended to the higher floor. Eventually, it came to a halt and the blast doors hissed and withdrew. Gaëlle led the way through the immaculate corridors to the operations room, where a coloured security man stood. He smiled at them and asked them for security passes. Gaëlle gave him hers and explained to him that Ward was an allied agent due for a meeting with the Head of the Service.

'Fine,' the man said, 'but I am going to have to search you and remove any weapons. It's a necessary procedure for all non personnel. I'm sure you understand.'

Ward said that he did and allowed the guard to remove his Beretta and his flick knife temporarily.

'Thanks for your cooperation.'

Gaëlle opened the door and they stepped inside the large room, filled with men and women working at the banks of computers, listening through headphones, and studying charts and maps on the walls. Ward immediately spotted Seymour Cartwright at the far end of the room, talking to an important-looking man in a stylish business suit. Cartwright turned around and saw Ward, his most senior agent, and broke away from the intelligence officers to meet him. 'Good morning, Agent 27S,' he said, thrusting out his hand for Ward to accept. 'I trust the party at Claude Victor's estate up in the French Alps was a success?'

Ward reached inside his jacket and removed a fresh packet of Marlboro cigarettes and slit the wrapper off with his thumbnail. 'I suppose you could say that,' he said, shaking his chief's hand then, then selecting a cigarette.

The other man with Cartwright came forward to greet Gaëlle. He was a rather short, stocky man who had a look of power and authority about him that Ward rather admired. He had greasy, balding black hair that was slicked back neatly and a well - trimmed moustache that drooped above the feminine mouth like a curtain of some sort. His hooked nose was rather big and didn't look right on the small round face. The grey eyes were cold and calculated, showing signs of stress and lack of sleep. He had a small scar on his left cheek which showed on the sunburned skin. Overall, the man looked quite ugly and revolting, but carried an air of self importance about him nevertheless. 'Ah, Agent 345',the man said in English, with a thick French accent, 'I've been looking forward to the report on last nights' events. It will be interesting to see what that millionaire Victor is really up to.'

Cartwright stood next to the plump man with the moustache. 'Allow me to introduce you both,' he said. 'This, 27S, is General Gaston Kretzmer, the Director of the DGSE.' The General's feminine mouth cracked into a warm smile. 'And this, my dear General,' Cartwright continued, 'is Frank Ward, Agent 27S from the Directorate of Operations Department in the Central Intelligence Agency. He is one of my most valued and capable operatives.'

The General and Ward both exchanged greetings and shook each other's hand. Ward noted that the small hand was dry and cold. 'It is a pleasure to meet you, General,' Ward said.

General Kretzmer put his arms behind his back and stood up straight, making himself appear taller than the man actually was. 'Likewise, Mister Ward. My CIA counterpart has been telling me many things about you and your past adventures. I must thank you for coming to my aid and rescuing my best female agent, Gaëlle, from the Chinese hit team.'

Ward turned towards Gaëlle Dumas and grinned. 'It was nothing, General. I'm glad Mister Cartwright assigned me the case. Since that morning, Gaëlle and I have become - er - close friends.'

General Kretzmer nodded and kept looking at the two spies of opposite countries. 'Did you ever find out who wanted you dead, Agent 345?'

'Yes,' Gaëlle said abruptly. 'Claude Victor was the one who put a price on my head all those days ago. It turns out that he was the one who stole the two nuclear warheads and the American missile guidance hardware.'

Gaëlle and Ward watched as their chief's eyes nearly popped out of their sockets in disbelief. Cartwright swallowed and turned towards Ward. 'Is that true?' he said.

Ward took several drags on his Marlboro cigarette and dropped it into a small office bin under a computer desk. 'I'm afraid so, Sir,' Ward explained regrettably. 'I unveiled the truth about it last night at Victor's castle fortress. He has contact with the controller of the feared Chinese Triad society in Hong Kong, and has paid them a large sum of money in Chinese currency to kill Gaëlle, steal the warheads, and the guidance system from our government laboratory in China.'

General Kretzmer and Cartwright swapped worried glances. 'But ... but,' the General stuttered, 'why did he want Agent 345 dead? And why did he steal those warheads and the missile hardware?'

Gaëlle started to talk before Ward could reply: 'I happened to be the one investigating the disappearance of the warheads. An insider in the DGSE must have informed Victor and given him my personal address. He thought it would be more sensible to kill me rather than risk himself being caught. As for the theft of the warheads and the American missile guidance system, Agent 27S and myself are still trying find out why.'

Cartwright could feel his body become numb. God only knows what Victor intended doing with them! He had to sit down as he could feel his legs weakening. 'Did you assassinate Claude Victor or recover the stolen hardware?'

Ward and Gaëlle shook their heads. The General bit his lip and said: 'Le 'OH, merde!' He turned to face Cartwright, whose face was already looking deathly pale. 'I don't know about you, Cartwright, but I'm going to insist on Agent 345 killing Claude Victor and relocating the warheads and your guidance hardware. I think it is of vital importance to my country that this Monsieur Victor is eliminated.'

Cartwright got back up again. 'I agree. Agent 27S, you will work alongside Agent 345 again on a mission to destroy Victor and bring back the stolen weapons and hardware. If Victor's intentions are criminal, he could use the warheads as a token of extortion and world-wide blackmail.'

Ward and Gaëlle grinned at each other, both overjoyed to be working with each other once again. The General walked over to a wooden desk beside a large screen relaying satellite images and lifted the receiver off a telephone. Cartwright and the others watched him. 'Hello, yes, this is General Kretzmer speaking,' he said urgently down the instrument. 'Put me in contact with the Heads of the Directorate of Intelligence and Operations Division at once.' There was a long pause. 'This is the General. Alert your divisions to a threat called Claude Victor. Have your team load his profile onto the mainframe computer in the Operations Room. Then, use the satellite imaging to locate his exact whereabouts. If he is at his castle in Mount Blanc, I suggest military action to commence. Thank you.'

The General used his linen handkerchief to wipe perspiration from his forehead and walked unhurriedly towards Cartwright and the two agents. 'The Directorate of Intelligence is searching for his records and is going to use satellite photography to locate Victor. I've also alerted the Operations Division and I will give them further warning if the military and an SAS team are required.'

'Good. I'll contact Langley HQ and update them. They might have something on him that may prove useful,' Cartwright explained.

In front of them, on a huge screen on the wall, a black and white photograph of a man flashed onto the screen followed by information and a brief dossier. The DGSE logo was in the top right hand corner. Ward looked up at the hideous face that belonged to Claude Victor, the ruthless gangster who was responsible for many gruesome killings. Those glassy, almost animal-like eyes stared at him directly from the screen. The photograph looked several years old, as the deep, swollen bags beneath the eyes were not in existence, and the wrinkled flesh looked more youthful.

The General looked up at the screen. 'Ah it appears the Directorate of Intelligence has located the Claude Victor file. Now lets see -,' the General began reading the text, 'No criminal records or history of past crimes. CIA, MI6, FSB, DGSE, Mossad, you name it, he's clean. Known to work with a man called Marcus Hillman, who is apparently an ex-convict. Apart from that, everyone else in his organisation is clean. Victor has also been rumoured to participate in illegal street races, prostitution and gambling.'

Ward bit his lip. 'Doesn't exactly tell us much. How about your live satellite. Can you locate him?'

The General swallowed and talked quietly to a woman at a computer. He turned towards Ward hesitantly and said: 'It may take a long time. Sometimes it takes minutes, hours or even days.' He paused and looked thoughtful for a few moments. 'Tell you what, you two visit the armoury section and pick up weapons that you think you may need. Our armoury as you fully well know, Agent 345, is stocked with various types of guns, rifles and explosives. Ammunition of all kinds are also available in the firing range. Once you've checked out your new equipment, you can return to your hotel, relax, and wait for my call. Okay?'

Ward and Gaëlle looked at each other and agreed. 'Thank you, General,' Ward said as they headed towards the door. They said goodbye and disappeared through the exit of the Operations Room and headed for the lift.

Hours later, Frank Ward and Gaëlle Dumas had returned to the Deluxe Double Suite in the luxurious *Le Meurice* hotel in Paris. They sat in the elegant living room, sorting through various munitions that they had received from the armoury section of the Direction Générale de la Sécurité Extérieure. They sat in the green leather armchairs beside the glass-surfaced coffee table, handling various guns and weighing them expertly. Trays of ammunition and special armour - piercing bullets were laid out on the mahogany dining table, along with a small box containing six fragmentation grenades. They were MK2A1 Pineapple grenades, loaded with PFC caps that detonate on impact once the pin has been removed. Ward had selected these due to their average weight and durability. He doubted whether they would need them on this particular mission, but they were always good weapons for concealment and could easily take out large groups of enemies.

The other weapons that they had selected included a Colt King Cobra, with a barrel measuring six inches. The revolver had been in production since 1986 and discontinued in late 1990s, although the DGSE still had a few available. It was technically similar to other mk.V revolvers, and can be described as direct successor to the Trooper Mk.V. King Cobra featured a more modern design with full length under-barrel lug and solid top-barrel rib. Sights were fully adjustable. All King Cobra revolvers were made from stainless steel. Like the earlier Trooper revolvers, the King Cobra is an all-around, versatile gun, suitable for sport, duty, self defence and even hunting. However, Ward found them useful for taking out car engines from a distance and stopping men in their tracks as a shotgun would do. He regarded it as a powerful gun and whilst quite heavy and large, it was one of his personal favourites. He preferred his Beretta for more stealthy, delicate kills, and for the concealment value. Despite this, the King Cobra provided more fire power than the Beretta, but would have to be hidden in a car or suitcase. It wasn't suitable for being carried on the body.

The final weapon that Ward and Gaëlle had withdrawn from the armoury was an Uzi 9mm sub machine gun developed in Israel by Usiel Gal, and manufactured by IMI. Uzi had been adopted by police and military of more than 90 countries, including Israel (now only in reserve), Germany and Belgium. More compact versions, Mini and Micro Uzi, are adopted by many police, special operations and security units around the world, including Israeli Isayeret, US Secret Service etc. This ergonomic SMG has a magazine housing inside the pistol grip, making it easier to reload in tight situations. Through previous experience of working with the Uzi 9mm, Ward favoured it above other SMG's because of it effective range and rate of fire.

Frank Ward put his silenced Beretta 84FS Cheetah down on the table and poured himself another glass of Russian vodka, and then poured one for Gaëlle. He sat back in the comfy chair and sipped the strong drink. His headache had returned and so had the pains in his legs and torso. He was thinking of how he could destroy Claude Victor and recover the two missing warheads and the newly built missile guidance system developed in the government weapon facility based in Hong Kong. Victor knew who he was - his cover had been blown, as had Gaëlle's. He had many contacts and informants - he possibly already knew where Ward was staying and how long his booking would last. He would have his men combing Paris searching for him, with orders to bring him back dead or alive. Ward realised that now he knew Victor's secrets, the criminal wasn't going to allow him to stay alive and would hunt him down. It would possibly be wise to switch hotels and register under fake names. That might throw Victor's men off the scent long enough for the DGSE's Directorate of Intelligence to locate him so that Ward and Gaëlle could follow him. Claude Victor was a wise man and would surely not stay at his castle fortress up in the mountains like a sitting duck waiting to be attacked by the French and American military. No, he would leave the country and try and get away. But where would he go? General Kretzmer and Cartwright had probably already alerted the intelligence community. Surely the evil gangster couldn't escape surveillance.

Ward stood up and walked over to the writing desk in the corner of the room and collected his gold-plated cigarette case and brought it back over to where they were sitting. He opened the lid, revealing ten or eleven Marlboro cigarettes (his favourite brand!) and selected a long, thin one and put it in his mouth. He offered Gaëlle one, but she declined.

'I'm just going to have a cigarette,' he informed her, heading out onto the balcony. He glanced at his watch. 'It's eleven now. Listen out for the General calling. Once we know where Victor is, we'll pack our bags and head to the airport if necessary.'

Gaëlle sipped her vodka and said: 'OK.'

The night air was cool and refreshing as Frank Ward stepped out onto the stone balcony that was connected to the Deluxe Double Room. The streets outside the hotel were unusually calm, as was the traffic. The Parisian cafés were beginning to close for the night, and one or two men and women were walking their dogs through the romantic Tuileries Garden exactly opposite the street from the *Le Meurice* 5 - star hotel. He reached into his trouser pocket and removed his Dunhill lighter and flicked back the metal cylinder and held the end of the cigarette in the flame. He inhaled the smoke pleasurably and dragged it down into his lungs and then let it all out between his teeth in a faint hiss. He had taken up smoking when he was in the American Army. Since there was little drink in the base to help him drown the guilt of having killed, cigarettes helped him relax and weaken his conscience. He smoked much less now - five a day was his limit, although he didn't even quite reach the limit most of the time. Cartwright and his predecessor had always told him that he should give up; that smoking was affecting his physical fitness and his stamina, even though Cartwright often enjoyed cigarettes himself. His explanation was that agents in the D.O section need to be as fit as possible in the field. Ward tried to give up and even used those nicotine patches, but after a while, he got bored and decided to carry on with the habit.

It was while Ward was daydreaming, that two silver BMW's came around the corner and came to a halt expertly in front of the Tuileries

Garden entrance. Ward finished his cigarette and crushed it with his foot as he tried to make out the drivers and passengers. Something was not right. He watched as the passenger door of the first car opened and a familiar figure emerged. Ward swallowed and his mouth opened in disbelief. He stared unblinking at Marcus "Menace" Hillman, Claude Victor's bodyguard and chief executioner. It was definitely him all right. The predator features, the well - built body, the bulging muscles under the sports jacket. Ward could feel himself going dizzy. Victor had tracked them down already! He knew where they were staying and now was going to eliminate them! More men emerged from the two cars. Ward recognised the hard, blunt faces and the stony eyes. The other passengers were a mix of Hungarians, French and Germans thugs, all recruited by Victor supposedly as 'staff,' but instead, were hired killers. *How Ward had underestimated Victor! Why didn't they get out of here earlier?* Ward counted the total number of men. Eight, including "Menace" himself. The men all looked up at the hotel, and one drew a small automatic at the sight of Ward on the balcony. "Menace" turned and told him quietly to put the gun away for the moment.

Quickly, Frank Ward ran back inside the room and found Gaëlle sitting in one of the antique leather chairs, reading a free women's magazine which had been put in every room. 'Gaëlle! Get up! Victor's men have found us! They are outside!'

Gaëlle looked up from her magazine, her face contorted with a combination of shock and fear. 'What?' She cried, confused. 'What are you talking about?'

Frank Ward collected his Beretta from the table and handed it to Gaëlle. '"Menace" is here, along with several of Claude Victor's heavies,' he explained quickly. 'They're here to kill us. Take my Beretta and stay in the bathroom. I'll lock you in and head outside and take care of them with the Colt King Cobra. There's ten rounds in the gun.'

Gaëlle Dumas, Agent 345, took Ward's Beretta 84FS Cheetah and weighed it in her hand, while Ward picked up the new Colt King Cobra and loaded it with .38 ammunition instead of .357 to reduce recoil and noise. Once the cylinder was loaded with six shots, the maximum capacity, Ward grabbed hold of Gaëlle's arm and pushed her into the bathroom.

Ward ran his fingers through his black hair and put his arm around her shoulders. 'I won't be long,' he told her. 'Hide in the bath behind the shower curtain. I'll try not to let them get inside the hotel, but if they search the room, stay quiet and still. They might not find you. They'll probably go to the car park and check if you've tried to escape. If the worst comes to the worst, well .. you've got the death pill. Right?'

Gaëlle looked at him nervously, and he noticed she was trembling. 'But what if you get killed? I'll never see you again,' she asked.

Ward pulled her close and she opened her mouth ready to receive his tongue. She moaned softly, running her hands through his hair and clawing at the back of his neck with her fingernails. He pulled away and looked at her. 'I took that risk when I joined the Central Intelligence Agency, Gaëlle,' he told her slowly. 'So did you. If either of us dies tonight, then that's just how it works. If this is the last time I see you again, I just want to say I love you.'

Tears were forming in her eyes as Ward backed out of the marble bathroom towards the door. 'I love you too,' she replied.

Clutching the powerful Colt King Cobra in his right hand, Frank Ward ran out of the Deluxe Double Suite and down the corridor. In the rush, Ward had forgotten to pick up the keys and left the door unlocked.

He holstered the heavy handgun in the waistband of his trousers and sprinted down the grand corridor towards the main staircase. Ward hoped that none of them had got inside the hotel yet. He would have to keep them at bay, especially "Menace". He burst through the reception area, ignoring the stares of porters and guests as he threw himself out of the entrance and onto the deserted street. He gripped the butt of his Colt, and pulled it out, before taking cover behind a concrete pillar supporting the overhang on the entrance above the steps. He poked his head out from where he was hiding, and pointed the gun in the direction of the cars, his finger itching on the trigger. He was expecting one of Victor's men to let off a shot, but there was only silence. Nothing. Ward waited a few seconds, and hesitantly came out from behind the pillar to see the two empty BMW's.

Where the hell had they gone? Had they sneaked inside the hotel? Or were they hiding in the shadows, ready to shoot him dead in the street?

Cautiously, Frank Ward edged down the steps leading onto the pavement, and turned 360°, moving the long barrel of the Colt King Cobra with him. He ground his teeth nervously, and could feel beads of sweat gathering on his forehead. His eyes were darting in every direction and searching the dark shadows in the corners of the building.

They had vanished!

Slowly, Ward crept up towards the first silver BMW and glanced inside. There was nothing in the car, except a cell phone and a few papers. He turned around and walked towards the large entrance to the famous Tuileries Garden, which is the most central park in Paris. It stretches its "*à la française*" alleys and lawns along the Seine river from the Louvre museum to the Concorde square. It was designed in 1664 by Le Notre, the gardener of the King of France Louis the 14th, and the Versailles park designer. The Tuileries Garden is spread with basins and statues.

Where they hiding in the park? Did they want him to walk inside so they could gun him down silently and hide his body in the bushes?

Ward, Agent 27S, walked into the park, gravel crunching underneath his shoes. All was silent. There was nobody around anymore. Would there suddenly be a roar of gunfire? Followed by screams and blood? Ward's body was now pumping with adrenaline, and his eyes were concentrated and alert. His finger was resting on the trigger, ready to be pulled at the sign of movement or voices. Ward bit his lip until it bled, and stayed focused and quiet. He was going to kill - he had to kill, or they would kill him. He tensed himself; his grey eyes fierce and sharp. It was then he saw part of a Hungarian face exposed in the pool of light from the streetlamps. Then came the shiny muzzle of a gun, taking aim.

Frank Ward lifted his gunning arm and balanced it on his other, training the gun on the figure lurking in the shadows. The Colt King Cobra spat once, quietly. The round caught the man in the chest, and the impact send him flying backwards and into the trees, like the force of a shotgun bullet. The Hungarian didn't have the opportunity to scream - he died instantly and was now thrown back onto the ground in a pool of red.

Ward spun around, searching for more opponents. There must be some more hiding in the trees. Suddenly, as if reading his mind, another of Victor's men leapt out of the bushes and onto the path, standing in front of the lake. He fired, but the shot went too high. Ward cursed and crouched down, his eyes searching in the direction of the shot. The killer fired again, this time only missing Ward's chest by a few inches. Agent 27S reacted quicker this time, and could make out the dark figure standing beside the water. He aimed at the man's right leg and squeezed the trigger. The man cried out in agony, as he was thrown backwards into the icy water with a tremendous splash. He stayed under for a few moments and then his head resurfaced and he tried to tread water but couldn't. The water was turning slightly red and he begged for Ward to pull him out. He ignored him and left the man splashing and cursing in the water, struggling to stay afloat.

Frank Ward headed across a lawn and crouched down in the shadows of a huge tree looming over him. His mouth was dry and his face was covered in beads of sweat that glistened in the moonlight. Ward held the Colt King Cobra tightly and pointing north as he lay down in the damp grass, his fingers wet with dew. He couldn't see any movement or rustling in the trees. There was no sound except for the occasional car driving down the street past the entrance to the Tuileries Garden. He certainly couldn't detect any hidden gunmen. *Could they see him? Was he just lying there, still, waiting for them to put a bullet in his skull and kill him?* He willed himself to observe more closely and notice anything suspicious. It was like a game of cat and mouse. They were all cats, and he was the mouse; being hunted. The minor difference was that he wasn't running away from the threat; Ward was facing it and hunting them too.

Hell, where was that "Menace" guy? He was the one that Ward was more focused on. "Menace" was a brutal killer, who had slaughtered many people both at Victor's request and for his own enjoyment. He was a sick man - somebody who took pleasure in destroying the lives of others. Ward presumed that "Menace" was a crackshot, possibly with the same accuracy as himself. In that case, it was going to be a matter of who pulls the trigger first.

Remaining silent, Frank Ward wiped the perspiration from his face and balanced his gunning arm on his other, the long barrel of the King Cobra pointed a few inches from the ground. There was the sound of crunching leaves behind him. Ward was alert and listened intently, moving his finger up and down the trigger. The crunching leaves continued. *Was it a rabbit?* No, surely not. The noise was too loud for a rabbit. Ward turned his head in the direction of the sound and caught sight of a large foot behind a bush. It was one of the men! The person ran out from behind the trees and crossed the lawn, carrying a Browning M.9100.

Ward sprang to his feet and aimed the gun at the person's head. 'Stop there, and drop the gun or you'll get the first bullet in the leg,' Ward threatened. 'Don't try anything stupid, either.'

The tall man stopped still in his tracks and reluctantly turned towards Ward and looked down the long barrel of the powerful King Cobra. He flung up his arms and slowly allowed the Browning to fall to the grass. 'Good,' Ward said. 'Kick it away from your reach and then come closer.'

The killer did as Ward had instructed, and obediently stepped forward into the light from the streetlamp. Ward's body went numb when he realised who it was. "Menace" Hillman stood there, defenceless, staring down the instrument of death. Ward smiled. '"Menace"'. He said coolly. 'Normally I frown upon killing in cold blood. In fact, I hate it and do not enjoy it at all. However, I'll enjoy killing you, you cruel bastard!'

"Menace" glared at Frank Ward, his cold eyes showing anger but not fear. He did not seem to care that he was going to be shot. 'Go ahead, Ward,' he dared, 'shoot me! It won't change a thing. You won't live another day to snoop around Claude Victor's affairs. Neither will the girl.'

Ward ground his teeth, and began to wonder where to shoot first. He was a monster and would suffer for his crimes. He didn't deserve a painless death. 'We'll see about that, "Menace".'

With satisfaction, Frank Ward pulled the trigger of the gun, just after he noticed "Menace" nod his head at something behind him as if making a signal. "Menace" hurled himself to the ground and collected his gun, avoiding Ward's shot. Before Ward could take "Menace" out, bullets roared all around him, bouncing off tree trunks and the ground. Ward swore and crouched down to avoid the rapid gunfire, and watched as "Menace" Hillman and two other tough - looking thugs ran out of the entrance of Tuileries Garden and vanished from sight.

To hell with them! he thought. *There was no time to think about them now!* He was being fired at by three of Victor's men lurking in the shadows out of sight. Ward dived for cover amongst the trees and shrubbery in the grand central alley of the gardens, lined with shady, chestnut trees, manicured lawns and a gallery of statues. He quickly discovered protection behind a thick tree trunk as various pistol rounds rebounded from the ground. He could hear one of the men screaming instructions to the others. Ward got down on the grass, trying to keep his body behind the trunk which was serving as a shield from all the shooting. Ward examined the cylinder of the Colt King Cobra. Three rounds had gone, only three remained. *Could that be enough?* He didn't bring any spare ammunition with him. If all his bullets were used up, he would have to use his flick knife. It would be inaccurate and not good for long range. He was surely outnumbered. The gunfire from the killers continued to smash into the tree, sending bark and shrapnel raining down on Ward.

The shooting was slowing down now, and it appeared that one of the killers had run out of bullets. Ward recognised the click of the empty firing pin. He took the chance and sprinted out from behind the tree and across the lawns, ducking and swerving like a rugby player to avoid the bullets. He turned briefly and let off a shot which caught one of the men in the shoulder and sent him sprawling to the ground in agony. He hoped he had severed a bone or artery. There were only two men now - which one of them had no rounds spare in his gun? One of the men was running after him, jumping over the low hedges and building up speed. Ward turned briefly and saw the enemy closing in on him. He guessed that the man was perhaps a trained athlete before Victor recruited him into a life of crime. Ward suddenly stopped still, and within a second, spun around and delivered a high kick using his right foot which connected painfully with the killer's jaw. The man grunted and fell backwards, stunned. Agent 27S didn't stop at that; he swung his fists and smashed his opponent in the nose, sending a small amount of blood splattering over his face. Dazed and possibly unconscious, the athletic brute toppled backwards and fell into a prickly rose bush planted in the flower bed.

Once again everything was silent. Frank Ward stood still, his body stinking of sweat, blood and gun powder. Some of the men's blood had stained his white cotton shirt, which was now filthy and partly torn by the rose bush. He wiped his face with his shirt sleeve and tucked the Colt King Cobra back into his waist band and walked purposefully towards the exit. It was then he realised that "Menace" and a few others had escaped earlier in the confusion of gunfire. *Where had they gone*! Ward's heart suddenly sank and he swallowed. My God, Gaëlle! *Had they got her*?

Quickly, frantically, Ward sprinted towards the entrance with every ounce of energy he had remaining in his body. He had a terrible feeling that something bad had happened. *Damn, why had he let* "Menace" *get away*? *Why hadn't he shot him on the spot*? He ran out onto the pavement and stopped to catch his breath. Some of the killers were emerging from the grand entrance of *Le Meurice*, and were making their way towards the two parked BMW's across the street. Amongst the "heavies" was Marcus "Menace" Hillman, and he was running towards the passenger seat of the first BMW, wielding his Browning M.9100. He caught the sight of Ward crouching behind the second BMW and the gun kicked sharply, bouncing off Ward's King Cobra. Stunned, Ward cried out and dropped his gun as the evil executioner "Menace" scrambled into the back of the car. Ward wasn't going to let him get away this time. With his powerful Colt King Cobra out of reach, Frank Ward retrieved his trusty commando knife from his shoe heel and aimed the weapon at "Menace". He threw the knife with force and it caught the villain in the right thigh. Ward heard "Menace" grunted audibly as he felt the wound before disappearing inside the car.

Frank Ward collected his Colt King Cobra from the tarmac and felt angry and disappointed with the knife-throwing. He had aimed higher and had hoped to either pierce the heart or the lungs - two of the most vital organs in the human body. Normally his knife-throwing skills were accurate and always on target. However, this time, his aim was poor. The second BMW roared to life and before Ward could fire, it had vanished down the street and hurtled around a bend leaving only a faint cloud of dust behind.

The first BMW with "Menace" inside started up shortly afterwards and sped away in the opposite direction. Scrambling awkwardly to his feet, Ward ran onto the road and took up the traditional shooting stance as he watched the driver perform a crazy hand - brake turn. The tyres screeched loudly on the pavement. The BMW was now heading straight for him, increasing in speed. Ward stood still and firm, gambling whether to shoot or run. The BMW was only a few yards away now. Ward aimed and was ready to shoot. His target was the actual vehicle engine. If he could hit the engine, it would either stop the car or blow it up. While he had decided on the target, the BMW was now only a few metres away. There wasn't any time to shoot. At the last moment, Ward threw himself out of the way, the bumper just clipping his shoe as he crashed to the ground.

He lay on the floor for a few seconds, tasting the blood in his mouth and searching his body for injury. If he had decided to pull the trigger, the BMW would have flattened him on the road and mowed him down. He was very lucky. Agent 27S turned his head slowly to see the BMW getting away. Ward swore and collected his Colt King Cobra. He crouched on the floor, and the gun exploded in his hands. The bullet shattered the back window with incredible force, sending shards of glass showering down upon "Menace". In a final attempt to take out the front tyre, Ward made the Colt bark a final time, the round simply bounding off the metallic paintwork. Ward examined the cylinder and found there was no more ammunition left. With bitter disappointment, he watched the enemy vehicle disappear into the moonlight. Wearily, Ward tucked his useless gun into the waistband of his trousers and walked purposefully up the concrete steps of *Le Meurice* hotel.

How could he let them get away like that? Especially that "Menace" guy! It was then as he scolded himself silently for his poor shooting, that he remembered Gaëlle, his lover, upstairs in their room. "Menace" and the others had come out of the hotel! *Had they ... had they killed her?* Ward swallowed and sprinted through the reception area towards the elevator section where he ran inside one and selected his floor. As the elevator began its slow ascent, Ward kept repeating to himself, : 'She's fine. She's fine. She's fine.'

Frank Ward stood outside the Deluxe Double Suite and reluctantly gripped the cold, brass door handle. He didn't want to go inside. *What if she was dead? What would he do if she was there, lying in a pool of her own blood? How the hell would he live with himself?* He took a deep breath and calmed himself down; preparing himself for the worst. He reached inside his pocket for the key but couldn't find it. He tried the handle and found it was unlocked. As the door opened, Ward's stomach churned and he willed himself not to vomit immediately. The living room, which had been furnished elegantly in Louis XVI style, was now a shambles. Tables were overturned, glass was shattered all over the carpet, and trays of guns were scattered across the floor. Expensive ornaments lay broken and in pieces and sophisticated artwork had been ripped from the walls. The whole place was covered in smears of red.

'Gaëlle?' He called, his voice timid and shaky.

There was no reply.

'Gaëlle?'

Frank Ward closed the door behind him and advanced further into the room. The gold and white wallpaper was stained with red, as was the light brown carpet and the furniture. *Was it blood?* He took a few steps towards the bedroom and discovered the door was open. Hesitantly, he poked his head around and saw a crumpled figure on the golden king - size bed. He gaped in horror as he recognised the golden hair, that was now hiding the pretty face that he adored so much. It was Gaëlle. Her clothes were soaked in blood. She was lying so incredibly still.

'No,' he cried. 'For God's sake, no!'

This wasn't happening, he told himself. He must be having some kind of terrible nightmare. It wasn't real. But Ward couldn't wake up. He was standing there in the room, alive. He stared down at Gaëlle - the woman that he had made love to, the woman he planned to marry. Her throat had been slashed horribly from ear to ear and her body was covered in multiple stab wounds. Blood was everywhere. Trembling he reached down and felt for a pulse, knowing that he wasn't going to find one.

'Gaëlle,' he said softly, his voice shaky, 'I'm so sorry.'

The trail of blood on the carpet indicated that her body had been dragged from the bathroom and into the bedroom, where her body had been dumped on the bed. He stroked her soft pale cheeks, that were already deathly cold. He brushed the locks of golden hair out of her face, and slowly locked his mouth onto hers for a final time. Her lips were stiff and parted. He kissed her for a few precious seconds, and then pulled his mouth away from hers. 'Goodnight, darling.' He stood up straight and tried to come to terms with her death. He loved her so much, and now, Gaëlle had been killed. It was all his fault. He had forgotten to lock the door. "Menace" and his gruesome pals must have raided the room, destroying everything and finally destroying his true love. He turned away from the obscene sight on the bed and put his head in his hands. *What was he going to do?*

His thoughts were interrupted by the telephone ringing outside in the wrecked living room. Frank Ward rushed out of the bedroom and spent five minutes searching through the mess for the phone and receiver. Eventually, he found the instrument hidden underneath an overturned table. Gripping the receiver tightly, he held it to his ear, breathing heavily.

'Agent 27S?' The voice enquired. It was General Kretzmer, the head of the French DGSE.

'General!' He said, struggling to gain control over the situation. 'Get over here with a few of your men and the police. Something terrible has happened here.'

Before the General could reply, Ward had slammed the receiver down on the base and pulled up a chair that lay on the floor. He found his Beretta 84FS Cheetah that he had given Gaëlle lying in the bathroom. He examined the magazine and as he sat waiting for the police and the DGSE agents to arrive, he thought about how this would affect his mission. The Claude Victor assignment was now no longer a mission like any other. With the death of Gaëlle Dumas, his girlfriend and future wife, the mission had become a personal vendetta against those that were responsible for her death. He was going to kill Victor and "Menace" and avenge Gaëlle if it was the last thing he would ever do. Bitterly, he sat back in the chair and thought about how he would seek ultimate revenge against the two people he hated most in the entire world.

9/ BACK ON TRACK

WITHIN A MATTER of minutes, the Rue de Rivoli streets surrounding *Le Meurice* was packed with ambulances, police squad cars and pedestrian vehicles which belonged to high ranking members of the D.G.S.E.

The police had managed to barricade the whole road surrounding the hotel, keeping curious members of the public away from the crime scene. Guests in the hotel had been locked in their rooms and were not permitted to leave until the investigation was over. The Tuileries Gardens were also sealed off, where paramedics, police and D.G.S.E agents were working to locate the bodies and survivors of the assassins. The dead were bundled into black body bags and then carried into the back of the ambulances to be identified and then sent to the morgues. Survivors would then be arrested by the police who would then hand them over to the *Direction Générale de la Sécurité Extérieure* for questioning. While members of the team were working furiously in the gardens, others were inside *Le Meurice*, questioning Frank Ward, taking photographs of Gaëlle, and carrying out other procedures necessary in a situation like this.

Frank Ward watched grimly as the paramedics hauled her gruesome corpse into the body bag, blood still trickling from her severed neck. He tried to stay still and calm, but he was shaking all over as a uniformed paramedic zipped the bag up. He felt so useless. He couldn't do anything for her now. There was nothing in the world he could do to bring his future wife back. He swallowed as he watched two men carry the bag out of the bedroom. Ward watched them disappear through the front door and then returned to the ransacked living room, where a professional group of police officers and crime scene investigation men were searching the room for fingerprints and any clues. A toad - faced man with a matt of untidy ginger hair came from across the room scribbling notes down in his pad. He was Detective Inspector Jean Hugo of the French metropolitan police. He had already asked Ward a few questions concerning the death of Gaëlle Dumas and the men in The Tuileries Gardens. He had explained that he was a member of the American Central Intelligence Agency and that he was working with Gaëlle on a confidential mission. General Gaston Kretzmer, the head of the D.G.S.E, had also backed up his statement.

'Monsieur Ward,' the Detective began, running his long fingers through his tangled hair, 'do you have any idea who those men were that tried to kill you, and succeeded in taking away Madame Dumas's life?'

Ward selected a Marlboro cigarette and lit it carefully with his Dunhill lighter before replying, 'They were professional hit men sent by Claude Victor, the owner of the Kraken International Cooperation. You've probably heard about him. Recently, Gaëlle and I unveiled Victor's criminal activities. He must have wanted to silence us.'

'Well don't worry, Monsieur Ward,' Detective Hugo said, 'The D.G.S.E are dealing with him. Over the next week or so, we will search our criminal records database and also those of the French secret services, in order to identify the bodies of the gunmen and the survivors as well. We hope that the survivors will crack and talk. Hopefully they'll inform us of where and when Victor employed them. Thank you for your cooperation, Monsieur Ward. You can leave here now, get a bite to eat and rest in a bed and breakfast for the night. We've finished questioning you for the time being and it would be helpful if you left us to search your room for evidence. I'll contact you on your cell phone if we need any help. Your clothes and belongings will be sent to you as soon as possible.'

Ward forced a smile and thanked the Detective. *The man was right*, he thought. He would end up a wreck if he stayed here any longer. He was starving, too. A comfortable bed and breakfast would do him nicely. He said goodbye to General Kretzmer and headed towards the elegant table in the living room where his polyester jacket was draped over a chair. He waited until he thought that nobody was watching him, then he secretly hid his Beretta and the Uzi 9mm in his folded garment. Quickly, he walked out of the Deluxe Double Room without looking back. Frank Ward left the hotel where the torrent of emergency vehicles were still parked. He removed his car keys from the breast pocket of his cotton shirt and located his 2006 Chevrolet Z06 Corvette in the large hotel car park. Ward unlocked it automatically and climbed into the comfortable leather drivers seat and put the jacket on the passengers seat. *He would need them for when he was going to go after Victor*, he decided. After all, he had no idea when the police would return the rest of the munitions and his belongings to him. They would be in there for weeks. Frank Ward slipped his Beretta into his shoulder holster and put his jacket on over it to conceal it from view. He then proceeded to hide the Uzi 9mm SMG in the weapons tray under his seat, fitted by the CIA free of charge. If he needed anything else, he always had the contents of the weapons tray. Ward shoved the keys into the ignition of the Chevrolet and waited for his vehicle to growl loudly as the engine started. As he reversed out of his parking space and headed for the exit, he couldn't stop thinking about Gaëlle, and how it was his fault that she had been killed.

Within thirty minutes of driving around the twilit streets of Paris, Frank Ward had eventually come across a small but welcoming Bed and Breakfast motel on Avenue des Tilleuls and noted the '*VACANCES D'EMPLOI DISPONIBLES*' sign in the large front window, overlooking the garden. The three-storeys high building looked pleasant enough with a delightful mixture of Colonial and Hispanic architecture. Bedrooms and suites in the front of the house all had a view of the park with its beautiful old trees.

Ward yawned audibly as he slowed down and pulled the Chevrolet over into an unoccupied parking space. He glanced at his silver watch and the dials informed him it was ten past midnight. *Hell, was it that time already?* Ward turned off the engine, locked the car and pocketed the keys and began walking around the front of the building. Lights were on in various rooms and the reception area. Some of the more youthful guests would just have returned from the clubs and bars, he guessed. As for the staff in the reception, they were probably ready for closing for the night. Ward approached the front door and pressed the bell. He waited for a few moments until a small, ratty - looking female in her forties with steel - rimmed spectacles appeared and opened the door.

Frank Ward grinned and apologised for calling at such a late time. Since he was fluent in French amongst other languages, he began to talk in the native tongue: 'As I was driving by, I couldn't help noticing the vacancy sign in the window. I've been busy recently and I'm extremely tired. Please may I have a room for the night. Hopefully I should be out of here by eleven. I've got to meet with somebody tomorrow morning.'

The ratty woman adjusted her spectacles and glanced at her watch. 'It's quite alright, *monsieur*, you'd be surprised at the number of guests we have at this hour,' she smiled warmly and gestured with her hand to come inside, 'please follow me into the reception and I'll have a look at the rooms we have available at the moment.'

'*Merci.*'

He followed her into the grand reception area and then across the wine red carpet to the reception desk in the corner beside the olive green three piece sofa. The walls decorated in golden wallpaper were lit up by a pool of light from the lamp on a small mahogany table. The whole design and colour scheme looked charming and elegant, personalised by the refined choice of furniture. The short receptionist went behind the desk and flipped through a few papers in the guestbook. 'We have a single room available on the first floor. Number 8. Would that be fine?'

'Yes,' he replied, 'that would suit me nicely.'

'Good,' she said. She reached up where several room keys were hanging on hooks on the wall. She searched for the correct key and handed Number 8 to him. 'Name?'

'Michael Goodwin.' (This was one of Ward's many official CIA aliases).

'Thank you very much, *monsieur*. That will be forty five euros, please.'

Ward nodded and reached inside his jacket, removed his brown wallet and took out the money that he had exchanged from dollars to euros on his arrival. 'There you go, plus a ten euro tip.'

The receptionist smiled from ear to ear again and gladly accepted the change. She stuffed it into the cash register and watched as the handsome, masculine man headed towards the staircase. 'By the way,' she called after him, 'breakfast is at nine.'

Sleep had been almost impossible, and the few hours that he managed to doze off were filled with horrific and vivid nightmares. He had imagined Gaëlle standing before him in his bedroom, her naked body covered in blood and stab wounds, gore still pouring from the thick cut in her throat. He had screamed and screamed until she disappeared and he awoke, shaking uncontrollably and covered in beads of perspiration.

Frank Ward held his head and rushed into the small bathroom where he vomited in the lavatory for a few minutes. He tried to forget about the nightmare and continued his usual morning ritual. He exercised on the floor, showered for ten minutes in hot water and then changed back into his crumpled dress shirt and trousers that he had worn the day before. With the money in his wallet, he decided he would freshen up after breakfast and buy some new clothes from the shops on Avenue des Champs-Elysees. Then, he would collect his Toshiba Satellite 1.73 GHz Pentium M Laptop from the Chevrolet Corvette and using the CIA access codes to enter criminal records, he would look up the Chinese criminal chief that he had spotted in Claude Victor's castle during the conference. Hopefully, if he could identify the man correctly via Identifinder, he could build up a likeness of the man which should than match the real person, and give details of his crimes and past, plus his most recent sightings. That way, he might lead him to Victor and his operations. He would *persuade* him to tell Ward everything he knew about Victor's plan. If he located the Chinese gangster, he would contact the Paris Branch of the CIA where Cartwright would be. He was hoping that if he presented this information to his chief, he might send him after Victor and his Oriantal contact from the Hong Kong Triad society.

Three hours later, following the consumption of the delicious breakfast consisting of four or five *crêpes* (thin pancakes that originally came from Brittany in the west of France). The chef had filled them with various ingredients such as ham, cheese and a few small mushrooms. It was fantastic! Once he had washed it all down with two mugs of black coffee, he collected his Chevrolet Z06 Corvette from the Bed and Breakfast car park and headed for Avenue des Champs-Elysees, where he purchased a number of expensive garments from a tailor's shop. He had selected a few dark linen jackets, cotton shirts and woollen trousers. Ward had even found a pair of matching rectangular cufflinks! He returned to the hotel feeling clean and refreshed in his new clothes. He took out his Toshiba laptop computer from the spacious trunk of his car and took it up to his room, Number 8, pausing to acknowledge the ratty - looking receptionist on the way through the door.

Frank Ward assembled his laptop computer on the writing desk in the corner of the room and pulled up a chair, before turning the computer on. He waited for a few moments until the black screen suddenly opened onto his desktop page. He typed in his password and accessed an icon, exclusive to members of the Central Intelligence Agency. It was the crimianl records programme, that was available to members of the world wide espionage group which included MI6, MI5, the Federal Bureau of Investigation, the Israile Mossad and the FSB, the successor of the Russian KGB. He stabbed at the keys and typed in his code number '27S' and watched as the screen opened onto a page listing the various intelligence organisations. He selected the CIA, and browsed down through the list of hyperlinks, and clicked on the '3-D Visual Identifier' system. This sophisticated hardware allowed him to input physical characteristics, that manipulates sketches of the individual targeted, until it resembles the subject. The data is then programmed into the criminal records, and if the resemblance is accurate, the background of the target and recent movements will be provided.

He sat back in his chair and thought back to that night when he spied on the conference meeting up on Mount Blanche. He could picture the menacing, frightening face clearly in his mind, although some features he had forgotten. Firstly, he selected the nationality of the subject and the estimated age, and watched as the skin on the blank face turned a slight yellowy brown colour. He remembered the small brown (almost hazel!) eyes that had resembled shotgun barrels, and the delicate fine nose. Now the mouth! *What was it like again?* Of course! He experimented on the programme and made the lips smaller and fuller to match the target's mouth. He programmed all the information into the laptop and could see the similarity between the picture and the real man whom he had seen days ago. The hair, if his memory was serving him correctly, was fairly long and jet black, with a smooth, wavy texture. It was slicked back immaculately. He reached for his cigarette case as he stared hard at the picture he had built up on the laptop. Ward flicked back the oxidized jaws of his Dunhill lighter, and lit the Marlboro cigarette. Satisfied with the picture, he clicked 'SEARCH' and waited for a background and location to flash up on the screen.

Within minutes, the ingenious device had matched the visual picture and a new page came up, showing a file photograph of the real man. 'Kazuki Masaharu,' he read from the screen, 'convicted murderer and gang leader. Known to participate in illegal CD, VHS and DVD sales and arms dealings. Planner and strategist for the Hong Kong Triad society. Known to recently have been offering Triad 'services' to other villains in another scheme to gain money and fund criminal activities. Mother German, father Chinese. Brought up in Beijing by grandparents following parents death. Gained criminal record status at age of twenty one. Arrested once for shooting a policeman in the head with a double - barrelled shotgun. Last sighted - 27/04/07 in Tianjin, China by a Mossad agent working undercover. *Why, that was yesterday!* '

Frank Ward grinned and inserted a small floppy disc into his laptop and saved the page onto it. Then, he put the floppy disc into his pocket, packed his laptop away and hurried out of his room. Before he left, he returned his room key to the receptionist, thanked her for her services, and started the car.

Station P, the French branch of the Central Intelligence Agency, was located in the lively centre of Paris. It was within a legitimate business called *Rene's Café*. Open from seven in the morning, and closed at nine at night, the café was merely a front for the CIA's monitoring HQ in

France. Station P works closely with the D.G.S.E to gather intelligence and keep terrorists and criminals under constant surveillance.

The Chevrolet Z06 Corvette drew up outside Station P, where customers of *Rene's Café* were already sitting outside at the tables, sipping coffee, tea, and French hot chocolate. As Frank Ward emerged from his sports car he guessed that the cover did *very* well. He locked the car and made his way past the tables outside the café and disappeared inside. More people were seated inside, in the comfortable seats beside the large, French windows. Ward walked right towards the back of the room, took out a small swipe card and ran it through a swipe machine beside the door that read 'STAFF ONLY - STORAGE ROOM' in French. The swipe machine turned green, and the automatic door retracted. Ward replaced his swipe card and disappeared inside.

Walter Greaves, Cartwright's Chief Of Staff, was sitting at the far end of the room in a leather swivel chair at a bank of computers with several other CIA technicians. He was wearing head phones over his ears and sipping a warm cup of coffee, provided by the café. *It was a nice little cover*, he smiled to himself. Not only did it rake in money, but there was always a warm drink whenever needed.

'Morning, Walter.'

It was a familiar voice. A voice he knew too well and was very fond of indeed. He spun around on the chair and looked up as his closest friend in the agency, Frank Ward, who was coming into the room. He smiled and put the mug down. 'Morning to you, Frank,' he replied amiably. 'Are you alright? I've heard about that business with the French girl. You must feel terrible.'

Ward nodded and sat down next to him. 'I'm trying to recover,' he explained, softly. 'I feel that I'm responsible for what happened.'

Walter Greaves shook his head and took his headphones off his greying brown hair. 'Don't feel guilty, Frank. It happens in this line of duty all the time. She was a spy just like you. She knew that she would be risking her life joining the world of espionage. Spying is a dirty profession. I don't know why I'm in the business.'

Ward produced the small floppy disc containing the Identifier page on Kazuki Masaharu. He pushed it across the computer bench towards Greaves. 'I'll get revenge on Victor and his men for killing Gaëlle,' he vowed. 'I want both you and Cartwright to have a look at what I've found this morning on the 3-D Visual Identifier program. Where is he?'

The Chief Of Staff thought for a few moments and then answered: 'He'll be in the Communications Room I think. I'll see if he's available to come here.' Greaves got up from his chair and walked towards a small desk against the wall and picked up the receiver on the base. Holding the instrument against his ear, he pressed nine, which was the room number for the Communications Room. It rang a few times until it was answered.

'Cartwright speaking.'

'This is Greaves, sir. Agent 27S is here with me in the Computer Suite. He says he has something to show us. Are you busy?'

'No, not particularly. I'll down in a few moments.'

Seymour Cartwright, the current D.C.I.A strolled into the Computer Suite two minutes later, looking exhausted and tired as usual. The heavy bags that drooped under his grey eyes showed the stresses and complications of his job. He noticed his Chief Of Staff and Ward sitting at the computers, and he found a chair and sat down next to them.

'Morning, 27S. The police and D.G.S.E still haven't found anything yet. I've just been talking to General Kretzmer. One of the surviving gunmen took a cyanide capsule when questioned about his connections with Claude Victor. Apart from that, we haven't learned anything new.'

'You will in a few moments, sir,' Ward assured him, sliding the compact floppy disc into the computer. The monitor flashed and Frank Ward opened up the file and the face of Kazuki Masaharu erupted onto the screen. 'Using the new 3-D Visual Identifinder, I made up a picture of the Chinese Triad leader who attended Victor's conference at his castle fortress. The likeness proved to be accurate, and using the criminal records, it identified him as a man called Kazuki Masaharu. If you would care to read his background?'

The Chief Of Staff and Cartwright leaned forward and studied the text on the Chinese gangster. A few minutes later they exchanged amazed glances at each other and turned towards Ward.

'He was last spotted yesterday in Tianjin, China by a Mossad intelligence operative. Supposing he is there with Claude Victor? After all, he was the one that stole the American missile guidance system for him from the laboratory in Hong Kong. What if Victor needed his services again?'

'Good thinking, 27S,' Cartwright complimented.

'If you could give me permission to go Tianjin as soon as possible, sir, I could follow up this lead and look for this Kazuki Masaharu. Station C, the China branch, could then aid me in the field. Once I've located

Masaharu I can follow him and see if he takes me to Victor. I can also question him on what Victor is going to do with the missile guidance hardware.'

Cartwright bit his finger nails and toyed with the idea. 'You may be right, 27S. My only worry is that you may have decided to make this assignment more personal since Madmoiselle Dumas's tragic death. If I send you to find this Masaharu chap, I expect you to continue this mission professionally and objectively. Do I make myself quite clear?'

'Very clear, sir,' Ward said.

'Fine. I'll have my men book you on the next available flight to Tianjin, Agent 27S. I'll also alert the head of Station C to meet you over there on your arrival, to help you with your mission.'

Frank Ward got up from his chair. 'Thank you very much, sir. I'll contact you at Langley Headquarters when I arrive at the airport.'

He then pushed the chair under the desk, said goodbye to Greaves and his chief, and disappeared out of the door.

** *

An hour later, in his small office in Station P HQ, Cartwright sat at his desk with his Chief Of Staff opposite him. His long, pointed fingers were laid on the metal - surfaced table and he knocked the ash off the end of his cigarette. He lifted his head wearily and looked into the eyes off his second-in-command. 'Have I done the right thing, Greaves, sending 27S to China after that Chinese gang leader?'

The Chief Of Staff lifted his glass of bourbon whisky to his lips and sipped his drink. He placed it back down onto the desk and replied, 'I know Frank Ward well, sir. He always comes out on top and will use his instincts for tracking down both Claude Victor and Kazuki Masaharu. He's a good agent, the best I've ever seen since I came in from the American Air Force ten years ago. He won't give up. Just give him time, and I assure you, he'll find something important.'

Cartwright sighed. 'I do hope you're right, Greaves. I don't want 27S to take the mission too personal. I agree with you. He's the best we've had in the CIA for many years. Of course,' he said, laughing, 'I don't tell him that.'

10/ AN OLD FRIEND

SIPPING HIS CHINESE cocktail, Kazuki Masaharu gazed dreamily across the still morning ocean and watched as the sun was beginning to rise. It was a breathtaking performance that was so moving and fantastic, it almost made him wish that he had not become a criminal and instead, decided to enjoy the world and its many marvellous secrets.

He swallowed a mouthful of the traditional cocktail and decided that he actually enjoyed it. It was made with a combination of rum, grenadine, a few dashes of curaçao, more dashes of maraschino liqueur, Dash Angostura bitters and three or four ice cubes. All mixed together in a cocktail shaker before being strained into a glass made the drink both satisfying and enjoyable.

Despite his life of greed, murder, theft and prostitution, Kazuki Masaharu respected the good things in life and loved to live well, not caring that he was living off blood money. It was all a game to him. He liked to think that all the miserable men and woman he had executed over the years had all helped finance his life of luxury. He smiled as he took out one of his Cuban cigars and inserted it between his small, full lips and lit it casually with his lighter. He inhaled a lungful of smoke and continued to watch the ocean move slowly in the breeze, the surface of the water coated in orange from the rising sun.

Ever since he had stolen the missile guidance hardware from Hong Kong for Claude Victor, the man had engaged his services as a temporary bodyguard and a hired gun. A few of his other more experienced members of the Traid society had come along with him to carry out illegal deeds. Victor said that he couldn't have his own men, especially that man known as "Menace", to do the dirty work in case the police or intelligence groups connected them to him. Masaharu and his men were to carry out the more 'complex' duties. Plus, he needed them to protect Victor's island home off the coasts of Beijing where 'Operation Launch' was going to take place.

He had to admit though, Claude Victor and "Menace" freaked him out. That was the downside of the job. They were both so fascinated by death, especially "Menace". The thug would boast often to Masaharu that he had killed over fifty men, most of them in cold - blood by sadistic methods such as hacking them to bits with axes or probing their organs with sharp blades. "Menace" bragged that he was a master of torture and could keep victims alive for several hours whilst inflicting a severe amount of pain. Victor, on the other hand, wasn't as gruesome. He was still, however, a maniac with a mania for money and power. Masaharu hated him. Victor oozed authority and could have a man sent to his death with his army of thugs. He would keep going on about being the richest man in history and claimed that he had more power in his fingernails than God himself has in his entire body!

The good parts of the deal were the money and the luxurious life that Victor shared with him. The money which had already been exchanged for the theft of the guidance system, could improve the Triad society sufficiently, and help buy better munitions and recruit extra men. It could also cover police bribes and failed operations in the past. Victor had also promised him the sum of two million once Operation Launch becomes a success. Masaharu was very eager to collect the money. While Masaharu and his men were working for Victor, they were also staying on board his luxurious yacht, *Le dauphin*. Basically meaning 'The Dolphin' in French, it was built for Claude Victor several years ago in Paris. It was more than one hundred and twenty feet of luxury, like a floating hotel. It was complete with more than fifty luxurious bedroom suites, a swimming pool, sauna, entertainment room and much more. With a hull of aluminium and magnesium alloy, two Baudoin seven-hundred-and-fifty horsepower diesel engines, Kohler generators, Naid stabilizers, *Le dauphin* could move her seventy tons at a continuous running speed of sixteen knots. Superb electronics included: Sat-Com with Telex, autopilot, on-board computers that assisted the ship's management and relayed data to and from anywhere in the world. It was fantastic, and when Victor didn't require his 'unique capabilities,' he would simply lounge on deck or swim in the pool, enjoying the peace and relaxation.

He tapped the end of his cigar into a glass ashtray on the table on the sundeck of the massive yacht, and turned his attention away from the setting sun and onto the magnificent figure of Linda Pascal, Victor's new fiancé, relaxing with a suspense novel on a sun lounger, wearing no more than a revealing black and white bikini. The reasonably short hair, the flirty emerald - green eyes, the sensual mouth. *God, how attractive she was!* Her figure was terrific and sexy, like one that belonged to a famous catwalk model. Her breasts jutted out perfectly under the bikini top. Since Victor first introduced him to her at the party back in Paris, he couldn't help but long for her to be his fiancé rather than Victor's. *Why did she like him?* He resembled the walking dead! *Did she know about his criminal connections? Or was she just with him in a bid to inherit his large fortune?* He remembered what Victor had said to him a few days ago, :'If I catch you messin' around with my girl, I'll slit your throat with a bowie knife and cram your organs into your mouth.' Victor laughed afterwards, leaving Masaharu unsure whether the man was attempting to pull off a joke, or was threatening him.

The double doors leading out onto the sun deck opened and Claude Victor walked unhurriedly towards Kazuki Masaharu sitting down at the circular table. The strange man, "Menace" Hillman followed him out, a bandage tied neatly around his muscular thigh. Since the incident in Paris, "Menace" had developed a noticeable limp. The knife, thrown by Frank Ward, barely missed a main artery, which if severed, would have instantly caused the man to bleed to death. To some extent, Kazuki Masaharu almost wished that the bastard Ward had killed "Menace" so that he and his men would be given the chance to eliminate the American agent. If the job had been performed by himself, Ward would have been killed by now. After all, the spy deserved it. Masaharu had rather been hoping for the chance to avenge the deaths of his Triad men following the failed assassination of the French agent.

Claude Victor put a cigarette to his lips and sat down next to Masaharu. 'Good morning, my friend,' the criminal said softly, his foul - smelling animal breath enveloping Masaharu. This morning, Victor was wearing a white polo shirt beneath a dark grey sports jacket. As he sat down, he extended the bony, fragile hand of a skeleton. Reluctantly, Masaharu took it and was shaken by how cold the palm was. It was as if the hand was dead completely. 'I trust you are enjoying yourself on my yacht, Mister Masaharu.'

Kazuki Masaharu exhaled a cloud of smoke from his nostrils and lounged back in the chair. 'Yes, monsieur Victor. I'm exceptionally comfortable here.'

'Good,' Victor said, smiling his twisted, toothy smile.

"Menace" Hillman sat down next to them, his fiery eyes alert and watchful. Masaharu got the feeling that Hillman wasn't particularly fond of him either.

'I wanted you to know that my team of staff over at my island home near Beijing has recently finished building the Operations centre where Operation Launch will commence,' Victor explained. 'Now that Stage One is complete, I require a few of your most elite enforcers to go over there and guard my home until the day of the launch. The rest will stay here on my yacht, including yourself, where you will protect the Missile guidance system down in the vaults.'

'That's fine with me, monsieur Victor.'

'Excellent. Now I require your services. My men back in Paris have been keeping tabs on our friend Frank Ward since the evening of the failed attack, led by "Menace". It seems that he has located your files on the criminal records, Mister Masaharu. He will heading over here to Tianjin as we speak. I don't want him to interfere in my plans again. He knows too much. I want you and your men to keep a look out for him and kill him discreetly before he makes contact with his headquarters on arrival. Let his death be a particularly painful one, "Menace" - give him the gun.'

Marcus "Menace" Hillman reached inside his jacket and removed a single action Desert Eagle Mark XIX pistol from his shoulder holster underneath his left armpit. Silently, he examined the magazine, noted that it held seven rounds, and then pushed it across the surface of the table towards Masaharu. The Chinese gangster weighed it expertly in his hand, as a trained killer would do, and tested the firm grip. Satisfied, he fitted it into his own holster and thanked "Menace".

'Use this gun,' Victor instructed, puffing casually on his cigarette which hung from the corner of his mouth. 'Do it *cleanly* and stuff the body in the trunk of his vehicle and burn it to bits to destroy the evidence. Got me?'

Kazuki Masaharu grinned slyly, eager to wreak revenge on the American thug who cost him several men. 'Don't worry, monsieur Victor. I've got a personal score to settle with our mutual friend, Mister Ward.'

Claude Victor got to his feet heavily and looked Masaharu coldly in the eyes. His hideous, wrinkled face was deathly serious. 'You'd better eliminate him, Masaharu. I won't give you another chance if you fail. I won't tolerate it one bit. I'll show you what happens to anybody who displeases me.'

Victor turned around slowly and looked towards his gorgeous fiancé, Linda, who was absorbed in her novel. 'Would you mind going to your cabin, darling?' Victor asked, softly. 'I must talk privately to Mister Masaharu, please.'

Linda Pascal looked away from her novel and slipped her bookmark between the pages. She sat up and looked at her lover, adoringly. 'Of course, Claude. How long will you be?'

'Not long. I'll send Mister Hillman to collect you once we've finished.'

'Ok.' The remarkable tanned figure got to her feet and walked towards the double doors with the elegance of a fashion model. She disappeared through the door and vanished.

Kazuki Masaharu felt uneasy being left alone with these two sadistic creatures. The hairs on his neck stood upright and his palms began to perspire. He could sense that something bad was going to happen. He swallowed and watched Victor's gruesome mouth twist into a cruel grin.

'Now that we are alone, Mister Masaharu, I can show you the price of failure that I will inflict on people in my employ.'

Shit! What was this monster going to do to him?

"Menace" suddenly dived on him from behind, knocking the wind out of Masaharu's body. The strong man threw the Chinese gangster onto the floor with a grunt and seized him with his muscular arms, underneath the armpits. Kazuki Masaharu was shocked and attempted to struggle free from the powerful ogre behind him. He could feel "Menace" Hillman's large fingers biting hard into his biceps as he held him there tightly in front of Claude Victor.

The French criminal reached down towards his belt and slowly unsheathed a long Freeman Hunter knife, designed by Gerber Knives. Victor wrapped his crooked fingers around the polished pear wood handle and held the sharp, stainless steel blade upwards where the light reflected on the metal. Kazuki Masaharu tried to swallow but he found that he couldn't. His stomach churned violently and tied in a knot. Masaharu thought this only happened in novels, not in real life. But no, it existed, and Masaharu, the brave but sinister murderer, had never felt fear like this in his lifetime. Victor slipped his thumb into the finger guard and used the grooves in the wood for a perfect grip.

He certainly knew how to handle the weapon. He had killed before with this knife, Masaharu knew it. Whether he had killed a deer or a human being, Claude Victor was definitely not a virgin at destroying life with this 3. 25 inch blade. A cool bead of sweat trickled down Masaharu's cheek and hung on his chin for a few seconds before it dropped onto the stiff collar of his shirt. Victor reached forward with his free hand and grabbed a handful of Kazuki Masaharu's black hair and forced his head back violently and put the hunter's knife against his throat. The Chinese crook looked up with his blue eyes, and for the first time, he looked scared and frightened. Masaharu sensed his demise in a few, long moments that would seem an eternity.

'I would kill you if I wanted or needed to, Masaharu,' Victor snarled. 'Just you remember that. I hold Operation Launch in a much higher regard than your life. To me, you bear hardly any significance to me at all. I could replace you and your men to continue your work. I'm paying you well, am I not?'

Masaharu swallowed and said, 'Yes, I'm pleased with my salary.'

'Good,' Victor spat, 'I've hired you for work and I don't expect you to fail me again like your men did in Paris, when I told you to kill the French agent. If she had died ages ago, we wouldn't have had the security breach at my castle, nor would we have the problem with Frank Ward, the American agent. Got me?'

'Yes,' he replied.

'This is a punishment for not eliminating the French agent all those days ago.' Victor slowly raised the Freeman hunter knife above his head and his crazy eyes were wild with excitement.

'Please! No! Monsieur Victor! Don't hurt me! I'll do better!'

Claude Victor ignored Masaharu's cries for mercy and brought the blade down forcefully onto his right arm. Kazuki Masaharu screamed loudly, roaring and shouting obscene curses into the sky as the knife cut deeply through his flesh and his vein. "Menace" released his victim and allowed Masaharu to fall to the floor in agony, a crumpled figure. Blood was seeping out through the wound and most of his sleeved arm was covered in red. Some of the gory mess had dripped onto the polished wooden deck.

'Let that be a lesson to you, Masaharu,' Victor hissed through his bent teeth. 'I spared your life because I like you. I think you are a capable man. However, others haven't been as lucky as you. Next time, I'll kill you. Now, get a few of your Triad men together and get down to Tianjin Airport and eliminate our friend, Mister Frank Ward.'

With that, "Menace" and Victor marched away, leaving the bleeding figure screwed up in a ball on the deck in extreme pain. The bleeding was getting worse. Kazuki Masaharu pulled back his sleeve and looked at the gory wound in disgust. He put his hand over it and added pressure to stop the bleeding. He now had no doubt in his mind that Victor hadn't been joking when he said he would kill him if Masaharu messed with his fiancé. Victor was clearly a madman and now, Masaharu knew he was capable of anything.

On the top deck, one of the crew had heard the deafening screams and the foul language that had been yelled to the heavens. As he mopped the deck, he instantly knew that somebody else had angered his boss, Claude Victor.

Ward had never been to the urban area of Tianjin before, but from what he had heard, it was a comfortable city with a lot of beauty, especially around the swampy coasts. In the hilly far north, the Yanshan Mountains pass through the tip of northern Tianjin. The highest point in the city is Jiushanding Peak on the northen border with Hebei, at an altitude of 1078 metres. Then of course, there are the many natural rivers and reservoirs. For example, there's the Hai He river (basically meaning "sea river"), that runs through Beijing and Tianjin. It is 1,329 kilometres long, and connects with several other smaller rivers within the Tianjin Municipality.

The urban area of Tianjin is located in the south-central area of the Municipality.

As well as the main urban area of Tianjin proper, the coast along the Bohai is filled with a series of port towns, including Tanggu and Hangu.

Tianjin's climate usually consists of hot, humid summers, due to the regular monsoons, and dry, cold winters, because of the Siberian anticyclone. Spring is dry but windy, and most of the precipitation takes place in July and August. Tianjin also experiences occasional sandstorms which blow in from the Gobi Desert and may last for many days.

Frank Ward walked through the airport terminal towards the Customs area, carrying a small, battered suitcase in one hand and a thin, black leather briefcase in the other. It was warm already, and he could feel the sweat gathering underneath his armpits (Damnable Tianjin summers!). Ward took his luggage to the Customs officer, flashed him his passport and CIA identification card, and signed the necessary papers for permission to bring his Beretta into the city. Once he had signed a few things and allowed his luggage to go through the X - ray machine, he thanked the man and collected his cases before heading purposefully towards the exit. His Chevrolet Corvette, which Cartwright had sent ahead on a special cargo plane, had been parked in the car area. As he approached the automatic door leading out of the terminal block of the TSN airport, he noticed the suspicious Chinese gentleman behind him, walking with exaggerated slowness. He noted the hideous scar that ran down the left side of the cheek, and the cruel, hardened eyes that belonged to somebody who was a killer.

Kazuki Masaharu? No, this man behind him was bald. It can't be! *Or was he just being over suspicious?*

Agent 27S ignored the Chinaman behind him now and mixed in with the mass of tourists leaving the airport. He hoped that if the man was following him, he would soon lose him in the crowd. Ward kept moving and headed towards the massive car park at the front of the airport. The Chinese man was still behind, watching him and talking rapidly in Tianjin dialect through a cell phone he was carrying.

What the hell was he saying?

Ward was now sure that the Chinese man was watching him in particular. It must be one of the Triad gang members on loan to Claude Victor. *But how the hell did Victor know that he was in Tianjin? And how did he know the flight number?*

The Chevrolet Z06 Corvette was parked at the rear of the car park. Cartwright had insisted on Ward taking his car over to China. He said that it would be more reliable than a rented car. Ward unlocked his car and dumped his luggage into the passenger seat and looked back that the Chinaman would be behind, spying on him, and reporting his movements through his cell phone. Frank Ward climbed inside his car and took out a map of Tianjin that Walter Greaves had given him. It had the quickest route from the TSN Airport to the Station C Headquarters in the central part of the city. He laid the map down on the dashboard and felt for his Beretta in his holster, secured below his armpit. He hoped he wouldn't have to use it today, but he wasn't going to take any chances this time. Cartwright had arranged for Ward to meet the head of Station C at the shipping warehouse, which was basically a cover for the Chinese branch of the agency. Ward reversed out of the parking space, and watched as the Chinaman put away his phone and rushed across the parking lot towards a parked black Land Rover with tinted windows. Frank Ward watched him carefully and sped out onto the streets. If the Land Rover was going to follow him, Ward was going to put up a chase.

***

In the row of cars behind the Land Rover, two men were sitting inside a large, blue van. The one in the passenger seat watched as Frank Ward's sports car left the car park, followed closely by the 4x4, into which the

Chinaman had just climbed. The passenger pulled a set of earphone walkie - talkies over his ears as the driver started up the engine.

'Boss?' The man with the headphones enquired.

'Yes?' Came the reply.

'Ward has just pulled out of the car park. A van full of Chinese assassins has gone after him. Should we follow?'

'Go after them,' his chief ordered. 'Make sure no harm comes to my friend, Mister Frank Ward. I want him alive. Understood?'

'Yes, sir.'

With that, the van tore out of the car park and came out of the road behind the other two cars, keeping quite a distance between the Land Rover and themselves.

***

Frank Ward kept switching glances between the road, the map, and the Land Rover behind. According to the map, he was in Zhanggui Zhuang, Dongli District, about 13 kilometres (about 8 miles) away from the downtown area of Tianjin, where the Station C Headquarters was located.

The black 4x4 was gradually gaining on him. *If only he could see inside the windows and make out the others inside the car!* Ward looked up into the rear view mirror above his head and slammed his foot down harder on the stainless steel pedal, so that the accelerator was now on the floor. The dial on the speedometer was now touching seventy. The Land Rover appeared to be doing the same.

The chase was on.

The Chevrolet Z06 Corvette hurtled around the corner at high speed, and Ward used the hand brake to manoeuvre around the turn. There was a terrific screeching of rubber, and Ward wrenched the wheel to correct it and continued. The Land Rover managed the tight turn too and was now drawing close to Ward's car. Agent 27S sounded the car horn several times, and swerved quickly before driving up onto the pavement. He overtook a car in front, and then pulled aggressively at the wheel and managed to get a bit ahead of the Land Rover. There were a few moments when the 4x4 went out of sight, but soon it came back into view and increased in speed.

In the Land Rover, the bald Chinese Triad agent cursed and sat hunched over the wheel, determined to get closer to the Chevrolet. Kazuki

Masaharu was sitting next to him, his injured arm wrapped in a cloth to keep the bleeding under control. He reached underneath his jacket and retrieved the Desert Eagle "Menace" had given him. He flicked off the safety catch and gently lowered down the passenger window. 'Get as close to the car as possible, you fool! I'll try and take the tyres out with a few well placed shots. Just stick behind him and floor the pedal!'

Masaharu, the leader of the Hong Kong criminal group, the Triads, extended his head out of the window and balanced his gunning arm on his other, allowing his gun to roar twice. The first shot went completely wide, although the second was more accurate and bounced off the bumper.

It was no good, he thought. They were out of range. As soon as they were close though, he was going to continue shooting.

Ward's eyes shot directly up towards the rear view mirror. His heart skipped a beat when he realised that the gunman in the Land Rover was *none other than Kazuki Masaharu!* Victor was definitely onto him now. Frank Ward cursed for having underestimated Claude Victor. He would have minions working all around France watching him, reporting his every movement. Hell, that ratty receptionist in The Linden House was probably working for him for all he knew! As Ward turned around another corner and drove through a red light, he noticed a blue van following behind the 4x4, matching their speed. *There must be more of them! There was no escape now! Ward was done for!*

The shot that had hit the rear bumper of the Chevrolet wouldn't have done any harm at all. It wouldn't even have scratched the metallic platinum paintwork. Since Cartwright had offered to reinforce his vehicle with complementary 'extras' as he had put it, the whole of the exterior of the car was armoured and immune to bullets.

It was then thinking about the armour - plates surrounding the Chevrolet Z06 Corvette, that Ward remembered another one of the useful pieces of equipment installed by the CIA's Weapon and Gadgetry Department. Ward reached towards the armrest and opened the lid which revealed a button that activated the smoke screen dispenser device. This was a hidden nozzle inside the exhaust pipe that emits a thick cloud of smoke for ten seconds, completely blocking the view of the vehicles behind. Ward grinned and pressed the button. Instantly, a torrent of cloudy, black smoke ejected from the exhaust, leaving the 4x4 and the blue van behind. Ward increased in speed so that he could get as far away as possible before the ten seconds ran out. He tugged at the wheel and veered left out of sight. By the time the smoke had disappeared, and the assassins in the 4x4 and the blue van could see the road again, the enemy vehicle was nowhere to be seen at all.

Ten minutes later, en route for Station C, Frank Ward noticed the sign advertising the gas station, and since the Z06 was low on fuel, he slowed down and pulled over beside one of the pumps. It was a self service facility and Ward climbed out, then swiped his card for five hundred Yuan, the Chinese currency. The Central Intelligence Agency was paying for his hotel, his food, and fuel. He picked up the nozzle and shoved it into the petrol tank of his car and watched as his money increased on the digital screen. However, moments later, a blue van pulled into the station and stopped next to Ward's pumps. *It was the van that had chased him earlier along with the Land Rover! They had found him!*

One of the men, who looked American, climbed out of the van, and glanced over at Ward and then turned away. Frank Ward surveyed the situation he was in and analysed all possibilities, should they try anything. The Beretta was in his shoulder holster. At the first sign of trouble, he could easily whip the gun out and shoot to kill if he thought it was necessary. The lights flashed on the pump, signalling that the tank was full. Ward screwed the cap back on and looked cautiously past the Z06 and watched as one of the men approached him. The man appeared to be nearer to forty than thirty and supported a heavy stubble. Ward guessed that the majority of his body was muscle. He looked like a hardened type of man, maybe a bouncer for a night club or something like that.

'Mister Ward, please come with me. My chief is waiting for you.'

Frank Ward, Agent 27S, clenched his fist and was ready for lashing out with his arm if the man tried anything.

'Really? Well I'm not going anywhere, so you can tell your chief that he will have to talk to me before sending you to pick me up.'

The expression on the man's face was now more serious. 'I'm afraid, Mister Ward,' he said calmly, 'that I must insist.' The man started to draw a gun from its hidden place underneath his jacket but he wasn't fast enough. Ward hurled his fist in his direction and slammed him back against the petrol pumps. The man grunted and staggered backwards in shock, and Ward knocked the pistol from his hand lashing out with his foot, sending the man sprawling face downwards onto the concrete ground. The injured man tried to grab his gun but Ward snatched it up and removed the loaded magazine. Then, he drew his own Beretta and pointed it at the figure.

'Hold it!' came a powerful voice from behind. Ward stopped and felt the cold muzzle of a pistol jab him in the back of the neck. 'Hand over the gun real slowly and turn and face me. Try anything and we'll give you a third eye. There's three men including myself all with a gun trained on you.'

Ward swallowed. The game was up. He couldn't do anything, or one of the three gunmen would shoot him dead. He felt a hand reach up towards his, and in a second, his Beretta had been taken away from him.

'So far so good,' the man behind him said slowly, 'now face me.'

Frank Ward did as he was told. A man with greying hair, and roughly the same height as himself was behind him, a Glock 18 pointed directly at him. 'Shame about what you did to Jerry, Mister Ward. He don't like being roughed up like that. Now, let's head back to the van and get movin'. My boss is going to be real pleased about seeing you.'

As he was marched towards the back of the blue van, Ward found himself confused and baffled as to who these men were. *If they did work for Victor, why were they American? Victor didn't employ Americans, surely?* Jerry, the man whom Ward had attacked, followed them to the van and opened the rear doors, gesturing with his gun to go inside. Ward shot him a hard stare and asked what was happening to his car.

Jerry replied, 'I'll follow the van in your car until we get to our destination. Hand over the keys.'

Ward felt like beating the pulp out of Jerry again. He simply glared at the man and ignored his question.

'Jerry said hand over the keys,' the gunman behind him repeated. 'Do as he says, wise guy, or I'll blast a hole through your back.'

Reluctantly, Ward dug into his pocket, produced his car key and dropped it into the hard paw of Jerry's hand.

He had no idea where he was going or why they were 'kidnapping' him. Ward sat down in the back of the van, and the greying - haired man climbed in with him, sitting opposite with the Austrian Glock 18 gun. Ward toyed about with the idea of launching himself at him, but decided against it. The man looked a pro - it was something about the way he held the gun, the casual manner showed that he was a quick shooter and not one of those men that regret it, either. Jerry shut the rear doors and locked them. Ward could hear his footsteps walking away towards his

Chevrolet. The engine started up moments later. It coughed a little and was soon away.

The journey was over in a matter of minutes. The van came to a halt and the gunmen unlocked the rear doors and told Ward to go out first. He did and looked up at the large, dull square building that announced itself as the 'TIANJIN SHIPPING WAREHOUSE - EST. 1972.' Ward genuinely couldn't believe his eyes. *Why the hell had they brought him here? Why had they taken him to Station C Headquarters?* Frank Ward turned around to get answers from the gunman. The man smiled, tucked his Glock 18 back in the waistband of his trousers and handed Ward his Beretta back.

'Sorry for bringing you here like this, Agent 27S,' the man smiled. 'Our boss, the Head of Station C, told us to go to the airport and watch you leave. He wanted to make sure that Claude Victor had not sent any of his heavies to eliminate you. Sure enough, there was that Land Rover full of assassins. We followed you to make sure they didn't do any harm. Then, you used that smoke screen and we lost you temporarily. We figured that we had to find you first before the assassins did, so we searched around the area and spotted your car. We decided that you probably thought that we were sent by Victor too, so instead of trying to convince you, we played it your way and brought you here safely.'

Ward grinned and realised the whole thing now. He extended his hand and shook the man's hand.

'Kyle Wood, Station C branch,' the man said.

'I guess you already know me. By the way, who is your 'boss'?'

Kyle grinned, the handsome smile filling the whole creased face of his. 'He told me that you already knew him. He said you two were old friends. You'll see him again in a few moments.'

The Chevrolet Z06 Corvette appeared behind the van and Jerry got out and handed Ward his keys.

'I apologise for attacking you like that,' Ward said softly, 'I thought you were one of Victor's men.'

Jerry rubbed his right hand which Ward had hit to knock the gun away. 'Nothing but a sore hand,' he shrugged casually. 'It'll heal in a few days. Glad to meet you.'

He and Ward shook hands, and Ward noted the dry palm.

The rest of the CIA agents climbed out the car and the men headed up to the concrete steps where the noises of the sawing, and machines working, were already audible. They walked through the great storage area of the 'warehouse', where large cylinder drums were stacked, and crates of all sizes were shelved. The warehouse was lively with people working and doing their jobs. They reached a door at the end of the warehouse that had a 'NO ENTRY' sign above it, with the Chinese translation underneath.

'This is where the shipping cover tapers off,' Kyle Wood explained, unlocking the door with a small key. 'From here onwards, are all the Station C offices.'

Ward nodded and he was led through a long corridor with several rooms on both sides, some with the doors open. There were offices crammed with people, and computer rooms where technicians were working furiously, stabbing at the keyboard. Others were communication rooms where workers were using computers to position the CIA's global satellite on enemy land, where live footage would then be relayed on the screen. They approached an elevator and Jerry programmed the floor, prior to them all going inside. There was a few seconds to wait as the elevator ascended a few floors, and then the great blast doors retracted.

'The Head of Station C is waiting for you in that room -,' he pointed to a door at the end of the hallway, - 'we'll be outside if you need us.'

'Thanks.' Ward moved towards the door eagerly, and rapped his knuckles on the wooden door. He was dying to find out who his 'old friend' was.

'Come in,' boomed the familiar voice.

But who was it?

Ward opened the door and stared in amazement at his close friend sitting ten feet away behind a massive, black desk that was tidy and uncluttered. A flat screen computer laptop, a telephone, and a metal ashtray were the only items on the surface of the desk. The man grinned.

He hadn't changed at all. The untidy, straw - coloured mop of hair, the medium built body, the rounded, handsome face, and of course, the unmistakable Western accent that belonged to Albert Dawson. He remembered when he first met Albert in the Chinese Dragon Casino. He had provided him with vital information about the Sharp assignment. He had been a strong ally and a loyal friend.

Hell, if it wasn't for him, Ward would undoubtedly be dead by now!

And now, here they were again, in Station C headquarters in Tianjin. Dawson was wearing a Western, light brown jacket that hung loosely around his big, broad shoulders and trousers with a black tie. He had a cigarette in one hand, and a half - empty glass of vodka martini in the other, which if Ward remembered correctly, he preferred straight up with a twist. His smile was charming and he too, seemed pleased to see his pal again.

'Well, if it isn't Frank Ward!' The loud Western voice exclaimed. 'How the hell are you? How's the arm?'

Ward was still lost for words. He was so surprised and shocked. *But why was Dawson here?* He was in the Directorate of Operations Department like Ward, if he remembered rightly. His number was 12R.

'I'm fine, Albert,' Ward announced. 'My arm is healing. But, how are you? And why are *you* here?'

Dawson winked at his friend and pointed to the leather armchair opposite him at the black desk. 'I'll explain everything in a moment, my friend. Please sit down and I'll get you a drink and a cigarette.'

Frank Ward nodded and sat down heavily in the comfortable chair while Dawson was busying himself fetching a bottle of Ikon Russian vodka from the drinks cabinet behind him. Ward smiled. Dawson had even remembered his favourite drink. Whilst Dawson poured him the drink in a cocktail glass, Ward looked around the pleasant, spacious office. It was not furnished in Chinese design at all. The whole room looked completely Western. The carpet was a creamy yellow, as were the walls on which framed paintings hung. There was a bookshelf against the wall, a large, bulky safe and of course, the drinks cabinet behind the large, rectangular desk. An interactive screen was attached to the right hand side of the wall, presumably where satellite imaging would be viewed. It was all very modern and stylish - very much like Albert Dawson's elegant taste.

Dawson sat down and handed his friend the cocktail glass and produced his slim line, silver cigarette case. 'These are Zhong Nan Hai 8mg cigarettes. They're the best Chinese brand. Ever since I was sent out here, I switched from the Marlboro to these. Personally, I prefer them to American cigarettes,' Dawson explained, pushing the opened case across the desk to his pal.

Ward took one, put it between his lips and lit it quickly. As he inhaled the smoke, he had to agree that this cigarette was probably the best he had ever tasted. The richness of the tobacco was fabulous.

'Now,' he said, 'tell me why you're here.'

Dawson sipped at his drink and began: 'Not long after Cartwright became the Director of the Central Intelligence Agency, Station C was monitoring espionage activity in the Caribbean. However, the work in the islands dried up, and Station C relocated to China, and the British SIS took the Caribbean. It was then Cartwright decided to send me over to Tianjin as the Head of the Station since I had been in the agency for a few years. Ever since that day, I've been over here.'

'Do you like it working in China?' Ward asked.

Dawson shrugged casually. 'It gets quite boring most of the time. I'm usually stuck behind this bloody desk signing documents or working on the computer. It 'aint like the old days where I was always out in the field on some kind of dangerous assignment. It's just not the same. I suppose I can't really complain, though mate,' he said colloquially, 'the money is nearly double what I used to get. You don't know how happy I am to be working with you again.'

'I'm pleased too, Albert.'

'Now tell me about our mission, please,' Dawson said, exhaling a lungful of smoke through his teeth with a faint hiss, 'Cartwright only explained a few things briefly on the telephone.'

'We're dealing with a French businessman who is secretly working as a criminal. His name is Claude Victor. Maybe you've heard of him?'

Dawson nodded, 'Yes. He's the rich industrialist who created the Kraken International Cooperation.'

'Exactly,' Ward said. 'The other culprit is a man named Kazuki Masaharu, the leader of the Chinese Triad society in Hong Kong. He was the one who tried to kill me as I came here. Well, here's what I know already. Victor stole two French cruise missiles from the Air Force by switching them with the fake warheads on a test launch. Victor's men must have sent them off course in mid air. A French agent from the D.G.S.E was investigating the theft when Victor demanded that Masaharu send men to intercept her before she found anything out. I was sent to protect her and that's basically how I got involved. Victor then had Masaharu and his men break into an American Government lab in Hong Kong and steal a missile guidance system -.'

'Yes,' Dawson interrupted. 'Station C was investigating it.'

'- the French agent and myself attended a party at Victor's castle, undercover where I overheard a meeting between Victor and Masaharu. The Frenchman was paying the Chinese gangster off for stealing the guidance system. Soon afterwards, our covers were blown and we had to escape. The following day, once we reported, Victor found us both and ultimately killed the French agent. The next day, I found out where

Masaharu was hiding and Cartwright sent me here after him. I presumed he would be with Victor.'

'Interesting,' Dawson said thoughtfully. 'From what I know, Victor doesn't have any property here. I don't understand it.'

Ward smiled. 'I've been doing some more research on the plane over here. Claude Victor owns his very own yacht, *Le dauphin*. It's usually docked at Tianjin harbour when not at sea. Do you know where it is?'

'Of course,' Dawson replied, 'it's the largest comprehensive international trade port in North China.'

'Excellent. In that case, I propose we visit the harbour tomorrow morning and see if *Le dauphin* is there. We'll watch the boat and see who's onboard.'

'Great idea,' Dawson exclaimed, cheerfully. 'I'll arrange it. Now, I guess you're going to need a place to sleep while you're in Tianjin?'

'Yes. I'm sure I'll find an adequate hotel.'

'Why bother? Stay with me at my house. It's only a few streets away. Plus, we'll be able to catch up on the old times. We can even get drunk every night!'

Ward finished his drink and killed his cigarette in the ashtray. 'Albert,' he grinned, 'I can think of nothing better.'

11/ THE INFILTRATION

IT WAS A calm Sunday afternoon. The Tianjin harbour wasn't busy at all. In fact, there were only a few workers bringing in some squid or seafood that had been caught during the morning. Tianjin Harbour is a multi functional and international trading port, which possesses the largest modern container terminal in China. Tianjin Harbour, with an annual handling capacity of 24 million tons and having shipping lines with all continents, links with over 300 harbours in the starting point of the shortest Europe-Asia Continental Bridge.

Frank Ward parked the Chevrolet Z06 Corvette in an isolated area of the docks and Albert Dawson retrieved a medium - sized suitcase from the boot. Ward turned off the engine and walked around to where Dawson was looking over the equipment that Station C had provided. Packed tightly into the case were two handguns, a sub machine gun, an assault rifle and a few multi - purpose commando knives. The pistols were Ward's Beretta 84FS Cheetah and Dawson's Browning 9mm. The sub machine gun was an Uzi, and the assault rifle was a gas operated Chinese QBZ-95.

'We've got a deadly artillery here, Albert.'

His friend grinned. 'We aim to please. We've also brought a powerful set of binoculars to allow us to see who's onboard. I wonder if your theory about Kazuki Masaharu is right.'

'I sincerely hope so,' Ward said to his associate. He slipped his Beretta into his shoulder holster and fastened the case up before lifting it out of the car. They made their way across the harbour and walked for a few minutes before the magnificent *Le dauphin* came into view. Ward was taken aback by its beauty and grandeur.

'Not a bad yacht eh?' Dawson chuckled.

Ward ground his teeth and thought of all those people who had been killed brutally and savagely to pay for this boat. Now that Ward thought about it that way, *Le dauphin* wasn't beautiful at all. 'It is all paid for by blood money,' Ward told him.

Together, the two CIA agents found a discreet hiding place quite a distance away from Claude Victor's yacht. They sat down heavily on a raised platform and removed the binoculars from a small compartment of the suitcase. The binoculars were specialised ones that prevented the magnified image from being ruined by shaky hands. As soon as you press the "Stabilise" button the image becomes superbly clear, taking out the "shake" and absolutely transforming the view. It is like using them on a tripod on steady ground, but without the need for the tripod or the steady ground! The binoculars were almost unbelievably good, magnifying 18 times through 50mm object lenses, with a high level of image stabilisation - they are far more powerful than would be practical without it. Measuring 8x6, the binoculars were easy to use and were weather resistant.

Frank Ward put the binoculars to his eyes and zoomed in on the deck located at the stern of the ship. He pressed the "Stabilise" button so that the image was perfect and clear and focused them on the people gathered around the tables and leaning on the railings.

'I see three men and a woman. Two of the men are sitting at one of the tables with a drink, apparently playing cards. They are Chinese, most likely working for the Triads. The other is Claude Victor.' Ward felt the hatred build up inside him as he spoke the name. Just looking at the man again made his blood run cold and revenge boil up inside him. He thought of Gaëlle, and remembered seeing her body, ripped open in a violent and savage way. The moment was still vivid in his mind and in his heart and he knew he would never be able to forget it.

Ward buried his thoughts for the time being and focused on Victor. 'He's talking to a girl in a bikini. I think it's his fiancé, Linda Pascal - yes,' he decided, 'It definitely is her.'

'No signs of Kazuki Masaharu?' Dawson asked.

Ward shook his head dumbly and handed the binoculars to his friend to allow him to look.'Probably a late sleeper,' Ward suggested.

'Maybe you're right,' Dawson replied. 'Either that or he isn't on board.'

'I'm pretty sure he will be,' Frank Ward announced confidently. 'It only makes sense that way.'

'What do you mean?'

'Well', Ward explained, 'why would Claude Victor be docked over at Tianjin in China of all places? It would be one hell of a coincidence if Masaharu happened to be here and not be involved with him.'

'I guess you're right.' Albert Dawson reached inside his pocket and produced a square packet of Zhong Nan Hai 8mg cigarettes. He slit open the cling film wrapper, opened the box, and took out two cigarettes. He handed one to Ward, put his between his lips and searched for his lighter. He patted his trouser pockets and located it before lighting it quickly.

Dawson passed the lighter onto his associate and looked back into the binoculars.

'There's another man on the deck now,' Dawson confirmed. 'It might be Kazuki Masaharu. He's certainly Chinese.'

Ward looked at the ship with his own eyes. He saw the man, but it was too far away to identify. 'May I see?'

'Sure.'

Albert Dawson handed him the binoculars and Ward focused the lenses on the new arrival at the stern. He zoomed in on the face and immediately recognised the cool, fierce face that belonged to the Chinese warlord. He grinned. 'It's definitely him, the Chinese bastard,' Ward said through clenched teeth. 'We're making progress, Albert. Masaharu and his Triad men are still under loan to Claude Victor. That means that they're up to something. I don't know what they have planned yet, but I'm determined to find out.'

'Do you think Victor has the missile guidance system on board, Albert?'

Dawson thought for a few moments. 'It's likely', he said. 'From what my men have told me, the yacht is highly guarded and all security are armed. There's underwater cameras, CCTV on board, you name it. If there's one place Victor would keep it for safety, it would be on *Le dauphin*.'

'There's only one way to find out, then.'

'I don't understand', Dawson said, his confusion matching the expression on his face.

'I'll come back down here at nightfall and go and search the yacht for the missile guidance system. Even if I don't find what I'm after, I can kill Claude Victor.' Ward said, his eyes narrowed with a hint of revenge.

Albert Dawson laughed quietly, 'You've got to be crazy, Frank. If you think that you can single handily break onto the world's most highly guarded yacht, you've got another think coming. There's no way you'd get off *Le dauphin* alive, with the guidance system or not!'

'I'm not crazy, Albert', Ward said seriously, 'I'm doing this for my country. God only knows what Claude Victor is going to do with those cruise missiles and the guidance system. Whether he's selling them on or firing them, I must stop him, either with your help or not. Now or you going to help me tonight?'

'What do you have in mind?' Albert Dawson asked hesitantly.

'For starters I'm going to need you to drive me down here and wait for me to finish. If I take longer than one hour, leave immediately. That means that I've not made it -.'

'But Frank -.'

'Listen! I'll need Station C to provide me with a wetsuit and scuba diving equipment. I'm going to swim deep down so that the cameras underwater don't spot me and so that the bubbles from my oxygen tank are not as visible. Then, I'll find the ladder leading up, and search the ship. I'll take a few commando knives and that's all. A gun or anything else would attract attention, silenced or not.'

Dawson swallowed. 'I still think you're making a mistake doing this.'

'Look Albert,' Ward demanded, 'will you bring me down here tonight or not, with the equipment?'

'I will, but don't blame me if something happens.'

'Don't worry, Albert. Nothing will happen, I promise.'

The moonlight reflected on the glimmering water, as it moved gently up and down in the light, night breeze. The cold water lapped against the side of the magnificent yacht, *Le dauphin*, making the boat move up and down so slowly that it was barely noticeable.

The Tianjin harbour was completely deserted and silent. The only noises were that of the water hitting the wooden docks and piers, and the night security talking to one other on Claude Victor's yacht, whilst patrolling the decks and corridors with handguns holstered at their waists. Two of the guards in particular were patrolling the quarterdeck of the ship, joking and having crafty cigarettes while on duty. They patrolled a preplanned route and they would follow this route back and forth until sunrise, when they would return to their cabins and rest, and the morning security would take over.

Frank Ward had been watching their routine for fifteen minutes now in the same spot that he and Albert Dawson had been monitoring the yacht that afternoon. Using highly detailed night vision goggles provided by Station C, Ward could clearly watch the guards' movements and memorize their path, for when he was going to sneak on board. *He would have to be careful*, he decided. Since the ladder was located at the stern where the security would be patrolling, he would have to pick the right moment before climbing up. If worst came to the worst he would have to subdue them with his commando knives. It would be extremely difficult, though. By the time he had taken one out, the other might have time to draw a gun, or worse, alert people of his position. He watched them a bit longer, zooming in when necessary.

The goggles are a very handy piece of gadgetry, Ward decided. Built up with an objective lens, an eyepiece, a power supply, an infra red illuminator system and a light intensifier tube, it works on light-amplifying technology. This technology takes the small amount of light that's in the surrounding area (such as moonlight or starlight), and converts the light energy into electrical energy through the front lens. This light, which is made up of photos, goes into a light intensifier tube that changes the photos electrons. The electrons are then amplified to a much greater number through an electrical and chemical process. The electrons are then hurried back into visible light that you see through the eyepiece. The image will now be clear green-hued amplified re-creation.

Ward took the night vision goggles off his head and put them back in the suitcase filled with weapons, that he and Dawson had brought down earlier. They had decided to leave it here until tonight to save bringing it back down again. Besides, there was already enough equipment to bring here before nightfall. Albert Dawson had contacted his men at Station C and told them that he required a wetsuit, an under water torch, breathing apparatus and goggles. It took the men a few hours to find such things, but in the end, they found the scuba gear that would be important for Ward's mission tonight. Frank Ward opened the main compartment of the suitcase and located his commando knives and the US SP5 Bowie Survival Knife. The survival knife features a 10 inch 1095 Carbon Steel blade made of epoxy powder coated carbon steel. It was more suitable for close range rather than throwing, and kept in the sheath that was attached to his belt underneath the wetsuit that he was presently wearing. Once he had managed to get onboard the yacht, he planned to take it off and hide it, for when he needed to leave. He wore a plain black T - shirt and a pair of casual, navy trousers underneath. The rest of the throwing knives and the lock pick Gaëlle had given him were fastened to his belt by a wire, so that he could ensure that they were in a reachable place.

Ward zipped up the case, hid it away from view and then met Albert Dawson who was sitting in the Chevrolet Z06. 'I'm ready, Albert', he told him, his voice confident, even though that he knew himself that there was a big chance he would never leave *Le dauphin* alive. 'I need you to give me the scuba gear.'

Dawson, whose face was normally calm and relaxed, now looked gaunt and terribly concerned. 'OK', he said opening a satchel containing all of the equipment. 'Can you see any guards?'

'Yes, there's two of 'em patrolling the quarter deck area where the ladder is. I've timed how long it takes them to complete one lap of their area, so I should be able to get on the yacht when they are away.'

Albert Dawson handed his associate the two cylinder oxygen tanks that would be fitted onto his back, his goggles, flippers, mouthpiece and underwater torch. Ward spent a few minutes putting on all of the gear and going over it all meticulously in case something wasn't put on correctly. He walked over to the edge of the harbour now and bit firmly into the rubber mouthpiece and held it tightly between his teeth. Then he crouched down, spat into the goggles to prevent them from steaming up, and then washed them in the icy water. Ward's heart was pounding against his chest. He couldn't believe what he was about to do. He was risking his life; about to face what was possibly going to be his death. If this plan failed, he would be killed mercilessly by Victor's men. The least that could happen would be that he is spotted but manages to escape. Even that outcome could cause Claude Victor to panic and bring forward whatever he was planning. Ward's palms were sweating already. He took a massive deep breath and then turned around to Dawson who was watching him from the car. It was then he gave a thumbs up sign, and dived off the harbour, vanishing from view with a quiet splash.

As Albert Dawson watched his friend jump into the cold water, he felt a tear come to his eye. He knew that he may never see his friend again. What was most upsetting was that Frank Ward seemed so confident. He didn't appear to be aware of the dangers or the outcomes of what he was about to do. Although he may never return from the yacht, Dawson admired Ward's courage and bravery. The man was a hero to his country and would give up his life if he thought the United States of America was in danger. Frank Ward deserved a medal for his loyalty and services, Dawson thought as he reminisced some of the dangerous situations that his friend had been through. The Sharp affair all those months ago seemed like an eternity. Not only did Ward's brother die, but Frank nearly did also. And despite the man's fear in the situation, he triumphed over the villain. It was as Albert Dawson thought back to his friend's many encounters with danger, that he suddenly had confidence and belief in Frank Ward. He smiled and wiped the tear away.

'Come on Frank', he willed to himself, 'You can do this.'

The water wasn't as cold as he had expected it to be. Yes, it was cold Ward admitted, but not freezing. As soon as he struck the water, he clicked on the underwater torch so that he could have at least some vision in the murky, black water. The Aqua Lung torch was a simple ergonomic shape that gave six hours of perfect, white light once fitted with batteries. It was a handy tool, but even with it, Frank Ward was struggling to see where he was swimming.

It was disorientating, really. Ward could barely see anything and couldn't hear. With the lack of vision underwater, he didn't know how far he had descended. He remained cool and calm though and moved the beam all around ahead of him, making sure there was no obstacles. Ward kicked his legs strongly and firmly like a frog, whilst using powerful strokes with his muscular arms. With the two forces combined, Ward was moving quickly and powerfully in the water.

Ward had always been an exceptional swimmer who was very strong. In fact, he had even considered being a life guard when he was younger. Being brought up in Los Angeles, he would visit the beaches every day with his two younger brothers, Joe and Peter. They would have races in the sea, muck around in the sand and admire the life guards. When he was a teenager, he won several swimming medals and certificates after doing hundreds of lengths in a pool for charity. He remembered once he had finished that he had been so proud of himself.

Concentrate! Ward willed himself. *Keep going and look out for Le dauphin!*

Ward continued, trying to breathe normally through the rubber mouthpiece. It would have been easier if he had snorkelled, but with the underwater cameras, his cover would be blown instantly. He had to swim *underneath* them and then resurface and find the ladder. Despite his poor vision underwater, the rubber fins made it definitely easier and more comfortable. With the slightest kick, the split blade of the fins deflects to form a pair of wings that slice through the water with reduced drag. They enabled him to glide effortlessly through the water.

Within minutes, a large white shape loomed above him: the hull of Claude Victor's private yacht, *Le dauphin!* The cameras! Quickly, Ward dived downwards, kicking his feet madly and cutting through the water with his free hand. He had to get as far down as possible until he reached the stern. If he was caught on film, the guards would probably put on wetsuits and go after him with CO_2 guns. After all, they were probably prepared for such happenings. Ward swam a little further, and when he thought he had gone down far enough, he stopped and resumed his slow, gliding technique, made up of occasional kicks of his legs, strokes of his arms. He didn't want to make many bubbles, either, in case a guard happened to spot them. It would make them highly suspicious. *Hell, the dangers were great!* This was the most dangerous, frightening thing he had ever done. His confidence was merely covering up his fear. After all, he was only a human being like any other. It was his determination and devotion that would pull him through. Plus his bravery!

Now he was below the stern! He had made it unnoticed! Relieved, Ward swam out from underneath the massive, white - painted shape above him, and quietly broke the surface with his head. He pulled the goggles from his eyes and trod water for a while as he took in his surroundings. It was so good to see again and hear the sound of the water lapping against the side of the boat! He clicked off the underwater torch with his thumb and grasped the side of the ladder with his free hand. Ward kicked off his flippers and allowed them to sink to the bottom of the harbour. He couldn't carry everything up the ladder with him; he was going to have to dump his wetsuit, oxygen tanks and the rest of his gear in a safe place while he was searching the boat.

He listened for voices or footsteps.

There weren't any.

Taking the chance that the guards weren't patrolling past him, Frank Ward hauled himself up the metal ladder, slowly and carefully and unsheathed the US SP5 Bowie Survival Knife. Holding the deadly weapon carefully and at an angle ready for attack, he climbed the last few steps and stood onboard *Le dauphin*.

There was nobody in sight. The guards had either just gone past him, or were on their way back from the off stern area. Moving like a cat, Frank Ward hurried barefoot across the deck looking for a place to strip off his scuba gear. He found a secluded area in the shadows where crates of what were probably food and resources were stacked. Ward looked around and dropped his goggles, torch and oxygen cylinders before shedding his 'rubbery skin'. Now, he was wearing the dark T - shirt and the casual slacks that were plastered onto his body.

Time to get to work, he decided.

Ward crept cautiously from behind the crates, the shiny blade of his knife glinting in the moonlight. On such a warm night like this all the companionways would be open, he thought. Stealthily he moved down the outer side of the yacht, heading for the broadside where he expected the cabins to be. It was then he heard noises approaching. Ward swallowed and flattened himself against the wall and reached for a small commando throwing knife.

The footsteps were drawing nearer. Nearer and nearer. Then a man coughed before he came into view. Ward didn't have chance to see the face before he grabbed a throwing knife, aimed and released it. The guard's eyes widened in surprise as the silver flashed through the air and impaled him through the neck so suddenly, that he didn't have the opportunity to reach for his Heckler and Koch or scream. The man gurgled for a few moments, and bled horribly from the mouth, before he crumpled to the floor. Ward guessed that the knife had penetrated an artery in the neck and that death had been instant. As Ward approached the figure on the floor, the tongue had protruded from the revolting lips and the eyes were staring upwards unseeing and unblinking. Frank Ward knew now, after killing several men, that these were the terrible signs of death. Ward stood there for a few moments while he decided what to do with the body.

He certainly couldn't leave it here. Somebody would find it. Ward reached down and seized the corpse underneath the arms as he dragged it across the floor towards the rail surrounding *Le dauphin*. He hauled the body to its feet and pushed it against the rail so that the limp arms dangled over the side. Then Ward grabbed hold of the feet and lifted them upwards, sending the dead guard over the side of the boat, where he crashed against the side of the harbour. This absorbed most of the fall, so that when it slid into the icy water, there was very little noise. Ward looked over the side. The body moved up and down in the breeze simultaneously with the boat. He hoped that nobody would discover it before he had chance to leave.

Ward left the rail and listened attentively for voices or sound and then advanced towards the cabins. A small lifeboat hung from the near beam just aft of the broadside. He could make out the shape in the darkness. Ward thought back to this afternoon when he had studied the yacht through the binoculars. He had seen Kazuki Masaharu emerge from the cabins on the broadside and then walk towards the quarterdeck.

Now where was the door? Ward's planned strategy so far was going well. He intended to find Claude Victor in his bedroom suite and demand where the missiles and the guidance system were kept. Then, he would swiftly execute the fiend and locate the hardware. That was his plan, but he knew that the slightest mishap might wreck the whole thing. He hoped that Victor was alone in his cabin. Ward would have to be quick to clasp his hand over the ghastly mouth before the living zombie could scream.

Frank Ward ran his fingers through his wet, black hair and felt against the sides of the cabin block for a door. He couldn't see one in the darkness. He could faintly see his reflection in the porthole windows. His cruel, hardened eyes stared back at him, and his jaw was set in a determined, sombre line. After a few moments of feeling the walls, he gripped a cold handle with his left hand. Ward grinned and switched the Survival knife from his right hand to his left, before slipping the picklock into the hole. He fiddled around with it for a few moments until the lock retracted and the door swung open, leading down into the cabin area, where the crew, the Chinese Triads and Claude Victor and his fiancé would sleep. There was a small close - carpeted step leading straight down into the well - lit corridors, which were panelled in polished mahogany. The walls were decorated simply in a light blue, that resembled the sky. Ward's movements were exaggerated, slow steps, so that he would not awake anybody in the cabins. His bare feet made no noise as they touched the carpet. He quietened his breathing and advanced like a snake unhurriedly down the corridor, noting the brass plaques on each door reading the room number.

35, 34, 33.

Ward presumed that Victor's suite would not be a number but rather an 'Owner's Stateroom.' If not, it would be one of the earlier numbers.

29, 28, 27.

The hallway branched out to the left and the right now. Ward looked down the right corridor and noted the nearest room number. 49. That must be where the rooms start. Using this theory, Frank Ward headed down left where the numbers were continuing to decrease. At last, he came to the 'Owner's Stateroom'. Excitedly, Ward gripped the door handle and reached for the picklock. Now, he was going to get revenge for Gaëlle. Fiddling with the picklock, Ward gripped his US SP5 Bowie Survival knife and holding it horizantly, prepared to open the door.

Slowly, Linda Pascal, Claude Victor's new fiancé, turned the page of the paperback thriller she had been reading for a few days now. It was a good book; full of suspense, exciting and enjoyable. She had been finding it hard to put it down since she started it. The thriller was written by the

'Queen of Suspense', Mary Higgins Clark, whose books Linda simply adored and craved.

Linda read another three pages, and then decided to put it down and go to sleep. She was exhausted and slipped her bookmark into the novel between pages 82 and 83, reached across to the polished wooden bedside table and placed it face downwards. Before she turned off the light, she sank back against her pillow which was propped up against the bedpost and pulled the covers close up to her neck, covering her small breasts.

She reached down and felt her bare back where her flesh had been ripped off from the long tails of 'The Corrector'. The Corrector, as Claude named it, was a nine tailed whip. The oiled cowhide tails were roughly twenty - four inches in length, and the 13 inch flexible tapered handle, gives the whip slightly snake-like characteristics. Kangaroo hide overlay the handle. Recently, Claude had used 'The Corrector' on Linda on many occasions. There was nothing she could do about it except bear it. It was painful. For the slightest mistake, like questioning Claude's instructions, he would haul her onto the bed, rip the garment from her back and sadistically whip her violently for several minutes. She would scream, but the cabin was soundproof, and he would beat the tails down furiously and tear away her skin.

The man was a monster. She hated Claude Victor, her lover. The man was not a human; he was, a beast. When she had first met him in 2001 in Nice, France, he seemed so charming and sophisticated. Claude had taken her to an exclusive restaurant where they dined all evening, eating exquisite cuisine from around the world, and drinking expensive wine. It was a fabulous night. She loved him because it appeared that he loved her. She didn't mind about his frightening appearance. Afterwards, he brought her back to his yacht, *Le dauphin*, and made mad, passionate love to her. Ever since then, though, the love making had stopped and so had the nights together. She barely saw him, and when she did, she would anger him and be punished with 'The Corrector'. He was always doing business with various men, and then if she was around, he would tell her to go away. Secretly, Linda Pascal suspected Claude of being a criminal. He was always so secretive, so alert and cruel. The men he associated with, such as Marcus Hillman and the Chinese 'businessmen', were frightening too. Linda was gradually fearing for her life. Some evenings, when Claude was drunk, he would pull a gun out of a drawer and threaten to shoot her dead. Although she wanted to leave him and run away, she knew that Claude would track her down, and maybe kill her.

Nobody runs out on Claude Victor. This was what Claude had said once when she told him she didn't love him. He punched her in the face, resulting in a horrible black eye, and used the evil instrument 'The Corrector'. He tortured her once too. Her strapped her down onto the bed naked, and released a golden-bodied scorpion onto her body.

'This', Claude Victor had hissed, 'is a *Leiurus quinquestriatus* scorpion. It is known more commonly, however, as the 'Death Stalker'. As its name suggests, my darling, it is extremely lethal and its venom is often fatal to human beings. This will teach you to dare to answer back again, Linda'.

The scorpion had crawled slowly up her right leg to her horror, its eight legs moving slowly and carefully. The pedipalp claws were pinching at her skin inquisitively, detecting her fear through the tiny hairs on its armoured body. Claude Victor had left the scorpion there for an hour, allowing it to inject small amounts of venom into her, causing her much pain. By the time he had removed it, the Death Stalker was on her left breast. Linda knew that she would never forget the scorpion torture, or the regular beatings with 'The Corrector'.

Linda settled down in the bed and pulled the covers up to her chin, her golden hair framing her face. She longed for a saviour; a handsome man to come along, defeat Claude, and take her away and love her. She deserved to be loved. She hadn't done anything wrong in her life. Sadly, she closed her eyed and prepared herself for sleep. She didn't hear the door open softly and the wet figure dressed entirely in black gently approaching the bed, a knife clasped in its hand. The figure knelt down, before moving fast like a cheetah; slamming his hand down on her gaping mouth and holding the shiny blade to her neck. Her emerald - green eyes stared into his, filled with a combination of fear and surprise. She studied the man's face. It was cruel and ruthless, but nevertheless, didn't hold the sadistic quality that Claude Victor or Marcus Hillman had. It was the kind of handsome face, she decided, that could smile.

'Move, talk, or call for help', Frank Ward snarled, 'and you're dead'.

Linda swallowed, feeling the coldness of the carbon blade on her skin. She nodded slowly, and the powerful hand came away from her mouth. The knife, however, stayed at her throat.

'You', Linda said softly, 'I recognise you from the party in France'.

Ward nodded. 'Where's Claude Victor?' he asked, angrily. 'Why isn't he here? Is he on board?'

'No', Linda Pascal replied, 'he's at a meeting'.

Ward ground his teeth. He was disappointed. He wanted to kill Claude Victor and avenge Gaëlle's horrid and particularly brutal murder. 'Where is the meeting?'

'I don't know, -'.

Ward applied more pressure with the knife and grabbed hold of her left arm tightly. 'Tell me everything or I'll break your arm. That isn't just a threat, Linda'.

'I believe you', she said, tears rolling down her pretty cheeks, 'He mentioned he was having a conference with a Chinese businessman and his associates who often come onboard *Le dauphin*. I think he said they were going over to the Chinese man's home on the coasts of Tianjin. I don't know anything else, I swear!'

Kazuki Masaharu! He has a home on the coasts on Tianjin! Then that would be where Ward would get answers from Masaharu.

'You're doing well', Ward said, his voice now calm and more gentle. His sudden rage had now vanished. He put away the knife in the sheath at his belt and sat up. Linda sat up too, not realising that in all the struggle, the covers had slipped down to her waist, exposing her neat, round breasts. Embarrassed, she pulled the covers back up to her neck and wiped her tears away.

Linda asked puzzled. 'Who are you?'

'I work for the Central Intelligence Agency in America.' Ward decided he didn't need to lie. He sensed that the girl herself didn't like Claude Victor that much. She had already provided him with lots of vital information without too much *persuasion*.

'You're after Claude', she questioned, 'aren't you?'

'He isn't exactly the man that you and the rest of the world think he is, Linda Pascal', Ward explained, presuming that she didn't know of her fiancé's criminal actions.

Linda smiled simply. 'I knew it', she said confidently, looking at Frank Ward. 'He's always away and has some really strange people under his employ. That Chinese businessman is one of them. He scares me to bits. What has Claude done?'

'That's classified. I'm afraid I can't tell you. What I can tell you is that when I catch him, his punishment for his many crimes will be death. He's wanted by the entire intelligence community, you know'.

Linda lay down on the bed face downwards, the hideous scars and cuts on her back revealed. Ward gasped and carefully ran his fingers down one of the thick wounds.

'He did this to you?' Ward demanded.

'Yes', she answered simply.

Ward leaned forward towards Linda. He felt extremely sorry for her. She turned towards him, and slowly, his lips touched hers. His tongue was insistent, and managed to penetrate her lips and wrestle with hers.

They were interrupted by a harsh rapping on the door of the Owner's Stateroom. Linda pulled away immediately.

'Open the door. Now!'

Linda Pascal swallowed and asked Ward to pass her silk robe that was hung beside the bed.

'Open the door this second, Miss Pascal!'

Quickly, she put the robe on over her naked body. Ward motioned towards the door with his hand, and he unsheathed the Survival Knife. 'Anwer it. I'll be behind the door.'

'*Open* it!'

'I'm coming!' Linda explained, coming across the room. Ward hid behind the door, holding the knife to her back. Gingerly, she unlocked it, and faced the men in the doorway. Ward poked his head around carefully. It was "Menace" Hillman, clutching a Desert Eagle gun. Two of the crew were behind him on either side, themselves, armed. Ward was glad to see that a bandage was around "Menace's" leg. At least the commando knife had done some damage, he reflected.

'What did you want, Marcus!' Linda demanded. 'I was trying to get to sleep'.

'An intruder has slipped aboard *Le dauphin*.' "Menace" hissed. 'We've found the body of a guard in the waters. Seen or heard anything?'

'Nothing at all', Linda insisted. 'Now will you go away?'

"Menace" Hillman gave her a cruel glare with his predator eyes, a glare that Ward recognised. He then said: 'Stay in this cabin. I don't want you distracting my men as we search for the intruder. Got it?'

'Yes'.

With that, an anxious and worried looking Marcus Hillman marched off with his men, and Linda clicked the lock.

'Did I do alright?'

Ward managed a smile. 'You did great'.

Linda walked over to the window where a blue leather club chair was positioned, providing a fantastic view through the blind-covered, bullet - proof windows that overlooked the calm, night waters. She watched the brute Marcus Hillman rushing down the decks with men, searching for the intruder who was hiding in her own bedroom.

'You'd better leave', Linda told him, turning around briefly. 'If they catch you in here with me, Claude would have us both killed.'

'Don't worry, I'm going', he said, unsheathing the long knife from his belt. He gripped the door handle and listened for noises outside the cabin.

'Thanks for helping me.'

'I want to help you. Claude is such a pig, a … a monster. By the way, what's your name?'

'Frank Ward.' With that quick reply, the handsome man with the knife had slipped out of the door and vanished from sight.

Linda sat down heavily on the blue chair and reflected on the situation. She had just betrayed Claude. If he ever found out, he would kill her violently and painfully. That was how he was. But, this Frank Ward, the man who claimed to work for the Central Intelligence Agency, might just be her saviour. He might be the man, her prince, that she had imagined would rescue her. Linda opened a drawer from the antique dressing table and found her nail varnish. She applied the paint onto both her finger and toe nails, and then inspected them carefully. Linda smiled. She knew that she would be seeing a lot more of Frank Ward in the next few days.

The CIA agent squeezed onto the deck out of the cabins area and hugged the wall. Shadows of figures were dancing across the wooden floored decks. Men were approaching! Instinctively, Ward sprinted north towards the quarterdeck, his bare feet hammering against the deck.

'I heard something!' cried one of the crewman.

Marcus "Menace" Hillman turned towards the man, his evil face bathed in the moonlight. Sweat was trickling down his face like icy tears. His cruel, hard mouth set, and his anxious finger stroked the trigger of his Desert Eagle.

'Split up', he instructed. 'I'll head 'round the quarter view. You Sam-' Hillman said, motioning towards one of the crew with his gun, 'run down to the forecastle. Bill, you go to the stern area and I'll meet up with you there. Shoot to kill. I've got a pretty good idea who the intruder is.'

The two crew members, clutching their weapons, acknowledged their boss with a slight nod and then rushed off to their allocated areas of *Le dauphin*. "Menace" Hillman grinned, something that he rarely did. As he examined the magazine of his Desert Eagle, he said: 'I've got you now, Frank Ward.' Then, the ruthless killer sprinted forward towards his own area, in search of his arch enemy.

Ward had run to the stern and located the stacks of food crates where he had hidden his scuba equipment. Crouching down, he fastened the twin oxygen tanks onto his back carefully and clenched the rubber mouthpiece with his teeth. The noises were drawing nearer. One of them belonged to "Menace". Ward stood up and knew that he would have to get away. There was no time to pull on the wetsuit. It would take too long. Ward clutched his knife and ran clumsily towards the stern. He gripped the rail with his hand and carefully climbed up, so that he was balancing on it. It was at this moment that "Menace" appeared. A few gunshots sounded nearby, bouncing off the deck and the rail.

'Quick! He's getting away!'

Ward had no time to face his opponent. Standing up straight, he assumed the dive position and slowly, toppled forwards. As Ward fell, he hoped that the mouthpiece wouldn't come loose or the oxygen cylinders. He had had a matter of seconds to attach them to himself.

Had he done it correctly?

There was nothing he could do now about it. Like a spear, his arms entered the freezing water first, followed by the rest of his body. A shockwave of pain and surprise ran through Ward's body as he struck the water. The coldness made his body numb. Without a wetsuit, he could not warm his body. It was like a million needles hitting him all over. The bullets that were flying down in the water brought Ward out of his paralysed state, and he swam like hell, deeper and deeper, not knowing where he was as going. The rounds were whizzing down slowly, leaving trails in the water.

Frank Ward wondered whether they could still see him. Even if they couldn't see his body, they would see his bubbles. That must be what was giving them the indication as to where he was. Swimming through the thick curtain of darkness, Ward used his usual stroke to get as far down as possible, to stop or at least lessen the amount of bubbles reaching the surface of the water. As Ward swam, he could make out the fantastic white stern of the *Le dauphin*. Ward came up with an idea, and quickly swam underneath.

If he stayed under the boat for a few minutes, "Menace" Hillman and his two gunmen would think he was dead, either by the bullets, or by drowning from staying underwater for so long. He just hoped that

"Menace" hadn't seen the scuba gear on him before he dived. If he had the plan would be messed up. Ward could only pray that he hadn't.

Hiding underneath the great shadow of the yacht, Ward waited patiently in the darkness, treading water. He wondered how long he had been on the yacht. He had told Albert Dawson that if he took longer than an hour to drive away. Ward hoped he was still there, and that "Menace" and his men thought he was dead.

Back on the stern of *Le dauphin*, "Menace" Hillman emptied his entire clip into the water, hoping that one of his shots would destroy Frank Ward. After another three rounds, the pin clicked, signalling that it was empty.

'*Matrice, espion!*' "Menace" screamed angrily, throwing the useless gun to the ground, where it skidded across the wooden planks.

'The spy must be dead, Mister Hillman', said one of the crew.

'I'm not so sure', "Menace" hissed. 'That guy has a nasty habit of surviving my attempts on his life.'

'But he's been down there for *three* minutes! No man could hold his breath that long!'

'Alright', "Menace" snarled, looking down into the water expectantly, waiting for Ward's body to float to the surface, spreadeagled like a starfish. 'Send down two frogmen. I want you to retrieve the guard's body and find Frank Ward's. Understood?'

'Yes, Mister Hillman', replied one of the crew.

'Now go.'

The two crewmen walked away towards the storage area where the divers gear and C02 Harpoon guns were stored. They decided they'd arm themselves, just *in case*. "Menace" Hillman gripped the bars of the rail tightly, and gazed down into the water, on which the crescent moon was reflected. He knew he should feel pleased that Frank Ward, the American agent was dead. But he wasn't. He had wanted to kill the man himself. He imagined how he would do it. "Menace" decided that he would tie the man to a chair naked, and using the ancient art of chakra torture, probe his most sensitive organs with the deadly tools, inflicting as much pain as possible. Chakra was one of "Menace" Hillman's favourite torture methods. He decided that it made the victim most uncomfortable. Still, "Menace" reflected, at least the man had had a painful death. Drowning is caused by the filling of the lungs with a liquid, causing the interruption of the body's exchange of oxygen from the air, leading to asphyxia. It was a distressful death all the same. "Menace" pulled himself away from the rail and sat down at one of the empty tables on the deck. Eagerly, he waited for Ward's soaking corpse to be brought to him.

While all of the three men on the yacht were distracted, Frank Ward unfastened the oxygen tanks and the mouthpiece and allowed them to sink down to the bottom of the harbour bed. He then gripped the side of the harbour, and with all the energy left in his exhausted body, hauled himself up. He immediately spotted the outline of his Chevrolet Z06 Corvette in the darkness (what a relief!) and sprinted towards it. He watched Albert Dawson look on in amazement as his friend ran to the car door, dripping from head to foot with water.

'Frank! You made it!'

Ward smiled and asked his friend for the towel.

'Sure! Here', Dawson handed him the towel to dry himself.

'Get the engine running Albert. We've got to get the hell out of the harbour before Victor's men discover that I'm still alive.'

'Find anything out?' Dawson enquired.

'I'll tell you on the way back.'

With that, Ward ran around to the passenger side and climbed inside. Albert Dawson turned the keys in the ignition, and with a spray of gravel, the car had vanished into the night.

12/THE END OF KAZUKI MASAHARU

WARD LIFTED THE warm mug of Chinese green tea to his lips and sipped gently, allowing the warm liquid to run down his throat. He winced slightly in distaste - like many other foreigners, he found it too bitter. The leaves used for the green tea come directly from the tea bush, via a drying - out process that preserves the flavour. He put the mug down gently on the table and looked up into the tired face of his friend, Albert Dawson, who was drinking the bitter stuff himself.

'I don't know how you can like that green tea', Frank Ward smiled.

Dawson shrugged. 'I suppose after being out here for a while I just got used to it. I've got used to everything here now, but I still can't find my way around. It's just so crowded and busy. My biggest surprise when I came here was that there were more bicycles on the roads than cars', Dawson laughed, raising the mug to his lips. 'Hell, most of my staff ride a bicycle to work!'

'It's certainly not what I'm used to back in the United States', Ward added.

He was sitting in Albert Dawson's study the following morning after sneaking onboard *Le dauphin*. He was still exhausted. His body ached from the furious swimming, and the combination of adrenaline and fear. Most of all, he hadn't had much sleep last night. He couldn't stop thinking about Linda Pascal. She was gorgeous, the kind of woman that you would expect to see on the front covers of the Playboy magazines on the shelves, posing topless . He had been attracted to her very unique build back at the castle fortress. She looked fantastic in that dress she had worn. It was not only her beauty that made him long for her; he also felt sorry for Linda. The lashes on her back showed the great amount of painful torture she would have endured by Claude Victor. He wanted to love her and care for her, treat her with respect and make mad, passionate love to her, but then again he thought of Gaëlle and how he was responsible for her death. Women were not safe being in love with him. The Grim Reaper was following Ward and taking away those precious to him. The same thing had happened all those months ago (an eternity!) when his brother Joe was gruesomely executed. This was what upset Ward and made him not want to fall in love again.

'Have you stopped daydreaming yet?'

Ward suddenly broke out of his thoughts and picked up his mug. 'Sorry', he said. 'My thoughts were elsewhere.'

'So are mine, Frank', Dawson explained. 'I'm thinking about what you told me last night, about Kazuki Masaharu's home on the coasts of Tianjin.'

'Yes.'

'Well, "on the coasts of Tianjin" isn't what I'd call exact. The coastline of Tianjin is around 153 km! We need to get the address and quickly so that you can 'have words' with our yellow - skinned friend.'

'I agree.'

'I've got a friend in the Tianjin council. Maybe if I ask real nicely' Dawson suggested, 'he'll give out the address.'

'Try it', Ward said, 'have you got the number.'

'Sure.'

Albert Dawson, his light grey suit hanging loosely around his broad, authoritative shoulders, reached across the desk and snatched up the telephone receiver and held the instrument up to his ear. He waited for a few moments for somebody to come on line. Ward took this opportunity to select one of Chinese Zhong Nan Hai 8mg cigarettes (he had brought three packets at the local store this morning once he had run out of his American Marlboro) and clenched it between his lips.

'Hello, Mao Yang?'

'Yes', came the reply in Chinese. 'Who is this speaking?'

'Albert Dawson.'

'Greetings friend! It has been too long.'

'It has', replied Dawson. 'I need a favour.'

'A favour?'

'Yes. I'm after a man named Kazuki Masaharu, a Chinese terrorist who controls the Triad society. He operates mostly in Hong Kong, however he's here at his home on the coasts of Tianjin. I need his address so I can commence with the necessary arrangements.'

There was a pause. 'This information is extremely confidential. I wouldn't give it out if this man wasn't a threat to my country. Now, let's see. I'll put you on hold while I look it up on the computer.'

'Fine.' Dawson collected his notebook from its place beside the telephone and took out a biro pen from his shirt pocket. He started 'doodling' on the paper impatiently whilst waiting for his friend Mao Yang to come back on the phone with the valuable information.

'Albert?' Came a voice down the line five minutes later.

'Yes.'

'Mister Masaharu owns a property on the south coast of Tianjin like you said. Here is the address I've found on the database -.'

Mao Yang continued to read an address down the line, which Albert Dawson quickly scribbled down word for word onto the pad.

'I've got it all down', Dawson grinned, pushing the pad across the surface of the desk where Ward caught it before it fell off. 'I appreciate your help very much, Mao. I'll talk to you soon. 'Bye.'

'Goodbye, my friend.' With that, Mao rang off.

'Well', Albert Dawson exclaimed, slamming the receiver down on the base, 'there you have it. Kazuki Masaharu's address. Tell me, what do you intend doing?'

'I'm going to get him alone and *force* him to tell me where the missile guidance system and the warheads are being kept. If we can get hold of them, it will stop whatever Claude Victor is planning.'

'Good idea', Dawson decided, letting the smoke out of his mouth in slow, casual blows. 'What equipment will you need?'

Frank Ward sank back in the armchair and gazed out through the armoured windows of Dawson's office onto the busy roads of metropolitan Tianjin. Already at seven in the morning, the streets were lively with people on bicycles riding to work and taxis ferrying sight - seeing tourists around to places like Mazu temples and the Luzutang (boxing rebellion museum) located in the urban area.

'I won't need much', Ward admitted, killing his cigarette in the ashtray and getting to his feet. 'Just that Israeli Uzi 9mm that I brought here. It's in my car. I have a fitted silencer for it too. It will be a suitable weapon for this particular situation.'

'I agree', Dawson said.

'I'll go and collect the Uzi from the Chevrolet', Ward explained, heading for the door.

"Bye.'

Abruptly, Ward turned around as he reached the door; a new thought having sprung into his mind. 'Wait', he said, 'I'll need a remote bomb.'

'For what?'

'I'm going to hide a bomb near the house and then take care of Masaharu. Once I've got what I want, I'll escape, get a good distance away from the bomb radius, and then detonate it. The explosion will not only destroy Triad funds, but it will kill several Triad gang members, severely affecting their organisation. It may even cause the group to close down.'

'Brilliant!'

'As the English say, I will be killing two birds with one stone', Ward smiled, 'Can Station C provide the bomb and the detonator?'

'I think so', Dawson grinned, 'We've managed to get an array of weapons and scuba gear. Who says we can't get a remote bomb?'

'Excellent. I'll be back in half an hour to pick it up from the armoury section. Then, I'll go and pay Kazuki Masaharu a well deserved visit.'

***

The black-ten passenger Lincoln limousine started up and drove forward out of the gates, the morning sun beaming down on the still ocean of Tianjin bay. Claude Victor sat in the back of the limousine, his bony, dead hands clenched together tightly, his shrivelled, translucent white face cold and calculated. He lay back in the soft, grey leather seats and poured himself a stiff, alcoholic drink from the exclusive bar. He downed the entire glass in one, solid gulp and then turned on the super cold air conditioning to cool him down.

He had just received word of the incident that occurred last night on *Le dauphin*. The American agent, Frank Ward, the man he believed was dead, had somehow risen back to life. It seemed that Ward had been given invincible qualities by God. He was appalled by Marcus "Menace" Hillman's detailed story of how it all happened. He had told him how Ward had managed to sneak onboard, kill a guard with a throwing knife, and then leap off the boat and then apparently 'drowned'. Although Hillman was a strong, powerful man, he lacked the superior brains that Victor had. People were becoming suspicious of him, Victor decided. Bodies were piling up and it was becoming more difficult to hide them away and dispose of them before the police could put two and two together.

Operation Launch, the plan that he had spent two years of his life scheming and gradually putting into action was less than a week away. The missile guidance system was being transferred by train with "Menace" to Beijing, where it would be locked up in Victor's Kraken International Cooperation offices. The warheads, too large to disguise, were being taken by *Le dauphin* to Victor's island, where the whole plan would finally end up. However, he was being presented with problems. The CIA, British SIS, the Mossad and Interpol were all hunting him down. The Chinese police were gradually learning of the his connections with the Triads. Above all, though, was the problem with Frank Ward, the man who never seems to die. He was still out here, uncovering Operation Launch and following the trail. No doubt he tracked down Kazuki Masaharu and then found Victor. He had to be stopped. That was why he had just spoken to Masaharu. Victor had demanded extra Triad men to assist in Operation Launch and the security to be upgraded. Masaharu had agreed, and having accepted some money, asked that fifty more gang members come down from Hong Kong immediately.

Frank Ward had to be destroyed. He couldn't risk the failure of Operation Launch, on which he had already spent so much time, money and effort. Claude Victor looked out of the black tinted window, his face sombre and for the first time in his life, concerned.

***

Lurking from behind the shrubbery, Ward had watched Claude Victor, his nemesis climb into the back of the Lincoln limousine. Ward had found the luxurious house alright, and had parked his Chevrolet Corvette a few streets away so that no Triad men would recognise it.

Having looked at the house, it could have easily belonged to a Chinese emperor. It was fit for a God to live in. The main entrance of the resplendent home, beside the three - car garage, was built up of a heavy platform and a large roof that floats over this base, made of baked stone tiles. The roof was curved, and made up of several rich, rainbow colours, which emphasised the supreme grandness. Some parts of the roof, however, were built up of blue roof tiles to symbolize the sky. The roofs were almost invariably supported by brackets, with the wooden columns of the buildings, as well as the surface of the walls, tending to be red in colour. On the door, and the red columns, were stencilled Chinese dragons emblems. Some of the rooms in the estate had terraces that overlooked the gardens below. The gardens followed both an East and West style, containing a large Olympic - sized swimming pool at the right of the large imperial estate. Ward noted that the design of the gardens was very *a*symmetrical. Like Chinese scroll paintings, the principle underlying the garden's composition was to create enduring flow, to let the patron wander and enjoy the garden without prescription, as in nature herself.

Having got a good look at the place, he had tried to find a way in. The walls were far too high to climb and were topped with vicious metal spikes and a curtain of barb wire. He looked at the large, golden gates and saw that a sign announced that they were electrified. There didn't seem to be any way inside. The security was highly efficient. Kazuki Masaharu, Ward presumed, didn't have many visitors. A few moments later though, the limousine with Claude Victor inside had started up and the gates had opened. The chauffeur had driven the 120 inch luxurious vehicle out of the gates, and before they shut, Frank Ward was lucky enough to be able to sneak inside and hide behind a Chinese parasol tree, its immense leaves providing excellent cover for him to get a look around the gardens and observe the guards.

Crouching down in the soft, manicured grass, Ward slung the light, olive - green satchel off his back and slowly unzipped it. He removed the recoil - operated Uzi SMG and slammed in a fresh magazine containing 32 rounds and then searched the satchel for the Avenger silencer, constructed of CNC machined stainless steel and aerospace quality aluminium. With a length of only 11.5 inches and a weight of 20 ounces, the Avenger silencer for the 9mm Uzi sub machine gun series is the smallest, lightest, Uzi silencer in its performance class. Once he had found it amongst the satchel's lethal contents, he fitted it calmly onto the muzzle of the SMG and laid it down delicately on the ground for the time being. He zipped up the bag and put it over his shoulder, and waited calmly like a tiger for the Triad guards to come into view. Like the previous night on *Le dauphin*, it would be sensible to observe the guards movement patterns, so he could determine the dangers.

He waited quietly behind the parasol tree for a few deathly silent minutes before the first guard came into view. He was a Chinese man, presumably in his early thirties. He had a plain, severe, rounded face, with a dry complexion like a walnut. The eyes were bored and uninterested as he walked past the flowerbeds, filled withflowers such as orchids, camellia and roses. He carried a South Korean USAS-12 shotgun, manufactured in the late 1980's and the early 1990's. He held it upwards, the 460 mm barrel towards the sky; the metal glinting in the morning sunlight. He was wearing a scruffy - looking, cheap brown jacket, grey slacks and a half unbuttoned white shirt. His hair, which had not been combed neatly into place, hung over his brow untidily. He marched past the tree where Ward was watching him from along the east side of the house, and lit a cigarette.

Judging by the man's expression and his relaxed manner, Kazuki Masaharu rarely had any trouble.

Ward grinned. *There's a first time for everything,* he thought.

He waited for the guard to finish his cigarette and walk past the main entrance and down the west side of the estate. Once he did, Frank Ward decided it was time to get moving. He crawled out from underneath the tree and with his Uzi held in his arms, he sprinted across the front lawn and past the Oriental granite water fountain. The morning sun made shadows grow under the long exotic trees. He crouched down beside the large three-car garage. Two of the green doors were open, revealing a Mitsubishi 4WORK Shogun 4x4, a yellow Lotus Elise and a Ferrari Testarossa.

Kazuki Masaharu definitely did have a nice collection of cars. Ward heard voices. Two guards, obviously having a break near the main entrance, were talking in rapid Tianjin dialect. Despite its proximity to Beijing, Tianjin dialect sounds different. He waited again and then the voices faded away.

They must have returned to duty, Ward decided. He moved out from behind the concrete garage and moved past the Olympic swimming pool, a Western feature added to the garden. The mixture of styles looked slightly strange, but still, Masaharu's wealth showed through. There were a few seats around the pool and a few drinks tables with sun umbrellas positioned above. The sun chased the shadows under the table as he passed the pool and came to the rear of the estate. Ward crouched down, flattening his back against the wall. There were no signs of guards in the area. Ward tore the green satchel off his back and searched inside for theremote - controlled bomb. He worked quickly, and removed the small, circle - shaped bomb, packed with 2.5 pounds of C4 high explosive. It had a special trigger system built inside, so that when the button was activated on the detonator, the bomb would explode. He laid the Uzi down on the grass and put his satchel back on his back. Ward seized the bomb with both hands and put it down carefully in the flowerbeds, framing the back of the house. He buried it partially in the brown earth behind the flowers to camouflage it from the human eye. With the bomb successfully planted, Frank Ward got to his feet and reached for his gun.

It was then he felt the cold metal against his neck; the long barrel of a shotgun pressed against his flesh. He stopped still and watched as a large hand reached down and prized the Uzi SMG away from his fingers. The man with the shotgun behind him paused to examine the gun, and then tucked it in his trousers. The man then grabbed Ward roughly by his shirt collar and pulled him upwards, pressing him against the wall, while his greasy, violent hands rushed down the sides of his body, searching him professionally for more weapons. Then he tugged the satchel from Ward's back and put it around his own.

'What the hell do you think you're doing here?' The guard demanded. 'Turn 'round.'

Ward did as he was told. He was looking down the long barrel of the gas - operated shotgun and swallowed noisily as a wave of nausea passed over him. He then looked away from the barrel and looked at the guard who had found him. It was the same man he had seen patrolling the grounds earlier. The bored, hazel eyes studied the intruder and he shoved the barrel into Ward's stomach, driving all the wind out of his body. Ward grunted and felt the urge to vomit. *Had the man spotted him planting the bomb?* If so, what would he do with him? Shoot him on the spot? Surely he would notice the detonator in the satchel!

'Kazuki Masaharu would like a few words with you.' The Chinese guard smiled, the horrid grin filling the whole of his jaw. The badly - cared for, yellowing teeth glinted in the sun.

'So would I', Ward spat.

The guard reached forward and grabbed Ward's right arm, his large fingers holding the intruder in a vice - like grip. Then, pointing the USAS-12 shotgun at his spine, ordered him to move.

'If you try to struggle,' the man warned, 'I'll pump your back full with the twenty rounds in this drum detachable magazine. That ain't a threat, either you Western thug. Once, I emptied three magazines into a guy's leg. In the end, there was nothing left but a pool of blood.'

Again Ward resisted the urge to be violently sick. 'Don't worry', he hissed, 'I believe you.'

The guard opened the back screen door and motioned with the shotgun for Ward to enter. He did so, and the guard closed the door softly behind. They were in a large, superbly decorated room, filled with various Chinese antiques, and Oriental styles. Like the magnificent exterior of the property, the room could belong to an Emperor's palace. The floor was surfaced in polished wood, partly covered with large, colourful mats and rugs. A few comfortable chairs were assembled around the room, with square, red cushions placed on them, decorated with Chinese calligraphy patterns. The walls were decorated with large scrolls bearing Chinese figures, and framed Asian paintings, some depicting landscapes and bamboo, while others were of creatures such as tigers and cranes. As Ward walked past, he felt the hard eyes of the tiger glaring at him, almost as if he was about to pounce right out of the picture. Placed upon ancient mahogany tables were small bonsai plants. There were also some 'mini bonsai', which measured only a few inches or less. They are produced mainly from cuttings or layering, but also from seed. The colours of some, such as the Golden Bellflower and the Flowering Quince, were so bright and exquisite. As the guard ordered Ward towards the twisting wooden staircase in the corner of the room, Ward noticed some *Peijing* that had been placed by the window and the door. *Peijing* is the hobby of creating miniature landscapes. For example, the landscape might consist of artificial rocks or woodwork or it may consist of one single piece of natural rock or wood. Miniature rock gardens also contain pavilions and terraces, trees and flowers, sailing boats, people, birds and animals, all very much reduced in size but nevertheless life-like, presenting vivid figures more real than those on landscape paintings.

'Don't stop', the guard said in his terrific English.

Frank Ward gripped the bamboo rail and climbed the steps up onto the second floor. The stairs led onto a long, plain corridor, with doors on either side. The guard pushed Ward towards the nearest door on the left and opened it.

The room was an office, decorated in Asian culture. In the centre of the room was a large desk of dark wood, with patterns of a dragon carved into the legs. On the right hand side of the room were a black and gold set of Japanese *samurai* swords, mounted on a solid wood tabletop display stand with a lacquered finish. The swords in the set include a Katana, Wakizashi, and Tanto Black. The crafted swords measured 440 centimetres and were made of stainless steel. Scabbards were tapestry covered and accented by black and gold woven cords which highlighted the tightly woven cord on the handle. The floor, like the main room downstairs was covered in a rug made up of fiery colours such as red, yellow and orange. A balcony led out from the back of the room behind the desk, overlooking the front of the garden. A triangular clock was positioned on the desk beside the golden pen holder. A figure was sitting behind the desk, his long arms laid out flat before him, and his face staring upwards at the new guest. Ward could hear the double doors close behind him.

'*Ni hao*', the guard greeted in Chinese. 'I found this Westerner prowling in the gardens.'

The man behind the desk studied the intruder. 'How did he get inside?'

'He must have sneaked inside before the gates closed.'

Frank Ward looked at the man sitting across from him. It was Kazuki Masaharu, the leader of the Chinese Triad society and the most feared criminal in all of the Eastern world. He sat there, relatively calm and relaxed, the gun barrel eyes fixed upon him. Masaharu ran his fingers through his long, wavy black hair, and realization spread across the ruthless face as he too recognised the other man.

'Frank Ward', Kazuki Masaharu said, his voice quiet and harsh. 'I'm not at all surprised to find you here. I presumed as soon as I returned to Tianjin that you would track me down, and use me for bait to get to Claude Victor. You're quite a clever individual, Mister Ward.'

'What are you and Victor planning, Masaharu?' Ward demanded. 'I know he paid you to steal the American missile guidance hardware, and the warheads from the French Air Force, too.'

Masaharu sniggered. 'You know too much to live, Ward', he hissed. 'You've stuck your nose in too far into both mine and Victor's affairs for long enough. I am merely doing confidential business with our mutual friend.'

'How much has he paid you?'

The gun barrel eyes were becoming tired of Ward's questions. The authoritative mouth fixed into a sadistic position, and the steely brown eyes focused on the guard standing behind Ward, the shotgun pointing upwards. 'Zun. Treat Ward to a lesson that nobody should ever annoy me.'

Zun smiled, the whole walnut face becoming creased. 'It would be my pleasure, boss.'

Before Ward could react, Zun lifted the USAS-12 shotgun up in the air, and brought the barrel down with considerable force on his back. Ward screamed in agony, more of a high - pitched grunt, and with all the wind forced from his body so suddenly, collapsed in a heap on the floor.

'So much for an "invincible opponent" as Victor described him', Masaharu grinned, staring down his long, fine nose at the crumpled figure on the floor, as if looking down the sights of a gun.

Zun nodded, reaching down, and hauling the spy to his feet again. Ward felt weak, as if his spine was broken. The blow could have killed him if aimed more directly at the spine, but fortunately, Zun had only meant to cause him pain, which he had done. Masaharu laughed out loud, a cruel sinister bark like that of a Doberman dog. He was obviously relishing the moment of watching the great Frank Ward, "the ace of the CIA", squirming in agony.

'Now that you understand how to respect me, Ward' Masaharu continued, fiddling with a ball - point pen, 'we can continue talking. Remember, you're not in a position to ask questions. If I wanted, Zun could snap your neck with just one karate blow. You see, Mister Ward, Zun is an expert in all Chinese martial arts. He's been training for many years, even since he was a little boy. He has even mastered a few Japanese fighting arts, including *kendo*.'

Ward didn't reply. He knew that the chances of him getting out alive of Masaharu's estate was very slim. Zun was carrying a powerful shotgun which could easily kill him with one shot. As for Masaharu himself, he was probably carrying a gun. Even if he wasn't, the rack of Chinese swords was easily in reach.

'Ever since you interfered with the assassination job involving the young French agent, I've been eager to avenge the deaths of my most experienced and loyal enforcers. Do you have any idea how many of my Triad men you murdered?'

'No', Ward said, uninterested.

'*Six*', Masaharu said through clenched teeth. He said the word slowly with meaning, as if he wanted to inject it into him. 'Another three were severely injured. If you weren't there, not only would a number of my men still be alive, but the French girl would be dead and we wouldn't have had that security breach up in the French Alps. We also wouldn't have had you sniffing around and following me to China. You've messed things up big time, Ward. I was overwhelmed with excitement when Claude Victor gave me the task of killing you. Now I'm even more pleased that I can end your miserable life in my home and take the enjoyment of watching you wriggle on the carpet before you die.' Slowly, Masaharu reached inside his dark brown jacket and produced a single action Desert Eagle, conceived in 1979 in Israel. Ward recognised the gun - he had spent a few hours training in the fire range at Langley headquarters with this particular gun. He liked it for its nice size and impact. He called it "the smaller version of the Magnum". He never thought he would be staring down the barrel of one, though. Masaharu flicked the safety catch "off" and aimed it at Ward's stomarch.

'Blow me to hell if you want, Masaharu', Ward snarled, 'Even once I'm dead, the Central Intelligence Agency will come right over here with several men and storm the place. They know I'm here.' Ward smiled, 'If I die, Masaharu, you die.'

Kazuki Masaharu didn't appear concerned. In fact, his expression hadn't changed at all. 'I don't fear you or your government, Ward', Masaharu admitted grimly. 'If they come for me, I'll go off to one of my other homes and lie low until the heat dies down. Now, lets get this over and done with. I can't wait to tell Victor the news.'

Masaharu's finger hovered over the trigger. He lifted the gun and slowly applied force on the trigger. Ward had to do something. Quickly, he struck out with his arm at Masaharu, his clenched fist connecting with his enemy's jaw. Masaharu made a stunned noise that sounded like, 'Oomph!', and was sent crashing from his chair, where his head collided with the wall. The Desert Eagle fell to the floor a metre away from where the dazed Masaharu lay. Ward spun around facing Zun, whose face showed confusion. Before he could lower the shotgun to blow a hole through Ward's chest, Ward assumed the attack position and stood less than a yard's space away. As always, Zun had the barrel of the shotgun tilted upwards, foolishly. Ward seized it at the stock and slammed the barrel upwards, where it smashed into Zun's nose. He'd gotten the angle just right: bone splinters from the bridge of the nose had been pushed up and penetrated the brain. Zun stood there for a few moments, rocking backwards and forwards, and slid to the floor sluggishly, stone cold dead.

With Zun out of the way, he was all alone with his enemy, Kazuki Masaharu. While he had been dealing with Zun, Masaharu had managed to shuffle forward on his stomach and grab hold of the Desert Eagle. He aimed his gun slowly, his mouth bleeding. Ward saw the glint of metal just in time, and kicked the gun away, where it skidded across the floor and went onto the wooden balcony.

'It's just you and me now, Masaharu! This is to pay you back for what you ordered Zun to do to me -'.

Ward extended his leg, and with applied force, kicked Kazuki Masaharu hard in the chest, causing the gangster to cough horribly and moan in pain. Then Ward got a handful of Masaharu's black hair and yanked him upwards, making Masaharu scream. Frank Ward pushed him up against the wall and reached down to Zun's body and tugged the shotgun from his lifeless fingers. Pressing Masaharu against the wall with his knee, he lifted the heavy weapon with both hands and pushed the barrel underneath his chin. Instantly, Kazuki Masaharu's brow began to perspire.

'Now that I've made you uncomfortable, Masaharu', Ward smiled, 'you can answer a few important questions. If you pass on any, I will blow your evil head off your shoulders. Got it? Nod slowly if you understand.'

Masaharu did as he was told.

'Good. Now let's begin. I'll give you to the count of three to tell me where the missile guidance system is being kept. You can do that can't you?'

'But, but, I can't tell you -',Masaharu stammered, swallowing. His mouth was dry and burning.

'One.'

'Please! I can't say anything!' Screamed Masaharu imploringly.

'Two.'

'Please!'

'*Three.*'

'Alright', Masaharu said quietly, 'I give in. It's being transferred tomorrow from *Le dauphin* to Claude Victor's Kraken International Cooperation Offices in Beijing. I don't know the exact location.'

'That had better be the truth, Masaharu.'

'It is! I *swear!*'

'Fine', Ward said, 'Where are the plans giving the details of what you and Victor are up to?'

'The plans for Operation Launch are in Victor's safe in his offices in Beijing, too. Now please, let me go! Victor would kill me if he knew what I've told you.'

'Operation Launch?' Ward was sure he had seen those words before. He just couldn't remember when.

'Yes. That's the code name of the plan involving the warheads and the guidance system. I don't know anything else about it. I just provide the security men for the operation and the equipment.'

'I knew that you would talk', Ward mused, 'I thought that you might value your life.'

Kazuki Masaharu smiled. 'You obviously don't, Ward', he snarled, 'Anybody that gets in my way *dies!*' Quickly, Masaharu managed to push the barrel of the South Korean shotgun away from his chin, and kneed his opponent in the groin. Ward's reflexes were too slow. He cursed and spun around with the shotgun. Masaharu had removed a Katana sword from the display stand and had pulled back the black and gold scabbard. He hold the sword expertly and the long blade glinted in the light.

'You'll never live to use that information, Ward!'

Masaharu lunged forward with the Katana, the sword slicing through the air only a few inches away from Frank Ward's body. Ward caught Masaharu's arm and pushed him away and managed to grab hold of the Wakizashi and remove the decorative scabbard before his enemy came back again.

Kazuki Masaharu was obviously a skilled sword fighter. His actions appeared to flow without effort. He had probably learned the art for many years, and was particularly good with the Katana. As for Ward, he had barely practised sword fighting. When he was in his teens, he and a group of friends often went fencing at the local Leisure centre. There, he had learned how to control his breathing, maintain his balance, the importance of timing and the most important aspect of all, the mental game. Good timing is the most critical factor in one's attack. No matter how fast, or difficult the shot, if it is not timed so that it hits your opponent, it will have no effect.

However, Ward had forgotten most of the techniques that he had learned all those years ago. Not only was he not as skilled as Masaharu, but his sword, the Wakizashi, was much shorter. One of the main uses of the Wakizashi was to fight indoors, where the low ceilings of feudal China and Japan would make use of the long katana nearly impossible.

This was Ward's *only* advantage.

Masaharu kept coming with the Katana, swinging the long weapon violently and destructively. Ward tried to keep his opponent as far back as possible and block the attacks. He decided if he was going to win this death battle, he was going to have to keep up his defence and hope that Masaharu would eventually become tired. If he tried attacking with his smaller, less capable sword, Ward would definitely be killed. Some of Masaharu's attacks were clumsy and dangerous in a bid to surprise Ward. The tip of the long sword was catching on the walls and ripping holes in the paper. Masaharu swung the Katana heavily towards Ward's head, but within a second, his opponent raised his sword and blocked the attack. Masaharu darted to the left and lunged with the tip of his sword. He managed to cut Ward's right arm slightly, sending Ward off - balance. Blood was running freely through Ward's dark jacket. Masaharu laughed sadistically and swung again. Ward dived onto the ground and rolled across the floor as the Katana swooped over him. To Masaharu's annoyance, he jumped to his feet and continued battle, despite the flesh wound on his arm.

Kazuki Masaharu was quite impressed with Frank Ward's fighting talent. He was proving to be a worthy opponent, an amateur *samurai*. Normally, Masaharu would impale his opponents with his trustworthy Katana within seconds. However, Ward was doing well. He couldn't understand it. It is widely agreed that the Katana, or *Dai-to,* is the single most perfect sword ever developed. Its power and finesse made it a nearly indefeatable weapon. It is made with a curved *ken* (blade) set into a long *tsuka* (hilt). The steel of the blade would be forged by master craftsmen, heated and folded over 200 times. Although the Katana was very powerful, it was also much lighter than European swords and could be handled with confidence and grace.

So why was Masaharu suddenly feeling worried? Could he sense that he was going to die?

While Masaharu was thinking to himself, his concentration had faltered and Ward managed to stab Masaharu's leg. The villain yelped in agony and reached down to the wound, dropping his weapon. The Chinese gangster fell to his knees, blood trickling freely onto the rug. He looked up at the figure above him, and the last thing he ever saw before he died was the look of anger on Ward's face. Then, with a single blow, Frank Ward chopped through Masaharu's neck with the Wakizashi. The blow severed the evil head right from the neck, and with a horrid gush of blood and a gargling noise, Kazuki Masaharu's head rolled across the rug and came to rest at Ward's feet. The brown eyes stared upwards in disbelief, the mouth open in a wide O and the tongue protruding like a snake from the ghastly, pale lips. A pool of thick red blood had circulated around the head. It had been so quick that the hands on the headless body were still trembling. As Ward looked down upon the head, he only wished that Masaharu's death had been much longer and painful.

Still, he was dead.

Frank Ward dropped his sword and smiled. He was pleased with how he had coped with the Wakizashi. The cut was still bleeding. Ward wasn't certain how serious the wound was, but he decided that applying pressure on it would stop the blood seeping out. He crouched down beside Masaharu's corpse and tore a piece of his jacket sleeve off and tied the material tightly around the arm as a make - shift bandage. He rushed across the office to where Zun lay and located the olive green satchel that contained the bomb detonator. Ward pulled out his Uzi SMG from the waistband of Zun's trousers and walked purposefully towards the closed double doors. Putting his ear against the door, he waited until he was sure nobody was in the corridor before opening the doors. He looked around, and with his free hand, locked the double doors, concealing the two bodies inside.

Agent 27S walked towards the wooden staircase, holding the silenced Uzi 9mm ahead of him, ready to spray any opposing threat with bullets. With the Avenger silencer equipped, the shooting would be almost silent, thus allowing Ward to hide any bodies and escape stealthily before the Triad thugs realised he was there. Ward moved down the creaky spiral staircase, gripping the elegantly shaped bamboo banister with his free hand for support. Ward glanced at the ornamental fan hanging on the wall, the translucent folded paper was decorated with Chinese symbols and ancient calligraphy. He rushed out into the main room again like a cheetah and ducked down behind a mahogany table supporting a fantastic Banyan Fig bonsai plant. It was then a figure came into the room; a Portuguese man with a toad - like, rather shrivelled face. The face, heavily creased with baggy, hanging bits of flesh, revealed that the man was roughly fifty. The salt and pepper hair was short and well groomed, as was the delicate moustache. He wore a black cotton shirt and a pair of cheap slacks and sneakers. The eyes, nearly invisible behind the almost opaque sunglasses, were looking around the room. A small firearm was tucked into a shoulder holster secured underneath the left armpit.

He hadn't yet seen the intruder hiding near the stairs.

Ward leaped up and stitched a vertical line of bullets up the centre of the man's chest; the several rounds drilling through the Portuguese's flesh, ordering the blood and arteries to part in their paths. The man mumbled something in Chinese that Ward didn't understand, and clutching the wound, fell to the floor. The great body crashed against the wood, and the sunglasses smashed on impact. Ward crept up to the still body, and grabbing the corpse by its limp legs, dragged it across the polished floor and concealed it underneath the stairs. Once the main bulk of the body was hidden away from view, Frank Ward ran towards the door that he had come through earlier with Zun, and found himself at the back of the estate where he had successfully planted the remote controlled bomb in the flower bed.

The only sounds were the morning chattering of the birds amongst the flowering Chinese tallow trees, the attractive red heart - shaped leaves blowing in the early breeze. There was certainly no traces of human movement nearby. Like a snake, Ward edged out from behind the rear side of the luxurious estate, and moved down the left hand side, sprinting like a gazelle. He passed a miniature lake that was three metres deep. The water was dark and misty, and a statue of a red dragon's tail was positioned in the water, giving the lake an Oriental feel. There were also two stone Sumo wrestlers that were extremely lifelike. The eyes were staring and the whole body was detailed. Ward was now at the front of the house, and standing right in front of the electrified gate. However, it could be opened from the inside by a small switch attached to the wall beside it. Ward ran over to the controls and activated it. Slowly, with a sluggish groan, the gates withdrew, and the intruder slipped out onto the streets unnoticed.

Giving one last look at the fabulous building which would soon serve as Kazuki Masaharu's crematoriam, Ward walked slowly (so as not to look suspicious) the few blocks distance to where he had parked his Chevrolet Z06 Corvette. He climbed inside and removed the detonator stick. With no regrets, Frank Ward flicked the switch.

There was a mighty explosion and Ward felt as if Tianjin had just experienced an earthquake. Even though he was well out of the bomb radius, the tremble on the ground still vibrated his car. He could see as thick, black clouds of smoke billowed out of the shattered windows, and the flames were licking out of the coloured roof tiles. The wooden columns supporting the main entrance overhang collapsed in the blast and the whole thing fell to the ground. The entire building was an inferno in a matter of seconds. Frank Ward had never experienced a fire growing so quickly. *It must be the wooden interior*, he thought. That would provide good fuel for the fire. The whole of the blue sky, that had looked so dreamy, was now a vicious torrent of red and orange, filled with ugly black clouds of smoke. Even where Ward was sitting, he could imagine the Triad gang members rushing around the gardens, wailing and screaming as their bodies were alight. The human fireballs that would be trapped inside the doomed estate would be pleading for mercy and rolling on the ground. Within fifteen minutes, the mansion had crumpled to the ground, just a pile of concrete and wood. The estate was now just a bonfire, the antique items that were inside the house now feeding the hungry flames, allowing them to live.

As Ward started the engine, he felt the satisfaction of making excellent progress in his assignment. Not only had he uncovered vital information, but he had eliminated his secondary target Kazuki Masaharu, and practically destroyed the Chinese Triad criminal society in the progress.

He pulled away from the kerb in his sports car, the powerful V8 engine growling like a tiger as it tore off down the street

13/ THE KEPT WOMAN

THE WARM WATER poured down over Frank Ward's head, instantly releasing him from the sleepiness and exhaustion, that he had been fighting against before getting out of bed.

He had been so comfortable. Ward hadn't had such a dreamless sleep since before he joined the Central Intelligence Agency. Since then, his dreams had been replaced by vivid nightmares, tugging at his conscience. He was overridden with guilt for those he had killed; their ghostly, gory bodies kept coming back to haunt him. However, last night, he didn't suffer. He was feeling happy at the moment. So far, the assignment was picking up, and the most useful information had been received from Kazuki Masaharu yesterday.

The whereabouts of the American missile guidance hardware, an essential piece of military equipment. He had to recover it as part of his mission objectives. He also knew that the data of 'Operation Launch' was hidden in Claude Victor's offices in Beijing.

So, obviously, this is where he and Albert Dawson were going.

Already, Ward had a reasonably good idea of what Victor, the corrupt French science genius, was planning. Since yesterday, Ward had crossed out of his mind, the idea of reselling the guidance system and the two nuclear warheads at a higher price. The code name of the whole, evil plan hinted that the warheads were going to be fired, with the aid of the guidance system.

But where? America? England? France?

At the moment, Ward had no idea, except for the information he had gathered over the past few days. He would have to take extra precautions now. The death of Kazuki Masaharu and the explosion at his estate might have frightened Claude Victor off. He might believe that the Chinese police and the intelligence community had connected himself and the Triad society together. If so, he would be cornered.

Frank Ward stopped thinking for a moment, and reached up into the glass shower cabinet to get the body gel, and began rubbing it over his skin. He then looked upwards towards the water until his eyes were blood - shot and the tiredness had completely gone. He now felt alive and ready to continue the day. Albert Dawson had gone to Station C at seven this morning to finish the business and hand over to one of the officials there. Whilst he was working, he would also look up the Bullet train's shuttle schedule between Tianjin and Beijing. They had decided to leave Tianjin at mid - afternoon, so that they still had the chance to complete the business up at Station C.

Ward had always looked forward to travelling on the high - speed Bullet trains. Known in Japan as *Shinkansen*, it is a network of high - speed railway lines operated by Japan railways. Since the initial Tōkaidō Shinkansen opened in 1964, the network has grown to connect most major cities on the islands of Honshu and Kyushu with running speeds of up to 186 mph in an earthquake and typhoon-prone environment. However, more recently, a few *Shinkansen* projects have opened in China, including the line connecting Tianjin and Beijing. Dawson had told him how comfortable the Bullet trains were. The seats were like those of airplanes, and the train included a lavatory installed with imported equipment to collect waste, so as to avoid pollution along the rails. Dawson estimated the journey would take seventy nine minutes.

Ward turned the knob on the controls that shut off the water and, opening the glass door to the cabinet, stepped out onto the cold, white tiled floor. He was rather looking forward to breakfast and some warm green tea. Although he disliked the stuff due to the bitter taste, it would be good to get his brain in gear. He was working towards building up a perfect strategy which could destroy Claude Victor and his scheme, 'Operation Launch.' He dried his masculine, well - built body with a towel, wrapped it around his naked waist while he began the process of shaving, looking in the square mirror above the curved sink. He picked up his electric razor and began to get rid of the light stubble on his chin. Ward always preferred to be clean shaven.

After about three minutes, when Frank Ward had nearly finished shaving, he thought he heard the front door of Albert Dawson's house close gently with exaggerated quiteness.

The breeze perhaps? But surely Albert wouldn't have left the door open?

Curiously, the CIA agent put his razor down on the top of the sink slowly, and felt for the Beretta 84FS Cheetah which was located in the pouch of his shoulder holster that lying on the toilet seat. In Ward's profession, one could never take any risks. With the firearm in reach, Ward quickly snatched the Beretta by the non - reflective black frame and flicked off the ambidextrous safety catch with his right thumb. He knew instantly that his weapon was fully loaded with thirteen rounds. He had examined the magazine before he showered.

Now there was the sound of footsteps coming from the main hallway leading towards the bedroom. They were delicate and soft on the carpet; the intruder was taking a great deal of care so as not to be heard.

But they had been.

Ward steadily unlocked the door and moved out into the hallway silently; the water was still dripping from his wet, dark hair. Ward was now in a brightly coloured corridor in Albert Dawson's apartment in one of the showpiece tower blocks. Although the place had an Oriental feel about it, Dawson couldn't live solely with Chinese decor; which explained the mixture of Eastern and Western styles. The corridor connected the bathroom and the spacious kitchen. The intruder had gone through the living room and through the hallway leading towards the stairs and the downstairs bedroom. In the corridor, Ward passed a polished, mahogany cabinet, containing sets of valuable jade figurines.

The footsteps were getting slightly louder. Frank Ward's instincts were telling him that whoever had come intended to assassinate him. That may explain why the intruder was heading for the bedroom.

However, Frank Ward was not stupid. He took his Beretta everywhere with him and even slept with the gun beside him.

Ward had now reached the door leading into the comfortable but small living room through which the intruder had come in order to reach the bedroom. The living room, although lacking size, was very beautiful and would immediately give any guests warm hospitality. The room, decorated in so many cheerful colours that combined well, looked very different. A three-piece leather sofa and an armchair (very American indeed!) rested against the walls with a low brown table in the middle of the room. A circular aluminium ashtray was placed on the table, filled with several butts and squashed cigarettes. Dawson, unlike Ward, was a chain smoker. He could not decrease the amount he smoked in a day, no matter how hard he tried.

Ward edged through the room, his teeth clenched tightly together and his finger wrapped around the combat - style trigger. He walked through the room, following the imaginary steps which the intruder would have taken and approached the corridor that led to the staircase and the downstairs bedroom. Purposefully, the ruthless spy moved in an unhurried pace to the bedroom door. Through the glass he could see the arm of the intruder behind the door. In a flash, before the intruder could react, Ward hurled the door open and allowed his strong fingers to grasp the arm. With all his strength, Ward hurled the intruder forward in the darkness, and the figure crashed onto the unmade bed with a muffled cry. Ward dived on him like a tiger, pinning him down on the bed with his left arm and holding the snout of the Beretta to the forehead.

'I'll give you one chance to tell me why you're here', Ward whispered, 'or I'll you'll get a hole in yer head. Got it?'

The intruder tried to wriggle out of Ward's grip, and in the process, the morning sun from the window caught the face in the light.

To Ward's amazement, the intruder was a woman!

The golden locks of hair, the emerald eyes. Ward recognised her instantly. The intruder was none other than Linda Pascal.

For once, Ward was absolutely speechless. 'Linda? What the hell are you doing here? I could've killed you!'

Linda Pascal sat up on the bed and Ward hesitantly withdrew his Beretta. *Had the woman come to kill him? Had Claude Victor sent her to seduce him? Was it a trap or not?* Ward was utterly confused and couldn't get an answer from all the possibilities. Linda brushed the hair out of her face and locked eyes with Ward. Her beautiful, warm eyes showed desperation and fear.

'I wanted to see you', she said softly.

'How did you know where I was?'

Linda lowered her head with regret and guilt like a small child about to confess to their parents. 'I've been watching you closely since the night you came onboard *Le dauphin*. I figured that you would be staying in Tianjin, so I visited all the main hotels in the town enquiring about you. Nothing came of it. However, whilst shopping in the urban part of Tianjin yesterday morning, I happened to see you leave this apartment in your Chevrolet Corvette.'

Ward was taken aback by the confession. The girl had obviously not been sent to kill him or try to seduce him. Linda was obviously not following him under orders. Ward was certain of that. *But why? Did she love him?* Did that kiss on the yacht mean more to both of them than either could have imagined?

'How did you know that it was my Chevrolet?' He enquired.

Linda smiled slightly, giving a glimpse of her pearl - like teeth. 'While "Menace" and the crew were searching for you, I watched out of the window and saw you drive away. I managed to scribble down the first few numbers of your licence plate before you vanished. When I recognised your car, it was unbelievable.'

Ward said: 'Clever. But you still haven't told me why you're here. Why do you want to talk to me.'

Linda reached forward slowly and placed her elegant hand on his. She swallowed and said, 'I need your help.'

Ward didn't understand. 'How can I help you?'

Linda Pascal's gorgeous face suddenly hardened and became sombre. The normally gentle eyes had been replaced by determination and revenge. The mouth was clenched tightly. 'I want my fiancé *dead*.' Linda hissed the word ruthlessly. 'And you must kill him for me.'

Frank Ward now understood why Linda had come to visit him. He thought back to the night he stealthily intruded onto Victor's yacht and saw the hideous scars on her back where her fiancé had brutally beaten her. Claude Victor, as Ward had suspected, treated Linda terribly. So terribly, in fact, that she wanted him dead.

'Don't worry, Linda,' he assured her, 'I will kill Claude. Not only do you want revenge but so do I. He killed somebody very precious to me not long ago.'

Linda nodded and her voice became fragile. Tears emerged from her eyes. 'If only you knew the ordeal I've been through. He tortures me regularly and beats me almost daily with his whip. I hate him!'

'But what about the engagement party in Paris? Ward asked. 'Didn't you love him then?'

Linda shook her head. 'He forced me into it. All he wanted was the publicity and the media attention. He wanted, as usual, to be in the spotlight and back in the public's thoughts. He doesn't love me, and I don't love him.'

'How long has he treated you like this?'

'For the past five years. He threatens to kill me regularly and locks me up in my cabin on board Le dauphin most of the time. He only lets me outside occasionally to go to the shops and to dine in restaurants. Even then, he has his men watching me and, reporting back to him. I'm a kept woman and a prisoner. I have to sit in my luxurious room aboard the yacht, usually for hours, staring dreamily out of the window and hoping for somebody to set me free and love me.'

Ward wanted to free her and love her like she said. He couldn't bear to think of the vicious, violent torment that she would have endured for years. He wanted to rescue her from her gloomy, horrid world and take her back to America and care for her with respect as she deserved. Linda had probably never experienced love before from a male partner. Quickly he wrapped his arm around the back of her neck and pulled her into his arms. Their mouths connected in a passionate kiss. Their mouths moved together for a minute or so, and they collapsed onto the bed, their arms wrapped around each other's body. Finally, when they pulled away they looked at each other with hunger in their eyes and both knew that the beginning of a fantastic relationship had begun. Now, both of their lonely lives would be brightened up and they would have each other.

'I also came to ask you a second question', Linda told him, her hands linked around his neck.

'Really?'

'Yes. Would you be my rescuer and take me back to America with you once you kill Claude?'

Frank Ward grinned and kissed her softly on the cheek. 'Of course, darling. From now on, you won't be a prisoner any more. Once Claude Victor is dead and my assignment accomplished, we can go back to the U.S. I live in Virginia. My home is your home.'

Linda smiled and instantly her face showed relief from the fear and torment that she had carried around with her for the past five years. Now she knew that she had a lover, a man who would care for her and make love to her. She was free.

'How long will it be 'till you kill that *monster*?'

'Maybe a few days', he admitted. 'I don't know, but I do know I'll get him in Beijing.'

Linda's brow furrowed. 'How did you know that Claude was planning to go to Beijing? I was just about to tell you.'

Ward ran his fingers through Linda's smooth, golden hair.

'I took your advice and paid that strange Chinese man a visit. He told me everything.'

Frank Ward pulled his body away from Linda's and walked slowly over to the large windows where a small bedside table was positioned. It was there that Ward's packet of Zhong Nan Hai 8mg lay along with his Dunhill lighter. As he looked out moodily at the buzzing traffic outside, he began to light himself the first cigarette of the day. Linda sat up on the bed and adjusted the strap of her casual green T - shirt that had slipped down her arm in the struggle.

'I've heard what happened. You killed the Chinese man and destroyed his house. Claude is very frustrated.'

'Good,' Ward grinned, exhaling a cloud of smoke before advancing back to the bed. 'Are you going with him?'

'Yes', Linda replied, 'We're going on *Le dauphin* with the rest of the crew. He says he must sort some work out at his offices there, some documents involving the NASA space program.'

'Hmm hmm. And that's where I'll be going too', Ward stated. He offered Linda a cigarette.

'No thank you', she refused, 'I don't smoke.'

Ward shrugged and placed the opened packet neatly back on the surface of the table.

'Whatever he's up to, I'll find all I want to know in that building.'

Linda opened her sensual mouth in a protest, her attractive eyes pleading with him. Quickly she got up and gripped Ward by the arm.

'Please! Don't go there!' She implored, 'Claude Victor has a whole army of men over there. Plus, he's even more alert since you killed his business partner, the Chinese man. There must be another way!'

Ward said briskly, 'It's a chance I've got to take, Linda. If you want your fiancé dead and his twisted scheme stopped, I must go after him *there*. You must understand that.'

'*Please* be careful,' she begged softly.

'I will be,' Frank Ward informed her, 'I always am.'

Linda was still very sceptical about the idea and couldn't bear the thought of him being killed and her undergoing the horrible, fiendish torture of Claude Victor. However, the handsome man was a CIA agent and obviously very confident. He had promised he would kill Claude and free her - and she trusted him. She embraced her new lover and clung to his muscular body tightly and reluctantly became acquainted with the idea. After a few silent, affectionate moments had passed, the couple parted and Ward killed his cigarette in the ashtray.

'Have you had breakfast yet?' He enquired, looking her squarely in the face.

'No.'

'Neither have I. Let's go and get a bite to eat in town and you can tell me all about yourself.'

'Will you tell me about you?' She asked with an adorable grin, revealing the neat rows of white teeth.

'Of course. I've just got to get dressed and finish shaving and we'll go. Help yourself to a drink from the refrigerator in the kitchen. I'm sure my friend won't mind.'

'Okay'. Linda flashed him another gorgeous smile that lit up her whole face as Ward headed out of the bedroom to the bathroom where he would conclude the shaving process and rid his jaw of the slight stubble that had gathered over the past eventful days.

After three or four minutes, Frank Ward and the lovely Linda Pascal emerged from the front of the typical Chinese home of a working class person. The exterior of Albert Dawson's home was far from the magnificent architecture of Kazuki Masaharu's property, but still, the house looked modern and well - cared for. There was a small but beautiful garden in front of the large window, consisting of a manicured lawn surrounded by pretty flowerbeds and a granite water fountain built in the middle.

Ward locked the front door with the spare key given to him by Dawson and felt crisp and refreshed. He felt clean after the long shower and felt better knowing that his jaw was clean shaven. He was wearing a dark single breasted suit, made by the Italian company Enzo Tovare. Ward liked the classic suit style with hip pockets on the jacket and the comfortable virgin wool material. Most of Ward's suits were made by Enzo Tovare, whom he considered to be the ultimate producer of quality clothes. Ward slipped the key into his pocket and escorted Linda along the concrete path and out of the gate to where the platinum Chevrolet Z06 Corvette was parked in the shade of the morning sun.

'Do you know any decent places around here, Linda?' Ward asked as he unlocked the vehicle electronically with the button on the fob.

'Yes,' she said helpfully, climbing into the luxurious passenger seat. 'There's a nice place in the urban area where I often have lunch when I've been shopping. It's called "The Red Dragon." It's a Cantonese restaurant specialising in seafood. I trust you like Chinese food.'

'Of course I do,' he mumbled as he gripped the wheel tightly with his hands and slowly reversed out of the area and accelerated out onto the road. Ward noted the time on his wrist watch and then verified it on the car radio. It was nine fifteen. As the journey progressed, Linda began giving him instructions, telling him when to turn left or right. Ward found himself not concentrating on the road particularly - but more on the fabulous, divine woman sitting beside him. Her whole body was so desirable and Ward couldn't pick out a single flaw that damaged her beauty. Her clothes made her more attractive also - they were so simple but looked great on her. She wore a plain, light green strap top and casual creamy white trousers that ended above her small feet, which rested in a pair of flip - flops. Every few minutes he turned briefly towards her and admired her, knowing instantly that her smile was her most appealing feature. It was just so warm and pleasant. When she beamed, Linda looked happy, and to a stranger, nobody would know of the horrific torture and abuse that she had suffered. She was a brave girl, just like Gaëlle Dumas had been (*Rest In Peace, my love!*). After a relatively short and relaxing drive, Linda pointed out the restaurant at the end of the street on the right hand side. Ward slowed down and drove into the small car park beside the building. There were two other vehicles in the parking lot - a Honda Civic and a large industrial truck. Ward eased the Chevrolet into the nearest vacant space and turned off the engine.

It was as Ward pushed open the car door that a thought flashed into his mind. He cursed himself for being so clumsy and turned abruptly towards Linda, who had already emerged from her seat.

'Linda - are you sure that Claude hadn't had you followed this morning?'

She smiled again, 'Don't worry yourself, Frank. I thought of that before I even left *Le dauphin*. I walked around aimlessly for a while to see if Claude had sent his "guardian angels", as he calls them, to watch me. I didn't see anybody, so cautiously, I walked up to where you were staying.'

Ward was doubtful. *Was she sure? What if she had been mistaken and Victor's men had followed her?* There was nothing he could do about it now anyway. At least Ward felt reassured knowing that he had his trusty Beretta firearm concealed in his holster. It was a comfort at times like this, knowing that one has a weapon at hand.

Ward got out of the Chevrolet too and together they walked out of the parking lot and approached The Red Dragon by the main entrance. It looked like a respectable place from the outside. Ward could see immediately through the massive double windows that it wasn't very busy at all. There were only one or two of the tables occupied by people. They didn't look Chinese. Ward decided that the local people were probably at work and that most of the customers dining here during the morning would be tourists wanting to try some Cantonese cuisine.

Ward and Linda walked through the front door together and stood by the entrance waiting for one of the staff to come and escort them to a table. The restaurant was a large room with a well - stocked bar in the centre, behind which many alcoholic drinks were stocked. An Englishman, Ward presumed, was sitting on one of the leather-surfaced stools, talking to the short, wooden faced Chinese bartender who was cleaning a glass. There were several tables around the room and booths in the corner for larger groups. The walls were decorated in Chinese artwork and the CD player on the bar was playing the popular rock music of Cui Jian, a Beijing based musician, song writer, trumpet player, song writer and composer. Having no footsteps in which to follow, he is the pioneer of Chinese popular music. Upon their arrival in the restaurant, a uniformed pretty Chinese lady approached them, a broad grin on her delightful face.

'Welcome!' The waitress exclaimed in good English. 'May I get you a table for two? Or are you expecting more people?'

'No thanks, a table for two would be fine,' Linda said, before Ward had the chance to speak.

'Follow me please,' said the uniformed waitress.

Ward and Linda followed her past one of the couples sitting down at the tables. They were happily eating *Xiaolongbao*, also known as soup dumplings. It can be filled with hot soup and meat or vegetarian fillings, as well as other possibilities. The man and woman were peeling the dumpling off the lettuce leaf, taking care not to break the dumpling skin. They were talking quietly amongst themselves whilst eating and complimenting the chef on the *Xiaolongbao*. They acknowledged Ward and Linda Pascal as they walked past with a civil 'hello'. The Chinese waitress found them an adequate table near the window overlooking the busy urban streets outside.

'Will this table be fine?'

'Yes', murmured Ward. 'Thanks.'

The Chinese lady grinned and said amiably, 'I'll just go and get you a menu.' With that the waitress turned on her heel and walked back towards the bar, stopping briefly on the way to ask the other couple with the *Xiaolongbao* if everything was all right with their food. They said it was and she hurried towards the bar to collect a menu.

Linda pulled one of the seats out and sat down heavily with her back against the door. Ward slipped into the seat opposite her. 'It's a nice place,' Ward said looking around.

Linda nodded, her arms resting out in front of her on the table. 'I think so too.

They do some nice dishes here. And the price isn't that bad either.'

Ward was relieved. He didn't have much money in his wallet. 'I'll pay for the meal,' he announced.

Linda's face set into a decisive expression. 'Don't be silly! I'll pay.'

'But it was me who suggested going out and having breakfast!'

Linda Pascal smiled; again, her face was golden and content. 'Let's make a deal', she suggested. 'I pay for the meal, you pay for the drinks.'

Ward sighed and gave in, having sensed defeat. 'Fine,' he said reluctantly.

The Chinese waitress returned with a square laminated menu and put it down in the middle of the table. Linda picked it up first and studied the dishes carefully. The waitress had her notebook out and a pen ready.

'Can I get you some drinks?'

Ward looked at Linda inquiringly, 'What would you like to drink, Linda?'

Linda looked up for a few seconds and looked at the waitress. 'I think I'll have a bubble - tea smoothie, please.'

'Sure', said the waitress jotting it down in her notebook, 'And for you?'

Ward wasn't sure what to drink. He didn't feel like any green tea and it was too early in the morning for anything alcoholic. 'I'll have the same, please,' Ward announced, not even knowing what the drink was.

The waitress said that she would go and fetch them their drinks. Ward nodded and looked at Linda.

'What is a bubble - tea smoothie?'

'Oh, it's just hot tea with an assortment of fresh fruit', she explained, 'it's nice - it's usually my preferred choice of drink unless I want something a bit stronger.'

Ward nodded again. The smoothie sounded alright (surely it can't be as horrible as the green tea!).

'Have you decided on anything yet?' Ward asked, beginning to feel ravenous at the thought of food.

Linda took a final look at the menu and delicately pushed it across the table for Ward.

'Yes', she said, 'I think I'll have Elegant Egg Foo Yung.'

'What's that?'

'A Chinese omelette.'

'Sounds nice,' Ward admitted, glancing at the other available options himself. 'I'll have the Egg Drop Soup. The menu says it includes tomatoes and chicken.' Linda nodded in agreement and Frank Ward placed the menu back in the centre of the table.

'Tell me about yourself', Linda asked smiling.

'You first,' Ward insisted.

'Okay, but will you promise to tell me about you next?'

'Yes.'

'Fine. I am thirty one years old. I was brought up in Perpignan in southern France. I was one of three children, the only girl. My two brothers, Jean - Pierre and Henri were both older than me by a few years. My mother didn't particularly have much money, and could barely afford to feed and clothe us on her low salary as a maid in a wealthy man's house. My father, you understand, was jobless after it was revealed he stole some money from the company he worked for. Now, the family was even poorer and my father began drinking heavily most nights, and having violent arguments with my mother in his terrible drunken state. Sometimes he even abused *me*,' Linda paused and swallowed, her past haunting her as she thought about it. Ward put his hand over hers reassuringly and comforted her. After a few minutes she continued.

'My mother threw my father out onto the streets after his violent acts became more frequent. We heard nothing of him for a few days, but then his body was discovered in a disused warehouse alleyway. There was a gun in his hand. He had shot himself in the head - death was instantaneous. We were all in mourning for months and couldn't come to terms with my father's suicide. My mother eventually got a better job by the time I was in my early teens, and was earning more money. My brothers and I supported her to by helping with the housework. At school, I was doing well and excelled particularly in geography. When I left school, my mother couldn't afford to put me or my brothers through university, so I got a job as bar maid in a nightclub. It was a decent job and I gave some of my earnings to my mother whilst saving up for a house of my own. After a few years of working at the nightclub, I was spotted by a wealthy fashion designer. He decided that I would be a great model on the catwalk. I accepted his job and I had been doing it until I met Claude. We first saw each other in Nice whilst I was doing some modelling work for a magazine. Ever since that fateful day, my life has been a living hell.' Linda smiled, 'That is until I met *you*.'

Ward's face was full of understanding and he felt deep sadness for Linda's violent and troubled past. The things she had overcome were amazing. The waitress returned with the drinks and carefully placed them down on the table so as not to spill them.

'Ready?'

'Yes,' replied Ward.

He then told her what he wanted to order. Linda did too. The waitress exchanged a brief smile and picking up the menu, hurried off towards the kitchen.

'Now you tell me about yourself,' Linda said.

Ward cleared his throat and began, 'I am thirty four years old. I was brought up in Los Angeles with my two younger brothers, Joe and Peter. My parents, Sandy and Michael had both grown up there and owned a spacious house near one of the surfing beaches. My dad was a life guard and patrolled the beach, and my mother was a hairdresser. As children, my brothers and I spent most of our spare time on the beach with dad, either swimming or playing volley ball. I finished school and first decided to go to colleague and study mechanics. However, I had wanted a career in the American Army since I was a young boy. When the opportunity arose, I left college, became a soldier and went into the Gulf War in Iraq.' Ward paused and sipped a little at his drink.

Linda, completely fascinated by Frank Ward's past said, 'Go on.'

'It wasn't at all what I thought it was like when I was a child,' Ward said grimly, 'There were bodies littered across the ground, their bodies ripped apart by shrapnel and riddled with bullets. Blood was everywhere. I was surrounded by blood and the dead - it was horrible. Also, I had to *kill* for the first time. It was a dirty business. I remember the bullet from my gun striking the man in the chest and the body flying backwards. I remember vividly the shocked, frightened expression on the soldier's face in death. We had a raid on our camp not long after I came into the war. Several of my closest friends, some that I've known since a kid, were killed. It was terrible. We managed to overcome the raid and vanquish the threat. I was out there for a few more months but hated it. There was too much killing and gore. I was fed up of treading on corpses wherever I walked. I managed to escape on a cargo ship back to America along with a few other comrades. When I returned home, I was met with tragic news. While I had been away, both my parents had had a tragic car crash. Both died instantly as the vehicle veered off a hill and exploded. It was the worst day of my life when I discovered that my parents were dead. I had been looking forward to seeing them on my return, but all I could do was lay a wreath on their graves. Then, years later, once I had gradually got over my parents' death, my youngest brother Joe was murdered. Joe was formerly in the Central Intelligence Agency and was in the same Directorate as I'm in now. He was killed by an American drug baron whom he was after. On receiving news of my brother's death, I was determined to avenge him. I joined the CIA after hard training and countless hours at the firing range and exacted revenge on the drug baron, Sharp and destroyed his cocaine production business. During that mission, I was shot in the arm-', Ward stopped and pulled back his sleeve revealing the hideous scar on his left arm. Linda winced. 'I've recovered and was assigned to recover a piece of missile guidance technology stolen days ago in Hong Kong and two nuclear warheads. Since then, I've since discovered that Claude Victor is responsible and that is why I'm here.'

'You mean that Claude has stolen *nuclear warheads*!' Linda demanded quietly, shocked.

'Yes,' Ward said calmly, 'I didn't want to tell you before. I wasn't sure if I could trust you.'

'I didn't realise it was as serious as that! So is Claude a terrorist or something?'

Ward answered Linda's question with a quick nod. 'He's working with a Chinese criminal organisation called the Triads. That Oriental man who often stayed on your yacht was the leader of the Triads. That's why I killed him.'

Linda was stunned for a few moments. 'I see,' she said finally. 'Anyway, I hear that your past is pretty much as horrible as mine.'

Ward cleared his throat. 'Yes, we have been unfortunate. But that's why we're both together now - to love each other.' Ward said it and meant it just as much as he had when he said it to Gaëlle.

Linda grinned and agreed happily. They finished the bubble - tea smoothie in silence and waited for a few more minutes for the waitress to return with their breakfast.

'Here you are,' the waitress said, handing Ward his Egg Drop Soup.

'Thanks,' said Ward dipping his spoon into the thick liquid.

'*Bukequi*. Can I get either of you another drink?' enquired the waitress, noticing the empty glasses.

'I'm alright at the moment,' Linda announced.

'So am I.'

'Alright then. *Qing yong can*!'

'*Tie how chuh luh*!'

'What?' Ward asked, blowing the soup on his spoon to cool it down.

Linda looked up. 'I said "delicious" in Chinese. This Elegant Egg Foo Yung looks lovely.'

Ward looked at the Chinese omelette which she had ordered. 'Indeed.'

They finished eating their different breakfast courses practically in silence, except for occasionally commenting on the food. Once they had finished, the waitress returned to collect the empty bowl and plate. Ward thanked her and began to get his wallet out of his pocket ready to pay the bill. Linda had thought alike and placed a few yuan notes onto the table ready to pay for the meal. A few minutes later, the Chinese waitress came back to their table and read out their final bill. As Linda had announced, she would pay for the food, Ward would pay for the drinks. The waitress responded to the money with a discreet nod and invited them to come again. Then she was gone.

'I've really enjoyed this morning,' Linda said amiably.

'So have I,' Ward agreed. 'We'll meet again soon.'

'Where?'

'Beijing. The day before I search Victor's offices.'

'But where shall we meet?' Linda enquired.

'At the Beijing Opera', he told her smoothly, 'There you can bring me an architect's blueprint of the floors on the building. That way I should be able to find my way around easily and get out quicker. Do you think you can get hold of one?'

Linda thought for her few seconds and she bit her lip. 'Yes', she said, 'yes, I think so. I think Claude keeps one in his desk drawers. I should be able to get hold of it for you.'

'Great. I'll see you there then.'

'What day and time?'

Ward shook his head , 'I can't be certain. Give me your mobile number and I can contact you there. If Victor's with you or you're being watched, ignore it. But if you're alone, answer, and I'll give you the details. Understand?'

'Yes.' Linda then took her napkin and printed her number onto the fine material. She then handed it to Ward, who pocketed it in his trouser pocket.

Ward leaned across the table and their lips touched for a few moments in an affectionate kiss. 'Good girl. I'll see you at the opera. Make sure you're not followed.'

'I will', Linda said confidently, and with a final goodbye, and made her way out of the restaurant where she flagged down a nearby taxi and climbed inside.

Standing on the opposite side of the street, pretending to be glancing at a row of Chinese magazines standing on a rack outside a shop, was

Marcus "Menace" Hillman. Turning his face away he watched his target give the driver instructions and the car drive away. Quickly, he reached inside his jacket and withdrew his cell phone, updating his boss on his fiancé's most recent whereabouts.

'You'll never guess who she's been having breakfast with!'

'Who?' demanded Claude Victor in a deathly cold voice.

'Frank Ward, the American spy.'

14/ THE TRAIN TO HELL...

AT ABOUT TWO thirty, Albert Dawson had finished clearing up some business and returned home to his comfortable house where he found his friend and fellow CIA agent waiting for him in the living room.

'Everything going well at Station C?' Ward asked.

Dawson nodded and gently closed the door behind him. As always, Albert Dawson looked bright and alert. His sombre face was split into a smile. He was wearing a light-brown crumpled suit and brown leather shoes. His straw - coloured hair was combed neatly and parted to the left.

'Yeah. Pretty quiet all morning. Sent a group of men to Shenyank after a hired Japanese assassin. Wanted by the Israelis as well as our American superiors. The Mossad have been searching the world for this lousy son - of - a -bitch for years, but we found him. Known to have murdered at least twenty men, including two from the FBI and five from the CIA.'

'Have you got tickets for the Bullet train?'

'You bet ya,' Dawson said sitting down heavily on the three - piece sofa, 'The two tickets are waiting for us at the Tianjin station. We're due there at four. Journey takes about thirty minutes. What have you been doing all morning? Not sitting in this boring place for hours I hope?'

'No. I had an unexpected visitor come here this morning,' Ward explained.

Dawson's eyes widened. 'Not Victor's men!' He exclaimed. 'They don't know you're here, do they?'

'No,' said Ward. 'Not from Victor's men. From his *fiancé*, Linda Pascal.'

Albert Dawson was stunned. His mouth was open in a wide O of disbelief. 'Why the hell did she come here? Did our man send her to kill you or something?'

'She came to see *me*. Victor had absolutely nothing to do with it. I can assure you.'

'Sure. She says that. That doesn't mean she isn't a lying son-'.

'Stop!' Ward said, cutting off Dawson before he had chance to finish his sentence. 'She tells me she hates Victor. He beats her regularly and tortures her. Victor has her followed most of the time by his cronies and threatens to murder her if she ignores him.'

Dawson swallowed and nodded, finally listening to his close friend. 'I see,' he said slowly, 'But why did she come to you?'

'She came to ask me - beg me - to *kill* her fiancé for her.'

'What did you say?'

'I promised I would.' Ward then continued to tell Dawson about going out for breakfast and talking about their pasts. Then, he told his friend the final details of the next arranged meeting at the Beijing Opera.

'The Beijing Opera? Why there?'

'It's a better meeting place than a restaurant or a bar. Everybody's eyes will be on the stage, not on us. Nobody will notice us at the back talking about Victor's offices.'

'What about her. Suppose she's tricking you and goes and tells Claude Victor everything! Or, she might get caught stealing the blueprints! What if she doesn't show?'

'She will,' Ward told him lighting a cigarette. 'And she is not a liar. I trust her and she trusts me. She *will* be there because she wants Victor dead. Plus, she loves me.'

Albert Dawson gave a sigh and a dry chuckle. 'Frank - you sure do have a great way with women! All it seems you do is click your fingers and you've got one of the most gorgeous women in the world in your arms. Why can't you teach me how to do that?'

Ward smiled and exhaled a lungful of smoke. He said behind the misty cloud covering his face, 'Albert - I can't teach you all of my secrets. If I told you that, I'm afraid I'll have to kill you.'

They both laughed audibly and Ward offered Dawson a cigarette which he gratefully accepted.

'I'll go and pour us a stiff drink,' Dawson announced, lifting himself up from the sofa. 'Then, we'll head to the station. I've got a feeling that we're well on our way to catching Victor in our fishing net. We've almost got him!'

Frank Ward looked up, his handsome face serious. 'We haven't got him yet. My friend, we've still go a hell of a long way to go yet before I can wrap my hands around that murderer's throat!'

Later that day, the drive to the airport was a mad rush for Frank Ward and his companion. Due to various traffic problems on the way to the station, located in the city centre to the east side of Jiefang Bridge, spanning the Haihe River, Ward found himself skipping lights and breaking the speed limit.

Ward turned to Albert Dawson, his best friend since the Sharp affair, who was sitting in the passenger seat beside him in the Chevrolet Z06 Corvette.

'What time did you say our train leaves?' Ward demanded, wrenching the wheel furiously as he overtook a van and manoeuvred around a tight bend at about fifty miles per hour.

Dawson consulted the time printed on the daily train schedule. 'Four o'clock,' he said, shaking his head. 'It's ten to now.'

'Crap!' cried Ward. 'We'd better not miss it or Victor will be well ahead of us!'

'Stop talking and keep floorin' that accelerator!'

Frank Ward bit his lip and increased in speed, watching the needle on the speedometer gradually increasing.

'We'll make it,' he said confidently.

Five minutes later, the American platinum sports car hurtled into the large car holding area beside Tianjin station, the largest of the four railway stations in Tianjin. Ward found a space and drove the car into it.

'Pay the parking,' Ward told Dawson, 'whilst I get our cases out.'

His friend acquiesced and went in search of one of the car parking machines.

Ward carefully removed his black slim line attache case, in which he had crammed a few of his clothes, his laptop, and spare clips for the Beretta. He extracted Dawson's case and locked the car. He could hear footsteps approaching. Albert Dawson was running towards him, out of breath from running.

'The parking is paid for. Here's a ticket,' he said, handing Ward the piece of paper which he displayed on the dashboard.

'Ready?' asked Ward.

'Time?'

'Three minutes left to board the train,' Frank Ward announced glancing at his watch, 'We made it after all.'

Together, the two spies walked out of the car park in a hurried walk towards the station. They pushed through the busy throng of tourists and Chinese people returning home. The whole atmosphere was bustling and people were pushing past each other carelessly, nearly knocking Ward off his feet.

'Are the train stations in China always *this* busy?' Ward asked as a tall Chinese man collided with him before pushing past him roughly.

Albert Dawson fought his way through the crowds to his friend, using his suitcase both as a shield and something to push people out of the way.

'Yes unfortunately,' Dawson admitted. 'The stations are becoming very crowded like they are in Japan. In Japan, they have people called "pushers" who simply cram the trains with people in the rush hour.'

After a further two minutes was wasted jostling and weaving in and out of the crowds of people, the super - fast bullet train was soon in sight. The train had two horizontal blue lines on the side of the train, beneath the windows. They made their way to the entrance, and Dawson handed the tickets to the uniformed attendant standing beside the door. He directed them to their seats near the front of the train. Frank Ward sighed as he collapsed into the luxurious blue chair beside the window.

'I'd hate to go through those crowds every day,' he confessed.

Dawson grinned and put the suitcase and Ward's attache case up into the storage compartment and sat down next to his partner.

There was a few seconds silence, finally broken by Dawson, 'What do you think Operation Launch is all about?' Albert Dawson enquired, keeping his voice quiet so that none of the other passengers would overhear.

Ward turned towards him, 'I'm sure Claude Victor intends to fire the warheads at specific countries. On that I'm almost certain. Still, we have two questions to figure out until the whole thing makes sense.'

'What are those questions?'

'What motive Victor has for launching the warheads and what countries he has targeted.'

Dawson's brow wrinkled. 'I'm not sure Victor needs a motive. He could just be a maniac and want to be a mass murderer. We know he craves attention - maybe he just wants everybody to know his name and fear him.'

Frank Ward shook his head. 'I don't believe your theory. I'm sure Victor has a motive behind the whole plan, most likely extortion.'

'What about the countries?'

'I think the countries targeted will be wealthy countries, thus allowing him to benefit largely from blackmail if that's the motive. I have no idea. But soon we shall know everything that we need to know about Operation Launch and we can prevent it happening.'

'I agree.'

Upon Dawson's statement, the train started and the doors on the train closed with a mild hiss. Within seconds, the bullet train had progressed in speed and was travelling steadily at eighty miles per hour. In the next few minutes, the *Shinkasen* would have advanced to its maximum speed of one hundred and sixty four miles per hour.

** *

Meanwhile, while Frank Ward and his companion were trying to figure out Claude Victor's evil methods, Marcus "Menace" Hillman said a few words to the Chinese man beside him and got up, a sports backpack strapped around his polyester jacket. Carefully maintaining his balance as the bullet train sped along the tracks, he headed towards the lavatory. Noting the 'VACANT' sign on the lock, the sadistic French killer pushed open the door, stepped inside the small room and locked the door behind him. A twisted, cruel grin on his predatory face, Hillman slung the backpack off his shoulder and put it down on the toilet seat.

He unzipped it quickly and removed the hi - tech explosives provided by Claude Victor. The bomb, which only measured about fifteen centimetres diameter, had an impressive explosive radius. The bomb was triggered by an inbuilt timer that could be set manually. Smiling, "Menace" Hillman pressed the button on the bomb and set the timer for ten minutes. Delicately, he then lifted the top of the cistern and laid it on the floor and put the bomb inside. The villain watched as the timer began to tick and excitedly replaced the lid of the water tank.

'I've got you this time, Ward', he mumbled silently to himself , 'At last, you're dead!'

Then, with a grin of satisfaction, imagining his enemy being blown to smithereens, he unlocked the door and returned to his seat beside his Triad friend.

** *

Ward lay his head back on the chair and glanced through an English magazine that was put in front of every seat. He was bored and constantly overlooking his assignment from various angles whilst reading the text. He decided that upon arrival in Beijing he would wire an update to the CIA Langley headquarters and make Cartwright and the Chief - Of - Staff aware of recent events. However, his mind was occupied by thinking about Linda Pascal. She would be waiting for him to make the cell phone call; waiting for him to set her free from her cruel, insane fiancé. He began to think about his future - would the Central Intelligence Agency be part of it? Or would he throw the job in and settle down with Linda? At the moment, Frank Ward was sick of death and blood. Everywhere he went he brought violence and destruction. Why couldn't he get a simple job like other people? One that didn't involve guns and knives and bombs!

Ward shook the thoughts out from his mind and turned towards Albert Dawson who was presently closing his eyes and trying to go to sleep in the gentle rhythm of the train. Ward nudged him slightly and the Texan opened his eyes and looked towards him.

'What?' Dawson asked.

'How much longer until we reach Beijing?'

Dawson yawned audibly and consulted his wrist watch. 'About ten minutes', he murmured quietly.

Ward nodded and continued impatiently to thumb through the magazine.

** *

"Menace" Hillman, who was sitting a few seats behind the two CIA agents, looked out of the window at the fast blur of colours as the world rushed by. He was thinking about the cleverly-devised escape plan that he, Claude Victor, and the remaining Triad men had thought up. It had taken some careful preparation and thorough organisation. Three minutes before the bomb was due to explode, the Bullet train would meet a large van parked in the middle of the tracks, having been positioned there by Victor's men. Due to the van being on a long straight section of the track, the driver would have time to see the obstruction and slow down to avoid the risk of derailing. When the train stopped, "Menace" would go to the toilet and jump off the train via the window, followed moments later by his Triad associate. They would then escape the bomb radius and be well out of sight before the bomb detonates and splits the *Shinkasen* in two; both Frank Ward and Albert Dawson perishing in the fiery blast.

Hillman unzipped his sports bag and removed a walkie - talkie and whispered into it. 'Is the van in place?'

'Yes, Mister Hillman,' came the reply in Chinese.

'Good,' "Menace" grinned, 'The van should be in sight in a few moments. I'll contact you once the bomb has done its job.'

'Understood.'

"Menace" Hillman smiled and replaced the walkie - talkie, and then repeated the conversation to his friend from the Chinese Triad society. The train was only seconds away from the van blocking the track...

** *

Suddenly, the bullet train decreased in speed so dramatically that it was really unexpected. The jolt sent Frank Ward forward in his seat, his safety belt preventing him from being propelled head - first into the seat in front of him. Ward regained control and dug his fingers into the arms of the reclining chair, and looked out of the window. Ahead, in the distance, he could make out a large grey shape.

What the hell was it? The bullet train was going very slowly fifty miles per hour now and doing about seventy; having dropped considerably from one hundred and sixty. Ward's question was soon answered when the bulky shape ahead became more clear - it was a large, 2005 Dodge Caravan.

'No,' Ward murmured through clenched teeth.

Albert Dawson looked towards his friend inquiringly and shuffled up in his seat so that he was sitting up straight. He then bent his head slightly and tried to look through the window. He was unable to do so and this prevented him from seeing a thing. 'What is it?'

'There's a minivan stuck in the middle of the track,' Ward explained slowly, 'We're heading straight for it. That's why we've slowed down.'

Dawson's eyes widened and he swallowed, 'A *minivan*!'

Frank Ward rested his jaw on his wrist and began to think. Was this just some joyrider who had stolen a car and decided to get rid of the evidence? Or was this related to Ward himself? Ward began to think of Claude Victor - the corrupt scientist and his enemy, the large, disgusting fish eyes and the transparent white skin and the clean, bald scalp. *Could he have set this up? But why?* Ward attempted to answer his own question but couldn't think of any answer. He cursed himself for being too suspicious.

The train had slowed down now and glided over the track, eventually coming to a complete rest on the specialised track. There were some worried comments from other passengers opposite Ward and behind.

'What's going on?' cried a desperate obese woman with vile, curly red hair, 'Has the train broken down? I knew we shouldn't have come on these wretched bullet trains! They're too hi - tech!'

Ward ignored the annoying tourist who was shouting out irritating comments. The speaker above the door connecting the next carriage sounded and the driver's voice boomed clearly. The man said something that Ward didn't understand in Chinese and then he repeated himself in American - English.

'This is the driver of the bullet train speaking,' came the voice through the speaker, 'Please remain calm. There is a vehicle - a minivan of some kind - parked in the middle of the tracks. I've been forced to bring the train to a halt to avoid a serious collision that could cause us to derail. We will contact emergency services to come and remove the vehicle as soon as possible and see if it can be identified. Until then, I'm afraid, our journey will be delayed. Possibly for an hour or so. I apologise personally for any inconvenience and I ask you to wait patiently and cooperate in this situation. Thank you.'

The speaker went off and immediately the carriage erupted into a chaos of voices and people complaining. Of course, the red haired woman had the most to say - she was moaning and whingeing. Ward struggled to hear himself think.

'Great,' Ward said with a touch of sarcasm. 'Thanks to some idiot who dumped the van in the tracks we'll be delayed.'

'Just what we need,' Dawson added with a sigh of regret.

The driver of the bullet train, a large Chinese figure with broad shoulders emerged from the cabin and implored the frustrated passengers to calm down. The red - haired woman started to complain again and say that she was due for a meeting in Beijing. The driver apologised sincerely and the woman dismissed it with an angry tilt of her head. With all the commotion, nobody noticed the large figure dressed in a sports jacket move down the aisle and make his way through the crowds of people, standing up and talking to the driver. However, Frank Ward noticed and couldn't help but feel that he recognised the man. Although he didn't get a good look at the man's face, there was something about the way he carried himself and the familiar dress.

The man in the sports jacket reached the toilet and unlocked the door. Before he disappeared inside, the man turned his head slightly, giving Ward a perfect view of the face he knew so well.

'Albert - it's "Menace"!' Frank Ward shouted, unfastening his safety belt.

'What?'

Before Dawson could continue, his friend beside him had leapt out of his chair and was pushing his way through the people, his Beretta clutched in his hand. Albert Dawson scrambled out of his chair and removed his gun too. He chased after his partner, screams coming from all around him as frightened people saw the gun.

'Move! Now!' Dawson instructed, barging his way through the people with his powerful body. He was soon standing beside Ward who was at the lavatory door, trying the door handle desperately.

'He's inside - we've got to get him!'

'Who? Tell me!' Dawson asked impatiently.

'Marcus "Menace" Hillman, Victor's bodyguard and enforcer.'

Ward stepped back from the door and with applied force, extended his leg and kicked at the door. There was a thud and a groan from the door as the lock was beginning to give in. Ward lashed out with his foot again. The door was nearly there now. With a final kick, the toilet door came crashing down from the broken hinges and the two men trampled over it into the small room.

There was nobody inside. The thin, translucent curtains were blowing slightly in the breeze through the opened window.

'He's gone through the window!' Ward pointed out. He crouched down and looked to see the killer sprinting up the grassy bank beside the track. Immediately, Ward put his leg over the ledge and then his other, allowing himself to drop the short distance to the ground. Landing on his feet, he balanced his gunning arm on his other and took aim at the figure in the distance. "Menace" was jumping over a wooden fence that led into a grassy meadow.

Phutt, phutt. Ward fired two rounds from his silenced weapon but both went wide by a few inches. By the time Ward had got off his two shots, Albert Dawson was standing beside him having followed him through the small window. Ward turned to see his companion and they both ran over through the short grass after their target.

Metres away, "Menace" Hillman removed the small detonator out of his trouser pocket and held the object tightly in his palm. When he had gone a fair distance away, he grinned, and applied pressure on the button.

The heat was immense and resembled that of standing next to a barbeque on a hot summer's day. The force was so powerful that it sent both Frank Ward and Albert Dawson crashing to the floor as clouds of fiery flames and thick black smoke erupted around them. Mud was sprayed on them as they covered their heads with their arms. The noise and the heat of the explosion was terrific. It was followed by screams and profanities both in English and Chinese from inside the ruined bullet train. Ward turned his head and looked towards the wreckage. In the area where he had been sitting, the train had been divided cleanly in two. One half of the train, the rear half, was still on the rails, but the other was lying on its side. Shards of broken glass and damaged metal lay strewn on the ground where Ward and his companion lay.

Ward lay on the floor in deep pain and wasn't sure whether he had lost a leg in the explosion. His entire body was completely numb and as he tried to explore his senses, he discovered that both his legs were intact as were his arms, which lay limply in front of him. His hair and right cheek felt wet. Unsure whether it was sweat or blood, he reached up to the area and brought the hand back in front of his eyes for inspection. There was red all over his palm. He was bleeding on the head. It wasn't too major, though, or he would undoubtedly be unconscious. He looked at his companion beside him who was lying face upwards, his face black with dirt and reddened with blood. His white shirt underneath his business - like jacket was also spotted in red blood stains. He groaned and tried to lift himself from the ground but failed. He was obviously in more pain than Ward, and more injured.

Ward tried to lift himself up and spotted a figure only metres away from him. The cold, ruthless eyes stared at him.

"Menace"! Filled with panic and anger, Ward pushed himself across the ground and reached out desperately with his arm for his Beretta, which lay inches away from him. He was too slow, and "Menace" Hillman lashed out with his foot and caught Ward directly under the chin. Ward groaned and could feel the shoe penetrating his skin. The force nearly lifted Ward from the ground. In agony, he tumbled back into the grass and tried to fight back. However, he was too slow. "Menace" Hillman retrieved Ward's Beretta from the ground and quickly held it against his ear.

'Take it easy, Ward,' he ordered, 'Any moves I don't like and I'll kill you. You should have died in that train. It would have looked like an accident. A technical fault with the electricity. Instead, you got away *again*. Only this time, you will die here in *cold blood*.'

"Menace" crouched down above Ward, his right knee on his chest to keep him on the floor. His left hand was positioned at his throat, and the other held the gun; the muzzle pressed against his head. Frank Ward looked up into the face of his enemy. The hawk eyes glinted underneath the lock of hair that had fallen from its place. "Menace" licked his dry lips.

'Say your prayers, spy,' the madman hissed with a heavy French accent. 'Draw in your final breath. This moment is going to be your last!'

Normally, Ward would have had a plan, a quick strategy thought up on the spur of the moment in order to escape. However, this time, none existed. Was he really going to die like this? Was his life about to be ended on a grassy hill with a single bullet to the head? Frank Ward sucked in his final breath and closed his eyes, waiting for the gunshot to ring in his ears and the bullet to penetrate his brain.

But no! That shot never came! Albert Dawson had managed to haul himself to his feet and silently creep up behind "Menace". Dripping with blood, the muscular built Texan dived upon the French killer, lunging at him with slow, heavy punches with his fists. He knocked him to the ground and wrestled with all the remaining strength in his body. Ward lifted his head from the ground and watched the violent struggle. He saw a glint of metal - the Beretta! Hillman had managed to get hold of the weapon. In a flash, the killer shoved the barrel of the pistol against Dawson's head, and at point blank distance, pulled the trigger.

'Albert!' Ward cried.

He watched his friend being launched backwards into the grass from the power of the shot. There was a single hole in the centre of his forehead like a third eye. The bullet had gone through the skull and into the brain, and out through the other side of his head. His face covered in blood, Albert Dawson fell to the ground, smashing his head against a rock.

Everything was still.

Dawson's head turned towards Ward who sat amazed and filled with grief. The once happy and genial face was now not smiling and the mouth was opened in surprise. One of his eyes was still open and staring at Ward, the other was closed. The tongue lolled from in between the red teeth. The lively, body that was always on the move was now limp and lifeless.

"Menace" Hillman looked at the gory body first, then at Frank Ward who was sitting up, shocked at seeing his friend being killed in a second. One moment he was alive and wrestling him, the next, he was lying on the ground, still and dead. The murderer was still holding the smoking gun.

Hillman got heavily to his feet and lifted Ward slightly off the ground by his collar. Ward was weak from the explosion and having seen his old friend die before him. He had no time to react and managed to catch a glimpse of the brutal predatory eyes before "Menace" slammed the barrel of the Beretta on the back of the skull. Frank Ward grunted and blinked several times before passing out. Hillman could hear police sirens nearby. They must be coming along with the ambulances to the bullet train.

"Menace" swore. They would find the body too quickly before he had time to get away. He would have to make Ward's and the other man's death look accidental. If he put them in the van and parked it on the other side of the tracks, another train would come and smash into them, thus destroying their bodies and any evidence. Pleased with his plan, Hillman slung the American over his shoulder and carried him back to the van parked in front of the tracks. He dumped Ward into the passenger seat and then made another journey back with the dead Albert Dawson, his limp arms dangling over Hillman's shoulder.

With both of them in the car, "Menace" got behind the wheel and tore away over the tracks and dumped the van on the other side of the tracks a mile or so away from the exploded *Shinkasen*. Hillman kicked open the door of the van and eased himself out of the seat. The unconscious Frank Ward was leaning against him. "Menace" could taste Ward's blood on his lips. He climbed out of the car, leaving the still alive secret agent lying over the two front seats, soaked in blood and mud. Within a few moments there would be a second 'accident', and there would be no remains of either Frank Ward or Albert Dawson left in existence. Nothing could connect him with their tragic deaths.

Smiling, "Menace" Hillman, Claude Victor's right - hand man sprinted away unseen towards Beijing where he would meet a contact there ready to take him back to Claude Victor's private offices. He was excited already at having the chance of explaining the terrific news to his boss.

Moments later, the police and ambulances arrived on the scene and began to search into what had happened, and to remove the injured and dead from the wreckage. Only a mile or so down the track was Frank Ward and the deceased Dawson, moments from being hit full pelt by a bullet train at high speed.

Minutes passed and slowly Frank Ward opened his eyes and looked around him. He knew instantly he was in a vehicle and felt the throbbing pains in his head. He could feel his hair matted with blood, and several stinging pains around his body. Uncomfortable, he shuffled his body, sat upright at the wheel and it was then he realised the situation he was in.

He found himself looking ahead at the train track. He mouthed a harsh obscenity and gripped the wheel tightly, his knuckles turning white. He could imagine the bullet train coming hurtling around the corner, the flashing lights and the brilliant noise of the electric powered machine.

Calm down, he told himself. *Just remain calm*. He breathed slowly and carefully and cleared his mind so he could concentrate. Taking in his surroundings, he frantically searched the ignition for a key.

To his surprise, it was still in the engine! "Menace" must have forgotten to remove it as he left! Quickly, he turned the key and felt the whole van vibrate and come to life in an instant. He could hear the roaring of the bullet train in the distance, moments from coming around the corner. Ward could see the glare of the lights coming towards him.

Wrapping his sweaty palms around the wheel, he turned sharply and slamming his foot down onto the accelerator, drove off the tracks and towards the steep grass banking beside it. The *Shinkasen* sped down the track seconds later and into the large, dark tunnel.

Frank Ward sighed and brought the vehicle to rest on the bank near the meadows and sucked in deep and exaggerated breaths of air. He sat there in the seat and covered his face with his hands.

What had happened? Albert was dead, and Ward himself was injured. He recovered after about ten minutes and searched the inside of his shoulder holster secured under the left armpit in search of his Beretta.

It was gone. "Menace" must have taken it.

Ward swore. He was bleeding, weapon-less and his Station C contact lay in the back of the van in a pool of blood as the process of rigor mortis began to engulf him. He had to sort himself out and get over to Beijing.

He couldn't be far away. It would only be a few minutes journey, perhaps. He remembered his promise to Linda Pascal - the cell phone telling her when to meet her at the Beijing opera. There she would help him get at Claude Victor. Determined to destroy Victor, his twisted scheme and his cruel enforcer, "Menace", Ward applied force on the pedals and cut through the empty crop fields towards Beijing.

He wasn't just after Victor as an assignment like any other. He had Gaëlle to avenge, Albert Dawson, and Linda, who had suffered greatly due to her sadist of a fiancé. Ward ground his teeth angrily.

'*I'll get you, Victor.*'

15/ THE BLUEPRINTS

LOOKING OUT THROUGH his office window, high up in the 50 storey sky scraper, Claude Victor looked down powerfully upon the city of Beijing below and instantly felt like God.

The cars and the people resembled colonies of ants, marching back and forth hurriedly. The other buildings and apartments below looked like dolls' houses, miniature and delicate. Victor felt, with a sinister chuckle, as if he could stamp down upon their houses and crush them into the dust, along with all the people inside. Soon, he thought, he would be God. Armed with the two nuclear warheads and the vital piece of missile guidance hardware stolen from the Americans in Hong Kong, he would eliminate hundreds, thousands, even millions of people in the human race. They would be as insignificant as ants! And all the while, Claude Victor, the billionaire, would become even richer and more successful!

Claude Victor laughed a demented, insane laugh, more of a dry witch's cackle combined with a tiger's roar. He felt the most powerful human being on the planet. Still with his morbid thoughts, the French industrialist walked back towards his desk across the wine-red carpet and poured himself a stiff drink from a bottle of Bourbon, adding two ice cubes. He stirred the drink slowly and carefully. He raised the liquid to his pale lips and swallowed half of the volume of the glass in one, solid gulp.

He returned the unfinished glass to the surface of his desk and collapsed into the comfortable leather office chair, and began sorting through the papers and documents on his neat desk. As he tried to read through the important pieces of paper, his mind wouldn't cooperate. Five minutes ago, he had been contacted by his reliable and loyal executer, Marcus Hillman, who had informed him of the long awaited news of Frank Ward's death! It had seemed that the ruthless CIA agent had met with an unfortunate accident when his car had got stuck on the tracks and hit by a bullet train, killing him and his passenger, Albert Dawson. Death had been instantaneous.

The smile hadn't left Victor's thin, ugly mouth since hearing of the news (smiles were very rare from Victor!). Now with his enemies clearly out of the way, he and his men could continue work on Operation Launch without delay. With only two days until the the operation comes into practice, Victor was making all the necessary arrangements. He had had the missile guidance system taken over to Victor's small island off the coasts of Beijing along with the two warheads. The equipment had also been installed.

His thoughts were interrupted by a harsh rapping on the modern, metal door. Victor looked up from the desk, and in a calm, unemotional voice said, 'Come in.'

The door opened and Linda Pascal came walking nervously into the room. She looked fantastic - she wore a cotton black and grey striped wrap over a long sleeved T-shirt, complemented by casual yet fashionable grey slacks. She wore little jewellery, just a few rings and a golden chain around her neck. Her face was divine as ever - her natural beauty showing through the small amounts of makeup added to the eyelashes, lips and cheeks.

Claude Victor was disappointed that the visitor was his fiancé, rather than "Menace". He was earnestly looking forward to congratulating him on killing Frank Ward.

'What do you want?' Claude Victor demanded harshly, 'You know I'm busy! Why don't you stay on the yacht rather than bothering me at my work?'

Linda said that she was sorry. 'I'll go in a minute; I just want to ask you where the Beijing opera is?'

'The what?'

'The Beijing opera,' she said quietly, 'originated in the 19th century. I figured that while you were doing business here, I might go and see it. There's nothing else to do!'

Claude Victor eyed her suspiciously and finally said, 'How am I supposed to know? Go and find out on the internet. I'm busy!'

Once Victor had finished ranting, the telephone buzzed and vibrated on his desk. Victor gave an irritated sigh and sucked in deep breaths of air through his crooked teeth and snatched the receiver.

'What?'

'I just thought that you might want to know, sir, that Marcus Hillman has just arrived outside. He says he wants to talk to you.'

Claude Victor smiled, 'I'll be down immediately.' He slammed the receiver down on the base and rose from his desk. 'I've got to go and talk to Mister Hillman. Go out somewhere and don't come here again. Got it?'

Linda nodded and watched as her cruel fiancé rushed out of the room. She could still hear his footsteps echoing down the corridor moments later.

She was all alone. Cautiously, Linda walked over to Victor's desk and pulled out one of the compartments.

The architecture blueprints of the offices must be in here, she decided. She had caught a glimpse of them before. She began searching through the cluttered drawer frantically, burying her hands through the folders and papers and pens.

It must be in here! She kept working solidly for the next six minutes, praying that Claude Victor would not walk through the door and catch her in the act. If he did, she would most certainly be punished severely for her actions and be lashed repeatedly with "The Corrector".

She shivered and her body went cold. Perhaps he would even live up to his threats of killing her in a brutal, violent way.

Eventually she found the piece of A3 blue paper, folded neatly into four. She laid it on the desk and unfolded it, using her hands to spread the paper across the table so she could read the writing. It was very detailed - it showed each room clearly on each floor, and where the CCTV cameras and hidden alarm systems were located.

Linda grinned. Frank would love it. She could hear footsteps approaching. Her heart skipped a beat, and for a moment, she didn't breathe. Then she returned to her senses and folded up the paper before stuffing it into her deep slack pockets. She jumped up out of the chair and made her way towards the door.

That very moment, Claude Victor emerged, his immaculate, finely tailored dark suit hanging horribly around his bony, crumpled frame. He shot a hard, icy stare at Linda and stepped into the room, followed by "Menace" Hillman, who was wearing dirty looking clothes and had a trace of dried blood on his face.

'I thought I told you to get out?' Victor shouted. He grabbed Linda roughly by the arm and pushed her over the threshold.

She winced in pain and turned towards her fiancé, but the door had been slammed shut.

Linda straightened her top and walked towards the exterior elevators, constructed with glass panelled cabs. The elevators would scale down the 50 - storey skyscraper in less than a minute, giving a fantastic view of Beijing. Linda pressed the number, stepped inside the cuboid shaped cab and removed her cell phone from her leather handbag. She checked her messages to see if she had received any texts.

Sure enough, there was one. She brought it up onto the miniature screen and found that it was from Frank Ward. It said to meet her at the

Summer Palace in Beijing where the opera house was located. The time was seven pm. Linda checked her watch. She had two hours to prepare herself.

The elevator stopped at the bottom of the offices. Excited, she walked out of the cab and found a taxi to take her to the coast where *Le dauphin* was docked.

Quarter to seven, Ward reflected, glancing briefly at his wrist watch. Linda should be here by now. The opera would start in fifteen minutes; if they were late in, they would be noticed by any of Victor's men (that's if they had followed her here).

Frank Ward stood outside the opera house built in the late 19th century under the instructions of Empress Dowanger Cixi inside the Summer Palace, which is mainly dominated by Longevity Hill and Kunming Lake. Ward decided it was a very magnificent and elegant palace. In its compact 70,000 square metres of building space, there are a selection of gardens, palaces, and other classical-style architectural structures and statues.

Beijing opera, known as *jing xi* in China, has been performed for about 200 years. It uses a combination of song, speech, music, mime and acrobatics. Clever use is made of a few pieces of scenery and props. Some of the most famous Beijing opera performers include Mei Langfang, Shang Xiaoyun and Cheng Yanqiu.

As Ward watched the tourists and Chinese opera lovers disappear inside the entrance of the opera house, he began to wonder if anything had gone wrong. Supposing Linda had been caught by her fiendish fiancé and tortured, or perhaps even *killed?* Or what if she had double crossed him and really been betraying him to Victor all along?

Surely not! Ward knew - he was almost certain - that Linda loved him and wanted a lasting relationship, just as he wished.

Ward straightened his suit and knew that he looked a bit scruffy. He had washed and showered but had no other clean clothes since his cases were left on the bullet train. He had driven the mini van into a quiet marsh area and had laid the corpse of his close friend in the high grass where it would gradually decompose silently. He had found it hard to leave him; the eye that was still open seemed to watch Ward as he returned to the car. Now, Ward was entirely on his own - Station C had lost track of him and he was currently unable to contact Cartwright at the CIA Langley Headquarters in Virginia.

With five minutes to go, Linda Pascal appeared from the busy throng heading towards the main entrance. She was smiling and looked terrific, wearing somewhat formal looking garments.

Linda Pascal obviously wanted to dress up for the opera and feel comfortable in stylish and expensive clothes. As Ward watched her approach him, he felt very uncomfortable about his creased dark jacket and crumpled cotton shirt and tie. All the other male guests were wearing black tuxedos or elegant dinner jackets and cummerbunds. Linda was wearing a long dress of heavy scarlet silk which ended diagonally a few inches above her feet on which Linda wore high stilettoed black shoes. The upper cut of the dress showed the top half of her perfectly formed breasts and the expensive material showered her fantastic figure perfectly. She wore a priceless sparkling diamond necklace and matching square earrings. Linda had applied red nail varnish to her fingers and toes. She wore little makeup on her face - Ward was glad - (he disliked it when women overdid makeup; it made them look tarty, like prostitutes). However, the makeup that she wore, the eyeliner and the lipstick, looked perfect. She carried a small, discreet leather handbag.

'I'm sorry I'm late,' Linda said, 'I've been in a bit of a rush. I wanted to make sure that Claude wouldn't find the blueprints. I took a lot of precautions.'

Ward embraced her and gave her a soft kiss on her right cheek. 'I see that you have managed to get it.'

'Of course I have. I managed to take it from his desk before he returned. I don't think he suspected anything - I just hope he doesn't notice it's gone missing.'

'So do I,' Ward admitted, feeling ashamed of himself for ever doubting Linda's bravery and loyalty. 'We'd better get in,' he announced after consulting his watch a second time, 'the opera will start in a few minutes. You can give me the paper in there. Somebody might see us out here. Hopefully everybody's eyes will be on the stage and not on us.'

Linda nodded. 'Shall we get inside then?'

Ward acquiesced immediately and handed their tickets to the man standing by the door. He escorted them towards their reserved seats near the back of the theatre, supplying a perfect view of the performance. Frank Ward sat down in his seat and adjusted himself so that he was comfortable. Linda sat beside him. Ward flicked through the programme sheet placed on his chair and looked at the synopsis of the opera. It was called *Beauty*, and apparently is one of the most famous Chinese of operas. It tells the true tale of a kidnapped princess who dies for her country.

Ward turned towards Linda, 'When it starts and everybody is looking at the show, hand me the blueprints. Do you think that you have been followed?'

Linda shook her head decisively, 'I doubt it,' she said, 'I was careful and looked to see if Claude had sent his goons to follow me. I'm sure he hasn't.'

'We don't know,' Ward replied, 'so act as normal as possible and don't attract attention to us.'

'Okay.'

The music started; a cymbal and gong played dramatically for a few moments. This was followed by wooden clappers and the *huquin*, a two - stringed fiddle. The heroine of the opera, the *dan*, came on stage wearing a colourful red Oriental robe and headgear, the face painted in bright colours. The *dan* was played by a male; in Beijing opera, all female characters are played by men. The *dan* character began to sing, throwing "her" voice across the room. The heroine was joined by more characters, a *sheng*, a male character and a *chou*, the clown. After the song concluded, the audience clapped. During the applause, Linda opened her handbag and handed Ward the neatly folded piece of blue paper.

Ward took the paper in his hand and quickly unfolded it. He studied the detailed map and took note of all the security alarms and guard posts. He then knew that breaking into this building would be much harder than he had anticipated. He turned towards Linda and whispered, 'Which would be the best way to get in?'

Linda bit her lip, thoughtfully, 'The place is heavily guarded. There are security men posted on every entrance and exit. CCTV cameras are also installed in a few of the major corridors. There are even some invisible hidden lasers that, when broken, trigger an alarm. I don't know how you can get in.'

'I *must*,' Ward insisted, 'I have only days to find out what Victor is really up to before Operation Launch begins. We have to stop him for America, you and I.'

Linda sighed and looked concerned. 'But how will you get inside? With the Chinese gangster dead, Victor is suspicious of everything.'

'Not any more.'

'What?'

'Victor thinks I'm dead - he has no more worries about his plans being found out. All I need to do is act as one of the staff and sneak inside unnoticed.'

'I don't understand,' Linda said.

Ward consulted the A3 sized map and pointed to something with his finger, 'The map shows that there is a small alleyway beside the building where suppliers unload goods to the neighbouring factory. Supposing I wait until somebody comes out of the building? I knock the person out and take his security clearance. Nobody would even notice me.'

Linda smiled, 'I like it. Usually people go out every hour for a smoke. If you can get one person alone, then you can get the pass card.'

'What about you? Will you be there.'

'Yes,' she answered, 'I'll be at the offices tonight until three in the morning; that's when Claude returns back to *Le dauphin* to sleep. I'll be there if you get into any trouble.'

'I won't.'

'Good.' Ward smiled and shoved the blueprints into his trouser pocket. He turned around and clasped Linda's hand in his as they watched the remainder of the opera together in silence.

16/ NIGHT DUTY

AT TWO IN the morning in the urban streets of Beijing, the air had become much colder than in the afternoon and the streets were less busy with people and traffic.

No noises existed, only the few cars passing through, and men and women returning from local nightclubs. Frank Ward sat crouched in the corner of the neighbouring alleyway next to Claude Victor's Kraken International Cooperartion offices. He had got rid of his Italian suit and now, instead, wore a casual black turtle neck sweater and some loose fitting slacks. He felt more comfortable and able to move quicker and faster in his new clothes. He had purchased them from a cheap clothes shop, emptying most of the contents of his wallet.

Ward had been waiting in the damp corner beside the large green paper bin for at least half an hour. He hadn't been watching the time. Instead he had been watching the large double doors leading out into the alleyway where staff on the night duty would come out during their break and have a crafty cigarette. It was then that he would pounce; pounce like a cat on the mouse. He had been idly twirling his Beretta 84FS Cheetah around his index finger whilst he was waiting, so that if anybody was to appear, he could quickly slam a magazine into the cartridge and fire away.

Of course, he didn't want to do that. This particular job required stealth and stealth only - Ward didn't want to use his Beretta - silenced or not. He didn't want to be seen at all or shoot. A silenced gun could still be heard, and also the painful screams as a man falls sluggishly to the floor.

Frank Ward reflected on his day. *What a busy day it had been!* First his unexpected meeting with Linda, followed by the breakfast, the bomb explosion, Albert's death and the opera. He was sure he was getting closer now to destroying Claude Victor's cruel and sadistic plans. Once he knew the details of the mysterious Operation Launch, he could act - and quickly! He could finally defeat the master criminal and stop the whole scheme. Ward thought of the people who had died because of Victor - Gaëlle and Albert Dawson, two of the people who were very close to him. Victor had tortured Linda regularly and brought pain and suffering to those who upset him. He deserved to die. Ward was determined to wreak revenge and destroy the two people hw hated most in the world - Victor and his powerful bodyguard "Menace" Hillman.

Ward had everything he needed. As well as his Beretta, he had three spare clips that he kept in his holster, the lock pick given to him by Gaëlle Dumas, the blueprint map, a gadget called the finger print scanner and his messy knife, only to be used in emergencies. He felt prepared for any situation that he might face during the next few hours, for what could perhaps be one of the most difficult and dangerous jobs he had ever undertaken since working for the CIA. Ward knew that he was risking his life, but he wasn't afraid of doing so. Ward had risked his life many times during his career in the Army, and also in the American intelligence organisation.

Ward looked around him again at the spacious alleyway. It was quite long in width and length, enabling large cargo trucks to reverse and unload packages and crates into the factory next door. The alley was shared between both buildings. Around his hiding place were a couple of empty cardboard boxes, somewhat crushed and collapsed in the rain, litter and two rectangular dustbins, one for recycling paper and the other for waste.

It was in that instant that there came some footsteps from nearby, barely audible, but Ward heard them.

Since he had first joined the American Army, his ears had become very sensitive, to sounds of danger and any human sound. He was like an animal, a prey, listening as a predator approached. In less than two seconds, Frank Ward had attached the silencer onto the muzzle of the Beretta and inserted a fresh clip into the gun, loaded with six rounds. He directed the gun towards the double doors and watched as they opened with a deep sigh. A medium sized Chinese man came out of the building, wearing a business - like suit and square rimmed spectacles. The man coughed and walked over towards the green bin where Ward was hiding. He looked up into the starry sky and withdrew a cheap packet of cigarettes from his pocket and lit one. He inserted it between his lips and puffed on it excitedly, drawing the smoke deep inside him. He stood there for a few movements, leaning against the stone wall behind him, occasionally tapping the ash off the end of his cigarette. He had no idea of the man crouched inches away.

Ward prepared himself and waited until the right moment when the man turned his head in the other direction. Frank Ward then lifted himself to his feet and appeared to fly over to where the staff member was standing. The man in the suit managed to mumble a startled cry and tried to get a glimpse of his attacker before Ward pushed his face downwards into the top of the large industrial dustbin. There came a sickening splat as the face hit the plastic bin and Ward knew that with the amount of force applied, he had knocked the man out stone cold.

The man began to slide off the bin, his limp arms dangling over the edges. Ward grabbed the man by his collar and turned him over. The man's face was bloody, his cheek was cut and the nose looked broken. Ward reached down towards the laminated security tag attached onto the man's jacket collar. Quickly and efficiently, Ward tugged it off and clipped it onto his own turtle neck sweater. Now he had the security pass, he would be able to walk through the corridors without anybody realising that he was an intruder. Ward slipped the Beretta back into his pocket and lifted the lid of the dustbin. He placed the unconscious man over the rim of the bin and dumped him inside where he fell amongst the rubbish.

'Goodnight,' Ward said calmly before slamming the lid back down and locking it in place.

Nobody would discover the unconscious man for hours at least. That gave Ward plenty of time to get what he wanted and then escape.

Frank Ward moved over to the large double doors where the staff member had just come through. Ward disappeared inside and found himself in a long corridor alone. The walls were surfaced in modern - looking silver tiles and the floor was carpeted in dark blue plush. The offices, as Ward expected, were very up -to - date. Ward walked slowly down the passageway as normally as he could, whilst trying to listen for sounds or look out for anything important. He went through the door at the end of the passageway and followed the signs that directed him up a small staircase towards the outside elevators. Ward looked around him cautiously and unfolded the architect's map, before carefully consulting it.

Claude Victor's room would be on the top floor of the Kraken International Cooperation Headquarters.

Ward replaced the map in its place and crossed the hallway to the elevators, ignoring the security guard who seemed to be looking at him. Ward swallowed and hoped the man hadn't noticed the bulge of the Beretta as he stepped inside the glass constructed lift. Ward looked at the magnificent view all around him. He could see all the building lights below. Feeling slightly nauseous and dizzy, Ward remembered that he was thousands of feet up in the air. Ward selected his floor and watched as the doors closed together. The elevator began to ascend and scale the skyscraper.

Moments later it stopped and the doors retracted. Frank Ward stepped out of the elevator and into a large square room filled with desks all occupied by hard - working staff looking at the computer monitor screens. Few of them looked up to see who had entered the room and Ward simply passed from one side to the other without raising any suspicions at all. Ward kept his eyes open all the time, observing everything and noting everything mentally that might be of any significance. He also memorised the locations of the elevators and where all the doors were in case he needed a speedy escape. Once he had scanned the room for anything of importance, he passed through another hallway.

Ward didn't see anybody as he passed through, and eventually came to a door that had a sign next to it. It read:

"PRIVATE!
ONLY HIGH - RANKING PERSONNEL
PERMITTED ENTRY."

The notice was written again below in Chinese. Ward grasped the handle and tried it. As he had expected, it was firmly locked. Ward tilted his head to the left and then to the right to check if anybody was watching him from behind. Satisfied that there was nobody around, Ward's hand vanished into his pocket and reappeared again holding the lock pick. He inserted the device into the keyhole and fumbled it around delicately for no less than twelve seconds before the door swung open and Ward disappeared swiftly through it.

Ward returned the lock pick to its place and made one or two nervous steps into the corridor before he heard voices approaching. He immediately confirmed that one belonged to non other than Marcus "Menace" Hillman. He could recognise the deep, forceful tone of Hillman's husky voice.

As the sounds became more audible, Ward realised that Hillman would see through the disguise and promptly recognise him as the spy whom he believed had perished yesterday afternoon.

Ward turned and ran to his left, hiding behind a wall, surfaced in immaculate, shiny tiles. He flattened his body against it, keeping his back straight and his arms close to him so as not to expose them. He didn't want to get caught now that he was so close to finding out the details of Claude Victor's devilish scheme.

Marcus Hillman came around the corner briskly, a large stylish black suit covering his muscular, intimidating frame. He was talking to a Chinese gentleman wearing a blue shirt and a golden tie. They were talking about something which Ward didn't quite catch. Hillman stopped suddenly and looked in Ward's direction with his watchful hawk eyes. For a few seconds, Ward's heart temporarily seemed to stop and perspiration gathered on his palms and under his armpits. "Menace" Hillman then turned towards the man next to him and they disappeared through the door on their right.

Frank Ward forced his head to look past the wall, his silenced Beretta held tightly in his other hand. Whilst he watched his enemy vanish from sight, he partly wished that he had emptied the whole magazine into Hillman's skull. He was glad he resisted. He was here to find out about the mysterious Operation Launch, not to kill Victor's chief executioner.

That would come at another time.

Ward moved out of his hiding place, certain that he was entirely alone, and scanned the signs on each door either side of him, for the private study of Claude Victor, the wealthy industrialist and mass murderer. After reading the signs on twenty doors, he located the room.

Excitement crept up his body and a smile formed on his face. Minute by minute he was drawing ever closer to completing his assignment and destroying Claude Victor. He wrapped his fingers around the handle with his left hand and held his gun in the other, supposing that the occupant of the office was inside. Ward rested his shaky finger on the curve of the combat - style trigger and after counting to three, pushed against the door with all his weight and jumped into the room.

Immediately he spun his gunning arm around, and focused his aim on the high - backed leather chair behind the large square desk, in the far end corner of the room. He stared at the spot and imagined the figure of Claude Victor sitting there, a sinister smile transfixed on the hideous white flesh, the fish eyeballs open wide and gazing at him. He thought of the snarling lips and the revolting animal breath and the skeletal, bony hand that should belong to a dead man.

However the figure was not there. The man Ward *despised* was not there, sitting in the leather reclining chair. Nobody was in the office except Ward, standing there with his legs apart and his arms outstretched, the Beretta handgun aimed at an invisible man. Finally, Frank Ward realised that there was nobody there and slowly put the gun away.

He looked around him at the spacious office. Apart from the desk and the chair, there was a neat row of metal filing cabinets lined up against the wall, a small glass table with four low blue armchairs surrounding it and a small box - like fridge behind the desk, no doubt to keep Victor's finest liquors and Bollinger champagne inside. The walls, like the rest of the interior building, were tiled in silver and the carpet was plush. A portable laptop computer was assembled on Victor's desk with a telephone next to it and IN and OUT trays. Ward made another check on the room for anything he might have not noticed. It was then that he saw a wall safe above one of the filing cabinets.

Just what Frank Ward had been looking for!

He moved over to the safe and upon closer inspection, realised that the safe was not locked by a combination, but by a thumb print device. There was a small pad on the front door of the safe on which a person would put their thumb. An inbuilt processor would then recognise the print and unlock the safe. Ward figured that the scanner was only programmed to recognise Victor and Hillman's finger- prints. From reading the blueprints, Ward knew that all safes and a few doors (those that led into the laboratories) were locked by finger- print readers. That was why Ward had brought along his finger print scanner device.

The finger - print scanner was a standard piece of equipment to all C.I.A agents in the Directorate of Operations Department. In recent years, fewer doors were locked by key and most are locked by thumb print readers. This is why the C.I.A manufactures such a device. Ward usually kept it with him at all times, as he would never know when it might be required. He had to admit that it was a useful tool. The Weaponry and Gadgetry Department had certainly surpassed themselves this time. The device was no more than ten centimetres long, a small rectangular machine with a miniature screen for copying the prints left on the scanner. It had all the Criminal Records programmed in its microchip, so that any criminal prints would be recognised.

Quickly, Ward reached up to the safe and pressed the screen on his device against the scanner. He waited for a few short seconds while the gadget copied the print last recorded. The Criminal Records identified the print as Marcus Hillman's. The safe then unlocked and Ward abruptly snatched the contents in his hands and dropped them on Victor's desk. He sat down and sorted through the papers, discarding the irrelevant documents into a separate pile to return to the safe. At last, he came across something interesting. It was entitled 'Operation Launch'. Ward flattened the paper on the desk and brought his eyes closer to the text. He began to read:

Operation Launch - The Final Schedule
Issued to all members of the operation

HIGHLY CLASSIFIED

The two nuclear warheads will be taken on *Le dauphin* to the island HQ along with the missile guidance hardware on the 5th April 07. Six members of the Chinese Triads are required on board to keep watch. Marcus Hillman and myself will also be on board. The rest of the men will already be at the island base, having all the required equipment installed inside. Upon arrival, the warheads will be loaded into the cruise missiles and prepared for firing in the launching area. With the guidance system set up, the coordinates of Taiwan, U.S.A and Tokyo, Japan (Ward's mouth opened in shock) will be programmed inside the machine. The warheads will then be promptly launched into the sky. The estimated time until the missiles meet their targets is three hours. Once destruction of the target has taken place, the whole island will be destroyed before any further evidence is found. The Chinese Triads will receive the final payment for their services and will return to Hong Kong before the police and intelligence organisations realise the partnership.

Thank you,

C. Victor

Frank Ward sat dumbfounded, still staring at the piece of paper. So that was what Operation Launch was about! Claude Victor was going to destroy Taiwan and Tokyo tomorrow, killing millions and wiping out everything in the cities!

Oh hell, oh hell, oh hell! But why? What motive has Victor got? Why has he spent a large portion of his fortune hiring criminal societies to steal warheads and the missile guidance hardware? He must have some reason as to why he is doing this! As Ward thought it all over in his mind, he couldn't explain it. The schedule mentioned no extortion or blackmail letters or video tapes. If extortion was Victor's motive, his terms would already have been received by both the American President and the

Japanese Head of State. Ward would have had news of this if it was the case; Cartwright would have contacted him or he would have heard it in the media.

Ward's mouth was dry and his head ached. He couldn't believe that Claude Victor intended to destroy two of the largest and most important cities in the world! If Victor pulled this off he would be the most feared terrorist of all time.

But no, Ward thought. Nobody would know that Victor was responsible. Everybody sees Victor as an inspiration and a lover of the world and science and the environment. Nobody would know that Victor is in fact one of the world's notorious gangsters.

That was another motive out of the way. Power. Victor doesn't want anybody to know that it is he who will fire the warheads. He wants to sit back and watch the chaos he has caused unfold, and know deep down that he is the responsible one.

So how does he benefit from it all? Is he just a sick - minded, homicidal maniac, obsessed with death? *No*, Ward decided. Operation Launch had been well calculated and excellently thought out. A maniac couldn't have planned it so well as Victor.

Claude Victor must have a logical reason, some way of benefiting hugely from millions of people dying.

Frank Ward knew that he would have the answer tomorrow before the warheads were fired. He just didn't understand it all right now, but he knew that Claude Victor wasn't going to succeed.

Fwip. Ward didn't realise what the faint noise was until he looked down onto the document and noticed a perfectly rounded bullet hole in the corner. The shot had gone through the paper and barely missed his shoulder. Ward looked up and saw the uniformed guard standing half in the doorway, a silenced firearm directed towards him. The Chinese guard advanced into the room, closing on Ward and gradually trapping him in the corner of the room like a captured mouse. The guard resumed aim and Ward hurled himself to the ground, using the large bulk of the solid office desk as a shield. He lay on his chest and found time to remove his Beretta from its place and locate the trigger. He used his sensitive hearing to determine how close the guard was to him. He could hear the soft footsteps on the sapphire - blue plush and the soft, almost unnatural breathing as the security man drew closer. Ward estimated the distance between the two men and positioned himself with his back against the desk. He sucked in deep breaths of air and as the guard stood behind the desk, Ward pushed back with all his might.

The desk fell over, Ward's weight having pushed it off balance. The great metal topped desk crashed down onto the floor with a loud thud, catching the security man off guard and forcing him to retreat backwards to avoid being hit by the falling desk.

This was Ward's opportunity to get out.

He jumped up to his feet and pounced at the guard, wrapping the fingers of his right hand around the man's throat and wrestling the gun away with his other. Ward's powerful fingers dug into the guard's flesh and he pushed his hand far back, twisting his wrist. In pain, the guard was forced to drop the firearm to the floor. Frank Ward applied pressure to the man's neck, making him make a few desperate gargling noises. The two men grappled fiercely, struggling and hitting each other at any given chance . The guard managed to lunge at Ward with his fist which Ward easily blocked, resulting in Ward driving his knee into the man's chest with all his might.

The man grunted like a wounded bull and tumbled to the ground in agony. The guard crawled over to his dropped weapon which lay at arms length ahead. He spun around clumsily in search of his target. The intruder had vanished through the threshold, and now the door was wide open. The guard swallowed and removed his walkie - talkie from its place and contacted the rest of his security colleagues. Once one of the men answered, the injured guard began to talk rapidly in Chinese, giving a detailed and full description of the American spy.

Frank Ward sprinted non-stop through the corridors, getting as far away from Victor's office as possible. He ignored the people staring at him, and some noticed the metal object in his hand. A woman cried out and alerted a nearby guard to him.

Ward didn't care. He just wanted to get away.

He sprinted, barging past people in his way and keeping a look out for any opposing security men sent to intercept him.

How could I get away, he thought. *Guards would be sent to block off all exits and elevators.* He was trapped!

Ward kept on running madly, trying to retrace his footsteps as best he could. Guards were pouring into the corridor behind him and came bursting through the heavy steel doors. Lead slugs hit the doors and walls all around him, some denting the steel tiles that framed the wall. The noise was deafening. Ward didn't attempt to stop and let off a few shots. He collided with a guard who was running towards him, signalling him to stop with his gun. Frank Ward barged into him like a rugby player tackling a member of the opposition and sent the man sprawling to the ground.

Following the signs, Ward managed to stay clear of the areas where he thought guards would be waiting for him. The hallway with the elevator cubicles was one of them. He disappeared through a heavy door and slammed it shut behind him, sliding the heavy bolt across.

He could hear the angry security men behind the door shouting and trying to smash the door down with their feet. Their attempts failed.

Ward was now alone in a long hallway with only a few doors on either side of the walls. They didn't look particularly important - Ward decided that they were storage rooms or something of that sort. He slumped against the wall and ran his fingers through his hair. He didn't know how he would get out alive. Ward tried to plan a meticulous strategy of what to do. His cover was blown and the alarm raised. Everybody in the building was most likely on alert by now and hunting him down.

At first Ward didn't notice the door nearest to him open slightly. He was too busy concentrating, but his eyes were experienced and he managed to notice the person emerge quietly from behind the door. He felt for the Beretta and spun around quickly, prepared to take out the guard with a silent shot to the head.

But no. It wasn't a guard at all.

Linda Pascal came over the threshold, still wearing the dress she had worn last night to the opera. Her face was pale at the sight of him. Ward knew that she was concerned.

'Frank - what's happened?'

Ward looked up and dropped the gun to the floor. 'I nearly shot you.'

Linda ignored him. 'Have you find out what you wanted?' She enquired.

'Yes,' he replied, 'but I was caught. Victor's men are after me.'

'How are we going to get out.'

Frank Ward put his head in his hands and tried to think. He puzzled ideas over in his mind until one suddenly struck him. An idea had come into his head, an idea that might *just* work.

'We're going in the elevator,' announced Ward getting slowly to his feet.

Linda's mouth opened in surprise. 'That's the first place where security will be waiting. You can't just walk into the elevator.'

'No,' said Ward calmly, 'We're going to jump inside.'

Linda didn't understand and turned around to watch Ward, who was firing several rounds into the large rectangular window. A huge spider web formed in the reinforced glass and Ward gave it a mighty kick that destroyed it. He grabbed hold of the frame and easily lifted himself up so that he was standing on the outside of the skyscraper building, his back flattened against the wall.

'What are you doing?'

Ward ignored her and made sure that he was perfectly balanced. He was on the highest floor of the fifty storey building. One slip and he would tumble to his death. He bent his legs so that he had more control over his body before he turned his head and extended his hand out for Linda to touch.

'Give me your hand.'

'What are you doing?' She repeated.

'Trust me.'

Linda swallowed and looked up into the greyish blue eyes of the man she loved. Obediently she placed her hand in his and he helped her up onto the ledge beside him.

'We're going to jump and smash through the glass roof of the elevator cubicle. When we're inside, we ride it down before anyone can stop us.'

'No Frank,' she insisted, '*Please*. We'll get killed.'

Ward's face was sombre. 'If we stay here any longer, we'll get killed. It would be a lot more painful than if we were to fall. Claude Victor is a sadist, he'll torture us before we die. We *must* take this chance - it's our only chance of surviving.'

Linda was still very uncertain and she shivered several times. Her whole body, especially her hands, was shaking violently with fear. Ward was scared himself and was aware of the possibilities of death. He just didn't show it so that Linda felt calmer. Gently, he put his right arm around her back and pulled her close to him so that her head was against his stomach. Ward, holding Linda in his arms tightly, confidently leapt off the ledge and descended down a full storey. Linda screamed, terrified as they drew ever closer to the ground. Ward braced himself and gritted his teeth as they fell above the glass elevator.

There was a terrific splintering of glass as the two people crashed through the thickened glass that was the roof of one of the outside elevators. The glass gave way under their bodies and still clinging desperately to each other, Frank Ward and Linda Pascal landed in the elevator. Most of the fall had been absorbed by the glass roof, preventing the bottom from smashing under their weight. Ward jumped to his feet before the guards standing in the hallway could react. They all stared with their eyes wide at the two figures standing in the elevator. It took them seconds to realise that Ward was the intruder and they had just jumped from a storey height into the lift.

One security man went quickly for his gun, shouting: 'Shoot the man! Don't harm the lady; she's Victor's girlfriend!'

Ward rolled to the side of the elevator and stabbed at the DOWN button on the control panel. The great, heavy doors rolled into place together, the bullets rebounding off the inch - thick metal. Taking in deep breaths, Ward selected the bottom floor. As the elevator gradually went down the skyscraper office building, Frank Ward turned around and faced Linda, the woman he loved and cared for so passionately. She was smiling.

She took Ward by surprise and wrapped her arms around his neck tightly and locked her lips affectionately on his. Eventually Ward pulled away and looked hungrily into her eyes, a startled smile having crept upon his lips.

'What was that for?'

'For saving my life,' she replied. She embraced him tightly, nestling her head against his.

Ward said quietly, 'Remind me to do it more often.'

Linda chuckled. They continued hugging until the elevator reached the bottom floor, which was mainly the reception area. The doors opened and the two lovers stepped out into the night. Whilst Ward had been busy infiltrating the offices, it had begun to rain lightly. The damp road glistened in the street lamps floods of light.

'Do you have a car?' Ward asked.

'Yes, it's parked just down the road.'

'Good.'

They sprinted together, getting as far away from the building as possible. Ward knew that Victor would send some of his men after them at any second. They had to get away. They located Linda's car, a red Mercedes - Benz E - Class Saloon. It was a quiet elegant car - the exterior boasted a V- shape front grille and bumper, distinctive front fog lamps, matching side -skirts, and a set of alloy wheels.

Ward turned towards Linda. 'Do you have the keys?'

Linda tossed the keys to Ward who caught them easily in his palm and unlocked the vehicle automatically. He climbed into the driver's seat and noted how comfortable the seats were. The seats inside looked attractive - designed in sand - coloured leather and black. The driver's seat included a manual lumbar support. He started the engine immediately and gripped the wheel tightly. He slammed his feet down heavily on the accelerator even before Linda had closed the door of the passage seat beside him. He pushed the car from zero to sixty two miles per hour in eight seconds, sped down the reasonably empty road, and didn't slow down until he turned around the corner.

Ward knew as he put the gear on its highest level that he was in for a difficult and dangerous car pursuit.

17/ PURSUIT THROUGH BEIJING

'WHAT THE HELL is going on?' Claude Victor demanded angrily He looked around him first at the crumpled figure on the floor, twisting in agony and then at the open door of the safe. He snatched his expensive cell phone up from the desk and dialled the number of his Head of Security, Marcus "Menace" Hillman. There was no answer at this moment.

An intruder had been in his office and broken into his safe.

Victor walked over to the wall safe whilst he waited for "Menace" to answer. He examined the door carefully. It had obviously not been forced with a hammer or anything of the sort. The finger print scanner device must have been manipulated. But how?

The ringing tone ended and a muffled voice came onto the line. 'Yes, boss?' Hillman answered in a breathless voice.

'*Who* has been in my office?' Victor demanded. '*Why* are there guards swarming the building? *What* the hell is happening!'

Hillman attempted to calm his employer. 'An intruder has been here, sir. I've sent the men to locate the perpetrator. Guards are on full alert. It appears that he has escaped. Don't worry, we'll get him before he gets away.'

'*Merde!*' Victor swore in French. 'Look, "Menace", this intruder can only be one man - Frank Ward!'

Hillman was confused. 'But sir-.'

Claude Victor interrupted his chief enforcer before he could finish. 'Yes I know,' Victor snarled, 'Frank Ward is apparently dead. But did you ever see him die? Did you watch him get killed by that damn train? He's alive you stupid idiot!'

'But-.'

'Just shut up and get out there with a few company sedans. Take the helicopter too and make sure that you kill him this time. If you mess this up again, you can guarantee a fitting punishment! Do you understand?'

'Yes, sir.'

'Now get after him!'

'Yes, sir. Right away.' The line went dead and a faint continuous humming sound followed.

Claude Victor stood frozen in his office, his great fish eyes bulging out of their sockets and his crooked, yellowed teeth clenched tightly. In a sudden fit of anger and rage, Victor hurled his expensive cell phone across the room at the metal tiled wall where it smashed against it. There was a loud noise as it hit the wall and fell onto the floor in several pieces. Then, Victor grunted and slammed his fist down on the surface of his desk belligerently.

** *

Outside the office building, possibly no less than a mile away, Frank Ward had managed to maintain a speed of ninety which he would cut down to forty or fifty on the corners and turns, depending how sharp they were.

Linda's fingers dug into the leather passenger seat. She looked uncomfortable and constantly glanced at the speedometer to monitor how fast Ward was going.

'Don't you think you're going a bit too fast?' Linda asked, nervously.

Frank Ward didn't answer for a few moments; he was concentrating hard on the road with his ruthless, sapphire - blue eyes. His hands were holding the wheel lightly as he manoeuvred around a right hand turn at sixty, constantly checking the rear - view mirror above his head to see if Victor's men were on his tail.

As he reached a straight road, he found time to answer Linda's question: 'No,' he said firmly and stubbornly, 'Victor's men will be behind us any second. You keep your eyes locked on the mirror and tell me if you see them.'

'Err… okay,' Linda replied in an shaky stutter.

They continued their escape whilst Ward occasionally applied more pressure on the accelerator, increasing the speed. Luckily for him, the Mercedes saloon had good handling and responded very well to his sudden jerks of the wheel. Ward noted that if he ever decided to get rid of his beloved Chevrolet Corvette, he may consider replacing it with a Mercedes - Benz E- Class saloon. With a top speed of one hundred and forty miles per hour and a 4 - cylinder in- line engine, it could be a suitable car to suit Ward's fast-driving hobby.

Meanwhile, three black sedans poured out from the large underground car park below the Kraken International Cooperation offices in pursuit of the intruder. On the roof of the modern skyscraper complex, Claude Victor's Robinson R.44 private helicopter was lifted from the helipad by the whirling overhead rotor blades. The aircraft hovered in the air for a few seconds before the pilot in the cabin headed forward with the dual controls. Victor had chosen the helicopter as his own private aircraft because of its modern design and excellent performance. It also seated up to three passengers and could cruise in the sky at a speed of one hundred knots. This was especially helpful in this case - tracking down Frank Ward, the CIA spy.

Marcus "Menace" Hillman was behind the wheel of one of the black sedans below, constantly in contact with the helicopter above. The pilot's job was to try and spot him and report the whereabouts to Hillman and the other sedan drivers. It had been discovered that Ward had taken Linda Pascal's Mercedes, suggesting that she was with him. Victor had given Hillman and his team of men orders to kill Ward but not harm her. Victor explained that he would rather have that pleasure himself, of torturing her with "The Corrector." Hillman knew that he couldn't allow Ward to escape this time. He had already made that mistake once, and if he made it again, Victor would most certainly punish him severely.

'...I think I see it,' buzzed a voice on the walkie - talkie transmitter, 'The red Mercedes - Benz! It's just two streets away.'

The helicopter pilot then proceeded to inform Hillman and the other two sedan drivers of the directions. "Menace" Hillman smiled wolfishly and followed them implicitly, staying together with the other two cars. As the slick vehicles hurtled around the next bend, the fleeing Mercedes was in sight.

** *

Linda took a brief look up into the rear - view mirror and noticed the three black sedans a few cars behind, driving recklessly and blaring the horn aggressively.

Surely these were Claude's men, she decided.

As she looked more closely, she recognised the frightening figure of Marcus Hillman hunched over the wheel in the nearest vehicle. Her guess had just been confirmed. She nudged Frank Ward urgently as he overtook the car in front.

'Frank - Victor's menare following us. Mister Hillman's with them!'

Ward darted a sudden glance at Linda and checked in the mirror to make sure that she was correct. '"*Menace*",' hissed Ward through clenched teeth.

Ward slammed his foot down on the pedals much harder, almost flooring the accelerator. Linda shrank back in her seat and watched as the needle flickered on the hundred mark. The tyres screeched at an incredibly high pitch as Ward jerked the wheel suddenly to the left and drove up onto the pavement with two wheels, forcing a Chinese couple to jump out of the way in order to avoid the Mercedes. Ward stayed on the pavement until he had overtaken three cars and then turned back onto the road, now much further in front of the sedans in pursuit.

Frank Ward could hear the whirring of helicopter rotors above him and leaned forward so that he could look up clearly through the windscreen and into the starry sky. Sure enough, he could make out the white outline of a private passenger helicopter from underneath, hovering above the road.

Must be after us too, Ward presumed.

He continued, the engine roaring enthusiastically and the wheel obeying his demands. The sedans occasionally drew back at the traffic lights when they were good to Ward, allowing him to get far ahead. However, they did come back too and used Ward's own technique to drive up onto the pavement and overtake. All the while, the sedan drivers, especially "Menace" blared their horns and shouted abuse to other motorists as they refused to let them past.

'Watch it Frank,' Linda warned biting her lip, 'One of the cars is getting a bit close.'

Ward's eyes shot up into the mirror and then focused immediately back on the road. 'Tell me if any get any closer than this or pull a gun or something.'

Linda nodded and acquiesced. *It was going to be difficult to lose them*, she thought.

*** *

Marcus "Menace" Hillman clenched the steering wheel tightly in his awesome grip, his long, muscular fingers wrapped around the leather. His fiendish eyes were locked on his target ahead, Frank Ward.

The man was an enigma, Hillman thought. For once, he had a worthy adversary, who was proving himself to be a real challenge, and a competitive, fighting opponent. But Hillman smiled.

No man was a match for "Menace", he smirked. *He* was the best.

Hillman made sure that he was in no danger of losing control and turned around, facing the back seat where two Chinese gunman were sitting, cleaning their Browning with a piece of ragged material. They examined their magazines with their sunken eyes and practised aiming like only professional killers would do. They rested their heads against the rests and eagerly waited for their chance to get some shooting practice at the Mercedes tyres. *It would be a challenge to hit them at such high speed*, the killers decided.

'When I tell you to do so,' Hillman ordered firmly, 'lower your windows and shoot when we are in range. Aim at the tyres and the petrol tank if possible. Make it look like an accident. With Operation Launch a day away, Victor doesn't want to take any chances.'

'Sure "Menace",' said the first killer.

He looked much older than the second and was wearing a shabby looking polo - shirt and crumpled jeans. The other was wearing a loosely - fitting sports jacket and badly - ironed trousers.

A fraction of pressure on the wheel and "Menace" had swerved over to the left this time, dodging in and out of a throng of traffic. He signalled with his arm for the other two cars to follow in the same way and continued the chase. He was now inches behind the red Mercedes and the other two sedans closed on behind.

** *

'Frank!' Linda screamed.

Frank Ward turned his head to see one of the sedan cars pulling up alongside him. He swore. "Menace" was driving and roughly keeping the same speed as the Mercedes - Benz saloon, perhaps slightly slower. The windows in the back of the saloons rolled down and Ward and Linda watched in horror as they saw the cruel faces of the gunmen looking down the barrels of identical Browning 9mm guns.

Ward opened his mouth to protest and quickly put his arm around Linda's back with his left hand and pushed her down.

'Stay down there and don't lift your head up!' Ward instructed.

Then, all around the vehicle erupted a fierce drilling of bullets. Rounds ricocheted off the exterior of the car, denting the paintwork severely. One of the stray bullets hit the passenger window and the broken shards of glass rained down on Linda. She screamed and tensed her body as Ward began to ram the enemy car.

Ward turned right to get some speed up before pulling the wheel sharply so that the left side of the Mercedes - Benz smashed against the sedan. There was an almighty crash as the two cars hit together with a further scraping of metal. "Menace" Hillman lost control of his car momentarily and corrected it before it veered off into a wall. He responded angrily by trying to ram Ward's car but Ward was prepared for it. He rammed back, completely breaking the side - mirror clean off the vehicle.

At the same time, both gunmen ran out of bullets and stopped to extract the clip. It was then Ward seized his chance. He slammed on the brakes of the car suddenly and watched as the speed dial shot down from one hundred to zero. Hillman didn't expect this and carried on, resulting in a dangerous head - on - collision with the large transit van in front. The saloon came to a halt, the front bonnet crumpled up and smashed against the back of the other vehicle. The windscreen and one of the other windows was shattered in the collision.

Ward carried on in the Mercedes leaving "Menace" and the two hit men behind in the ruined wreckage. The other two cars dodged in and out of the chaos and resumed the chase. The Robinson R.44 helicopter flew through the sky overhead, the pilot keeping a watch on the Mercedes.

Ward raced on ahead of the persistent sedan cars, weaving in and out of the traffic and ignoring the red lights. A car heading towards him swerved to avoid collision but instead hit another vehicle on the other lane. A pile - up of vehicles continued and it held the two sedans back for a short while. With the road blocked off, the sedans reversed and accelerated down an alleyway that led back out onto the road further on. Now they were back behind the Mercedes.

One of the sedan vehicles managed to bump the back of the Mercedes, making the whole vehicle jerk. Ward moved the Mercedes - Benz left and right to avoid them but couldn't. He increased in speed again and roared down the Chinese streets and drove through the market area. The stalls were almost empty and Ward smashed through them as a short - cut to get to the other side of the square. The sedans followed, destroying the wooden stalls and sending fruit and vegetables scattering over the ground.

Frank Ward stamped down on the pedals hard and heard the engine growl like some kind of animal. His attempts to outrun the sedans failed, and as he concentrated on avoiding the Victor's men, he didn't notice the concrete statue in the middle of the market square. He heard Linda scream and he managed to get a glimpse of the obstacle before the Mercedes smashed it head with a terrific crash.

The Mercedes - Benz was still and Ward lifted his head up from the wheel of the wrecked saloon and was glad he hadn't been knocked out in the crash. His safety belt had taken most of the impact and instead of being unconscious or even dead, he only had a gash on his arm. He winced in pain, shuffled himself up in his seat and examined the damage. The front of the car was all twisted and covered in marble, stone and glass. The car was half embedded into the statue. Ward remembered Linda and turned towards her. Thankfully she was alright, and had only suffered a minor cut above her right eyebrow.

Ward looked up into the broken rear - view mirror and could see the two sedans pulling up behind them. Quickly, Ward threw the belt off his body and seized his Beretta.

'Stay in the car.' He instructed, and Ward was already out of the car door before Linda could reply.

Ward knelt down on the cold floor and assumed aim. He directed his gun towards the windscreen of the nearest sedan. He fired twice and felt the satisfying recoil of his pistol as it spat twice. A large spider web formed in the top right - hand corner of the windscreen and the second shattered the whole thing all together. He could now see clearly that one of his rounds had been successful and was embedded into the driver's shoulder. The man's face was contorted in pain and he delicately nursed the bloody wound with a shaky hand. The other sedan was coming towards Ward at full speed.

The driver was going to mow him down! Ward waited until the last second and prepared his body. As the glare of the lights focused on his determined face, Ward did a side roll avoiding the oncoming car, spun around quickly and let off a further three shots. Two of his metal lugs went wide and bounced off the pavement, but the other hit one of the front tyres. The rubber exploded and all the air was let out. The sedan sank down on one side. The driver attempted to correct the car but lost control in the struggle. The vehicle did a nose dive into the ground and flipped three times and came to rest upside down, one hundred yards away.

Ward sank onto his knees and ran his fingers through the black hair, damp with perspiration. He walked unhurriedly over to the Mercedes and helped Linda out of the car. As she stepped out, the dust on the ground was blown around strongly. Ward and Linda both looked up simultaneously and saw the Robinson R.44 helicopter above. The driver leant out of the cabin clutching a small black object in his hand.

Ward looked at the object for a few moments and finally realised that it was a grenade!

'Run!' Ward instructed.

The driver put the grenade to his mouth and tore the pin out with his teeth. He dropped it and the explosive hit the ground. A loud explosion followed. Ward and Linda were luckily out of the way and narrowly avoided being caught in the radius of the projectile. The helicopter circled in the air and hovered over them. The driver reached for another grenade. Linda looked up at the airborne vehicle and then at the Beretta held loosely in Ward's right hand. Instinctively, she snatched the Beretta from him and aimed at the driver in the cockpit of the Robinson R.44. Ward ran to her to protest but Linda had already pulled the trigger. The bullet formed a hole in the windscreen and hit the driver in the centre of the forehead, moments after he pulled the pin.

Ward and Linda ran for their lives and jumped onto the floor as the helicopter exploded spectacularly in a terrific ball of flame. The rotors were blown off as the grenade ignited and flew like a giant Frisbee through the air. The doomed aircraft then tumbled to the ground sluggishly, still burning and causing black smoke. Like a great, ugly insect, the 'copter crashed to the ground in a heap, shrapnel raining down on the market - place.

At last there was silence and Ward sat up and looked at the burning helicopter and then at Linda in amazement.

'Did I do well?' Lind asked smiling.

'You did great,' Ward replied and then leant forward and found her mouth with his. He rewarded her with a kiss.

18/ THE ISLAND

WALTER GREAVES, THE Chief Of Staff to the Director of the Central Intelligence Agency sat in his swivel chair in his office, dozing. He was very tired and stressed over the horrible Claude Victor affair. Both he and Cartwright had been worried about Agent 27S as he hadn't been in contact with Langley Headquarters since he arrived in Tianjin and met up with Albert Dawson, the Head of Station China.

What was the matter? Had they made any progress? Was Ward alright?

These were just some of the questions that had been plaguing the minds of the most superior officials and the American President for the past few days. The CIA had nothing to go on and couldn't make contact with 27S. Cartwright had contacted Station C yesterday to ask them what was happening. The Station didn't know and explained that Dawson and Ward had gone over to Beijing by the *Shinkasen*. Neither of them had contacted Station C since.

Greaves had previously attempted to contact Ward on his cell phone. There was no reply. Whilst he sat with his head tilted back on the rest of his chair, he was awakened by the soft purring of the telephone on his desk. He stirred and shuffled up uncomfortably before opening his eyes. He adjusted to his surroundings and looked at his watch.

It was very late. There was only himself and a few other members of the department still in the building. Seymour Cartwright had retired home to bed a few hours ago, too. Walter Greaves opened his mouth in a massive, exhausted yawn. Then, reluctantly, he lifted the receiver and held it lazily to his ear.

'Chief Of Staff, speaking.'

'Walter?' came the reply from the distant line.

'Yes,' he enquired curiously, 'Who is this?'

'It's Frank.'

Walter Greaves's eyes open in bewilderment and he sat bolt upright, running his fingers through his fine, balding salt and pepper hair.

'Frank - it's really you! What has happened? Why haven't you contacted Cartwright or Station C for days?'

'It's a long story, Walter,' Agent 27S said, 'Albert Dawson is dead but I'm hours away from stopping Operation Launch.'

Greaves's brow wrinkled in confusion, 'Dawson's dead? What's Operation Launch?'

'Claude Victor's scheme. He intends to fire the two stolen cruise missiles at Tokyo and Taiwan-.'

The Chief Of Staff interrupted, 'Good God!'

'Listen!' Ward commanded, 'He will fire them with the aid of the missile guidance system today. It's six in the morning over in Beijing. I'm going over to stop Victor with the help of his fiancé, Linda Pascal. Operation Launch will take place on Victor's "Island HQ". Linda knows it. It's a small island not far from the coasts of Beijing. Inform Cartwright immediately. I'll contact you once I've completed the assignment.'

'But Frank -'.

Ward had already hung up the phone. Walter Greaves gently put the receiver back on the base and collapsed back into his chair and looked thoughtfully out of his large office window, where the Memorial garden was located on the hillside between the Original Headquarters Building and the Auditorium. A brass plaque set in fieldstone and inscribed with *"In remembrance of those whose unheralded efforts served a grateful nation"* ensures the fallen will not be forgotten by the living.

As Greaves thought of Operation Launch and the danger that Agent 27S was putting himself through, the Chief Of Staff shed a single icy tear as he lifted the receiver ready to break the news of Ward's progress to Cartwright.

***

On the Eastern side of the world in a run - down Bed and Breakfast hotel in the centre of Beijing, Frank Ward looked at Linda lying on the opposite side of the bed and smiled.

She was so beautiful. Her delicate, warm smile, her model - like body, those eyes of green pools of emerald. They clung to each other tightly, holding each other in their arms as they lay there between the sheets. Linda's legs locked around Ward's waist and they kissed affectionately and made long, energetic love. Afterwards, Linda nestled her head against Ward's chest and they just lay there, holding each other and thinking how both of them needed each other so badly.

'You know that tomorrow, I may never see you again,' Ward said softly, running his hands through her long, shiny hair.

'Why?'

'I could be killed,' he replied.

Linda pulled herself away from him. Her face had set into the granite look of anger.

'How can you live like this?' Linda demanded. 'How can you just go around killing people and risking your life so blatantly? Don't you ever think of other people? What would I do if you died?'

'You would move on,' Ward told her, 'But I would rather die than let millions of innocent people die. I am just one man. I am insignificant. If I can prevent others dying, I would give my one life to save them.'

'Don't you feel anything? When you shoot a man dead, don't you think of their family or their loved ones?'

'I *can't*,' Ward said, 'I *mustn't*. If I feel remorse or regret I wouldn't be very good at my job. I'm a hired assassin, Linda, paid by the government to eliminate threats to my country. Those I kill are themselves killers. It would be unprofessional to be sorry as I kill a man.'

'And tomorrow, you will kill Claude.'

'I will.'

'It's odd,' Linda murmured, 'But I'm not like you. When you kill him tomorrow I can't help but feel something. I did love him once, you know, and now I hate him. I can't just shut off my feelings like you and feel nothing.'

Linda dried her eyes and put her head back on the pillow next to her lover. 'What is going to happen when you kill Claude?'

'When my mission is complete, I shall take you back to America with me and you will live in Virginia in my home.'

'Will you promise me something?' Linda asked.

'I'll try.'

'Once you've completed this assignment, will you leave the CIA and settle down to a normal life?'

Ward paused and thought about it. He had thought of handing in his notice to the Agency several times. He too had had enough of blood and killing. He had had enough of the nightmares of those he had killed haunting him and his dirty conscience. He was tired of having a string of untidy, meaningless love affairs. He wanted, like Linda, to marry and perhaps have children. But could a man like him marry and father children?

After all, thought Ward. *I'm a killer. An assassin. A government agent.*

He smiled broadly, 'I promise.'

Linda grinned too and they kissed. Ward ran his hand down her smooth spine and squeezed both of her buttocks.

'How can we get to the island?' Linda enquired after a while.

They sat up and leaned against the bed rests and Ward lit a cigarette. He puffed on it thoughtfully and began to think about it.

'I presume Victor will have the island very heavily guarded, Linda. I also think that he will have cameras installed around the island too. Maybe he's even got a radar set up.'

'Possibly,' admitted Linda.

'It's going to be difficult,' Ward said.

Linda agreed and gave a quick nod, holding the duvet up to her chin.

'Where is *Le dauphin* docked?' Ward asked.

'At a nearby port. Victor should be leaving with his crew of men in two hours -'.

'-Along with the warheads and the guidance system,' Ward added.

'Yes.'

'Supposing we hid on board and disguised ourselves as the crew. We could then get off unseen and get deep inside the complex unnoticed.'

Linda was sceptical. 'I'm not sure. Surely Victor would recognise us.'

'We've just got to be careful.'

Linda sucked in deep breaths of air. 'Okay. If we want to get on - board before Le dauphin heads off, we'd better go now.'

'Fine,' Ward said firmly, 'Get some clothes on and wait outside. Find a taxi. I'll get the equipment ready.'

Linda climbed out of bed and walked naked over to the front of the bed where her dress lay on the floor along with her thong and bra. She quickly got changed while Ward collected his Beretta 84FS Cheetah and fitted in a new magazine. He changed back into his turtle neck shirt and his slacks and assembled the gun in its holster pouch. He checked his pockets to make sure he still had his lock pick and the finger - print scanner inside. Once he was ready, he took the room key and locked it behind him and he walked out of the B & B. He met Linda standing outside on the pavement next to a taxi.

Linda climbed inside and Frank Ward paid the elderly Chinese driver. The man was a shrewd, bald man whose wrinkled and creased face resembled that of a toad. The brown eyes were bright though as he accepted the fare eagerly and started the engine. Ward slipped into the passenger seat and Linda gave the driver the directions to their destination.

Ward instantly recognised *Le dauphin* and pointed it out from all the other luxurious yachts docked at the port. It was just as he remembered it from the night he had crept onboard back at Tianjin harbour. The long hull glistened in the early morning sunlight and it reflected in the cold waves. Like a huge floating hotel, the yacht was beautiful and complex in design. The hull, made of fibreglass, also has two outer layers of Vinylester resin for blister resistance. Ward remembered the luxurious interior when he went inside, the owner's stateroom, the large cabins, and the main deck that is crafted with three distinct areas aft of the lower helm.

At present, there was nobody either on the deck or on the quarterdeck as far as Frank Ward and Linda Pascal could see. The reclining chairs and circular tables stood neglected in the shade of the large umbrellas. The sun chased the shadows underneath the tables.

Victor and the rest of the crew would be on the lower decks presumably preparing the warheads.

Ward and Linda were standing one hundred yards away from where *Le dauphin* was moored. The port was busy with people and Chinese fisherman preparing their boats to go out to sea to begin catching the fish. They had all the rods assembled at the stern of their boats and all their nets out on deck ready to throw overboard. There were also several cargo trucks littering the port area, unloading food and supplies to the yachts and boats, including *Le dauphin*. Other trucks were picking up yesterday's catches from the local fisherman, ready to sell on to markets and grocery stores. With all the people walking around and moving about, Ward and Linda were unnoticed in the middle of it all.

Ward looked over towards one of the cargo trucks and saw the driver climbing out, carrying heavy boxes and crates from the back of the vehicle up the gangway to Victor's beautiful yacht. The man had made several journeys now and was unloading the last few. His partner returned from the yacht and helped his friend lift them out of the truck. Ward saw this as an opportunity and quickly grasped Linda's hand.

'Come with me.'

'What's the matter?' Linda asked, struggling to keep up as Ward ran towards the truck.

Ward didn't reply and as one of the men bent down to retrieve a crate full of fruit, Ward hit the man's neck with his outstretched fingers. Using the commando cutting technique, his stiffened hand smashed into the man's throat, rendering him unconscious. His companion turned around startled, and looked first at Ward and then his unconscious friend. He raised his fist ready to attack him, but Ward was too quick and caught the man's fist in his own hand. Before the worker could call for help, Ward hit the man in the stomach and pushed him backwards into the truck.

The man was out stone cold before he slipped onto the floor sluggishly, spread - eagled.

'Quick,' said Ward, 'Get inside before anybody sees us.'

Ward jumped up into the storage area of the truck and helped Linda climb up. When they were both inside, Ward pulled the back of the truck down, hiding them from view. Linda could barely see Ward in the darkness.

Frank Ward crouched down to the man whom he had chopped on the neck and pulled him up by the back of his collar. 'Strip the overalls off the other man and pull them over your dress. Nobody should notice us in disguise.'

'It won't fit me very well,' Linda mumbled. 'He's a lot shorter than I am.'

'Just put it on and make it look as good as you can.'

Linda sighed and began to unzip the faded blue overalls from the sleeping worker. Ward did the same and after a few minutes, they began to put the overalls over their own clothes. Ward's fitted almost perfectly and he zipped it as close as he could to his chin, covering a bit of his face. As Ward stretched out his legs, he realised that his overalls were slightly baggy. Linda looked at herself and could see that the trousers came very short on her legs.

'Pity it doesn't fit.'

Ward smiled and lifted the back of the truck up so that the morning light filled it. They climbed out of the back and lifted the last two remaining crates out of the vehicle.

'Can you manage?' enquired Ward as they walked across the port towards the gangway of *Le dauphin*.

'It's a bit heavy,' Linda admitted, carrying the wooden container with both hands. 'I should be fine.'

They walked up the gangway without further talking, trying their best to keep their heads down as they walked through the entrance inside the yacht. As they passed anybody in the corridor, they turned away to hide their faces and attempted to look as inconspicuous as possible. They passed the saloon, decorated in creamy white and chocolate brown. The carpets were white and matched well with the leather two - piece sofas facing towards the large rectangular plasma screen television. The walls were panelled in wood and matched the brown theme of the spacious, large room. A wine cabinet stood beside the television, next to the small coffee table on which an ashtray was placed.

'Where are we going to hide for the journey?' Linda wondered.

'In Claude Victor's room,' Ward decided, 'He will be staying in the lower levels of the yacht in the conference room, perhaps discussing the final arrangements of Operation Launch.'

'Good idea.'

Unnoticed, they slipped down to the cabin quarters and located Victor's large room onboard. Ward tried the door and found that it was open. They slipped inside and locked it behind them and sat in the sapphire blue chairs waiting for the yacht to pull away from port.

Le dauphin started up and slowly began its journey to Prawn Island, as it is called. The large motor yacht left a widening, deep wake as it moved across the indigo - coloured ocean. In the stateroom, the humming of the engines and the spray of water could be heard, as it rushed across the sides of the fibreglass yacht . The only light poured through the partially shut blinds that covered all the porthole windows on each side of the large room, illuminating each of the sombre, severe faces sat around the table, gloomily looking towards the man sat at the head of the table. His long, twisted hands lay flat on the wooden - surfaced table before him, and he lit himself a cigarette. Only somebody who knew Victor very well would realise that he was actually in panic. The only clues that suggested this were his shaky hands as he lit himself a cigarette and the quivery elements in his usually aggressive, deep voice as he talked to his associates.

'We are in trouble,' Victor grumbled angrily. 'Frank Ward is still alive and well, and has succeeded in breaking into my offices. He knows all about Operation Launch - I found a letter that explained it lying on the floor. He had taken it from my safe. He has killed many of my men and no doubt has communicated to his superiors already. It is because of you idiots that the spy continues to succeed. In a matter of a few hours, the warheads will be fired at their countries, aided by the guidance system. That is, if Ward doesn't prevent it. The man is out there somewhere and knows too much. He also has my fiancé with him. She has double - crossed me and has obviously aided him in his mission. They must both be eliminated as soon as possible if they are spotted on Prawn Island. I wish to upgrade all defence systems over at the base. I want all my men to be vigilant and ready to kill them both if they show up. Do you understand?'

The men sat around the table all nodded energetically and looked adoringly at their boss.

'We may already have the world's secret services after us,' Victor spoke, hammering his fist down hard belligerently and hissing out each word for effect, 'And some scientists in China may have been sent to check all of the boats for radiation. As long as we maintain lookouts on the main deck for trouble and keep the warheads under constant watch, we should be fine.

On of the men sat around the table, a large greasy looking man with a particularly swollen face, raised his hand. Victor grunted; it was a signal for the man to speak.

'Supposing Ward shows up at Prawn Island,' the man said in a deep, husky voice, 'Shouldn't we interrogate him and see what he knows. I'm not sure I like the thought of us being under suspicion.'

'Good idea, Dylan. Personally I would like to see Frank Ward suffer considerably for the amount of interference he has caused for Operation Launch.'

"Menace" Hillman, who was sitting next to Victor turned towards his chief, excitedly, 'Please let me experiment on him, boss. I want to see how long I can keep him alive whilst torturing him. I wish to beat my current record.'

'Yes,' Victor said softly.

Claude Victor exhaled a cloud of smoke through his lips and said sternly, 'Upon arrival, the warheads are to be removed carefully by at least six or seven men to each of the nuclear weapons. Two transit trucks will be waiting near the jetty where *Le dauphin* will be moored. The trucks will then proceed to take the weapons right into the firing complex, position them correctly in the launching area, ready for the destination to be programmed into the missile guidance system.'

Again, the men nodded. As Claude Victor studied the serious - looking faces surrounding him, he paid particular attention to one of the men sitting three chairs down the table on his left. The man was Hungarian - one of Victor's many soldiers who had worked in his employ for seven years. His name was Vlad Polivenz. He was a small man who looked very fearsome at times. He had previously been involved in several murders in Hungary before moving to Paris and continuing his life of crime. He committed two grisly, savage murders whilst in France and made several shop and bank robberies throughout Europe. He was recruited by Victor as one of his hired guns and his identity was changed so that the police wouldn't associate the criminal with Claude Victor. Since the man had worked for Victor for a long time, he was trusted. However "Menace" Hillman had informed him that the man had been tipping off the Chinese police whilst in Tianjin. The police had offered him money for information.

Polivenz sat there, twiddling his ball - point pen between his fingers, his face vague and apparently uninterested. Victor noticed under closer inspection that the large hands twitched slightly, as did the rest of his body. Nervousness. The small man with a mop of balding, black hair now looked towards his chief, and stared at his employer.

He didn't notice Claude Victor remove his right hand from the wooden table and dig deep into his jacket. The hand stayed hidden from view for a few moments and then returned to sight, an ugly, metal object now clasped in the palm. The traitor took three seconds to realise what the object was. Victor steadied his hand and looked coldly down the snout of the double - action MAB PA - 15 pistol. The man's mouth opened and he stared in disbelief at the pistol.

The MAB PA- 15 rang four times continuously without stop. Each time the bullets emerged from the muzzle, the slide rotated the barrel and retracted to cycle the action. The unsilenced shots ripped into the man's chest, making a curved line of reddening holes in the man's white shirt. The man made a few painful gasps and his bloodstained hands hovered over his wounds. The fifth shot roared and hit the dead man accurately in the forehead, the force of the shot sending the leather chair backwards, onto the floor.

The men around the table gasped and lifted their bodies from their seats so they could see what had happened to their associate. They glanced back at their chief and employer, who had replaced the pistol in the hidden holster pouch secured beneath his left armpit. Around the crumpled body on the floor, a huge puddle of red grew around it, staining the blue carpet.

Victor smiled and looked at the blood. He remembered the capacity of blood a human body holds - ten pints - and thought that the amount of the red stuff on the floor was probably of that amount.

'I do not tolerate betrayal,' Victor said harshly, addressing the rest of the men around the table. 'Your former colleague, Vlad Polivenz decided to inform the Chinese metropolitan police department of our little scheme. As a punishment I ended his employment immediately - permanently. Linda - when I find her - will also endure a similar fate, but much more painful. Let this be a lesson to those of you who wish to deceive me.'

'Of course,' one of the men, a French thug, said.

'But what will we do about the Chinese police?' Another criminal enquired, a bulky Russian mobster.

'That,' Victor smiled, 'will be dealt with within the next few hours. A hit team will kill the two men aware of Operation Launch before they reveal details of the plan to others.'

'Brilliant!' exclaimed one of the men.

Claude Victor consulted his watch and killed his cigarette in the ashtray, blowing out the remaining cigarette smoke through his flared nostrils like a dragon. 'Now gentleman, we should arrive at Prawn Island in two minutes exactly. Please make your way onto the main deck and leave the former Vlad Polivenz where he is. He will be cleaned up later.'

The men around the conference table laughed heartily and departed from their seats, gathering their notes and pens from their places. Then, following Claude Victor and his bodyguard Marcus "Menace" Hillman, the men exited through the door and headed up onto the quarterdeck.

Both Ward and Linda were startled when the five gun shots echoed from the deck below. They both sat up straight in the comfortable blue chairs beside the small window (Ward had closed the blinds so that nobody could see them) and Ward had removed his Beretta.

Had those shots been warning shots? Had they discovered them hiding in Victor's stateroom cabin? Or had Station C come after them?

Ward cautiously drew the blinds and peered through the slit gaps. There were no men running around on deck and beyond the rail on the vast sheet of bluish grey, and no other attacking boats. Ward and Linda relaxed again and began to think out the plan.

'Have you ever been on this island?' Ward asked, leaning forward.

Linda closed the blinds again and faced Ward. 'Only once,' she said truthfully, 'That was before Operation Launch. It was a mansion and just another one of his properties. But since then, he has transformed it for "business purposes" as he repeatedly told me.'

'So I suppose you would know your way around, then?'

Linda considered briefly, 'I think I would,' she decided, 'but I haven't been for a while and the whole place could have changed considerably.'

'I understand that.'

'How do you intend stopping the cruise missiles containing the warheads being launched?' Linda enquired.

'Hopefully, I can prevent them being fired,' Ward admitted, 'but if not, I would have to alter the coordinates on the missile guidance system.'

'Do you understand how to work this device then?'

'Yes,' Ward said, 'Everybody in my department and the Intelligence section had information about the hardware sent to all of our office trays.'

'That's good,' she said noncommittally.

'But what if we can't stop the warheads? What if Victor kills us?'

'We *will* succeed, Linda,' Ward smiled, holding Linda's hand, 'But we must stick together.'

Linda leaned forward to embrace him but she stopped as they realised that the luxurious yacht had slowed down tremendously. *Le dauphin* veered right and came to a halt, presumably against the jetty. Both below and above, they could hear voices and talking as the men headed towards the entrance where the gangway would be lowered onto land. Ward got out of his chair, still wearing his scruffy, faded overalls. He opened the blinds again allowing light to pour into the fine, large cabin panelled in brown mahogany and carpeted in sapphire blue like the rest of the vessel. Ward looked out of the window and at the island.

From what he could see instantly, Prawn Island as it was called, was huge. Running around the coastal areas of the isolated piece of land was a white - sanded beach where the jetty area was located. There was room on the jetty for *Le dauphin* and also a small Morgan Marine speed boat, powered by a MerCruiser 4.3L V6 stern drive, achieving wonderful performances at around forty - five miles per hour and more. Further up the island, a large, square building that looked very modern and made entirely of metal and glass, dominated the skyline and stood above the trees and plants that concealed most of it. There was also a larger building next to it which appeared to have a sliding roof built into the top.

That, Ward supposed, was where the cruise missiles were going to launched. The island complex certainly had been under construction for the Operation Launch project. Apart from the beach and the speed boat moored at the jetty, the place seemed to be very daunting. Already, as Ward looked down below, he could see Claude Victor and a few of his men emerging from *Le dauphin* and carefully making their way down the lowered gangway. Of course, Marcus "Menace" Hillman wasn't very far away from his chief.

Victor talked to a few of his men and watched as two identical large, white transit trucks appeared from behind the trees and came thudding down the beach, sending showers of sand up in the air as the vehicles approached. They reversed and the drivers came out to open the doors ready for the cruise missiles containing the warheads to be taken off board. Victor signalled to some of his crew near the gangway to collect the weapons and they returned moments later, six men each carrying the large, torpedo - shaped missiles. The BGM - 109 Tomahawk missiles were brought down the gangway slowly and deliberately. Claude Victor oversaw the operation.

Tomahawk Land Attack Missiles (TLAM) are long-range, all-weather, subsonic cruise missiles with stubby wings. The weapon was originally designed in the 1970's as a medium- to long-range, low-altitude missile that could also be launched from a submerged submarine. Since then, they have been dramatically revised. The missiles were stored in and launched from a pressurized canister that protects it during transportation and storage and acts as a launch tube. These canisters are racked in Armoured Box Launchers (ABL). The missiles are known to be used often by the United States Navy, the Royal Navy, the Royal Netherlands Navy and the Spanish Navy. The TLAM's were powered by Williams International F107- WR-402 turbofan engines and fly at an average speed of about eight hundred and eighty miles per hour.

Both the weapons were loaded with difficulty into the back of each truck, the length of the missiles (five point six metres) almost reaching the end of the truck. Once the weapons were definitely secured, the doors at the rear of each van were firmly closed and Claude Victor climbed into the passenger seat of one van and Hillman climbed into the other. The remaining men, Claude Victor's most valuable personnel, climbed into the back of the trucks. The rest of the men, mostly consisting of Triad gang members, were already operating inside the launching complex. The engines of the trucks both grumbled and coughed a few times before reluctantly starting up with a healthy hum. The trucks advanced up the beach and struggled occasionally to get over the bumps. Soon, the vehicles holding the missiles had vanished behind the trees and were now right outside the two buildings.

Frank Ward moved away from the blinds. 'We've got to get out and off this yacht,' Ward announced, 'We haven't got long before the missiles containing the warheads will be positioned ready for launching in the second building.'

'What if we're spotted?' said Linda.

'We'll just have to be careful.'

Ward moved over towards the door and opened it slightly. He narrowed his eyes and looked through the thin gap out onto the corridor. There was nobody outside. Quickly, they both slipped over the threshold. Ward closed the door with exaggerated quietness, and armed with his Beretta, they moved down the hallway, treading carefully. They turned around a corner and climbed up the few close - carpeted steps that led up to the door leading out onto the broadside. Linda opened the door and got ready to sprint.

'Wait!'

'What?'

Ward stopped her in her tracks, put a straightened finger to his lips and directed his index finger towards a guard walking in the opposite direction. They waited until the man was definitely out of sight and then they advanced down the yacht and passed the bow view. They were heading for the forecastle area located at the bow of *Le dauphin*. They crept through the main deck area located at the bow, passing the unoccupied seats and tables dotted around. They stopped at the just off bow section and looked at the gangway that was now in sight.

Frank Ward looked down onto land. Two members of the crew, both with FAMAS G2 sub machine guns draped over their shoulders, scanned the men coming down the gangway efficiently, aiming the 488 millimetre barrel of the French SMG threateningly at the crew leaving the yacht. Ward and Linda waited for more of the crew to emerge from inside the yacht and exit via the gangway. They stayed where they were for five minutes until a group of five men, all Chinese, made their way down the gangway. Unnoticed, they joined them and huddled close together so that the guards armed with the weapons wouldn't spot them.

For a few seconds, Ward thought that one of the guards had seen them. The glaring eyes appeared to hover over them, and the man raised the FAMAS G2 a few inches. However, the man must have been looking beyond him and at somebody else on the yacht. A shiver went down Ward's spine as he walked past the two guards. They didn't look at him and together Ward and Linda passed the danger-zone and followed the other men up the beach. They trudged through the sand and progressed up the steep, white dunes. As they reached the top of the beach, Ward and Linda purposefully fell behind the rest of the group. When nobody was watching, they sprinted down the beach towards the grassy area before the two building complexes. They hid under the twenty foot Chinese tallow tree. The *Sapium sebiferum* (the scientific name) had large, attractive heart - shaped leaves. Ward and Linda sat down beneath it, seeking camouflage in the tall grass and behind the drooping branches.

They sat there for a while and both removed their faded overalls, rather like an insect shedding some sort of a grotesque skin. Their other clothes were revealed underneath. Ward, now wearing his black turtle - neck and his dark slacks, took out his gun and laid it on his lap defensively should any one come. Linda pushed the branches aside so that she could see the complex. The group of Victor's crew that they had followed were now walking through the entrance of the first building, which appeared to be the control room of Operation Launch. The second building, the one with the retractable roof, was the firing area where the Tomahawk cruise missiles containing the warheads would be launched, . The two transit vans were parked outside with nobody around them. The missiles would already have been removed from the backs of the trucks and assembled inside.

Linda drew back in and sat down next to Ward, her lover, wearing the lovely dress that she had worn to the Beijing opera at Summer Palace. She hadn't had the opportunity to change. It was unsuitable for running around in but it didn't matter. There were more important things than her dress. She reached across to Ward and put her hand on his arm.

'How are we going to get inside?'

Ward wasn't sure himself. Normally he would have made a very detailed plan beforehand, thinking of anything that could possibly go wrong. If he hadn't already got a plan, he would think one up in a matter of seconds, and usually, it would be good. But at the moment, he couldn't think. He had spent the past day planning how they would get here. He didn't know what to expect upon arrival. Ward decided to have a look and see if he could pick up on anything helpful that might get them inside. Ward scanned the two buildings prior to answering the question. From where he was sitting, a distinct gap separating the two buildings was visible. There was nothing in the alley but an emergency ladder leading up onto the roof, which had a large rectangular skylight. Ward put these things together and formed a plan in his mind.

'We'll get in through the roof skylight,' Ward said, pleased with himself for noticing the roof window, 'That way we won't be spotted near the entrance.'

Linda agreed and signalled this with an energetic nod. Ward then climbed to his feet and kept his Beretta 84FS Cheetah close to his body so that it was not easily spotted. With the frame being black, it was difficult to see against his dark turtle neck. Linda walked with him and they snaked through the long grass, looking left and right for guards as if they were children crossing an imaginary road. When they were satisfied that were currently alone, they sprinted the short distance towards the alleyway.

The circular control room was large and modern, built in three huge tiers with steel walkways positioned around each area. These were supported by steel girders. Elevators, as well as the many flights of stairs, provided key access to all three floors. The place was entirely metal - the walls, the floor, and the doors included. They all glimmered in the light created by the bright bulbs upon the ceiling and the hundreds of computer monitors dotted around the room. Men and woman (many Chinese) were all sitting in long rows, working furiously with extreme concentration at their own machine. The only noises in the room were that of the keys being stabbed on the keyboard. The eyes of the computer programmers were riveted on their monitors and armed guards assembled around the room watched them under instructions, and occasionally gave them a rough jab in the back with a pistol, to make them work harder.

This is what Claude Victor had told them to do.

At the front of the room, a large screen rather like those in a cinema, was built onto the aluminium - surfaced wall. The electronic piece of equipment showed the world map with both Taiwan and Tokyo highlighted in red dots. Next to this was a smaller screen, currently blank, that would later show the cruise missiles journey towards their respective destinations.

The third tier was mainly the workers' quarters. Victor had not allowed any of his staff to go home during Operation Launch. He had paid for them to live on Prawn Island to save them coming back and forth by boat. It would be too suspicious. The Chinese coast guards might investigate and keep the island under constant surveillance. The workers' quarters was where they slept, dined and spent their two breaks every day. They had done this over the past week while they worked in the main control room organising Operation Launch and plotting suitable flight paths for the missiles. Today, the most important day of the scheme, they would programme the missile coordinates according to the earth's plates and monitor the flights on the small screen should anything go wrong.

The second floor was offices and many spare rooms. One of these rooms, Victor (with the help of "Menace" Hillman") had transformed into a torture chamber where he punished staff for not obeying orders to work hard.

One of the great blast doors on the second tier opened with a slow whine and Claude Victor emerged and stepped out onto the walkway. He was wearing the fashionable dark French suit he had worn earlier, designed for him by an exclusive tailor in Toulouse. He was holding the small, silver case in which the missile guidance hardware was kept. Although the man seldom smiled, he couldn't help the fact that one managed to crease his lips as he moved down the staircase leading onto the bottom tier, gripping the railings with his long hands.

In less than one hour, he was going to be the richest man on earth, he reflected. And *the most powerful too!*

Surveying the many banks of computers with his grotesque, bulging eyeballs which nearly hung from their sunken sockets, Victor walked across the room and watched a particular man at work. The Chinese computer programmer, a veteran member of the *Black Tongs*, a former criminal society, was a short man with balding hair and metal - framed, square spectacles. The grey hair had been combed clumsily over the bald patch and looked ridiculous and amusing. His eyes never parted from the screen as his hands moved over the keyboard. The screen showed two sets of coordinates both large in print.

Victor smiled. 'Are these the final coordinates of Taiwan and Tokyo?'

The short programmer finally paused, and he turned towards his boss, adjusting his spectacles as he moved in his swivel chair. His face resembled Victor's slightly; it was pale and as the man talked, the teeth were crooked.

'Yes, Monsieur Victor.'

'Good,' he replied, 'Programme them into the missile guidance system immediately.' Claude Victor put the case down onto the workbench and unfastened the lid, revealing the small, technical device, capable of plotting the routes of cruise missiles. He removed the black object from the velvet lined interior and handed the gadget to the programmer who accepted it carefully in his hands. The programmer opened the lid and placed it down next to the monitor. The man scratched his head and fiddled with the wires whilst connecting the two machines together. Instantly, a box flashed up onto the screen reading:

TARGET COORDINATES DOWNLOADING

PLEASE WAIT

Victor gave a brief cackle of laughter, '*Fantastique*! Now wait, my friend, until they have downloaded. I'll inform you when the cruise missiles are positioned and ready for launching in the firing area. I will give you the instructions when to ignite them. Do you understand?'

'Yes, sir.'

Claude Victor acknowledged the man's answer with a nod and walked back up onto the walkway to find "Menace" Hillman, who was occupied in the torture chamber, making sure that one of the computer programmers would not go outside for a cigarette again.

Victor grinned. He rather wished that he hadn't requested the torture chamber to be sound - proof; he would get a high amount of pleasure from hearing the terrified, shrill screams of the man as "Menace" Hillman introduced his latest victim to his many torturing devices.

Frank Ward and Linda stood in the alleyway next to the metal ladder leading up onto the skylight. He presumed that the skylight also provided an emergency escape if the main entrance was somehow blocked.

'I'll go up first,' Ward said, 'I'll have a look through the skylight. When I can't see anybody around, I'll call you up. Got it?'

Linda said that she did and Ward temporarily holstered his Beretta whilst he gripped the sides of the ladder and began to climb up the steps. He was up in a matter of seconds and dropped onto the metal roof. He withdrew his Beretta again and made his way over to the closed skylight. He knelt down next to the roof window and carefully peered through the thickened glass. He could instantly see that the building was split up into three major floors. He could see a glimpse of electronics and computer equipment but couldn't see much more. There was nobody standing underneath the skylight as far as he could see. Ward tried the handle with his free hand.

It barely moved. The thing was stuck. Ward swore in frustration and decided to use the butt of his gun as some kind of tool. Holding his gun by the barrel, he smashed the underneath of the handle upwards. This forced the skylight window open with a high - pitched squeak. He laid the skylight window down on the roof and hurried over to the edge of the building where Linda was waiting in the alleyway below. Ward motioned with his arms to climb the ladder. He stood at the top ready to help her as she struggled up the steps in her dress and stiletto shoes. She reached out and grasped Ward's hand, and he lifted her off the top step.

'Are you going in first?' Linda asked, brushing her lovely hair from her face. There was a chilly breeze up on the roof, and the bottom of her scarlet dress of expensive silk ruffled in the wind.

Ward was already standing next to the open skylight. He turned towards her. 'Yes,' he said, 'It would be best. If there's anybody about,' Ward tightened his grip on the Beretta, 'I'd better be the first to go in.'

'I suppose.'

Ward crouched down and hoisted his legs over the open space. Holding the side of the skylight, he gently eased his body through the hole and allowed himself to fall through. He was suspended in air for a few short seconds and landed firmly on his feet on the walkway of the third tier. He looked up. The drop was slightly more than he had expected.

Linda's face looked down through the skylight, the late morning sun pouring down behind her. It lit up her genial face beautifully. Ward reflected, with a degree of sadness, because of the faint resemblance to poor Gaëlle...

'Just drop and I'll catch you,' Ward told her having thought of her stiletto|-heeled shoes. *Why hadn't she changed?*

Linda did as she was told and fell through the open space. A startled cry escaped from her mouth, and then she was prevented from hitting the ground as Ward caught her in his strong arms. He shushed her and looked around nervously to see if anybody had heard.

It didn't seem like it.

Slowly, he put Linda on the ground. Ward moved around uncertainly, unsure of what to do or where to go. The place was huge and divided into so many different areas and sections. He shrank back against the iron - plated walls and glanced over the railing and down below on the main floor. There were about six long banks of computer screens positioned around the room, all facing the two interactive screens before them. Ward surveyed the room carefully and narrowed his eyes, searching for guards. As far as he could distinguish, there were ten guards positioned on the main tier in the control room, immaculately uniformed in green combat clothes. Powerful SMG's, maybe Skorpion vz. 61's were slung around their shoulders. Double - action pistols and hand grenades were also strapped onto their belts.

How was he going to get down there unseen?

He watched a little longer, with Linda watching with him. Her eyes suddenly noticed something and she pointed it out.

'Look! Over there,' she moved her finger in the direction.

Ward couldn't see what she was talking about.

'What?'

'The elevator!' She explained. 'On the opposite side. It's heading down from the third tier to the first. If we head over there, we might be able to get down unnoticed.'

Ward bit his lip and sucked breath through his teeth. It was certainly risky. 'Well we've got to get down there somehow. The mainframe computer is down there, and the missile guidance system. We've got to stop those missiles from being fired!'

'Let's go,' Linda said and she started down the corridor.

Frank Ward continued looking down into the control room. He identified the missile guidance system that Claude Victor had hired the Triads to steal from Hong Kong. The tiny machine was connected to one of the computers in the nearest bank to the two large square screens at the front. He didn't care if he was spotted. He would just have to use his gun. He knew that he had to shut that thing off whatever happens. He turned and followed Linda Pascal down the long walkway and headed for the top elevator on the opposite side of the floor.

Below, in the control room, Claude Victor paced around the floor triumphantly, unaware of the two uninvited visitors on the third floor. He examined his wrist watch and compared it to the time on one of the many computer screens. It wouldn't be long now. It wouldn't be long before the cruise missiles were ready in the launching building. Whilst he was thinking, his group of technicians and nuclear scientists were examining the warheads and making sure that everything was correct, prior to them being launched. The technicians and team of engineers would also be checking the Tomahawk missiles jet engines which propelled the unmanned aircraft. They also needed to make sure that the TH - dimer rocket fuel and the solid - fuel boosters were all stored properly and okay. The missiles would then be assembled facing upwards towards the sky on their lifting wings. When ignited, the jet propulsion would launch them upwards in a terrific ball of flames, where the missiles guidance system device would then take control of the two flights and deliver the "flying bombs" to their destinations.

Victor passed the CCTV screen control panel on which the footage of all the cameras assembled around the island was relayed and viewed by the three members of staff who were sitting at the panel in their swivel chairs. As Victor passed he thought he recognised two of the people moving on the third tier. He swallowed and rushed swiftly over to the console to clarify what he had seen. His great eyes stared in horror, disbelief and panic at Frank Ward and his fiancé Linda Pascal. It was definitely them. He had been half expecting them today, but with his upgraded security team, he doubted that they would have been able to get here.

He suddenly burst into a fit of rage and grabbed the young man supposed to be watching the footage by the throat with his right hand. The other two men stared in amazement and gasped, terrified by the furious expression on their chief's face, not knowing the reason for this sudden temper. The man made a few gurgling sounds and his hands rushed to his neck as Victor's fingers bit into his flesh.

'*Imbécile*!' Victor bellowed, shoving the man's frightened face towards the screen, 'What the hell do I pay you for! Ward and Linda are here on the third floor!'

By this stage the man's face was turning a sickening purple. The trembling lips were icy and blue. Victor was suffocating the man. Finally, Victor calmed down and released the man, who stumbled off his chair and collapsed onto the floor, drawing in deep breaths of precious oxygen and rubbing his aching neck. Claude Victor turned and scanned the room for "Menace" Hillman. The French cold - blooded killer was standing nearby next to one of the staircases.

'"Menace"!' Victor growled.

The large, frightened man dressed in a dark sports jacket walked over to his boss upon the command and looked down at the man spread - eagled upon the ground.

'Have one of the guards dispose of this *débile* immediately as painfully as possible. They shall decided a fitting punishment for him.'

"Menace" nodded but frowned, 'Can't I kill him instead, boss?'

Claude Victor grinned broadly and his eyes held a sinister proposal. 'No, "Menace",' Victor said, chillingly, 'You have a better task. Send all the guards out and retrieve Frank Ward and Linda Pascal,' Victor pointed to the CCTV screen, 'They're on the third tier. Bring them to me in my office and then you will take them to the torture chamber. Agreed?'

'*Oui*, boss!' "Menace" looked eagerly at the screen at his number one enemy, 'I'll happily kill Ward in a most painful method. But what about Linda? Are you sure you want me to kill her, too?'

Claude Victor watched as one of the guards approached and lifted the man that had angered him up from the floor. The man protested and screamed as security seized him under the arms and hauled him roughly towards the exit. The guard removed his double - action pistol and shoved the muzzle against his forehead. Moments later, from outside, a loud gunshot echoed and moments later the guard returned. 'Kill the *chienne*,' Victor said brutally and coldly, 'I can't trust her any longer. She has betrayed me and helped Frank Ward on his mission. You can teach her a permanent lesson that nobody ever double - crosses me.'

"Menace" Hillman nodded and summoned the rest of the guards. They all assembled in a group, holding their Skorpion vz. 61's ready for firing. Led by "Menace" armed with a Russian AK- 47 assault rifle, the man marched up the staircase onto the second tier and climbed up another onto the highest floor. The men split up into two groups and searched the tier in opposite directions so that eventually Ward and the girl would be trapped.

Claude Victor watched the camera console as Ward and Linda searched through the corridors. He looked at Linda, so beautiful and divine; the woman that he had once loved. And now, he had ordered her death. *Why did she have to deceive him?* Bitterly he watched the screen and looked upwards at the team of security. Now, he didn't need her. She would just get in the way and create havoc like Ward had. Without regret he waited for them to be brought to him so he could have them killed. With them out of the way, Operation Launch would be unstoppable. And that was all he cared about.

He thought of the millions that would perish in the huge explosions when the nuclear warheads would explode and destroy Taiwan and Tokyo. Claude Victor's lips cracked into a wolfish smile and he hissed cruelly: 'The perfect kill.'

Frank Ward and Linda kept running, exploring the never- ending corridors that were all decorated in the same way. The walls were plain and boring and so were the rooms on either side. Some of the doors were open, revealing simple, plain bedrooms scarcely holding much furniture inside. It was like some kind of horrible, grotesque hotel on the third tier. Ward presumed rightly that this was where Victor's staff slept.

They had been running so fast and their adrenaline was pumping so hard that neither of them noticed the many security cameras installed on the ceiling, recording them as they went past and catching them within their lenses. Normally Ward would have been more careful in a situation like this but he was so excited and scared at the same time that his usual advanced vision had not worked to its full advantage.

Since the night when Ward infiltrated the Kraken International Cooperation Offices in down - town Beijing, he had constantly been trying to solve the mystery of Operation Launch. He had puzzled over his thoughts for many hours and he had come up with so many different solutions and motives to Claude Victor's fiendish scheme. He had used the process of elimination to get rid of ideas that he didn't think plausible or would fit in with Victor's character. The man was exceptionally greedy and wanted power, but at the same time, didn't want the world to realise that he was the master - mind criminal that he really was.

So why would he want to destroy Taiwan and Tokyo? How could he benefit? Financially perhaps?

Ward still didn't have the correct solution in mind yet, but his ideas were getting closer and closer and he knew that in the next few minutes, the secrets of Operation Launch that he had tried to find out for weeks, would be revealed to him. He would no longer remain clueless as to Claude Victor's insane and barbaric reasons to commit mass murder.

'There's the elevator!' Linda cried.

Ward returned to his senses and followed Linda towards the large steel box. Linda opened the huge retractable doors by pressing a button and they prepared to enter.

Then the shooting started.

19/ 'ONE LONG SCREAM…'

TEN ROUNDS DRILLED and clanged into the thick metal doors of the elevator next to where Ward and Linda were standing. Perfectly rounded bullet holes were made in the steel. Linda screamed and clung to Ward's body, filled with fear. Ward hadn't had time to react. He held his Beretta 84FS Cheetah tightly but knew without turning round that his lone pistol was outnumbered. The shots that had been fired at them were from an Avtomat Kalashnikova -47, better known as the powerful AK - 47 assault rifle.

'Drop the toy, Ward,' came a harsh, booming voice from behind them, a voice that by now, Ward knew only too well, 'That gun is no match for what I've got.'

Slowly, Frank Ward released his grip on the Beretta and allowed it to slip out of his hands, clammy with sweat. Linda looked at him with terrified eyes. Tears had formed and were beginning to trickle down her soft, bright cheeks. Her fingers clawed at Ward's body as she looked at him.

'*It will be all right,*' Ward whispered faintly.

Linda whimpered and replied with an uncertain nod. Ward turned around slowly to face their attackers. Marcus "Menace" Hillman stood at the front of the group of roughly fifteen, strong, brutal looking men. A twisted smile had creased Hillman's small, ugly lips and his predatory, eagle eyes stared down his hawk nose at the two frightened prey that he had finally caught. His facial expression and his intimidating body posture showed that he felt triumphant. Secured in both hands, he held the gas - operated rifle like a professional. Ward knew he mustn't do anything stupid - "Menace" would easily riddle them with bullets without hesitation.

'Kick the gun away from you,' Hillman instructed, 'Don't try anything stupid, *mon ami*, or my group and I will make strawberry paste of you and the *chienne*. Got it?

Frank Ward didn't attempt to grab his Beretta and start shooting. He knew that if he moved anywhere, he would be shot. Defeated, he kicked the gun away from his reach and sent it scurrying across the walkway near to where "Menace" stood. Hillman tilted his head slightly and ordered one of the men to pick up the gun. The guard did and tucked it into a calf holster.

'You two are coming with me,' Hillman grunted, moving the long barrel of the rifle up and down Ward and Linda's bodies.

Ward narrowed his ruthless eyes and snarled, 'What if we don't want to come with you?'

Hillman grinned and released a dry, sinister cackle from his lips, 'In your situation, Ward, I'm afraid you haven't got a choice in the matter.'

The group of stony - faced murderers advanced towards them on the catwalk, the security men brandishing their Skorpion vz. 61's. Linda flinched as a large, fierce - looking man built like a bull seized her underneath her armpits and held her tightly.

He pressed the barrel of the sub machine gun against her beautiful head, applying more pressure whilst she struggled. Hillman approached her and leant close to her face. His animal breath engulfed her and she tried not to inhale the terrible smell.

'Don't try and get out of this, Linda,' "Menace" hissed, 'You'll only make it tougher on yourself.'

The bull - like guard then lifted Linda off her feet and pushed her hard in the back with the gun and led her down one of the many metal stairways next to one of the huge pillars, leading down onto the second tier. Ward watched as his lover disappeared from view and two of the men grabbed him by the biceps. Their strong fingers ground down on his arm muscles, making his body ache. He protested with a few grunts and gave Hillman, his enemy, a manful, hateful glare. Hillman smiled and shoved the AK- 47 against his head as they headed for the staircase with the rest of the group.

'You won't get out of this one, Ward,' Hillman said with relish, 'I can guarantee that you never leave here alive.'

Ward ignored the comment and cooperated with the guards. He didn't want to struggle yet - he wanted to confront Claude Victor again at last. Then he would find a way of escaping.

Both Linda and Ward were brought by Victor's men to a blank door on the second level. There was no sign to inform what the room contained. The door, like the others in the hi - tech building, was solid metal. "Menace" Hillman knocked carefully with his heavy knuckles on the door, whilst watching Ward suspiciously should he try anything. Ward didn't make any effort to break free of the guard's awesome grip. He simply glared furiously at Hillman with a sincere lust to kill him.

There came a harsh and almost impatient reply from inside the room, a signal to enter. The voice inside had boomed and Ward and Linda Pascal recognised it. Hillman pushed open the door and advanced into the large room, holding the door open for the security team to bring the two intruders inside.

Claude Victor stood at the other end of the room, eying the two captives eagerly with his opaque eyes. His right hand held of a gun - a FN Browning M 1903 pistol. He directed the gun towards the two people he hated the most - his hand didn't move; it was as steady as a rock. A hideous smile transformed the fat, bulging lips.

Victor's lips curled. 'I expected you two to find your way here,' he hissed.

The rest of the security team had already left, leaving the three who were holding Ward and Linda. "Menace" Hillman stood further away, looking at his boss admiringly and then at his new prey.

Victor raised the Browning and waved it towards the door. 'You two guards can leave,' Victor said, 'If they move, I'll shoot them.'

The guards nodded as they received their instructions and at last their powerful arms slackened and they moved away, leaving Ward and Linda in pain and aching. Behind him, Frank Ward could hear the metal door thud firmly shut. He looked at the sadistic expression on "Menace" Hillman's face, and then at the two metal chairs that stood in the centre of the room. Perspiration gathered under his armpits and on his brow, and he tried to remain as confident as possible.

Linda looked desperately towards him. She was obviously frightened too, just as he was, but he was determined not to show it. It would only make matters worse.

Ward looked around the room uncomfortably. It was blank and depressing; the walls were all black and dark and the only light came from the large rectangular window that overlooked the catwalk and staircases and the first tier. The only furniture in the room was the horrible metal chairs and Victor's broad desk in the corner of the room, near where the criminal was standing. It had nothing upon it. A smaller table was at the other side of the room, on which a square suitcase was laid.

Claude Victor smiled a thin, cruel smile, 'It has been a long time, Ward, since I saw you last. Back at my engagement party in the French Alps, I believe. And since then, you've followed me all the way over here to Prawn Island near the coasts of Beijing in China. You are quite a CIA agent, Ward. I'll hand you that. You're not quite the fool that I underestimated you long ago.'

Frank Ward smiled stiffly but said nothing. He clenched his fists nervously and looked around the room for a way out. The door was an obvious escape. "Menace" Hillman would be able to stop them before they got that far. Besides, the guards had locked it as they left. It would take even longer to get out. The were no other ways except the window. It was dangerous though, and no doubt, thickened. The room, Ward reflected was like a prison cell.

Victor looked around the room and waved his hands. 'This is The Torture Chamber,' he said powerfully, 'Anybody who displeases me is brought here and is forced to endure a great amount of physical pain and punishment.' Claude Victor switched the FN Browning M 1903 between hands and moved over to his desk. He sank into the low chair behind it and raised his legs and laid them casually on top of the desk. He rested the gun on his lap and pointed the ugly muzzle at his two victims. If he needed to, he could easily pull the trigger. He looked at "Menace" Hillman, 'As you know, "Menace" specialises in torture methods and has spent many years in training. I made sure, when I brought him into my employment, that I paid to further his training. Now, I can admit, he is very talented. His ability is great. He shows no mercy and he practises regularly on live humans that I no longer have use for. He aims to keep his victim or victims alive for as long as possible.'

'You two are *sick*!' Linda snarled in disgust.

"Menace" Hillman looked sombrely at his boss. Victor looked at Linda.

'You, Linda, are in no position to insult either of us,' Victor said, 'If I wished, I could shoot you dead. Instead, I want you to endure hours of continual pain while you watch Taiwan and Tokyo being destroyed and wish that you had never betrayed me.'

Ward narrowed his eyes at Victor, 'Taiwan and Tokyo won't be destroyed. Operation Launch can never succeed!'

Victor grinned, baring his uneven teeth. The scars on his translucent, white skin showed red in his anger. 'Really? How will you ever stop it now? In less than five minutes, the Tomahawk cruise missiles will be launched and begin their mission. The estimated time for the missile to hit Tokyo is ten minutes. Taiwan will be destroyed in five minutes.'

Ward was not yet defeated. 'The Central Intelligence Agency has been informed this morning. By now, the whole intelligence community will be aware, especially the Japanese Secret Service and Chinese Intelligence.'

Claude Victor's smile vanished quickly. His eyes seemed to grow and he glared at Ward furiously. His finger hovered on the trigger and he hesitated at the thought of killing him. He decided against it. The man would be tortured. 'You *imbécile stupide!*'

Everything was quiet while Victor thought. 'It doesn't matter, anyway,' Victor laughed, dryly, 'Nobody can prove my involvement in Operation Launch once you two are dead. No matter what the CIA says, the world will not believe in them.'

Frank Ward raised his head slightly and looked at Victor. 'So what is Operation Launch all about, then? Why Taiwan and Tokyo? Surely you would want to destroy somewhere like Washington D.C?'

Claude Victor's head fell back and his mouth opened in a triumphant cackle. His eyes closed and his head came forward again with a smile beaming on his lips. 'It seems that you did not figure that one out! I would have thought that you would have come up with the solution long ago! Why do you think I should destroy Washington D.C? To kill the President? No I'm not bothered about that.'

Ward wrinkled his brow in confusion. 'So why?'

Victor spread his arms wide whilst keeping Ward in his sights. He raised a non - existent eyebrow. 'Do you want me to tell you the details?'

Ward said nothing.

Victor shrugged. 'Fine. I'll get pleasure in revealing it all to you. I can laugh once you see what an *imbécile* you have been.' Victor turned his head and exchanged smiles with "Menace" Hillman, 'It's not as if either of you will live another hour to pass on this information to anybody of any significance.' Victor cleared his throat and laid his left hand on the table, flat. His right controlled the Browning. He began: 'I'm one of the wealthiest men in the world. My past accomplishments have brought me my fortune of over fifteen billion euros. The Kraken International Cooperation makes over one hundred million a year. Money I don't need. Operation Launch is not simply about money but about power.'

'Power?' Ward repeated.

'Yes,' Victor said. 'I am obsessed with power. It is a huge mania with me. I enjoy being authoritative and handing out instructions. But, I'm greedy. I want more. I want the Kraken International Cooperation to be the biggest and best company in the world. I want to completely monopolise the industrial world and be one of the most significant and important living beings. That's why Operation Launch came around. You ask why Taiwan and Tokyo. Well,' Victor said firmly, 'I shall explain my actions. You see, Taiwan and Tokyo are both famous for their marketing and chemical companies and factories. Many of the things made today come from either the island of Taiwan or the busy city of Tokyo. It is with large companies and organisations from these areas that the Kraken International Cooperation competes. This also provides governments with merchandise and it's a matter of who gets in first. That's why I propose to destroy Taiwan and Tokyo. With all competition out of the way, Kraken International Cooperation will be the number one company and everybody will know of it and it's founder, Claude Victor.'

Ward snarled in fury, 'You mean to tell me that you will happily kill millions just to make you feel powerful? You would be a mass murderer and wipe out two cities just so that you can be one of the most influential figures in the world?'

Claude Victor shrugged again without a care. 'I'm not bothered about killing people. I've done so on many occasions. Only this time, it would be on a much larger scale. I don't sit back and regret anything. I'm not like you. I barely feel any emotion for anything.'

'I wouldn't regret killing *you*.' Frank Ward hissed through clenched teeth. Without thinking, he dived across the room towards the desk, ready to pounce on the gangster. However, he forgot about "Menace" Hillman standing behind him. The huge man caught Ward by the waist and tackled him violently to the floor, knocking all the wind out of Ward as he landed on top of him.

'Frank!' Linda cried. She bent down with an outstretched hand to help him.

Claude Victor got up from his chair whilst "Menace" assembled Ward's hands behind his back with some thick rope he kept in his pocket. He bound them tightly together. Victor approached his fiancé.

Linda looked up at the man she hated now. She drew her lips back and forced the words out of her mouth slowly: 'I *hate you.*'

Victor clenched his teeth and glared. Then, in anger, he raised his left hand and smashed it across Linda's face with cruel hardness, sending Linda onto the floor. Linda lay crumpled, sobbing into her hair which had covered her bruised face, whilst Ward watched, sadly.

"Menace" Hillman smiled and asked, 'Shall I tie Ward to the chair, boss?'

Victor looked at his fiancé in disgust and turned around momentarily. '*Oui.* Then the girl. If he resists damage him, but not too much.'

"Menace" tied the Ward's wrists together firmly so that the rope was biting into his flesh, almost cutting his blood circulation off altogether. It hurt but Frank Ward ignored the pain. He knew that there would be much worse yet to come. "Menace" Hillman got up heavily, hauling Ward off his feet with him, and man-handled him towards the metal chair on which he deposited him. Ward fell against the chair, and straightened himself without the aid of his useless hands. The killer then got to work on his legs and fastened his feet to the chair firmly. When "Menace" had his back turned briefly, Ward experimented with the strength of the rope on his ankles. They were firm and he was unable to lash out and kick "Menace".

Claude Victor moved over towards Ward, making sure he didn't try anything while "Menace" Hillman got to work tying Linda Pascal into the chair next to him. Victor pulled his own low armchair from behind his heavy, mahogany desk and sat down squarely in it, pointing the gun directly at Ward's chest.

Victor licked his lips and started to speak: 'Now "Menace" will begin the torturing business. I will ask first you Ward and you will answer whatever question I may ask you. If you refuse to answer me, "Menace" will inflict a reasonable amount of pain on you until you reveal what I wish to know. Understood?'

Frank Ward raised his head and looked at his enemy with blood - shot, defiant eyes.

'You won't get anything out of me,' Ward grunted, 'I'm not answering any of your questions.'

Victor sniggered arrogantly, 'We shall soon see about that, Ward. I don't care whether you survive this torture or not. If you do, I shall kill you anyway once you've suffered great pain. Whether you die painfully or not is up to you. If you want to die quickly, you answer my questions, if not, your death will be a long, slow living hell…'

'I've already made my choice,' Ward hissed, 'And that's not to speak. Kill me anyway you like but the army and military forces will be down here before Operation Launch succeeds. You'll be killed or at least sentenced to life in a state prison.'

Victor said nothing but ground his teeth. Ward sat uneasily in the uncomfortable chair, chaffing by his swollen wrists and his immobile body that was tied tightly to the chair. There was no way of escaping. He was forced to look down the barrel of the gun that drew ever nearer the more he twitched and moved...

"Menace" Hillman bent over the suitcase which was on the low table nearer Linda. He unlocked the catches carefully and raised the lid. From where Ward and Linda Pascal were sitting, they couldn't see the terrible things inside the "box of death" as Hillman often called it. Inside, all his "toys" were kept that he used to probe and torment his victims with. He selected a few tools carefully and took them out. Grinning, he closed the lid and locked the suitcase. The killer and sadist turned around and placed some of the objects in his hand down on Victor's desk but kept one object in his hand. He walked purposefully over to where Ward was strapped. He crouched down and got to work, shoving the fingers of Ward's left hand into the black device. Ward realised what it was and swallowed. He tensed his body and willed himself not to break. He knew that he was about to have his fingers crushed.

'That,' Victor boomed, 'is a medieval thumbscrew, or also known as a pilliwinks. It was an ancient instrument of torture throughout Europe and has been used many times to extract confessions from prisoners and such like,' Victor waved his hands and watched Ward's frightened expression on his grey face, 'It is merely a vice. The victims fingers or toes are slowly crushed creating,' Victor creased a smile, 'a *very*, *very* unpleasant amount of pain.'

Linda gasped and watched, terrified and frightened, as Ward's finger's were locked inside the evil, inhuman instrument. "Menace" made sure that the fingers wouldn't be able to slide out. He locked them in firmly.

'"Menace" had trouble getting hold of the Scottish thumbscrew. But since then, he has practised the technique and has used it many times. Now, he has perfected this and can make the pain more unbearable that you can ever imagine. Once your fingers are unlocked from that device, Ward, they will all be mangled and the bones in each and every one broken.'

Ward winced and prepared his body and his brain. He didn't care how much the thing hurt. He wasn't going to cooperate with criminals - especially Claude Victor; the man who had killed many people that Ward had loved and liked dearly. He wasn't going to breathe a word about his assignment nor about classified information involving the American government and the Central Intelligence Agency. As long as he could shut out the pain, he would be able to get through this alright. If his brain stayed focused and he continued and willed for him not to break or reveal any secrets, he would get through this. And once he did, he knew that he was going to kill Victor and "Menace" Hillman.

'Let's begin,' Claude Victor said without emotion, 'The sooner you two are out of the way, the better.'

"Menace" Hillman chuckled and got ready with the thumbscrews. His fingers were already on the twister ready to turn the device and lower the screws down onto Ward's helpless fingers.

'Now,' Victor said, 'Tell me the address of the headquarters of the CIA's Station China branch. I want to ensure that those who know what you know, die as soon as possible before they reveal anything.'

Ward shook his head. 'I'll never tell you.'

Victor narrowed his eyes angrily and drummed his fingers on the table. He showed no remorse.

'Twist the screws,' he ordered bitterly.

Hillman obeyed the order and happily twisted the device. The screws touched Ward's fingers and ground them slightly. Ward winced as some of the skin on his fingers was removed as the screws wore the flesh away from the bone. Linda gasped and leaned forward. She wanted to help her lover but the ropes restrained her and bound her tightly to the metal chair.

'I will ask you again, Ward,' Victor said softly, 'If you fail to comply, the screws on your fingers will again be lowered. This time, your bones will shatter under the weight. I will ask you a final time. If you refuse, your fingers will be mashed into a horrible mess. You can escape now with just grazed fingers if you answer my question. What's the address of the CIA's Station China branch?'

Ward stared up emptily at Victor. He prepared his body for pain and tensed his muscles. He clenched his teeth together so tightly that he believed that they would break. He had to keep focused and strong, mentally and physically, if he wanted to survive. Wearily, he shook his head.

"Menace" again tightened the screws, smiling wolfishly while he did so. He watched with pleasure as Ward screamed and writhed in agony on the chair, his face contorted in pain, fear and anger. Sweat poured down his face and he continued to scream, staring down at the bloody mess that had once been his fingers. The bones in each of them had been crushed by the thumbscrews, rendering them helpless. Ward's lips drew back from his teeth as his body rocked forward in a silent scream. In all the pain and the tension, Ward suddenly vomited on the floor horribly.

Victor looked at the spreading mess on the floor and looked up at the man he had believed to be invincible. Now, he was sitting in the chair, and by the look of his head and his body, unconscious.

Victor said harshly, 'Wake the man up immediately. When you bring him around, I can ask him the question a final time.'

"Menace" nodded and backhanded the unconscious man several times across the face. He did this repeatedly and the man slightly stirred. He was still half - unconscious and in no fit state to answer any of Victor's questions. The pain had shut down his body temporarily. Hillman climbed to his feet and took a cup of coffee from Victor's desk and emptied the contents on Victor's face. The luke - warm liquid made Ward awaken, and he spent several minutes taking in his surroundings and gathering himself together. The pain was still immense and the crushed fingers of his left hand were still bleeding freely from the wounds.

Linda sat sobbing, staring upwards at the ceiling so that she couldn't watch the man she loved suffering such horrible amounts of pain. She closed her eyes and wished she could close her ears - she couldn't stand hearing him scream.

Victor looked at the crumpled figure lying sluggishly in the chair. 'You know the question,' he said coldly, 'Give me the answer and I'll spare you any more pain. If not, it's about to get a lot worse.'

Ward glared at Victor through one eye. He was very dizzy and nauseous. The pain had taken over his body and his senses. He kept slipping into alight - headed state and nearly passed out on several occasions.

He managed a cold snarl: 'Never.'

Victor managed to control his temper. He breathed in heavily and clenched his teeth. His rubbed his clenched fist tightly, 'Damn you, Ward,' Victor hissed, 'I would have thought you had the brain to speak when you had your chance. Now "Menace" will tighten the screws for the last time. It will hurt more than it has ever done yet. You'll be begging me to kill you and to tell me everything. You've had your chance to have an easy death - now it will be just one long scream…'

"Menace" tightened the bolts. Ward yelped out in agony as the remains of his fingers were ripped away from the rest of his hand painfully. Now, through the masses of blood, bone and torn flesh, Ward could make out the ugly stumps that remained on the end of his palm. The rest was gone. This was the last thing he ever saw before the pain enveloped him again and unconsciousness took over.

Ward let out a soft moan from between his lips. He shuffled and opened his eyelids softly. He could feel pain and was hot and sticky from the sweat. He remembered about the thumbscrew torture and being strapped to the chair. He looked down at the end of his arm, wishing the whole thing had been some very vivid nightmare, but no, his fingers were gone. The blood and mess had been cleaned up now and energy and sounds came from the control room. Ward guessed that the Tomahawk Land Attack Missiles were being launched from the control room by the missile guidance system.

He looked around The Torture Chamber wearily, expecting to see Claude Victor at his desk watching him, but the armchair where Victor was sitting during the torture was now vacant and unoccupied. "Menace" Hillman was standing in front of the desk busying himself with the other tools he removed from the suitcase. Linda was still in her chair, sobbing silently to herself. Her face was bleeding badly, presumably from her torture.

They must have gone easier on her, Ward figured.

"Menace" Hillman was inspecting his tools delicately whilst watching what was going on through the large reinforced window overlooking the main tier. The computer programmers were hard at work as usual and Claude Victor was monitoring their progress and watching the missiles being launched on the smaller screen. Ward noted that Hillman had his back turned away from him.

Supposing I could get out, Ward thought desperately. He quickly tried to think of something. He had to get Linda and himself out before "Menace" decided to kill them. The missiles containing the nuclear warheads were being launched and he had less than five minutes to stop the first missile from reaching Taiwan. Then, he had to stop Tokyo being destroyed along with all those innocent civilians with it.

But first, getting out.

He was restricted. His legs he couldn't move at all. He couldn't try to pull the smaller table towards him. His arms were useless too, he could only move his wrists slightly; his arms were strapped down onto the chair. It was going to be difficult. He tried to remember what he had on him - in all the excitement nobody frisked him for weapons. He only had to kick his Beretta away. But he still had his CIA messy knife in his pocket.

If only he could get it...

He tried to move his right hand (his left was now no use whatsoever) as far away from the ropes as possible and down towards his pocket. He helped himself by raising his leg as high as possible so that it would be easier for him to reach. His fingers touched the material of his trousers and he pushed his arm down, clawing at his dark slacks until his managed to grasp hold of the tiny knife he kept for emergencies. He smiled lightly and removed the knife from his pocket.

Linda watched him in amazement as he started to use the sharpened blade to cut through the thick ropes that tied him to the chair. "Menace" Hillman was still occupied sorting and examining his torture equipment before replacing it in his suitcase. He hadn't turned around yet and noticed Ward freeing himself.

Ward didn't think at first the ropes would cut. He had been slicing away for at least sixty seconds before the ropes fell away from his sore and bruised wrists and gave him relief from the terrible chaffing.

Now for the feet…

Ward lifted his legs and bent down with the top of his body. He put the blade to the ropes again and pushed the messy knife back and forth like a hacksaw through metal. The ropes slackened around his ankles and they split.

He was free! Now for "Menace"…

Frank Ward lifted himself out of the uncomfortable seat in which he had been cruelly tortured and had the fingers of his left hand mangled. The pain was still unbearable and as he brought himself wearily to his feet, he thought that he would faint again. *But not now*, he told himself. *I'm alone with "Menace".I'm not going to waste his opportunity to escape.*

Linda watched as Ward held the small weapon tightly in his grip and raised the small knife ready for attack. He was now inches behind the killer now and then Ward brought the knife home.

The blade drove deep into "Menace" Hillman's chest. Hillman cried out a soft moan and spun around to face his attacker. He stared at Ward with glassy unblinking eyes, confused as to how his victim had managed to get out. He reacted. He tried to swing clumsily at Ward with his right fist whilst trying to pull the blade out of his chest. Ward ducked and easily avoided the punch.

Then, he went berserk. Ward hammered the man he hated with his tightened fists and planted several solid blows at his target. He felt his fist crash into "Menace" Hillman's jaw and another into his nose. He lashed out with his leg and caught the sadistic killer in the stomach. Hillman screamed shrilly like a wounded rabbit and tried desperately to counter - attack Ward's moves. The more Hillman moved, the deeper the knife penetrated inside him and the more he bled. He tried to back away but was stuck in the room. The door was too far away to reach.

Ward kept grappling with his enemy. He hit him with his right hand. The pain that had corrupted his body had now gone numb. He didn't care about pain any longer. Determination and revenge had taken over his body and it was this that pushed him to kill his opponent, that man who had killed several of those Ward held close to his heart. Through the blur of nausea and blood, Ward could make out "Menace" coming forward at him with large, outstretched hands. Ward responded too as the huge man fell forward on top of him, and before Ward knew it, they were both struggling on the floor with hands at their throats.

Ward dug his fingers deep into the flesh on Marcus "Menace" Hillman's neck, and tightened his grip around the throat. "Menace" did the same too and they rolled over each other, fighting to be in control. "Menace" drove his fingers powerfully into Ward's throat, his finger - nails clawing against Ward's skin. Ward wanted to be physically sick. He could feel numbness creeping up his body. His eyes stared glassily out of his own sockets and hard into his enemy's face. It was turning a livid, horrible purple and he expected that his looked like that too. He licked his dry lips and forced his body to give any extra strength into his hand.

Ward could feel himself either passing out or dying. He wasn't sure. He knew that it would be a matter of who would die first. He rolled over one more time, throwing "Menace" Hillman underneath his throbbing body. Ward ground his teeth and pushed his fingers harder and harder until he thought those on his right hand would break too. He could feel sweat pouring all over him and there was blood all over him; a horrid combination of both his and "Menace" Hillman's.

'Die… die… die…die!' Ward spat.

"Menace" Hillman wasn't giving in. His face had swelled and was now bright purple. The ugly, small lips were a light, chilly blue, and the eyes looked up angrily. Finally, the powerful hands at Ward's neck slackened and the fingers slowly slid away. Ward watched the face in amazement as the eyelids closed over the pupils and the horrible tongue protruded like that of a dog from his grotesque mouth.

Ward smiled and knew that this was the look of death. He had seen it many times. Relieved, he staggered away from the twisted and crumpled corpse. He crawled on his hands and knees up to Linda's chair and looked up at her.

'We've got to stop those missiles,' Ward said, breathlessly.

He began cutting away the ropes that bound Linda Pascal to the chair, severing them with the blade he had used to stab "Menace". When the ropes fell away from Linda's tortured body, she quickly got up and embraced him. They held each other for a few moments and then they got to work.

Linda walked over to the body of Marcus "Menace" Hillman who was lying spread - eagled, face - upwards on the floor. His dark jacket was now stained in bright red as was his white shirt underneath. She explored the insides of "Menace" Hillman's jacket and retrieved Ward's Beretta 84FS Cheetah and handed it to its owner. She then took Hillman's own pistol - his Desert Eagle - and kept it herself. She knew how to use a pistol - Victor had taught her once. She removed the magazine, checked its contents, and inserted it back in the cartridge and tucked the gun in the waistband of her trousers. She then tore a large piece of linen material from "Menace" Hillman's blood - stained jacket and handed it to Ward, who tied it over the remains of his fingers and made it into a temporary bandage to stop the bleeding.

Frank Ward, sweating freely and exhausted, was sitting in Claude Victor's armchair, examining the AK - 47. He held the large assault rifle in his right hand with his fingers on the trigger and balanced the rear of the gun with the elbow of his left. It would be difficult to shoot but he decided that he would be able to manage it. As long as his gunning hand was okay, he should be fine. There were twenty rounds still in the magazine; it would suffice and he always had his faithful Beretta if he ran out of ammo. He slipped the harness over his head and secured the back of the gun near his armpit and balanced it on his elbow. His right hand held the trigger.

'Let's go,' Ward said to Linda, who was crouched near the body, 'We haven't got long.'

Linda Pascal nodded and removed the Desert Eagle. The pistol was a heavy gun but she could hold it. She would only fire in emergencies - her shots weren't that accurate. Ward unlocked the door and slipped out onto the third tier. Linda followed.

Ward ran along the catwalk and threw himself down the flight of stairs. He stood near the railings, clinging to a steel girder that supported the roof for cover. His heart was thudding uncontrollably and his palms were wet. Under the heavy weight of the rifle, he wasn't sure he had the strength to fire. One of the guards on the ground floor spotted him and machine gun fire erupted in the room.

Bullets clanged and smashed into metal all around them and Ward could hear glass smashing behind him. He ducked and used the thick girder for cover, whilst responding with fire of his own. He took aim with the AK - 47 and felt the assault rifle vibrate in his arms as he sprayed the control room with iron slugs. People screamed ands the computer programmers abandoned their machines as their monitors exploded in the path of fire. Men collapsed on the floor, falling in the rain of fire, and Linda let off a few of her Desert Eagle rounds at two security men hiding behind a work bench in the corner of the room.

The stench of death had already taken over the room.

Ward watched one of the guards crouched underneath one of the many walkways, unsheathe a grenade from his belt, and yank the pin from the explosive with his teeth. Then, he hurled the bomb over his head towards Ward and Linda.

'Get down!' Ward cried, jumping onto the catwalk to avoid the explosive that sailed through the air. The grenade missed where Ward and Linda crouched and bounced back off the steel girder. It fell back down into the control room and landed in the middle of the banks of computers.

The explosion and sudden leap of fire and heat made the programmers scream. The huge fireball engulfed most of the room and many of the people in it, catching them in the angry flames and thick black smoke. Shrill screams followed and so did machine gun fire. All around them, Ward could see men on fire, rushing around helplessly as they went up in flames and fell to the floor, dead. As the fire spread and moved onto the second tier, men caught alight and tumbled over the railings to the floor below.

Ward watched the chaos unfold from their hiding place and could see Claude Victor struggling frantically in the flames on the first floor. Dead men lay where they had fallen and more explosions rocked the building. Catwalks collapsed as girders broke away in the mayhem and the metal walkways collapsed to the floor with a deep sigh, sending the men on them to their doom. Ward watched as the fire crept up to the missile guidance system and the mainframe computer nearest the large screen that showed the missiles as blue dots. They were quickly approaching the red dots on the interactive map that highlighted Taiwan and Tokyo. Thankfully, the flames destroyed the guidance system and permanently shut down the BGM - 109 cruise missiles flight courses. He watched on the cracked large screen that had not yet perished in the destruction as the two blue dots disappeared.

Ward turned towards Linda, 'We've done it,' he said wearily, 'The warheads will burn up over the ocean. Nobody will be harmed.'

Linda smiled and pointed over to entrance, 'We'd better get out of here before the flames cut us off and block the way out. We need to get off the island.'

'How?'

'There's always Le dauphin,' she said with a wolfish grin.

Ward nodded and dropped the AK - 47. The rifle was out of ammunition. He removed the Beretta although he doubted if there were many people still alive in the building. They rushed down the staircase as it began to give way beneath the fire that had spread beneath them. At the other side of the huge building, the structure surrounding the box - like elevators collapsed and the shafts tumbled to the main floor with a huge crash and explosion. Ward and Linda ducked and were overwhelmed by the heat. Ward watched desperately as a Chinese gang member ran across the walkway on the third tier, littered with bodies. There was a small eruption of fire and he was thrown like a rag doll over the railings and into the flames.

The lights on the ceiling flickered on and off as the electric supplies struggled and sparks rained down from the ceiling. Injured men cried out and tried to drag themselves towards the entrance. Ward wanted to stop and have a rest but he knew that he wouldn't survive if he did. The whole structure was tumbling down around him and the pillars and girders were splitting under the heat and weight.

Ward could smell burning flesh as he stepped and jumped over the dead bodies that had lost the battle against the angry fireball, which had spread so quickly in minutes. It was no longer a battle to stop the warheads, Ward realised, but a frantic and dangerous battle against death in order to survive. Burnt fragments of clothes were blowing about on the floor.

Ward heard the fierce roar of a second explosion behind him, much bigger than any of the others. He swore and Linda screamed as they fell back to avoid the flames licking around them. The yellow and the red was blocked out now as black smoke poured out of all the broken windows on the higher tiers and filled the building. His eyes hurt from the black smoke constantly being created as the flames spread and spread and grew and grew. The heat burnt his eyelashes and scorched his cheeks. Above the shrill screams of those survivors and the bellows and roars of the flames, he could hear Linda coughing and struggling to breathe in oxygen. The smoke had corrupted the air and made it difficult to survive. Ward was trying his hardest not to breathe in when it wasn't necessary, and only to do so via his nose. Breathing in through his mouth was much worse. A yellow flame towered above them, demolishing the third floor completely and destroying another elevator shaft. The flames would have bitten their way through the steel cables until the shaft couldn't be supported any longer. More explosions rattled the building and more debris fell down to the main floor, which was practically ruined. Tongues of red ran through flames and a man emerged from them, a human blowtorch staggering about before he collapsed onto the broken walkway and appeared to dissolve into the metal.

Frank Ward and Linda scrambled over a fallen catwalk that had collapsed and lay smashed, a twisted pile of metal. Ward ripped the temporary bandage from over his gory stumps and rammed the ragged material into his mouth to stop himself inhaling large amounts of smoke. He could see Linda struggling too. The bottom of her black dress was singed and charred. Her face, covered in blood and ash was contorted in fear and pain. She stumbled around helplessly, coughing and spluttering. She had inhaled a lot of smoke. Frantically, Ward bent down over a dead security man lying face down on the floor, surrounded by a circle of yellow and orange. Ward ripped some of the material from the jacket of his uniform and handed it to Linda who put it over her mouth. Ward then prised the man's machine gun from his lifeless fingers and slung it over his shoulder. He didn't know whether there would be people outside on the beach. They climbed over the dead and over the twisted metal and shards of glass, avoiding any burning obstacle ahead and finding ways around the angry fire that blocked off their paths.

The entrance was now in sight. The door had been smashed open, presumably by other people who had been lucky enough to escape while they had the chance. Many of the people who had been inside when the grenade landed in the control room, had been unable to fight against the growing ball of fire. Ward pushed Linda through first. She was near to the point of unconsciousness. He followed, leaving the doomed building and the few men who were still trapped inside.

Other men were sprinting and scrambling down the beach as fast as they could to get away from the control room building before the whole thing blew up along with the rest of the island. Some of the men were screaming and limping along, clutching injured skulls. Some others lay on the ground, dead, having inhaled too much smoke.

Linda started to run but collapsed in the sand. Ward turned around to find her and rushed over to his lover.

'It's alright now,' he told her, holding her in his arms, 'We're out.'

Ward breathed in the oxygen happily, sucking as much as he could into his lungs. His eyes were no longer stinging and the fresh air cooled him down. They lay there on the sand for a few moments, gathering strength and feeling both happy and lucky to still be alive, and not dead. They watched, at the top of the beach behind the high grass and the Chinese tallow trees, as the doomed modern building finally lost its battle against the fire. With a great moan, the building disappeared behind a huge orange and yellow cloud, and when it settled, there was nothing standing where the building had once been. The roar of the explosion shook the island and the trees and the fire spread onto the building next to it. They waited in the sand until they had both recovered enough to get up and make their way towards the jetty.

Frank Ward had no problem with any security men. They were too concerned about their own lives and were running frantically in every direction trying to get away from the doomed island. Some were trying to swim away but the currents looked to be too strong. It was suicide - especially with all the smacks of jellyfish that infested the waters. Many were not poisonous but those that had venom could be harmful or even fatal. Ward once had a friend who went to Australia deep - sea diving. In the reefs, he met a box jellyfish, a *Chironex fleckeri.* The water - dwelling invertebrate stung his friend with it's snake - like tentacles. When his diving friends hauled him to the surface, the poison had already kicked in and corrupted his body. He was stone cold dead.

They made their way onto the jetty, and saw Le dauphin's beautiful shape. The Morgan Marine speedboat was no longer there, and a fresh wake that had been made by the boat, was beginning to fade. Both Ward and Linda could see the power boat in the distance. One of the survivors must have taken it. As for the other criminal survivors, they wouldn't be able to leave. The gangway of Le Dauphin was still lowered and led up onto the broadside of the luxurious yacht that had more than fifty suites. They climbed the gangway and blanked out the sound of explosions behind them. They stepped onto the yacht and Ward and Linda turned around and watched the destruction of the other building. The island complex was completely destroyed and finally the fire was at rest. Black smoke poured out of the debris and filled the blue sky.

Linda Pascal lowered the gang-way whilst Ward made his way up to the commanding bridge, furnished in polished wood and sat down in the ivory - coloured leather chair. He wrapped his hands around the wheel and started the engine. It purred and he eased the great motor yacht away from where it was moored. When the stern of *Le dauphin* was pointing towards the distant Beijing, he increased the boat speed and glided away over the shimmering waves. He turned around and watched as Prawn Island got smaller and smaller until it had vanished completely from sight and he could only see the thin sketch of the black smoke up in the sky that showed the burning of Victor's complex. The boat's motion was rough as the yacht ploughed into the choppy Chinese fishing waters. The glimmering turquoise waters had now become darker and the cheap fisherman's boats were dotted around on the water.

Ward didn't care if the water was a little more choppy. He had driven many boats before - including his own father's speedboat when they lived in Los Angeles, and he had been a life guard on the beaches. He had never driven a boat of this size or beauty before though and he enjoyed it.

Linda Pascal came up from the main deck having been relaxing on a reclining chair and rubbing ointment onto her damaged skin. The cut on her face from "Menace" Hillman's torment in The Torture Chamber had now faded and she had put a plaster over it. It was not as bad as it originally looked. It was only a small flesh - wound. She sat down in the seat next to him and together they watched the sun. It was squashing into an orange circle as the afternoon began to draw into evening. The earlier sapphire - coloured sky had now turned a kind of romantic blood - red.

Le dauphin dipped under a small current in the water, rose up, and slapped a small wave hard against the hull. Ward eased the speed of the motor yacht up a few more knots and cruised over the ocean. The speedometer confirmed his speed at fourteen knots. Linda had mentioned to him before that *Le dauphin* could travel non - stop at sixteen, carrying her seventy ton with her. Ward looked around the yacht and thought of the marble kitchens, the lovely bedrooms and the heated swimming pool. This craft was quite something.

Linda locked her arm around his and looked at him with her emerald - green eyes. 'Turn the engine off for an hour or so,' she told him. She reached across before Ward could respond and turned the key in the ignition. The steady heartbeat of the engine faded away into the early evening and the only sounds were those of the water lapping up against the side of the aluminium and magnesium alloy hull. Overheard, a bird swept above the stationary yacht, searching for fish in the water and a place to land.

Ward looked at her hungrily and their mouths connected. They held each other for a few moments.

Linda got up out of her chair and began to descend from the bridge and onto the quarterdeck. 'Let's go into my bedroom. We'll lie down.'

Ward acquiesced. He pressed a button on the controls that released the anchor. He heard a splash below as the anchor broke the glassy surface of the water followed by the rattle of the chain. Finally, with a sickening thud, he knew that the anchor had hit the bottom. Ward followed Linda, forgetting about the keys that were still in the ignition. They walked together down to the lower decks and they soon found the owner's stateroom.

***

Silently, the stow - away on *Le dauphin* moved out of his hiding place after watching Ward and Linda go into the bedroom. He crept along the quarter deck, looking out at the vast surface of ocean surrounding the boat. There were no other fishing boats in sight - the fishermen would have hauled their large squid nets up, before heading back to the harbours and ports to unload today's catch ready to sell it on in the morning, to Chinese markets and Cantonese restaurants. The intruder climbed the metal ladder up onto the commanding bridge where only a few moments ago Ward and Linda were sitting, kissing passionately. He removed the keys and slipped them into his trouser pocket and made his way back down onto the quarter deck. He made sure he was quiet and moved stealthily across the boat, the sounds of his footsteps being overridden by the blowing wind and the moving waves.

The intruder crept down into the storage room, situated near the bedrooms. It was where the staff and crew of *Le dauphin* kept weapons and emergency equipment. The man inserted a wire into the hole and fiddled about with it until the lock opened. He pushed his weight against the door and stepped inside the small, claustrophobic room. The room was very dull and ill - lit, having no windows. The only light poured in from the wide corridor. The intruder examined shelves and searched drawers for their contents. Finally, on one of the top cabinets, the intruder found what he was looking for. He lifted the USA Winchester 1300 Marines pump action shotgun down from the top shelf and weighed the large weapon in both of his gloved hands. He ran a finger down the long 457mm barrel and searched many boxes of ammunition for the correct bullets. He eventually found the correct rounds and he inserted two bullets into the magazine.

One for Ward, one for Linda.

Then, he left the room abruptly and walked purposefully across the blue carpet towards the owner's stateroom where he had watched them enter.

20/ THE SCENT OF DEATH

FRANK WARD LAY ON the large bed in the centre of the luxurious cabin, staring up blankly at the light blue ceiling and feeling the pain again from his throbbing body. Whilst they had been running about trying to escape from the doomed complex on Prawn Island, he had ignored the pain and forgotten about it. Fear had taken over. Now, his body ached again, and Ward felt as if he was going to lose consciousness once again.

Linda Pascal was working at the other end of the room near the glass coffee table. She was preparing two drinks - a dark coffee for Ward and a frothy cappuccino for herself. She had changed out of her silk black evening dress that had been ruined and damaged in the flames. She had changed into her night dress taken from the large French *armoire* where most of her clothes were kept. She stirred Ward's drink mechanically and left it on the table ready for Ward to collect once he was ready for it. She climbed up onto the bed and lay down next to him.

'Why don't you take a shower?' she asked.

Ward looked down at the gruesome stubs on the end of his palm, all that was left of the fingers on his left hand. He ignored the question and said, 'I'd better get this checked out by a doctor in Beijing. It's probably all infected by now.'

Linda looked at him and at herself. 'We're lucky to be alive, you and I,' she admitted, smiling. She was happy now and content. She was no longer going to live a tortured and terrible life with her cruel fiancé Claude Victor. "The Corrector" above the bed would go forever unused and finally Linda could have all the love that she wanted and truly deserved. She knew that they were right for each other. They both had troubled lives, and needed each other's love and company to make up for the past.

Frank Ward propped his pillow up against the head rest on the bed and sat up. A wave of nausea passed over him and he fought the temptation to have a cigarette. He felt as if he needed one but in his state it would probably only make him worse. Ward reluctantly got out of bed and walked over to where the two blue armchairs were positioned by the circular porthole window and sipped his drink. He felt the soothing, warm liquid run down his throat and already he felt so much better. Most of the pain, apart from his finger stumps, had been created by the fire. The flames and smoke had made his head spin. He felt tired and sleepy.

He finished the whole cup of coffee in two solid gulps and walked across the cabin towards the door.

'I'm just going above deck to pour the dregs of the coffee overboard,' Ward called to Linda, who was relaxing on the bed.

'Okay.'

Ward grasped the door handle and pulled it back. He stopped dead on the threshold, his path blocked by the tall and frightening presence of Claude Victor, wielding a shotgun.

'Oh … my…', Ward mumbled.

Claude Victor glared at Ward menacingly with sunken, vengeful eyes. There was a deep gash above his right eyebrow, which was a bloody mess. The cut looked quite severe and so did the hard lines of Victor's ghostly - coloured face. It was probable that the injury had been sustained during the fire.

Victor lifted the barrel of the Winchester 1300 Marines a few inches, aiming the weapon at Ward's heart. A snarl gripped Victor's lips, 'Get back in the room, Ward,' Victor grunted bitterly, 'I am going to finish this.'

Ward gave Victor a hard stare and walked slowly backwards into the spacious cabin. He racked his brain and wondered what he had done with his Beretta and the Skorpion vz. 61 he had snatched from the dead guard's limp fingers. He was defenceless and weak. He couldn't fight and he didn't have any strength left in his bruised and damaged body.

Victor stepped into the room and looked around to see where his other hostage was hiding. He slammed the door hard, so hard, in fact, that the whole room shook and Linda Pascal got up off the bed to investigate. It was then that she saw the new person in the room. Her eyes widened and showed fear and her mouth opened in surprise.

'Claude - what… the … hell?'

Victor said nothing and moved the heavy shotgun between the two other people in the room, his long, skeleton fingers gripping the stainless - steel pump, and the others the trigger. His French suit, that had looked so meticulous earlier, was now ruined and burned in some areas. The expensive fabric was charred and the bottoms of his trousers were bloodied and stained. Victor must have injured his leg in the inferno that had demolished his island complex.

'Neither of you are going to get out of this alive,' Victor hissed, 'You thought you had escaped, but nobody ever gets away from me.'

Ward shifted uneasily from where he stood and looked around the room frantically for some kind of weapon. *He had to stop Victor!* Ward looked down onto the coffee table and considered the long, pointed letter opener. It might be good at close range, he reflected, but there was quite a distance between them. Ward looked at Victor; the crazy eyes, the eager fingers on the grip, the way he stood. Victor was not joking, he was going to kill them.

'Claude - no!' Linda cried from where she was standing beside the bed.

Victor suddenly pivoted with the shotgun, his face livid and obsessed. He pointed the shotgun threateningly at Linda. He held the weapon with ruthless hands. They didn't quiver.

'Shut up you scheming *chienne!*' Victor screamed, loudly, 'You betrayed me and humiliated me! I've got a bullet in this shotgun for you. Now, you can watch your new lover be blasted to pieces before you get pumped full of lead yourself!'

Linda drew back away from the shotgun and looked away. She cowered next to the bed, covering her face and blocking the sight of the shotgun away from view.

Victor sucked in deep breaths from between his crooked teeth and swung the shotgun back round again onto his first target. Ward looked at Victor and at the shotgun, deciding what to do. He knew he didn't have long before he must make up his mind.

Victor forced a smile and began to apply pressure on the trigger. He wanted to hear Ward scream and scream, and cry for mercy as his blood splattered against the wall. He felt the shotgun erupt in his arms, and he watched as Ward dived forward. He hadn't anticipated Ward's action. The man avoided the shotgun bullet which smashed against the wall, ripping a hole in the side of the cabin. Ward grabbed hold of the shotgun and tilted the barrel towards the ceiling so that Victor couldn't fire at either of them.

The two men struggled violently there on the spot, fighting viciously for possession of the Winchester 1300 Marines. Ward's fingers caught hold of the metal and he tried to jerk the weapon away and prize it from Victor's unwilling fingers. Linda watched, terrified, fixed on the spot by fear and unable to move. She couldn't guess who would get the shotgun.

Ward ground his teeth and pushed his weight against Victor trying to knock him off his feet. Victor dodged it and clung to the shotgun for dear life and held it in his arms. Ward risked losing possession of the gun and removed his left hand. He lashed out with his mangled hand at Victor's face and hit the man as hard as he could bluntly on the side of the face.

'*Eeurk!*' was the muffled noise that escaped Victor's mouth as Ward's knuckles connected with his jaw. Victor stumbled and fell away in pain, and his fingers slipped away from the Winchester 1300 Marines. Ward seized the powerful shotgun from Victor's arms and smashed his collarbone with the barrel of the shotgun. Victor made another startled noise and staggered across the room.

He swallowed and wiped more blood away from his face. He stared across the room at his enemy, Frank Ward, who was now pointing the long, horrible barrel of the shotgun directly at him. He knew he was going to die. The wicked aroma had filled the room; the scent of death. Victor dived to the right and snatched the ivory letter opener from the coffee table and hurled it towards Ward.

Simultaneously, Ward fired the shotgun. The letter opener sailed in the air like a silver arc and hit Ward in the chest. At the same time, the final round of the Winchester 1300 Marines blasted Claude Victor in the heart. Victor screamed shrilly and was flung backwards, smashed against the wall like a doll. He stood there, like a star- fish, staring out of his bulging fish eyes in shock and fury. His hands trembled and blood trickled from the grotesque mouth. Linda watched in bewilderment as a circle of red in the middle of Victor's chest expanded and then the figure crumpled to the floor, dead.

The letter opener bounced off Ward's chest easily without causing any pain. There had not been enough force behind it to have hurt Ward or indeed impale him. Harmlessly, the knife clattered to the floor. Ward dropped the Winchester and looked at where Linda was crouched. They both looked at each other.

'It's over,' Ward said with relief.

His legs were not responding and they gave way beneath his weight. He slid sluggishly to the floor, having aimed for the bed. His head hit the carpet and he lay there for a few moments, staring at the twisted corpse across the room, and then slipped into a state of unconsciousness once again.

Frank Ward and Linda Pascal spent the next two days in Beijing hospital, both under sedation. Ward had sustained the worst of the injuries including minor lung damage and severe blood loss, both from his fingers and a few other cuts and burns on his legs and arms. Linda's case was similar. She had inhaled a harmful amount of smoke and had been burned on her feet and ankles.

Doctors and surgeons had operated on Ward whilst he was in a relaxed, drugged sleep, attempting to do their best to repair the horrible stumps. They disinfected the wounds, removed the dirt and ash and certain bits of flesh. The fingers, obviously, couldn't be saved, and Ward's left hand was to remain useless for the rest of his life.

Frank Ward had now been awake for a few hours, and he was lying down with his eyes shut, feeling warm and comfortable in the clean sheets. The nurses had brought him some food; a strange Chinese vegetable dish and herb soup which he gratefully ate in a few minutes. He felt his energy being replenished as he lay there, letting his body heal and his mind. He was glad that his assignment was over and that he had prevented Operation Launch from happening. Claude Victor was dead and so was Marcus "Menace" Hillman, settling Ward's personal vendetta and the hit contract set by General Kretzmer of the French DGSE. The American missile guidance hardware had not been recovered though and neither the two stolen BGM - 109 Tomahawk missiles. They had been unfortunately destroyed, resulting in a huge sum of government money being required, in order to replace them. Still, Ward happily reflected, he had stopped the destruction of Taiwan and Tokyo and mass murder.

The double doors at the end of the ward opened and Walter Greaves, the Central Intelligence Agency Chief Of Staff emerged. The middle - aged man looked around at the neat rows of beds and searched through the sick people until he found Ward. He pulled up a comfortable - looking chair next to Ward's bed. Frank Ward's eyes were closed and he was trying to sleep. He didn't realise the Chief Of Staff was here.

'Agent 27S,' Greaves said softly.

Immediately, Ward's eyes opened and he turned his head abruptly to face the person who had called him by his secret code name. He stared in awe at his best friend in the CIA. He and Ward would often have dinner together in the staff canteen back at Langley Headquarters.

'What the hell are you doing here, Walter?' Ward asked with a broad smile.

Walter Greaves put his hand in his lap neatly and gazed around him at the blank white walls and the clean, white tiles. He replied: 'Cartwright received word that you and Linda Pascal were in a Beijing hospital suffering a few minor injuries. The CIA tracked you down and Cartwright asked me personally to come and talk to you about your mission.'

Ward cleared his throat and struggled to concentrate. The pills and many capsules that the nurses had given him to take with water were having an effect. 'So you want to hear the score, I suppose?' Greaves chuckled. 'Yes.' Frank Ward straightened his back and nestled his head against his thick pillows. He was comfortable.

'Well, Claude Victor is dead,' Ward explained, 'I killed him with a shotgun onboard *Le dauphin* after I destroyed Operation Launch. In the papers it will look like suicide, I guess?'

Greaves nodded, 'Yes it's already all over the headlines. Both the CIA and the French DGSE have mutually agreed not to let details of Operation Launch escape and get caught up in the media world. They want to keep the whole Operation Launch thing a secret. Nobody will ever know how Taiwan and Tokyo were so close to being wiped out.'

'It will be for the best. The missile guidance system is destroyed unfortunately.'

The Chief Of Staff acknowledged this with a mild shrug. 'Nothing you could do about it. It doesn't matter anyway. As long as it wasn't activated by enemy hands, the CIA would rather it be destroyed.'

'But how did I get here?' Ward enquired, his brow wrinkled, 'Who found us?' Walter Greaves gestured with a sweep of his hand towards a large, important - looking Chinese figure standing across the end of the ward, talking to one of the patients. He had tidy, salt and pepper hair, a healthy complexion and a warm, inviting smile.

'Doctor Zancuck told me on the way in. A fisherman saw *Le dauphin* the following morning and at first wondered if the owners had been eaten. There was nobody on deck and the anchor was lowered. Apparently, the fisherman thought that a giant squid might have got you. Anyway, he pulled his boat up against the yacht, climbed onboard and searched the rooms. He found you and Linda unconscious; she must have collapsed after you. He also discovered the dead body and immediately contacted the coast guard on the radio. They came and transferred you two and Victor onto the coast guard's boat. They took you both to hospital and Victor's body to the morgue.'

'Quite a story,' Ward said, grinning weakly. 'When do I get out of this depressing place? Has the Doctor said anything?'

Greaves shook his head, 'Not a word,' he admitted, 'but by the sounds of your injuries, another few days at the most. You're not expected to come back to Headquarters for a few weeks, especially with that hand of yours. I can guarantee you won't be doing anything active for a long time. Maybe you'll even have to leave the Directorate of Operations section. You'll be pretty damn useless without your left hand.'

Ward frowned.

'Bull,' he said bluntly, 'I can still shoot a gun!'

Walter Greaves laughed and got heavily to his feet. He stretched and gave a low, tired yawn. The muscles showed underneath his business suit as he extended his arms.

'Cartwright's orders, Frank.' Greaves started for the door ,'I'd better be off. There's some things I've got to sort out before I'm due back on my flight to the US. I'll be seeing you.'

Ward shuffled up in his bed.

'Wait!' he cried. 'Walter!'

But it was too late. The Chief Of Staff had already disappeared through the door. He was gone and Ward was once again left to think. *Why am I still working for the Central Intelligence Agency?* he thought. He decided that he was fed up with killing and being responsible for other people's deaths. He wanted to get away from espionage and codes and guns and everything else that he carried along with his work. Since he had awoken from his sleep and found himself alive and comfortable in a hospital bed, he was actually glad that he was still living. During his past assignments, he had dabbled with death on numerous occasions, not worried about the high and dangerous risks that he was undertaking. But now, it was different. He appreciated being able to see things and hear sounds and smell the sweet scents of the red flowers in the glass vase beside his bed.

And to him, the most important of all, Linda.

Ward smiled faintly at the thought of Linda and again, his pain was blocked out and he felt nothing. He loved Linda Pascal and wanted to live with her and be a normal person - not some top secret government assassin. He wanted a normal job; a job that he could talk about and actually *enjoy*. A job where he no longer needed his Beretta or his fists. He wanted to settle down and enjoy life, love and company. It was at this moment that Frank Ward, Agent 27S, decided to hand in his notice back at the CIA Langley Headquarters in Virginia, and resign permanently from the Directorate of Operations Department.

The next day, Ward's condition had dramatically improved and he felt in less pain. His severed fingers still hurt like hell and the nurse was constantly supplying painkillers with his morning cup of black coffee, along with his other prescribed medication, and his breakfast. The rest of his body - especially his chest - now felt much better and Ward was able to move about out of bed easily, without collapsing from the pain and his fatigued state.

Frank Ward was sitting up in his bed with his arms folded having just swallowed three painkiller capsules. Already, the tablets were taking effect and the gory stumps on the end of his left hand were numb. Ward gazed down at his hand. A fresh bandage has been applied to his left hand this morning when he awoke to prevent any infection.

Ward's mind still had not changed. He wanted to leave the CIA as soon he was discharged from the Beijing hospital. He felt certain that he was making the right decision.

I should have thrown it all in after the Sharp affair, Ward reflected.

After about an hour or so of sitting against his headrest supported by his pillow, and watching the nurses moving up and down the ward, attending politely to the sick elderly ladies over near the window, Ward decided to lie down and rest. He did so and thought happily of Linda. He was very anxious to see her again and hold her close in his arms. He wanted to tell her about his decision to leave the agency so that they could settle down together.

Where would they live? Ward thought to himself. Definitely not in Virginia anymore. The CIA would still be near him. Maybe Barcelona? Ward had always wanted to own a property in Spain. Or what about the West Indies?

Whilst Ward was thinking about his own and Linda's future, Doctor Zancuck passed by his bed, carrying a note - book underneath his arm and looking caringly at his medical patients with his charming eyes.

'Doctor,' Ward said quietly.

Zancuck stopped in his tracks and looked abruptly in the direction from where the sound came. He looked at the man with the light tan and bandaged hand and realised it must have been him calling. The Doctor moved over to his patient's bed and grinned broadly, a smile that revealed two immaculate rows of shiny, white teeth.

'Good morning, Mister Ward,' the Chinese man said in polite, accurate English, 'I trust that you are feeling better now after your breakfast and medicine.'

'Yes,' Ward said.

'Now,' the Doctor began, 'What is it that you wish to ask me?'

'When will I be discharged from here, Doctor?' Ward enquired, looking up with exhausted, sunken eyes at the tall figure that stood by his bed .

Doctor Zancuck smiled grimly and shook his head slowly, 'Maybe a week at the most. I'm sorry that I can't send you away earlier, Mister Ward, but your injuries were quite serious. If you had not been found when you was, I can guarantee that your injuries would have been fatal. Your makeshift bandage on your left hand was only tied very loosely. You could have easily bled to death. Also, the amount of smoke you inhaled could have killed you or at least given you long - term lung damage. I understand that your work is very classified and of high importance, but until you are completely fit I can't allow you to travel back to America. Until then, Mister Ward, all I recommend is to take the medicine and painkillers that I give you and get plenty of sleep and rest.'

'I understand, Doctor,' Ward said, 'But how is Linda Pascal?'

Doctor Zancuck considered the name and then remembered the patient, 'Oh yes, the woman who came in here with you. Her state of health when she was brought in was nowhere near as serious as yours'. She has only inhaled a minor amount of smoke that luckily hasn't left any damage. She also suffered a few third degree burns, mostly to the bottom half of her body. She is at the other end of the ward and should be out in a shortly. There is no need to keep her in here any longer.'

'May I see her?' Ward asked, desperately.

The Doctor bit his lip and toyed with the idea for a good few seconds.

'I'm not to sure that you will be able to do so in your current state of health -'.

Ward interrupted the Doctor and cut him off before he had any opportunity to speak.

'I'll be fine, Doctor. I've already had a friend come to see me yesterday.'

'Ah yes, that Walter Greaves,' the Doctor said, 'I remember his face. Go on then. You may go over and talk to her. But be careful with that hand of yours.'

Ward nodded and thanked him appreciatively. He watched Doctor Zancuck leave him after saying goodbye, and disappear through the white double doors of the ward. He could still hear his echoing footsteps out in the corridor outside. Ward eased himself over to the corner of his bed and laid his legs down on the cold floor. He winced in slight agony and discomfort as he stood on the floor upright, wearing the creased, light -

blue pyjamas that the hospital had supplied. Now that he was standing and could see the bottom of his legs and feet, he realised how badly burned they were, as well as bruised.

Ward moved away from his bed and walked across the ward, scanning the patients on either side of him for Linda Pascal. He eventually found her, sitting upright in her bed, idly flipping the pages of a woman's magazine which was kept in the waiting room. Ward smiled and was very happy to see her. Even wearing shabby, pink pyjamas and the fact that her silky hair was slightly messy, she still looked as attractive and sexy as she did when he first saw her back at the party in the French Alps. She didn't notice him straight away - her emerald eyes were fixed on the text with concentration. Linda finally looked up after hearing footsteps approaching, to see who the person was.

Linda's mouth opened widely in surprise. She stared at him, bewildered, before smiling.

'Frank!' she cried, 'I'm so happy to see you!'

Ward responded with another brief grin and carefully collapsed into the chair beside her bed. Linda put the magazine down and deposited it on her bedside table before opening her arms and clutching Ward in an affectionate embrace. Linda laid her head delicately on Ward's shoulder and nestled her head against his. Ward stroked her soft hair with his right hand; and as he brushed it out of her face, he noticed that the gash on her face was now stitched up and healing fine.

'You certainly look better than I do,' Ward said with a quiet chuckle.

Linda acknowledged the comment with a highly infectious grin. Her smile always appeared to pass onto whoever looked at her.

'When do you get out?' Linda asked.

Ward told her what Doctor Zancuk had told him earlier.

'I'll be out in a shortly,' Linda said.

'I know,' Ward replied.

'I'll be here everyday to keep you company until you get out,' Linda explained, kissing Ward chastely on the cheek.

Ward held Linda tightly and close to him. He felt so much better now that he had seen Linda. He felt comforted and happy. He knew that Linda felt the same too.

'What about the hand?' Linda said inquiringly.

Ward shook his head regretfully.

'I won't be able to use it again, if that's what you mean. Apparently, I've had an operation while I was in a sedated state. They've disinfected the wounds and removed bits of flesh and broken bone. The Doctor asked me when I first woke up if I wanted an artificial hand or not. I said not. I don't want to be walking around with a hook or anything.'

As Ward said this, he began to think of the largest American drug baron who operated throughout the U.S - Howard Sharp; the man who also killed Joe Ward. Sharp had had a hook on his right hand. Ward shuddered at the thought of the man - his jet black hair, the overpowering middle build and the mouth that always held a snarl. He told himself that Sharp was long since dead, and the frightening picture vanished abruptly from his mind.

He looked at Linda again, cleared his throat and finally prepared to inform her of his future plans for them.

'Linda,' Ward began, 'I've been thinking while I've been in this hospital about my last assignment. How we stopped Claude Victor from destroying Taiwan and Tokyo and everything else that happened. To put it quickly, Linda, I'm fed up of having death follow me around. I'm sick of having the role of the Grim Reaper - having the power to take away somebody's life. I no longer want that responsibility. That is why I've decided - once we get back to the US - to leave the Central Intelligence Agency.'

Linda's brow furrowed in confusion.

'What? You mean resign?'

'Yes. I am going to hand in my licence to kill.'

'Are you sure?' Linda asked incredulously. 'What will you do?'

Ward shrugged.

'I haven't thought yet,' he admitted, 'But it's for the benefit of both of us. Like you said back at the Bed and Breakfast, I could get killed at any moment. I take risks that any normal person wouldn't dream of doing. Since I came to, here in my bed, I was relieved to be still living and it felt good. That's why?'

Linda's mouth connected fully on Ward's and they kissed passionately. She slowly pulled away, grinning broadly.

'I don't mind what you choose to do,' Linda confessed. 'You've given me so much already since I met you and you have made me so happy. I want you to do what makes you contented.'

Ward shook his head.

'No I'm certain. I am leaving permanently and putting the CIA and undercover operations all behind me. I'm finished with spying. Somebody else can be 'Agent 27S'. From now on, I hold no code name.'

'I can't wait for you to come out of hospital. I wish you could come when I do.'

Frank Ward grunted.

'That's if I ever get out of this depressing place. Then, we'll go and live somewhere else.'

Linda's eyes narrowed again.

'But I thought I was going to live with you in Virginia?'

'You'll be living with me, but not back in Langley Falls. We will have a luxurious property in a warm, tropical country.'

Linda gasped.

'You mean, we could live in *Cuba*?'

Ward grinned, the smile filling his jaw.

'Anywhere you like. We'll have a large villa or something, overlooking the turquoise waters and the exotic palm trees.'

Linda Pascal was very ecstatic and excited. She kissed Ward several times and hugged him so tightly that all the breath in Ward's lungs was forced out of them.

'But we'll have to go back to Virginia for a while whilst I finish work at the agency headquarters. While I'm doing that, you can look for some nice properties in Havana or wherever you want us to spend the rest of our lives together.'

Linda ignored him and said simply: 'I *love* you.'

Ward looked at Linda, the woman he admired, respected and cared for. He stared hungrily into her eyes and wrapped his large hands around the back of her neck, pressing her breasts against his chest.

'I love you too,' he replied, 'and I always will.'

21/ A NEW LIFE

FRANK WARD GAZED reflectively out of the large, square windows that were positioned at the other end of the room in front of his large, metal - surfaced desk. He stared through the impregnable, ten inch glass out onto the New Headquarters Building Courtyard, that surrounded the two, six - storey office towers in which Ward's own private office was located. The landscaped courtyard was built up of a fish pond, flowering plants, trees, and a broad, grassy lawn. It was here that colleagues in the CIA could have lunch or meet up socially.

This, Ward reflected, was where he first walked to go and meet his future chief in his office, to be informed of his own brother's tragic and brutal murder.

Since he had flown back from Beijing to Virginia, Ward had spent his few final days in the Directorate of Operations Department sitting at his own desk, locked away from the world, surrounded only by past memories and thoughts.

He was also drafting the letter that he would leave on his desk for Seymour Cartwright to read, explaining his departure and why he was leaving the CIA for ever. He looked down at the piece of A4 paper and chewed the lid of his pen thoughtfully. He made a few adjustments to his writing, re - read it, and frustratingly crumpled it up and threw it to his right where he knew it would land in the waste paper basket. He outstretched his arm and grabbed another sheet of paper from his desk next to his IN and OUT baskets, both filled with documents and folders.

He wanted to make sure the letter was perfect, explaining everything that he wanted Cartwright and the other superior officials in the CIA to know. He didn't want to tell the DCIA personally - he wouldn't be able to bring himself to do so. A letter would show Wards' reasons better than words. He clicked the pen obsessively while he sat there, hunched over his large broad desk, thinking about what he needed to write.

As he brought himself to write the opening words, he put the pen down and looked at his open, leather briefcase beside him. All his possessions that he kept in his office had been bundled into the small attaché, many of the objects reminding him of his past assignments. Amongst the piles of paper and letters, there were objects that he had retrieved from the field and kept for sentimental reasons, either on the top of his desk or hidden away in the drawers. He turned his head now towards his case and looked inside. Two M67 fragmentation grenades, both with their pin fuses removed, were hidden beneath the piles of documents. The little steel spheres glimmered in the pool of light that was cast across the desk from Ward's reading lamp. Ward smiled and remembered the chase in Sarah Holmes's Land Rover during the Sharp assignment. He had used some grenades identical to the ones he brought back with him for souvenirs, to dispatch the enemies behind them on Suzuki SV 650 motorcycles.

Reminiscently, Frank Ward took his half - filled glass of Russian Moskovskaya vodka from beside his elbow and took a long, enjoyable sip. He swallowed the liquid and looked back at his attaché case. His Bianchi 4601 Ranger Viper Shoulder Holster, now worn and battered with age and use, was crushed into one of the compartments in the case, the black nylon fabric showing clearly. He remembered proudly as he was first equipped with his Beretta and holster by George Vex, the armourer in the Weapons and Gadgetry Department. The day was still clear in his mind. He could picture Mister Vex standing there, small and thin, studying Ward behind his steel - rimmed glasses, as he entered the office. Vex had left the agency a few months ago to attend to his dying wife in New York City. Ward was sorry to see Vex go - he was close friends with him and they would often dine together with Walter Greaves.

I won't be needing that holster any more, Ward thought, half - pleased and half saddened. Whilst he would be relaxing in the sun with Linda, walking together in the lively streets of Havana in the West Indies, the CIA would never leave his mind.

Frank Ward told himself to concentrate and closed the lid of his briefcase and locked the catches into place. He looked back at his letter and began to write.

After half an hour of writing furiously, scribbling out mistakes and errors in his letter, he finally sat back in his comfortable, high - backed office chair and evaluated what he had written. Ward addressed the letter to 'Cartwright, Personal '. Satisfied with his work, he read it out mentally to himself for a final time:

Sir,

By the time you have found this and started reading this letter, I will be long gone from my office and the Central Intelligence Agency. I have, as you probably already realise, resigned permanently and I am about to begin an entirely different life with Linda Pascal in the Caribbean. In the following paragraphs I shall present to you my reasons for handing in my licence to kill and say goodbye.

(1) During my last mission that you personally assigned to me in Paris, I have lost many people that I hold in high regard and close to my heart. I have seen these people being killed, their lives taken so cruelly away. Seeing this, I can only hold myself responsible and guilt will forever plague my conscience. I hate seeing people die, may of those that I've myself killed, and no amount of money could bribe me to stay here any longer. Compared to the vivid and frightening nightmares that I suffer from every night, money is not important.

(2) As shown in my personal records; my past has been bleak and filled with tragic memories and occurrences that I would rather not like to think about. Having my brother and both parents' lives shortened dramatically, left me in a depressed state andI attempted to cure this by drinking. I didn't care back then whether I lived or died. I joined the Central Intelligence Agency not only to seek revenge on my brother's killer but as another alternative to forget the stresses of life. Now, though, after nearly being killed myself in the field, I feel pleased that I am still living and I want to enjoy the rest of my life, rather than playing a gamble everyday that could mean life or death. I no longer want to die in a wild shootout, but instead, peacefully and happily with my loved ones surrounding me.

(3) As stated in my medical reports, I sustained a painful and traumatic injury whilst on my last case that kept me in a hospital in Beijing. I was tortured on my last mission as you know by the enemy, and lost all the fingers on my left hand. I had an operation which nursed the wound, but unfortunately they could not save my fingers from the horrible mess they were in. Now, my left hand is completely useless and is currently wrapped in thick bandages that I must change daily to prevent infection. Because of my very active role in the CIA, I also feel that my injury would make me pretty helpless. I certainly wouldn't be able to do as much of the action that I have done over the years. In fact I would be very restricted in what I could do.

(4) Before I started my last assignment, as you know (and disliked the fact) that I had a tasteless string of cheap affairs with various women; women that I would be able to sleep with and forget about my horrible and miserable life. For those single nights, I forgot about my problems and enjoyed myself. The only fault was that I never loved any of them. There has never been, for as long as I can remember, a girl that I have

actually loved so passionately, that I would like to the spend the rest of my life with. All I cared for then, was sex. But during this assignment, I met two women that I adored and admired and *loved*. I knew that I wanted to walk down the aisle with them as soon as I met each one individually. I suppose that it doesn't matter if I disclose the fact now that the first was Gaëlle Dumas, the surveillance agent working with the French Direction Générale de la Sécurité Extérieure. You first sent me to protect her from assassination in the military helicopter, and it was that moment that I knew I was actually in love. I saw it in her eyes too. A strange feeling took over my body, not a thirst for sex, but genuine love and care that I wanted to share with her. Our love didn't last long, though. As you may recall, Gaëlle was killed by Marcus Hillman (available on Criminal Database). Later on, though, I met Linda Pascal, Claude Victor's new fiancé. I fell in love again and we had an affair which eventually led to us both defeating Operation Launch, and preventing the stolen cruise missiles reaching their targets. Now, Linda and myself are together, and I value our relationship very highly. We intend to spend the rest of our lives together, living happily and no longer in danger. We hope to get married and have children. With all of our future planned, I can't risk my life for you and my country any further.

Now, we have reached the end. My time at the Central Intelligence Agency has mostly been a happy one and I have met many interesting people. I have learned many things about life from the agency and because of it, I value my life a lot more than before. I hope that you, sir, will continue to direct the CIA with the brilliant efficiency that you have since you've been my chief. As for me, I will still remember you - not as my boss, but as a close friend. Please find on my desk my Beretta 84FS Cheetah that I have carried with me for many assignments, and also my 'licence to kill' certificate. With these things, I shall also be leaving my code name behind - Agent 27S. I wish for my successor to be a determined and loyal individual, as I hope that I have been in your service. This is, sir, the final goodbye, not only to you but America as well. I will be sad to leave but happy and excited to start afresh.

Your obedient servant,
Frank Ward

Ward gently put his pen down on his large desk and laid his hands down carefully in front of him. He was satisfied with what he had written, and he decided that this would be the final copy, that Cartwright himself would discover, once Ward was gone from the building and the country.

Frank Ward swallowed and poured the remains of the Moskovskaya vodka from the bottle into his empty glass and poured the liquid quickly down his throat. He placed his glass back down onto the table and assembled it next to the bottle. Ward got up heavily from the chair that he had used on so many bleak Monday mornings, sorting through papers deposited in his IN tray. He lifted his heavy attaché case from his desk, loaded with all his equipment and personal belongings that he was taking with him. Ward left the letter on the desk inside the envelope and walked over beside the window to the coat rack where his dark linen jacket was hanging. Ward put his jacket on over his shirt and winced in pain as the material brushed against his bandaged hand.

Whilst Ward was putting on his jacket, he looked out of his office window for the last time and watched Walter Greaves, Cartwright's Chief Of Staff, hurrying through the New Building Courtyard. Ward was sorry that he couldn't say goodbye to his close friend but he felt that he had to leave quietly and unnoticed. He didn't want anybody to see him go. All that was explained in detail in the letter.

Frank Ward looked around his spacious office where he had worked for many months. The walls were plain and painted in a simple cream colour. The carpet was a melancholy grey, designed in an angular pattern. On the now vacant desk, the only item in the room that had given any hint of the occupant was a photograph of Joe, Ward's brother. It was now packed away in the case. That photograph had remained on his desk since he joined the service to remind him of why he joined.

Ward sucked in deep breaths of air through his teeth and turned his back on his desk for the last time. His hand hovered momentarily over the golden door knob before he pulled it open. He thought of Linda waiting back at their current house situated in the peaceful Langley Falls. For the first time, he was about to go and see a women whom he loved and cared about. He raised his head, blanked the CIA from his mind and stepped over the threshold without regret. He shut the door, abruptly ending his dangerous career and walked down the empty corridor, no longer Agent 27S.

He was about to start a life anew.

Printed in the United Kingdom
by Lightning Source UK Ltd.
119537UK00001B/400-492